SHE CAN, CAN'T SHE?

TALLIA FURY

Edited by Krystina Rhodes

Design, typesetting and publishing by UK Book Publishing

www.ukbookpublishing.com

ISBN: 978-1-915338-27-3

SHE CAN, CAN'T SHE?

CHAPTER 1

Her senses jarred with the uncomfortable truth. She no longer fitted her own life. It was the result of chipping away, at who she had been, to who she had become. She had five roles, none of them for herself. The first four were as a mother to her four children, all different as each child needed her for different skills, and the fifth as her husband's wife.

Imagine a beautiful place, towering snow-capped mountains that reached up to the sky that could be viewed from the second floor balcony of the house. Her life was nestled there in Scotland, which she was lucky enough to call home.

She found herself considering how far she had come, but contemplating where she would go. The daily routine stifling in its predictability where barely a ripple dared to intrude, she was looking for a sign outside of her fairy tale life. But didn't fairy tales have sinister things lurking to tempt you onto a different path? She had so much, but craved a challenge, a test. Her husband was undeniably successful, with his cobalt blue sports car that was rarely parked on the gravel drive, perfectly edged with white fences that were painted regularly. The house, terracotta coloured but threaded through with burnt orange saffron, yellow and cherry red bricks to break the monotony.

The four children, two girls and two boys, balanced the family structure. The girls, close in age, were playmates in their early years and the boys inseparable. Four pregnancies, no complications and relatively easy births, was she not just the luckiest woman? So what was wrong, a midlife crisis, or worse, an early menopause? She couldn't exactly pinpoint when the dissatisfaction had begun, but a peek into her future, when six would become two with the fast approaching retirement that would lead to pottering around the house most days, the children gone. Her and her husband in the garden; weeding, pruning the hedges, deadheading the flowers. They would sit and have coffee whilst he read the papers, her knitting for a grandchild, whom would soon fall to her as everything else had. Oh to fight to achieve, feel fear, a possible loss, even hunger and to have to find a way to put things right.

Had she have known what was coming, she might have been a bit less careless with her thoughts, and when a random event set these processes in motion, she was later forced in to thinking back and recalling the familiar phrase, be careful what you wish for.

For now her daily life continued as she expected. It began in a favourite spot at the kitchen table, the breakfast dishes and cups left in the haste of getting her children and husband off to the outside lives whilst she held the insider post. She chuckled a little at that. The kitchen area was higgledy piggledy as miss matched cups lined the walls hanging on hooks that were an array of all different colours, as were the plates and bowls. Her personality was here as she had been given free reign, an indulgence on behalf of her husband that claimed the kitchen to be a woman's domain, though not naturally hers by being a cook out of necessity and not out of joy.

She had a coffee with a book in hand as always, but she didn't want to read of the fictitious lives of others today as she turned the book face down on the kitchen counter. No more reading for a while, she decided, time to start a new story in her own life.

A clang of the doorbell startled her to her feet. She was wearing expensive mules trimmed with feathers, not her style at all, a gift from her husband Christmas last. Had she conjured someone? The door creaked open, a little oil was needed. A chore missed by her husband but something she could easily do if she wanted, she parked the thought in her head where it would remain. Before answering the door she freed her dark hair from the band that held it secured away from her face and viewed herself briefly in the large hall mirror. It was an interesting face; Noticeable eyes, a straight nose, full mouth. An asset was her skin, the result of the minimum of care, avoiding the suns harsh rays by always being in the shade as she was not overly fond of hot weather. Preferring rain and crisp cold days, which there were lots of in Scotland. Maybe she looked a little jaded, a result of too much giving, her husband gave her tasks such as to collect a suit from the cleaners or to take a pair of his shoes to the cobblers to be re heeled. He was oddly frugal considering he could easily afford to replace his shoes and these requests were always accompanied with a smile, a smirk he probably thought went unnoticed but she always saw it. It was disrespectful and had been there at the start of the relationship, but then you ignored it because early euphoria allowed you to.

CHAPTER 2

She opened the front door, "Mrs Chevelly". The gravelly voice robbed her briefly of air, it seemed to come from his boots and her gaze fell to them. Mostly undone laces haphazardly put through eyelets here or there, an accident waiting to happen, a frequent comment that was made to her sons as she tied one or the other of their laces. Her husband insisted on the old fashioned lace ups when they could just as easily have had Velcro straps. She had tried to teach them how to do them themselves but, whilst her older son sometimes managed with extreme concentration, no matter how many times they were shown her younger son was yet to master the skill.

The owner of the deep voice had magnetism, his smile revealing gaps in his teeth that she found perfect but imperfectly so, whilst hers dazzled in comparison. Her husband had paid to have them professionally cleaned as a gift, it was a painful process and she felt cheated. He was always critical of everything and chose what she would wear if he took her out, which was rare, other than to work functions where he could parade her as an extension of himself. She was always uncomfortable in these situations and sometimes felt a childish urge to show him up but quickly brushed these feelings aside, not wanting to look like a fool or risk the possibility of being punished later in some way.

His long lean fingers held a parcel and she noted that his eyes were blue, navy, and very dark and they held a mischievous twinkle. She was charmed and felt wrong footed as she scribbled her signature. He had imprinted on her consciousness and lifted her mood, but she quickly dismissed it from reality.

CHAPTER 3

Her first born Maisie was 16, an unexpected child in many ways, with hair just a tad off white. Marguerite's husband had been blonde as a child, but his colouring had settled to a darkish brown and her hair had always been a rich chestnut brown. Maisie had a mass of ringlets, where did they emerge from? Her eye colour also undefined, being neither blue nor green, and you were drawn to them. She was a lovable child though cruel at times and now a student at college, her second daughter was in her last year at seniors and the boys both at juniors. Marguerite stood at the kitchen window to get a better view, the mountains impressive as always. It had been raining earlier but now the sun was out and she was treated to a rainbow, 'a water gow' by Scottish expression, truly magical to encounter.

The house was large, five bedrooms, one for each of the children, with no crowded areas or bunk beds in sight. Marguerite and her husband's room an impressive white suite, extending to a balcony where they could admire their garden that was always abundant with varying shades of green and a riot of flowers, a myriad of colour. The boys spent many hours out there, kicking a football or playing out adventures with the aid of their handmade den which they added to daily with broken branches. Inside the den it was messy with comics, empty crisp packets, sweet wrappers and cups that were rarely ever returned to the kitchen, likely awaiting Marguerite's collection. She had a quick shower in the en-suite, immaculate fluffy white towels enveloped the heated towel rail, matching his and hers robes hanging on the back of the door, bottles of expensive bath oils, bubble baths and all manner of things arranged neatly on shelves. It was her responsibility to keep this room of all the rooms in the house pristine as her husband was proud of the bathroom and it had been very expensive, representing a level of success he had achieved and the only area in the house that was theirs alone. Fresh from the shower and dressed casually, Marguerite was ready for the onslaught of demands that would unduly follow.

"MUM!" her daughter's voice, alerting her to attend to her role as Maisie's mother.

"Hi Maisie, how was college? Did you learn anything interesting today"?

Maisie was studying textiles, but she took it for granted. Not appreciating that she could continue her education without being expected to contribute to the household income, simply believing it was her right. Tedious was the reply, accompanied by a sigh of annoyance at being asked. Marguerite had been to college, but that was a long time ago. At this later stage of her life, she felt trapped and a bit cross that her eldest daughter didn't relish her freedom more.

"I'm going to chill in my room" Maisie informed her.

There was no 'how was your day mum?' Likely thinking what could possibly happen in her mother's day that could be of any interest to her. Maisie was caught up in all that was Maisie 90% of the time, escaping to her room to text her latest love interest Mitac, the conversation with her mother over before it had even started. She had only just left him at the college gates, what was there to say so soon? But what did Marguerite know? She wasn't young anymore and today felt as though she had lost some weight of apathy, whilst enjoying a momentary lapse into unknown territory, a picture of a face appearing in her mind and that lazy smile. She smiled after Maisie, feeling sorry that she had those thoughts as it wasn't like her. If Maisie was happy that was all that mattered. Maisie's eyes suddenly noticing her mother and reaching into her mind, Marguerite felt disconcerted as most people did when Maisie looked at them in that way, thinking she would know their innermost thoughts. That was because the 10% of Maisie that was not reserved for her own self was engaged in pulling secrets.

Mitac was a foreigner. Marguerite, often pondering the idea of a non-Scottish non-English son-in-law wondered what he was doing studying with a group of girls in a textiles class. There was one other boy but it was a female domain, so a strange choice and an even stranger guy, but Maisie was not like her mother so she had been told. Marguerite believed that Maisie was going to do something extraordinary with her life and Mitac could be a part of that, or become just today's flavour to be replaced by a less exotic Scot or a straight laced British boy, but he had set a bar that none of the local boys could raise to. Marguerite hastily chose pizzas for dinner, a random selection intended to cater for all the varying requests she would have got had she have asked, but that was not an option today.

CHAPTER 4

Beattie arrived home, her waist length dark hair a sheet of silk flying behind her as a gust of cold air followed her in. Marguerites second daughter Beattie, who would choose it, she looked like a Beatrice, but Beattie she had soon became as it was easier for the younger children. People always preferred to shorten names but at least it wasn't B, though I expect she was called that on occasion. A kind of geeky child, massive bitter chocolate coloured eyes looked quizzically out expecting the best and mostly getting it. A child with an appeal to relatives, friends and even authoritative people, she seemed to charm them all. Marguerite remembered observing Maisie looking hurt when she'd heard someone say how adorable Beattie was, wasn't she adorable to? To their father, Maisie and Beattie were Rose red and Rose white, proud of their beauty and impeccable behaviour in his company, he would smile and look satisfied.

The boys, Frankie and Maurice, two bundles of playful fun causing chaos wherever they went, were adored just the same. Were they not all so very blessed? Marguerite often questioned how she and her husband had produced these exceptional children. Her husband was so straight minded that she was flattered the sparks that were evident in her children had ignited from her, laughing to herself as she hardly dared to ignite her own, but her trail of thought was suddenly disrupted by the smell of burnt food.

The overcooked pizzas were hastily divided out and delivered to the girls in their rooms, her and the boys at the kitchen table. After finishing their food the boys rushed out to the garden to play, climbing trees was their chosen activity today. Their father wouldn't be pleased about damaging them, but as he was rarely there to observe his sons, the broken branches became fodder for the den. Her mind travelled out to the mountains that she and her family, but rarely her husband, had spent so many happy hours. Walking amongst the bluebells in the spring, other times wild flowers and heathers; it was a staple to be seen all year round. The sky littered sparingly with ever-changing black clouds in the distance, always hovering, threatening rain or a storm. In the early years when it was just the girls, they could have been seen trailing along in colourful wellington boots with matching raincoats rolled into balls in a large knapsack, along with snacks and drinks. Maisie always dressed immaculately, remaining so on her return. Beattie however sported socks around her ankles, or one up one down, sometimes not even the same colour or pattern. She had always shown a flare at an early age for mixing spots and stripes and pulling off a look that nobody else would get away with. Now fifteen she was anxious to study fashion design and was, like most children, always in a hurry to grow up. Didn't they know being an adult was serious business?

CHAPTER 5

Marguerite's husband was not aware of Maisie's love interest, he didn't take seriously matters of the heart, which she thought was short sighted being that at sixteen hormones raged like no other time. Couldn't he recall the intensity or the urgency? Education, this was the foundation of a successful life, frivolity was for losers, not for his children and not for his wife.

Maisie was texting Mitac, the two M's together. He was Romanian. She knew her mother was sceptical, her dad didn't know, he always harped on about education opening all doors, unlocking hearts that was for later. Naive or perhaps just choosing to be, he cared for his children, supported them and his wife but beyond that he had no conception of emotional issues, nonsense. That was his wife's expertise as he was seldom aware it was required. Maisie was sad for this as she would have liked a male viewpoint, though probably not his, as he would just push away the conversation embarrassed and she was a dutiful daughter, always endeavouring to uphold his expectations. Mitac was captivating to her, a treat compared to local boys and she was fascinated by all things Romanian. Marguerite would listen to her and she would fancy she caught a wistful look, perhaps envy, she knew her mum was an outstanding person, but lately she had been elsewhere mentally but she remained loyal. Maisie was sure of her in the way she wasn't of her father.

For Beattie school was fun but she was keen to get to the next stage, her career, she had the skills already but they needed fine-tuning. She dared to break the uniform code at school, maintaining her habit of wearing mismatched socks and other students followed the trend. She disliked the uniform, it was practical but dull, why she had thought, and in the future saw herself designing a uniform which gave some individuality but was still suitable for school, so many ideas buzzing in her head. Today she was called to the school office, she didn't care really it wasn't the first time. It was a huge room; lots of chairs, filing cabinets housing confidential information about them all, a vase full of chrysanthemums brightened its sombre look. She was a popular girl, with the other pupils as well as the teachers, so she wasn't in serious trouble. The headmistress looked amused but persisted in telling Beattie that rules are important and one broken could lead to a revolution. She was amused at this overly dramatic statement but nodded in accordance. Later at the school assembly an announcement was made reiterating the uniform code then the subject changed to other school activities.

Beattie admired her sister but was careful with her as you could not be sure what colour mood would greet you. At the moment it was pink as Maisie was in love, but you had to be aware of purple and most especially black which was the mood that settled and made an impact on the whole house. Even her dad couldn't not notice but in his usual way skirted around any problems that could have caused it.

CHAPTER 6

Sweetness was very much a part of her sister Maisie's nature, but this could instantly sour with the wrong word or look. Her brothers were fun, occasionally annoying, but did little to cause disharmony in the house. Maisie was the one to do that but for now she seemed settled, not pink but purple, so not happy but not at danger level which was black. It was a sort of joke with them all, not of course funny to her. Beattie thought of their father, funny old thing needed to lighten up a little, they seemed a tight ship and he must feel outside of it, a lofty figure. Beattie saddened. Like Maisie, she would have liked to have conversed and more so laughed with him. Beattie was increasingly aware that her mother was fading but their basic needs were attended to, they were fed and had clean clothes so not entirely neglected. Her father should have noticed, it was obvious, to her but to a lesser extent her sister and brothers. If he noticed he did and said nothing, took their mother for granted. She was young but not a fool, she knew many marriages floundered and some of her friends had separated parents. Why was she having these thoughts? Perhaps she should give her father a nudge, but she felt sure he would just dismiss it as it would make him feel uncomfortable and she too liked to live in a harmonious house. With this in mind, she considered it was for her, the only one aware of the seriousness and potential upheaval that could follow, to have a word with everyone. Maybe even her dad, bring him back to them, but she knew he wouldn't listen and would say she was being unrealistic as her mother in his opinion had no reason to be unhappy, none of them did. He worked hard to give them all the possessions they could want or need. Beattie liked nice things but she didn't think it was the most important factor, she accepted that her father provided for them but was that just to make himself feel good?

Maisie's purple mood lingering these days, rarely pink, they were all determined by her love life. She was dabbling in the foreign pool, a choice now of two, between a Romanian and a Spaniard. What was the point in pursuing a foreigner? It could only be filled with problems, what chance did either have with a girl like her sister? She really needed someone to lower her agony levels not to raise them but Maisie seemed to like to live on her nerves, only happy in a distorted way if she was tortured. She was unaware of anything other than him, the Romanian, her college work was set aside, not concerned for anyone else in the house. Did she mean to be so selfish or did life only show that what related to her was all she could handle? But if she was in a good mood she could be nice.

Her brother Frankie, tall and gangly with facial features that promised to be dangerously good looking, very dark hair and brown eyes. He appeared the stronger character of the two boys, being older and very serious about protecting his younger brother. He didn't particularly expect anything from his father, he already knew it was futile and his father was not going to be the one to show him how to be a man in a good way. Maurice on the other hand was soft but their father was dismissive of that. Maurice cared if people were upset and it was a weakness in a boy, their father showed what could be achieved by hard work, but to the boy's holidays and expensive clothes became normal to them, like living in a big house, what else had they known? Maurice liked nothing more than a game of football with his dad but this happened infrequently as he did not take into account personality traits and definitely not his wife's. What was happening with her? He knew she was distracted but didn't think too long and hard, she would get past it he presumed, she was busy and had the family to think about, little time to indulge in daydreaming and fantasies. He was a busy man he had no time for any of that. He was a white collar worker, a common term for a man who works behind a desk. Beattie personally thought it was a front, a place to hide from his real self, who they weren't allowed to know in case they found that he fell short. He had done a good job of ironing out any visible weaknesses; they were all in awe of him, always wanting to show that they had skills he should notice. She didn't care too much for herself as she didn't need his encouragements; she had every intention of becoming financially secure in her own right. He thought her constant sketching and messing about with materials a passing fad. She was, she had told him, going to be a fashion designer, from a young age her defiant chin jutting out, she would stamp her little feet clad in expensive patent leather shoes, expressing her annoyance. She refused to dress in a way that suited her father on the rare occasion they were taken out on parade, as she later thought of it. They were polished, scrubbed and hair brushed, even Maisie's which was a disaster zone as her mother clipped it tight at either side of her face and sprayed it, daring a tendril to emerge. A credit to him, he admitted that much, so proud strutting with his brood behind him. On occasion they were taken to a business colleague's buffet or barbecue and they were admired, they were his trophies. She had seen mums expression, she too dressed to impress, but she could sense her true mother beneath her expensive outfits, bursting to explode or cause embarrassment by daring to speak out when she didn't agree with something she had overheard the men talking about. She noticed her mother didn't really join in the gossip with the other women; she stood alone even then, resisting temptation, until now it seemed. Nobody actually knew anything for sure, but it was clear to Beattie that she had something going on outside of them and the house, but what?

CHAPTER 7

The full length mirror by the front door, the check stop, was your hair passable? Your outfit, did it show your figure to its advantage? Her sons only taking a quick peek, her eldest daughter stayed a while but her younger daughter confident that she looked good, having done the necessary before leaving her room would fleetingly glance then be on her way. Marguerite had just returned from the school run, so was checking on her way in not out this time. It reflected a woman in her late forties, she looked at least 10 years younger so she had been told, examining her face for wrinkles and lines but her skin showed none of these. She was alone, a state which she had been happy with. She was in a house full of people at the start and the close of each day, but they were usually all unavailable to her, each active in their own lives. She was always on the side lines on duty to be pulled in for reassurance or to find missing objects, but who did she have to call on? Today she felt the need for company, wanted to be with someone, or somewhere where there were people that weren't her family. She didn't want female friends particularly, in general she found women didn't like her, she didn't care why, maybe because she looked too good, had too much, not her problem. She wouldn't turn away anyone in need of a smile or a quick chat, but she gave little away. Her eyes danced with the prospect of a day free of chores, she would dress with extra care, take herself off to the local town and indulge herself. She knew of a café, it was expensive, so she would sit outside with a costly cappuccino in her hand and people watch, who knows who could wander by. After that, she would aimlessly stroll in and out of the twee shops, maybe buy something for herself, hoping she wouldn't return with gifts for the children which is what she usually did. Her days seemed so regimented and she knew she shouldn't feel like this, but she felt unchallenged and unmotivated. This was a distraction to be out neglecting her chores. Didn't she have a pile of washing to attend to, covers to return to all the beds? The thought alone was enough. Her brain was screaming for stimulus, as was her body. Maybe she should take up a class on an interesting subject or join a gym, practical solutions safe, but that was not what she craved.

Her BMW gleamed on the outside, her husband took it to the car wash every weekend, but inside it was not so pristine. Cleaned just once a month, the boys usually left empty food packets and crumbs. Her husband had a no eating or drinking policy for his car, but it was rare they were actually in it. She was not a fastidious person and the high standards she tried to maintain were not for her, she preferred to be comfortable in the way she dressed and in her home. She had taken up smoking, an act of rebellion but maybe just a small one, he would be outraged even though they both smoked when they were younger, but now he considered it expensive and a waste of money. He could indulge himself in anything he wanted, as could she, but she had possessions and that was not an area that needed attention, it was she herself that did. Any vestige of youth had been replaced by a serious smug older man, his chosen persona of course, this was a natural progression in some ways but didn't we all want to hold onto something of our youth? She felt like a rebellious teenager as she bought a packet of cigarettes, thinking that perhaps smoking and a few indulgences would cure her discontent for the time being.

She arrived in the Scottish town. It had cobbled streets, quaint shops selling materials a haberdashery delight, a florist, delicatessen, a chic boutique very expensive where she and the girls had sometimes bought an item of clothing for a treat. There were also a few larger shops but you had to travel out into the bigger towns for a department store with more choice, she felt all she needed could be found here, it was a comfortable town for her, familiar. She found her way to the café. Table's wrought iron with matching chairs and colourful cushions, the terrace was cobbled so you had to be careful if you wore heels but today her chunky heeled boots meant it was not treacherous. Hanging baskets, lots of pots of different textures and styles were crammed with flowers, she sat at the table tucked away shielded from the breeze, it was almost warm. A typical petite Scottish girl arrived to take her order, the girl had small sharp features, she ordered a coffee and a pastry with jam and cream and lit a cigarette relishing her freedom, but was she as free as she wanted to be? A day off could be taken any time, but she felt that because her family were always so busy it was her duty to take care of everything related to them. She could have been more indulgent, protective of herself, but now she was at crisis point. A wink from an attractive younger man, was this all it took? It was the catalyst, but this feeling went much deeper.

CHAPTER 8

"Mrs Chevelly"! Was this possible that he would find her here? Her thoughts now reality, she noted the long eyelashes, how was it that the men often had longer thicker lashes? Her hazel eyes locked with his navy ones, the darkest blue. "Well hello" she replied in a flirtatious tone, she still knew how to do that. He stretched his long body as he took a seat near to her, his endless legs splayed luxuriously out in front of him, feet clad with those boots. Confidently, his hand seeking no invitation, reached out and with a finger stroked the inside of her palm as goose bumps raised at the nape of her neck, it felt delicious. "Marguerite" he said, "Rodrigo" she replied. He smiled, his eyes alight with mischief. "Italian?" she raised an eyebrow. "A little, my grandfather was Italian so I guess a part of me is too". They laughed as he took her hand in his and they sat like two lovers, as if they always had been so.

Rodrigo considered Marguerite. He was attracted to her and liked her enormously, he noted her age, guessing he was likely young enough to be her son. He observed the rings like sparkling trophies, she was another man's wife and he should feel bad, feel that solidarity with his fellow men, but no sense of decency prevailed. Life wasn't fair and if you were careless with something or someone precious, it was stolen from you. Marguerite was financially secure already, he had seen the house and he had little to offer her apart from himself. With no house of his own and no car, if he went anywhere he walked or used public transport and if in a hurry a taxi. He had a bedsit, very basic, and worked purely to pay for necessities and his own pleasure. Marguerite seemed uncomfortable and he could sense her conscience debating her next move. "Just a coffee with a friend" he reassured her and squeezed her hand lightly. She returned a weak smile, knowing that this was how they would justify their meeting and whatever she did now was crucial. "Let's meet here the same time next week" he said, breaking the awkward silence. It was said casually but she caught his expression, he wanted her to say yes. What was this? It wasn't sensible, but thought it was harmless as she could stop it anytime she chose. Stop what? She hesitated then nodded "next week" and as she took her hand back he could tell she was back in the role of Mrs Chevelly again. He wiggled his fingers in a gesture of a wave, thinking the soft approach would get him his prize and it worked as she called out after him, a sudden need to confirm the meeting "Yes, here the same time next week"! She watched him stroll away and stayed a little longer, lighting a cigarette her fingers trembling, recollecting her reaction and how she had handled the situation. Had she looked an idiot? A sex starved married woman she was and he probably noticed it, she knew that it was foolish, hadn't she read enough books? In real life you threatened to lose so much, but the thought of being with him, lying with him. She imagined them, their bodies entwined naked, it was unbearable to wait and then they would still just be playing. She must be patient and act with caution, she smiled to herself secretly.

The next week stretched interminably, intermittent with thoughts of would he? Could she? It was a licence to dream and she hadn't felt this way for a very long time, finding herself going through the motions of her life. She often caught the family staring at her but no one said anything, what could possibly have made their mother like this, she didn't go anywhere? But they had noticed the lack of focus on them. Maisie, usually engrossed with all that was Maisie, a situation with Mitac had arisen and a black mood surfacing. She was fierce and unpleasant to the boys who knew to leave her, quietly retreating out into the garden or to their rooms. Marguerite heard sobs from behind her closed door as she tentatively tapped but was ordered away, just as well Marguerite thought selfishly, she didn't want to hear about another love gone wrong. Beattie, usually full of optimism was preoccupied, she could usually be relied on to balance out Maisie's moods but it seemed that she too had a darker side. Marguerite hadn't noticed it was her that was causing the change in Beattie and she didn't try too hard to find the source of the change in Beattie's behaviour either. Marguerite thought of herself as the barometer, if she was happy the others would catch it, be placated, even Maisie would eventually allow Marguerite to coax her out of her mood and her room, until the next time. What vibes was she omitting now? She had mentioned the girls to her husband with concern, did they not seem out of sorts to him? He had brushed it away "What could possibly be wrong, don't they have everything?" He voiced dismissively. "Yes, apart from your attention" she replied, but the comment seemed to go unnoticed, ironically. Though he did care for them all in his own way, if he was aware of any change in her or the children's behaviour now would have been the time to mention it, but he chose not to.

CHAPTER 9

Mitac was an older student, his compatriots mostly Scots and a few English. There was another boy, Spanish, a flamboyant character who dressed to attract attention, he and the boy noticeable for being male and more so for being foreign. The girls here were not like Romanian girls that lead simple lives but longed for pretty things, the boy's smart clothes and cars, any car. Scottish and English girls were full of self-importance, always expecting to be first in the relationship. It was confusing but he liked their boldness. Maisie was demanding, a challenge for him to bring her to his side as an adoring slave and he knew he was fighting a losing battle. Maisie was formidable, had the look of a haughty princess as her eyes searched for his very soul and he felt it being plucked from him. He was the eldest son of a large family which was common place in his culture, unfairly responsible for his family but that was how it was, he had come to Scotland to fulfil that debt but also to make and take something for himself, an education that would hopefully make him wealthy and help his family to. Scotland was mystical and no less beautiful than his homeland, it had grandeur and atmosphere and the weather was often biting cold, he felt comfortable here but he must concentrate on his studies, ignore her presence as whilst in class nothing must distract him from his goal. The relationship had taken wings and he felt gratified that she felt he was worthy; her family were an enigma to him, being fed titbits about them but not yet being introduced into their home. He had briefly met Beattie, who had looked at him critically, what had she seen? A delusional man most likely, for thinking he could hold the blonde magnetic girl that was her sister. Her mother he had met whilst he and Maisie had been in the local village, he noted her looks, not much like Maisie but charismatic, her lively eyes assessed him then dismissed him and she had gone about her business, leaving them staring after her slim form belying her years. Maisie spoke highly of her. She had informed him that her dad was very Scottish, but what did that mean? He was very Romanian, of course he was, he probably wouldn't like her choice of boyfriend but it didn't matter as he didn't need to know or want to, she was to concentrate on her studies. Mitac could relate to that as for him it was the way out of poverty, for her more riches.

CHAPTER 10

Marguerite was working her way through her daily routine, it kept her balanced but only just and she knew she was not much use to anyone. Her house that was once immaculate was looking jaded, as was she. She tried to pull her family together but they were scattering without her fully engaged, she should be concerned but it was enough to deal with her own self. The boys needed her to help them but they rarely did anything alone, they had each other so needed no entertainment from her. She should be encouraging them to pursue different things as they weren't particularly alike other than in looks. Her eldest son was gangly and her younger son considerably shorter, but he could overtake him in later years. That was the interesting thing about children, they would just seem taller all of a sudden or start using different words, catch you out by saying something wise or funny, her younger son was perceptive but her eldest often spoke out without thinking. They were very different, which was probably the reason why they didn't annoy each other. She had a diversion now but as meetings could not be frequent this heightened the excitement and, whilst she would not always be available, she knew he would stop whatever he was doing to be with her if the chance arose. All these assumptions without actually having met again since the chance meeting, she was getting carried away.

Maisie was and always had been deeply involved in her own life in a big way, not really noticing the behaviour of the other people in the house unless it was in direct contact with her. Beattie, spending more time with unknown friends, lessening in her original self and a new more grown up version emerging. This was only normal

Marguerite consoled herself, pleased in a way, but you missed the closeness you get with your children when they were small. She worried about Beattie, who was not usually a concern, pushing herself through life with her realistic attitude. She was out so much now that it seemed unacceptable but she relayed her fears for her safety, keeping it light. Beattie often wore a shamefaced look, she knew her mother was struggling but said little to reassure her.

The walls of the Chevelly house teetered a little more as the days passed, they were all behaving oddly now. Even the boys had caught on that something was amiss, walking around with startled looks not being able to relate or understand, the football laying idle in the bushes and even the den became neglected as they too retreated to one or the other of their rooms to play video games that were previously not of much interest.

Marguerite and her husband were out of sync at dangerous levels now and the atmosphere was explosive as he began to be out of the house more after work hours. She felt relieved not to have his accusing eyes on her but annoyed he was an absent parent, but then had he not always been in the areas that mattered? She was resentful of this but retreated back as she had nowhere to run.

Mitac had gone to visit his family in Romania but didn't return for some time, his elderly grandfather had passed away and this involved a lengthy funeral. Maisie pondered his return, knowing that when he did he would have to get work in his free time, his family needing his money. With barely no time for her and she no concept of poverty, she became difficult and needy, Mitac thinking she was a spoiled child that got everything and appreciated nothing, but despite this the relationship continued.

Marguerite went to the café to sit at her table most days. Always freakily available, her cappuccino going cold as she recalled how their eyes had given away their desire, her pupils dilated and black, mirrored by his. Those kinds of feelings didn't just go away they had to be explored and acted on didn't they? A wiser woman would have

24

looked ahead, but she didn't want to.

Rodrigo passed the café, tempted to meander by every day, thinking it would become noticeable that he was acting like a stalker. He just wanted to spend even a few minutes with her, impatient and not wanting to wait until the arranged day, what if she didn't arrive?

Maurice had a slight cold but she wasn't overly concerned, only for the possibility that this could mean she wouldn't be able to meet Rodrigo. She hardly knew him but was already finding herself putting him before her children, a bad mother beneath the surface it seemed, she felt scared of the intensity of her feelings knowing he should be someone she should dismiss. Her children needed her so she began to double her efforts with them. Mitac, she told Maisie, would be fine. They were together in class, if not much out, but she would just have to be patient with him if they were to stay together. She felt it was becoming less like a relationship, he eventually appearing after working all hours, he had one free evening but it seemed this was only arranged to tell Maisie that he had yet another family issue, nothing to do with her, and he must make another short trip. Maisie, becoming increasingly paranoid, now doubted his return and Marguerite felt for her daughter. Love, in its many forms, seemed to cause as much pain as it did joy, but was it not still something we all need so desperately?

Beattie said she thought she too was getting the cold and felt unwell. Unfortunately she was right and on the day of the meeting she was confined to bed. Marguerite attended to her with hot drinks and food, mostly left untouched, Maurice's cold now just a sniffle, Frankie too showing signs of it. The boys still went to school and Marguerite felt tortured, questioning if she should leave Beattie, but she was rewarded as her husband appeared bleary eyed also not feeling too good, he too had caught the dreaded cold. He had muttered "I have a meeting at the bank later today, could you go"? She really was becoming something else, a sick daughter and a sick husband and all she cared about was herself and an almost complete stranger. She didn't like how this made her feel, but was pleased that her husband considered her able to handle a business meeting. She scolded herself, why had she not been more forceful, more actively involved? She had instead taken the submissive role when she wasn't that person at all, she needed to salvage herself but not like this.

The meeting at the bank allowed her to take extra care with her appearance but she kept it minimal as not to cause suspicion, not that her family would think her capable of duplicity. The meeting was regarding finance for a conservatory they didn't need, the patio doors already opening out to the garden with a huge terrace. Where could a conservatory possibly go without destroying what was already there? Marguerite went to the meeting anyway and the loan was approved effortlessly, with the paperwork in her bag she made her way to the café. She felt different now, stupid that she had even put herself in this position, but her heart, traitors that they are, told her different when he appeared. She had considered that he might have thought better of getting involved with an obviously married woman, teetering on the precipice herself, thinking maybe she could return to her life and her marriage and get more involved. If it was mundane it took two people to make it so and she was one of them, but the other didn't even know he was in the game. She felt annoyance at her husband's lack of perception and pondered how different today could have been had he have paid more attention to her. She was an observer of behaviour and in tune with it, would notice if he acted out of character, but perhaps she was a master of deceit, an element of her nature that hadn't yet been given a chance to emerge.

Despite her having only been to the café a few times her table, as it seemed now in the corner, was available. She lit a cigarette and without ordering, a cappuccino arrived, was she that predictable? She found she was a little irritated by this, maybe today she would have preferred a tea. She was arguing with herself and she was nervy, again this was rare as usually she was confident even if it was suppressed, playing out her submissive roles that were funnily enough a trait she disliked in other people. She considered that her husband should have noticed that she was smoking again, wanting him to cause friction, spark a response, but then he would need to get close enough to be aware of subtle changes in her behaviour. She had been his wife for years but felt he wasn't aware of her as a person anymore she was just useful, keeping the children at bay, making his life comfortable. The resentment built daily and she was ripe for this dalliance but really didn't want to jeopardise her family, she was getting ahead of herself.

A hand, the slightest touch on her shoulder and any resolve left melted away as she stared at him, he was just the sexiest man and she felt starved. Intermittent Sunday afternoon activity was all she had and for her husband it seemed attraction was not linked to affection or understanding and was just ignited as and when, like another chore. The promise of Rodrigo a guilty pleasure, losing herself to a place where only she and he existed, but the moment was broken when they both started to speak. They laughed, tension fading from her, but it was too late and she felt helpless to pull back.

CHAPTER 11

Maisie was in a stupor, nasty and cruel, upsetting the boys who didn't understand the change. Marguerite was concerned that they would grow to be men to inflict pain on women, with their father as a role model it didn't bode well for them and their future victims. How cynical was she? They were still very young, plenty of time to develop a caring side for women. They had sisters, surely that would help? Their father only had a brother so he had not had much insight into the female mind, though having a wife and two daughters should have gave him an idea.

Beattie, picking up the vibes, was getting sadder by the day, kept on about getting out there and having fun but not seeming to have any. What sort of fun, Marguerite pondered, alcohol, drugs, boys, the dangers were numerous. Beattie was blossoming in other ways, experimenting with make-up, her geeky look now slick, eyelashes heavily mascaraed she looked less like a child and Marguerite felt alarmed that her little girl was now leaving, never to return. Beattie, defiant, had stayed out late again several times and Marguerite didn't know where she was, who she was with or what she was doing.

The boys were back outside playing in their den, happily occupied in their kingdom of childhood, away from what was happening in the house.

Her husband seemed to have a lot of meetings recently, their authenticity not verified, but Marguerite doubted that she should worry. Couples after years of marriage just took each other's loyalty as a given. Dangerous, she reflected, knowing that if she were capable of straying then he was too. He never seemed overly interested in women, content in building his empire, but they were operating separately and that didn't bode well. That's just the way it goes when neither partner is interested in the other persons pursuits. Marguerite felt unneeded, but thought it wouldn't help to try and re immerse herself so instead she was daydreaming, time wasting. It was a wonder nothing was said, which just went to confirm further how little anyone was actually noticing about her. Nothing important was forgotten however, she attended any school related functions, it was mechanical, but she was barely there, fading. She needed Rodrigo to reassure her that she as Marguerite was special. She and her husband didn't attempt to talk about anything of importance, they conflicted at the best of times, and surely he must have picked up on the vibes of unrest? Was he completely stupid or perhaps he just didn't care? She couldn't believe that after years of being together he wasn't frightened of losing her, he most likely didn't consider her brave enough to revolt, but she was ready to fight, she couldn't accept this mediocrity any longer. It was a waste of a life, she felt devalued and she hated it, wouldn't accept it, or was this psychologically a way to get his attention? Didn't he realise what he could lose? But he was shallow, she knew it for sure, she was no longer perfect for him, no longer a puppet whose strings could be pulled, she was making a stand and the children were developing traits they too had kept undercover. He hadn't known what to do with them when they were good, so dealing with them as flawed he had no clue, the boys were easy but they too were neglected by her husband, Roly.

Their father, Roland the rat, a trifle unfair he wasn't but there was some resemblance, always scuttling away, though striding was probably more accurate. Marguerite had met him at Maisie age, laughable, as he had said Maisie didn't even know her own mind. Nevertheless how could Roly, without looking deep at the time invested and the money, the reflection of his life staring back at him, not question how his wife was moving in another direction or why? If he tried to make a difference now, could he? It all seemed too late.

Marguerite had already found a potential distraction, but it was so much more complicated than that. Regardless of the outcome with her and Rodrigo, which was an aberration, she could not continue and accept that this was all she was due. She wanted to scream at Roland but could already visualise his reaction, that smirk, which would remain for ever imprinted in her mind as representation of his true self.

CHAPTER 12

Marguerite had chosen Roland at a very young age and he had been just a few years older. How many people met a truly worthy partner that deserved to keep them for life at that stage? The end of personal dreams it seemed, when it should only have been the beginning. Having to consider another person when making any decisions, as oppose to just yourself, instead realising any dreams were now to be fulfilled through shared aspirations where compromises usually resulted in neither getting exactly what they wanted. Granted, at some point in all marriages there came a time where you felt stagnated, but this feeling could pass. Marguerite had allowed herself to become involved but now she felt starved of affection from her husband. Was that her fault, did she deserve it? Apparently so, she thought.

Roland, at his desk in the office where he shouldn't be and didn't need to be, but the house felt wrong and he couldn't function there, could only be at home when everything was going his way. His wife was looking younger every day; Girl like, maybe even more attractive now than she was when he had first met her, but he wasn't able to tell her that. His children were not placid but they all tried to be what he wanted, he could see it in their eyes. Almost begging for his approval, admire us Dad they said, I'm good aren't I? I'm clever? He hated that he couldn't tell them he was proud of them all. Roland knew he should kick a football around more often with his sons and he had tried on occasion, but their sheer joy actually made him feel sick, thinking how little he deserved it. He was selfish, that much he knew, but it wasn't natural to him to indulge in what felt like trivial time wasting pursuits when he had more important things to do, money to earn. He often found himself feeling impatient to get away during those times, but the boys would always run off happily after to play their own games, satisfied to have had a little attention from their father, if only for a short while.

His daughters, they were almost women now, but he barely knew what they thought or what they did when they weren't at college or school and it felt too late to find out. Marguerite gave into all of the children's demands which somehow made him the sensible one, he showed them the value of money and that it didn't just magically appear, it was earned. He was starting to feel things, his emotions emerging, but only thinking how it would affect him and not how it affected his family. He was worried that his wife had finally bored of him, but he knew she would always protect the children and find ways to give them all they needed, so he retreated back to his coldness, a barrier to protect him, that was now beginning to eat away at him from the inside. He remained stalwart however, continuing with his work and responsibilities as before. His wife, he presumed, was mostly at home. The children were her focus and with four, two of them teenagers, there was always something to do for one or all of them. She could go out when she wanted, spend his money, her life wasn't difficult. He had to go to work, make sure the bills were paid and in doing so was able to ignore the fact that the atmosphere in the house was turning dangerously icy. Maisie for one spent so much of her time in her room now, not speaking to anyone, but Roland continued to distance himself, not knowing how to deal with women's emotions and assuming Marguerite would deal with it.

Much later, he would come to realise that this time had been his chance to put things right, but hindsight is not useful.

CHAPTER 13

Maisie, she had to be certain of things, craved security. She pulled her fingers through her ringlets, perfect baby curls, but she hated them today as she arranged them haphazardly on the top of her head. Looking in the mirror her face was young, oval shaped, her compelling eyes gave character above her perfect little nose, the envy of Beattie, whose nose was straight though not large. It suited Beattie with her massive eyes. That's where people always looked, Maisie had said, when in her pink mood. She could be generous, moods allowing, and her smile was huge when she was happy enough to show it. She tried to smile now but failed, what was her future with Mitac? He had no money and even if he did get a good job eventually, most of it would find its way back to his greedy family in Romania. She also knew her father would not part with any of his precious money to fund a life for his daughter with a foreigner. He hadn't even met him yet but he didn't need to, it wouldn't change his view that he wasn't worthy of his daughter and this was already concluded without knowing him at all. Maisie thought her mother had sold out but that was not true. No doubt she had started out with the intention to stay married, had a family so it had brought her a lot, but she knew her mother was not in love with her father anymore. Instead she was falling for someone else and her parents rarely spoke, difficult to when her father was barely there, but Maisie was too wrapped up in her own anguish and had nothing left over for anyone else.

Beattie was mentally reviewing herself, she knew she wasn't behaving well and her parents would be horrified. Her father would lock her in her room if he knew. Her mother was trying to be modern thinking but was naïve, her friends took drugs and got drunk and Beattie was curious about the effects. She began sampling small amounts, drinking wine and tasting spirits, she had also started smoking cigarettes, rebelling. She used to be a bit like her mother, always the one to be cheerful and to do the right thing, dancing around people's moods, but right now she didn't care about being the favourite, she wanted to break out, experiment and live a little.

The boys were unsettled, eyes large and questioning, looking to their mother for answers but receiving just hasty hugs. They tried to catch their father's attention but he was always on his way to somewhere, only returning for meals and rarely then, so they barely saw him and if they did he would just pat their heads and be on his way, avoiding any meaningful conversation. It was hopeless and they too had become more engrossed in their own safe place, in the garden, in their den.

CHAPTER 14

Beattie wished now that she and her sister were closer. They thought differently but had the same parents so were therefore linked in the fight against parental control, or lack of it. Her father did try, kind of, and she felt pushed to change this, but her mother was so easily manipulated, what was happening to her? Beattie was not so unlike her sister, but equally not like her at all. Maisie was a sop, stupid about boys, but Beattie she had a power over them she was the one in control. The boy's looked at her but most wouldn't even dare to think they had a chance. Beattie knocked on Maisie's door and entered, her new rebellious self not waiting to be told to go away, or receive permission to be allowed through. What mood was it today?

"You need to be aware" she told her sister "that we need to be friends". "Of course we are, aren't we?" Maisie replied, the tone itself questioning whether in fact they were. Beattie didn't think so. "Something is going on Maisie and it's not good, I'm a bit frightened" Beattie said, also admitting that she herself was becoming out of control. Maisie quickly lapsed into talking about Mitac and how unhappy she was but Beattie ignored that, she wasn't listening to her. "This is about mum and dad, not you".

A sudden tap on the door alerted them to their mother's presence and they both turned quickly looking shocked, making it obvious that they had been discussing something that was not for their mother to be a part of. Marguerite would have liked the girls to be closer, to be friends, but she was aware of slivers of jealousy on both sides in different ways. They both asked if she was alright, with Beattie suggesting she was acting as though she was in some kind of 'dippy daydream'. "Am I"? Marguerite questioned, looking girlish and radiant. The girls didn't want to deprive her so dismissed the idea and said no more as they wrapped their arms around each other, united.

CHAPTER 15

For Rodrigo, time stood still, incapable of concentrating on anything other than Marguerite and when they could finally be together. Was she thinking of him too? He spent all his waking hours with her on his mind and dreaming of her when he was asleep, but had she thought better of pursuing something that had barely begun and banished it?

Marguerite noticed her husband had not returned home again that evening. Where the hell was he? One of the boys was coming up in a blueish rash, could it be meningitis? His eyes were becoming glassy and he was feverish, Beattie had alerted her mother to the situation. Alarmed and knowing they must act fast, they helped each other get Maurice to the car, covering him with a light blanket. Beattie wanted to go with them to the hospital but Marguerite said she was better to stay at home and listen out for Frankie rather than get him out of bed, she had to go. Beattie was afraid but had a maturity beyond her years and as she hurried her mother inside the car, she placed a beloved teddy into her brother's sticky hand and his fingers curled around it.

The hospital was a huge stark white building, looming threateningly on the other side of the town. This was another first, a visit to a hospital with a sick child, but alone to cope, well that was a given. A shiver crept up her spine as she was spotted immediately by two porters and, with a sense of urgency, a trolley was brought over and her son placed on it with the upmost care. Maurice was staring vacantly now, sweating profusely as he was whisked away leaving Marguerite to deal with the spiral of scattered outcomes that were competing in her head, her nails digging into her palms. She knew she should message or call Roly but didn't feel the need for him, being used to dealing with anything major or even minor without him. Her fingers hovered over her phone as she put her hand into the pocket of her light weight jacket; removing it, she scrolled through her contacts and stopped at Rodrigo's number. Could she? But within seconds the decision was taken from her as the phone buzzed into life, it must have already been in his hand, what did he actually do when he was on his own most nights? She didn't have time to consider this and answered hastily.

"I'm at the hospital with my son" she told him.

"I'm on my way if you want me there" he responded. Again, thinking of her and not him or the cost of yet another taxi, or the fact that her husband could appear. Marguerite decided she might be able to cope with him at her side, though coping was the only option, she didn't know yet if her son was seriously ill. Children could appear so fragile one moment, but then recover quickly in the next, so she settled as best she could. Hoping and waiting, waiting for him and waiting for news of her son. Had she been too wrapped up in herself to notice her son was ill? She was failing in her role, the fourth, as a mother to Maurice. Fortunately Rodrigo arrived quickly, genuinely anxious for her pain and concerned for a child he didn't know but understanding of her anguish. The nurse, not curious about the connection between her and him, clarified that Maurice was not seriously ill. It wasn't meningitis, just a rash. "Children know how to scare you don't they" she smiled comfortingly, confirming it was acceptable for Marguerite to let go of her breath now, which she had obviously been holding. "But he does have a fever so it's not a good idea to take him back out in to the cold just yet. We will need to keep an eye on him here for the time being". The nurse then hurried off to attend to other patients. Marguerite would have liked to have taken Rodrigo back to the house but Roly could appear, if he hadn't already, and it wouldn't be right. Beattie was taking care of Frankie, but where was Maisie? She suddenly realised that she hadn't seen her at all that evening, but felt unable to deal with that now on top of everything else. Rodrigo, recognising it was time for him to go home himself, put a light kiss on her dry mouth and assured her gently that he would call tomorrow.

Upon arriving home, Marguerite found Beattie asleep next to her other brother, but there was still no sign of Roly, so she sent a text to let him know about Maurice. A call would probably have been more appropriate, but she was reluctant to have to speak with him tonight, she was exhausted and didn't need or want his support. This really was a measure of the destruction of their relationship she thought, when she couldn't even call him about their son and found she didn't even want to, but she still expected a quick response; a message or a call, but neither was forthcoming. Fortunately Maurice was going to recover, but surely this should have been a time when parents put aside their differences? She considered how Rodrigo had risked encountering her husband, there for her regardless of consequence. He was of course high on love, but he had a kindness in him, he cared for people and was generous with his time and emotions, the softness in him and the coldness in her husband opposite spectrums. But we are what we are, all with different qualities; perhaps she and Roly balanced each other in many ways, she the giver and he the provider, an old fashioned concept that had worked well in years past. Roly was not a modern man, he was traditional and she had been forced into that role, taking years to chip away at her until she could bear it no longer. Nobody planned to break the marriage, it was a gradual demise and it was sad it had come to this, but she was helpless now to do anything. Roly just didn't seem aware at all and that infuriated her, he didn't see any of them really, not for who they really were and it was a waste, his children moving forward and growing to be strangers to him. Surely he would want to do something before that was too late too? She knew the children would welcome his attention, even now. She had watched them over the years, looking at Roly bewildered, nothing they did getting the kind of recognition they really wanted. He was proud of their looks and their good behaviour, even though they were rarely out as a family. His smugness sat horribly with her, knowing this wasn't their real children and that they were just acting on his behalf, not daring to upset him. Why hadn't she told him any of this before? Because he would smirk when she got emotional, and that would always stop the flow of conversation. She felt exasperated at the waste and what could have been had she have tried harder, had he have tried harder, but did it even matter now?

Rodrigo called, asking after her and her son. No news yet, will let you know she said, thanking him for the call. Just as the phone clicked off, it rang again instantly, Roly this time. His voice was stern, he had had a few drinks with some friends and was sleeping on the sofa as he couldn't drive, he explained, but it sounded lame he could have got a taxi. He asked after Maurice eventually, she said she didn't know yet, hadn't heard and would let him know. Repeating what she had just said to Rodrigo, her feelings for Roly took a further dip.

The next morning, Marguerite called the hospital as soon as she woke up and was told that Maurice could be taken home after checks had been done. He was awake and hungry, that was good news, and she felt overwhelmed with relief as strange thoughts entered in to her head allowing her to consider how different the outcome could have been. A caffeine fix, that's what she needed and she was still sat at the kitchen table with her coffee when Roly sauntered in. Automatically she rose to make him a cup.

Maisie appeared shortly after looking shifty, she must have been out all night and was likely expecting a telling off, alarmed at her father being there. But he just nodded blankly at her as Marguerite told of the turmoil last night with Maurice. Maisie's expression of anguish was followed by relief on two counts. One, that her brother was ok and two, that she had avoided an inquisition on her own whereabouts last night. A light one possibly from her mother, but extreme from her father definitely.

Now, other than Maurice, all the family were at home. Beattie joined them with Frankie and they were kind of like a real family again for a short while, as Marguerite gave Frankie a glass of milk, Beattie a coffee. When had she started drinking coffee? Another step towards being an adult, she noted. The clock ticked loudly on the wall, Roly's contribution to the kitchen décor. It was large and ugly, but truly significant in that moment, signalling in short bursts minutes never again to be shared all of them together as a proper family. They sat quietly; each in their own place in their own mind's, but thinking similarly that this too would soon become a memory to be placed with all the others.

CHAPTER 16

Roly had been in England on a business trip for a few days but decided to arrive home a day early, wanting to surprise his family. He had thought deeply whilst he was away, finally realising he was nothing without them and deciding he needed to make an attempt to turn around their opinions of him.

Walking through the front door, he noted straight away that every light in the house was on. No consideration for expense he thought irritably but stopped himself, trying to retain his mind set. His wife and children were spoilt but he had played a part in that, swaggering in a conceited way and lavishing them with possessions, but he hadn't planned on selling his virtues to them tonight. He continued to make his way through the house, following the sounds of chitter chatter and laughter which lead him to the front room. He entered but was suddenly stopped short.

Who on earth was this man in his house? A common man, youngish and good looking, perhaps he was a boyfriend of Maisie's he considered briefly. He looked a bit older than Maisie but maturity was good, though he didn't look very mature in an outrageous T-shirt with an obscene picture on it, paired with jeans and untied boots.

"What's going on here"?

Roly tried to sound cheerful, but panic began to crawl up his spine as he realised there was no sign of Maisie and this young man being a couple. The man was sat next to his wife and Maisie was stood the other side of the room. There was no physical contact but they looked as though they were together, he could feel it. No one spoke as they all remained rooted to where they were stood or sat, the boys started to grab at Roland playfully but he just responded in the usual way of patting their heads. His family were all together, which didn't happen often as they were mostly too busy participating in their own individual activities. Not today, it appeared. He watched the man stand up.

"Best be on my way" Rodrigo declared, but he seemed wrong footed and was looking extremely awkward.

"Who are you then"? Roly asked, trying not to show any accusation in his voice as he put a hand on Rodrigo's shoulder.

"Nephew of a friend of Marguerites"

His grip tightened slightly, "What friend"?

Everyone's eyes immediately turned to Marguerite, waiting for an answer to the question that nobody had yet got a definite answer to.

"A friend" Marguerite responded shortly, unwilling to give out any further information, knowing that even if she gave a name he would still question why Rodrigo was there anyway and further prolong the conversation.

"I see. Well don't rush off on my account" Roly said tightly, loosening his grip on Rodrigo's shoulder and instead tapping him on the back, a little harder than was necessary.

"It's cool" Rodrigo replied, desperately wanting to get out of the house, his confidence shaken. Roland was a big man and he was Marguerites husband and whilst nobody knew anything for sure, surely it was written all over their faces? Rodrigo made one last attempt to leave but Roly insisted he stayed and had a meal with them, forcing him to return to his seat and endure the rest of the evening.

Roly was seriously angry for a man who didn't profess to have feelings, least show them, but now he could feel every one of them building. Could he be the reason for the change in his wife? Surely she wouldn't stoop so low to consider a man so young, attractive or not? He himself couldn't have felt uglier than he did right now. He wasn't bad looking, but next to this stud he felt old, used and passed his best. He found he couldn't dismiss the idea, but wouldn't dare to voice it for fear of putting the final nail in the coffin that was their marriage.

CHAPTER 17

Marguerite and Roland sat at the kitchen table the next morning with coffee, neither of them interested in food. Marguerite looked so incredibly beautiful today, glowing even. Had she? Roly's thoughts wandered in to dangerously painful territory, he felt sick at the thought of his wife with that man but he knew he couldn't just accuse her. He tried to hold her hand but she looked at him with venom as she slid the rings off her left hand, they sparkled momentarily on the table.

"It's over" she said.

Was he hearing her right? His eyes were awash with tears and Marguerite felt a small tug of pain, she wasn't made of stone. He was still her husband and she again pondered on how they had reached this point and how careless it had been of them both. Roly felt untethered, floundering, not at all himself and his voice came out choked as he faltered at the words.

"Can I do anything"?

"No" she replied. "It's too late".

"So what now"? Roly asked, his voice barely a whisper.

"The children and I will stay in the house, I've looked after it unfailingly all these years so it is my right" Marguerites tone left no room for negotiation, her mind was made up. "You, I cannot decide for".

It all seemed so business-like. Roland's heart now set loose to feel was beating frantically, erratically, as though it might suddenly stop but continued on treacherously. There was no escape for him; he never thought he could be self-pitying as he debated daring to voice his fears and feelings. What did it matter now? Her silence confirmed it for him as he pinched his pale lips tight, his face white whilst she just stared at him, her eyes accusing, waiting for something he could not speak. He could see that she was about to try to explain herself but he chose not to allow it and instead held his hand up as if to say, no more. He couldn't bear it. For now, she was innocent, but he had lost her and she had just ended their marriage and he couldn't deal with hearing the truth. She had been his all these years, but had not realised until now his true feelings for her and he was devastated, broken. He needed to be alone.

"What will you tell the children?" he asked eventually, adding "They don't need me, I suppose. Of course, I provided the walls and roof, but you provided the glue".

Marguerite felt insulted. If that was his idea of a last ditch attempt to win her back it had failed, his seemingly newfound acknowledgement of her importance was bittersweet but just left her feeling cold. It was too little, too late.

CHAPTER 18

Maisie wondered where her dad had gone, the evening ruined by his arrival a day earlier than was expected. She had seen his initial expression of hope suddenly dashed at spotting an intruder, but he had gone along with it. Everyone, especially mum, was jumpy. Was that guilt? Her parents were separated, but what did that mean? They were still married, had a family, a house, it wasn't that simple, what was her mother doing? It was out of character and Maisie felt guilty for thinking it was fun without him there. He was her dad and she loved him, but he had made them feel like laughter and love were a crime. Ambition was the road to money and it seemed to be all that he was concerned with, but it had worked well for him she thought. Perhaps they should be more like minded, Maisie liked nice things, but her father seemed to miss the fact that the bricks in the road required love too and with that, anyone could achieve anything. Her boyfriend Mitac, like her father, was gone now too, would he return? Maisie felt unsure. She wasn't like Romanian women that were loose with their men and knew their place. Her father though, she would of course see him again somewhere, even if it wasn't at the house. Her mother presumably had something going on with Rodrigo, could she? She appeared so young now when Maisie had looked at them both together, masking the dramatic age gap slightly so it didn't seem as wrong. In her head she visualised Rodrigo's dark blue eyes lined with thick eyelashes that fluttered to his advantage, but somehow he still looked manly. He made them all laugh and played with the boys who soaked his attention greedily, happy to have a male addition to the house. Her thoughts then turned to her father, he was not a fun figure, he was a coward because he hadn't stayed to fight and she was so disappointed in him for that. She might have had some respect for him had he have at least tried to win her mother back somehow, but his absence had now became commonplace which said it all to her, he didn't care enough.

Beattie was extremely angry, tears threatening as she shouted, outraged that nothing had been said to her.

"He's left, just like that with no explanation"?!

Maisie and even the boys could have accepted a reasonable explanation at this point, but he had offered them nothing. Marguerite tried to hold her hand, it was icy, but her face was the opposite reaching boiling point as bright red spots appeared on her cheeks. Suddenly she turned to her mother.

"What's happening with you mum? You're not here with us are you, not mentally, and dad isn't either, if he ever was"!

Her voice was getting higher with exasperation, despairing of both of her parents, the boys didn't know what was going on but her parents were the ones acting like children now.

Marguerite felt helpless to stop the wheels of destruction that were in place now, had it all been her fault? But it's never just one half of a couple, she had always tried to be whatever everyone wanted but now no longer wanted to, not even for her children. They would grow up and have their own lives, she had to have someone just for her, but would her relationship with Rodrigo last if she didn't commit? At the moment she was just living for now and he was her oxygen.

CHAPTER 19

Rodrigo had been made aware of the situation and he was pleased, wickedly so, but he was not the cause. Marguerite had a choice and the house of Chevelly had been tottering long before his arrival. She could now be his, how long for he didn't know, but now was all that mattered. His family would tell him he was stupid, but how was he? She could give him everything he could possibly want or need and, right now, she most likely would. The future is of course unknown, but who cares? Perhaps Roly would return to try to reclaim her he considered, but doubted any success, he was a stranger to him but he felt he had had his measure and would prefer not to cross paths with him again.

Roly, now back at work, regretted all the hours he spent there at his desk. All the meetings he had invented, why did he always feel like he had to be seen to be in control? He should have been at home with his wife and children, such a credit to him, unbeknownst to them he had always been proud of them all and he was now deeply hurt that he had lost them. Why hadn't he just sent a colleague to deal with what now seemed like such trivial matters? These feelings sat badly with him, he felt like a monster. In his own way he thought he was right to devote himself to his work to enable his family to have a life of luxury, his father had done the same, but now he saw that that alone could not sustain a marriage. He thought briefly about their family holidays, those were the good times, they had become more and more expensive; better locations, fabulous hotels, and when they returned they felt revitalised, ready to resume their daily lives. Had these things been nothing? His family obviously wanted something else, but what? Marguerite must have been unhappy for a long time, he hadn't noticed, but now he had she was already lit from the inside with desire for another man. He too saw now that he hadn't taken much interest beyond education in his daughters, not paid enough attention to his sons. What sort of example had he set to them now on how it would be one day to be men? He had a small flat now, couldn't put himself on other people, not the very ones he had belittled, not to their faces of course but in his mind. The flat was soulless, basic and clean. Maybe his wife hadn't actually slept with this man yet? He considered this but deep down already knew that she had. Without actual proof or a confession though, maybe there was still a chance? Could he make Margarite feel the loss of him? She always contacted him by text now never called and only regarding things that she absolutely couldn't deal with herself, which were scant, so she must be dealing with everything perfectly well without him.

Marguerite, again at the table in the kitchen, couldn't find a sensible thought to act on. The children obviously expected her to keep everything together, considering their parents invincible as children do, however they clearly were not. Gradually, without prior notice, strangers were appearing regularly at the house. With Roly now not in situ the children had decided it was time to bring their outside lives in. Another boy, Gregg, had caught Maisie's attention, so Mitac had been put on the shelf for now to gather dust. He was a year older than her and was at the house now, in her room. Marguerite, relieved to hear her eldest daughter laughing again, left them alone not wanting to dampen any signs of happiness coming Maisie's way, and why would she? She should be allowed a boyfriend and to bring him to the house, however she knew Roly would never have approved, probably because he knew how 17 year old boys could be.

Greg was English but working in Scotland, he said he liked the fresh air, the landscape and the girls. He was dapper with an old-fashioned expression but it suited him, hair blonde and his eyes a pale grey, he was a bit of a bad boy, a player. Not like Mitac at all, who had a conscience and cared for his family, a characteristic which Maisie chose to ignore. Marguerite was hesitant to voice any concerns regarding the obvious sexual overtones. Had her daughter slept with Mitac? Most likely she presumed, but it hadn't been confirmed, and was she sleeping with Greg? Mitac had been left broken when he finally returned from Romania to find Maisie had moved on, but he had remained stoic, another good characteristic, accepting without retaliation. So much for true love! Marguerite didn't want to think of it as fleeting, she was a silly woman acting like a teenager, or was this a midlife crisis that hadn't been kept under control by smoking or being frivolous? Now she was relishing a glorious unsurpassed period of time where she felt no price was too high to pay! That was even more immature, she scolded herself, the cost would be too high and it already was.

Beattie was happy that Maisie now had free rein, a new boyfriend who was allowed in the house. But had her mother left her senses behind? Beattie was envious, she wanted her friends in the house, she was allowed a friend to tea but she was too old for that. Greg had a brother, she had seen the photo and overheard that he was going to be in Scotland to spend his holidays with Greg. He was luscious and she knew she would be introduced, what was his name? Melvin? Max? Mark? She couldn't remember, no it was more unusual, Mace, that was it!

CHAPTER 20

Marguerite thought ahead, the summer holidays were approaching and the boys usually went to her parents. They were a while away by car but still in Scotland and every year she and Roly would drive there together and leave the boys for a few weeks. They would chat with her parents for an hour or two, catching up face to face, they looked forward to it but this year she would be alone and she would have to take the boys by herself. Her parents hadn't seemed overly surprised at Roly's absence, or at least didn't voice it, assuming that he must have decided for the first time not to visit them. Had they noticed anything? They would rarely have got the chance, visits were infrequent to them and only very special occasions gave them the opportunity to go to the Chevelly house. They would have been concerned if their daughter and Roly were having problems so Marguerite didn't tell them the extent. The boys had been a bit bewildered and clingy when she left, but thankfully less so when she returned a few weeks later to collect them. Roly may not have been the ideal father in as much he didn't always do things that other dads did but he was a presence, a disciplinarian figure, and the change in the dynamics of the Chevelly house had unsettled them. Going to her parents was something they did every year and it reassured them that some things were still the same.

Marguerite pulled into the driveway, music was blaring from the house. They weren't close to other houses but sound travelled. A strange smell greeted her, pungent and intense but she was so innocent that she thought it was incense. Calling out her return, her voice was lost and she suddenly felt sleepy, busy day she thought naïvely, not relating it in any way to the smoky air that was making its way through the house. She struggled to make a coffee and feeling heavier by the second her senses finally alerted her to make a connection. Immediately she dragged herself up the stairs to Maisie's room and opened the door without knocking; the air was thick with smoke. She spotted an ashtray full with what looked like cigarette butts they had been smoking in the house, a definite no for the children who other than Maisie were too young to smoke. Marguerite rushed to open all the windows and switched off the stereo, feeling some relief at finding her daughter and Greg holding hands whilst very much asleep and fully clothed, the ashtrays contents would have to be a discussion for the morning. Marguerite felt out of her depth, she was a delusional woman and her daughter had been with a foreign man and now a druggie. Roly would be horrified and she was too about the drugs, obviously anything goes now with only her at the helm. If she were to call her father now and let him know what was happening, what would he say? He would most probably blame her and say that she was an unfit mother, likely act on it. She would sort this even if she didn't know what she was dealing with, it was normal for the young to experiment wasn't it? But she knew she would need to approach this problem very carefully.

CHAPTER 21

The next morning Marguerite awoke, semi refreshed but still muzzy as she remembered the events of last night, knowing she would have to deal with the situation immediately before she had the chance to stop feeling angry. She went and knocked on Maisie's door and, without waiting, pushed the door open. Her daughter was leaning against the boy and both of them looked exactly how she was feeling, the silence loud. Marguerite waited, following the rule of waiting for the other to speak first.

"Mum, about the boys..." Maisie mumbled, trying to get her mother onto a different topic. Usually mention of the boys made her smile which would make her more amenable, but it didn't work today. Maisie resorted to smiling helplessly as Greg tried to slip out towards the door, but Marguerite stood barring his escape route.

"So, what happened in here last night"?

"Oh nothing, it's just like a cigarette really" Greg knew what she was talking about straight away, trying to justify it.

"Smoking in the house is not allowed" Marguerite said, mentally reminding herself that she did, but that was just actual cigarettes and only when she was alone.

"Yes, I thought you would say something like that as I'm no expert on the subject, but I know the difference between cigarette smoke and something else".

Who the hell was this boy introducing her daughter to drugs? She was at fault again, trusting her daughter to choose a suitable boyfriend, but really with Maisie she knew that would never be the case and she couldn't be around all the time to supervise every second.

"Just get out" she told Greg.

Maisie looked upset but said nothing and let him leave. After he had gone she sunk into the chair beside her bed and started crying, her usual ploy to get her mother on side.

"No Maisie. Not this time. If I catch you partaking in this kind of thing again you will be staying in for a month, apart from college" Marguerite said, forgetting that college was actually closed for the holidays anyway. "And for now, no Greg, I don't want him here".

"But Mum..." Maisie pleaded.

"No" she confirmed firmly, making it quite clear that there was no room for negotiation, leaving the room and her daughter to stare after her. In her mind she recalled times when she had been told not to do something as a child, remembering that it usually just made it more exciting, but it didn't matter now. She had, had her say and she doubted she would be able to keep Maisie in for a month if it came to it anyway but honestly Maisie spent so much time in her room, it would be no great hardship as unless she took her phone away, she could still message and speak to people. Still, she had shown she wasn't to be messed with today, but was this what happens should she dare to default as a mother? It appeared to provide her children with a license to deviate as her daughters and even her sons, as young as they were, were becoming more attention seeking by the day.

Suddenly the doorbell interrupted her train of thought and she mentally acknowledged it but didn't get up to answer, it was still so early. It wouldn't be Roly as he had a key and often chose to walk in using the element of surprise to catch her out, knowing she couldn't collect herself. This was how he would operate nowadays, leaving her unable to get on, waiting for the next onslaught and not being able to have Rodrigo in the house without worry. Marguerite accepted this but she wasn't about to let him loose her anything that she wanted, however she now felt scared of her own husband, was that irrational? Marguerite got to her feet and out of habit briefly checked her appearance in the hall mirror, noting her pained

54

expression before finally opening the front door. She stood well back, as did the young man that stood there.

"Greg here?" the man enquired brazenly, his voice not sounding very pleasant in the slightest.

"Why would he be?" Marguerite replied as she shook her head.

"Maisie" he said, his stance impatient. "You're her mum aren't you?"

Marguerite, feeling disrespected by his tone waited, saying nothing.

"Greg around later?" he continued, staring hard at her and making her feel slightly uncomfortable.

Who was this man and what was his connection to her daughter and Greg?

"He owes me money" he said, answering her thoughts as quickly as they came.

Of course it was about money, wasn't it always, but what was it to do with her daughter? She felt no need to explain herself and instead pulled herself up tall, hoping at least to appear to be a force to be reckoned with, and shut the door after stating that no, Greg certainly would not be there later, if ever again. She peered through the hall window and could see the annoyance on the man's face but he didn't knock again.

Marguerite suspected that this was something to do with the situation in the house last night and knew that she would have to talk with Maisie about it again, but not until later as, for now at least, the man and Greg were both gone.

CHAPTER 22

The next morning Beattie was quiet, wondering if she was a part of last night's debacle. Maisie hadn't appeared so Marguerite text her, they sometimes did that as it was a big house and shouting wasn't practical. A clear message, straight to the point often made a greater impact… get to college or else. As expected Maisie soon appeared, looking subdued. "It's the holidays Mum".

Of course it was, Marguerite had forgotten.

Maisie looked thrown together, her ringlets defying her sullen look happily bouncing as she momentarily opened her mouth to speak further but clamped it shut upon noticing the look on her mother's face.

The doorbell rang again, but this time a police officer stood there and he wasn't smiling. Apparently a group of young people were very noisy last night, it was noticeable around here as it was usually a quiet area, and he reminded them that other people live in the vicinity. It wasn't serious but implied that next time it could be. Marguerite picked up the post, catching the looks of the faces on the photographs that lined the gallery wall. Faces of her once happy family, some capturing the best moments on exotic holidays, others captured faces beaming with a sense of achievement. Nostalgia swamped her as she scrambled past them, too choked to look again and pushing open the patio doors. The garden beckoned, untamed and rambling free, spreading without constraint and all the more beautiful for it, unlike her, so caught up even now in the confines of her old life and trying to pull the best parts of it into a new one. She gulped the nectar air greedily as it calmed and restored her, it never failed.

This house wasn't just bricks, it was her family home and it was the memories that brought it to life. She had been careless, allowing for a lost youth possibly she didn't know, but now the years of suppression that hadn't been noticeable previously were suddenly surfacing dangerously. She needed to concentrate, get absorbed; the house was in need of attention, it even smelt horrible. With the air freshener in one hand, spraying indiscriminately to eradicate any trace of evidence of cigarette smoke or otherwise that should never have been there in the first place. The other hand picking up odd socks, items of clothing and rubbish thrown randomly on the floor, nowhere near to a bin. Nobody remembered or respected any rules anymore, they were all embracing a lack of restrictions, and she could see how easily a house could become out of control without some level of expectation. Marguerite knew that some serious effort was required but she felt the tension dispel as she frantically moved rapidly from one room to another. It was so big, so full of too many expensive things and it looked austere as she considered the waste of money. Who needed the most expensive furniture, when it wasn't what you liked? Who were they trying to impress? So many pointless items filled the shelves, ornaments they didn't need or use. The house wasn't even open for people to admire, Roly hated visitors, and all of a sudden it was as though nothing really made sense any more.

Marguerite decided that not today but soon, she would have a garden sale. No too noticeable, a car boot. That could be fun for the boys, get them to get rid of some things that they didn't like anymore, they would likely be inspired by the idea of making some money of their own since they didn't often get given actual money as they were just bought things. The girls could clear out their wardrobes, that would be easy for Maisie but on the verge of impossible for Beattie who didn't dare to touch anything as to move a little bit the dust would show and then she would have to continue so better never to start. Did anyone really care about dust? Maisie did, her room was pristine normally and she would like the house the same and would often say as much to Marguerite, but she had too much going on at the moment to worry about the house. Marguerite wasn't the best housekeeper, she didn't like housework, it tired her but what else could she do? It was her duty, her work, she knew she could do so much more but had chosen to cut off any ideas that were solely for her, she was static in her resolution today.

Feeling pleased, she ridiculously called Rodrigo knowing it was not a good idea considering that she had just spent the whole day getting calm and rational but she threw it to the wind now. He was thrilled of course, said with such enthusiasm that he would be over soon to be with her and it was delicious to be wanted so much. All her earlier thoughts on nostalgia now set aside and instead overtaken with the excitement of thinking what to wear. Marguerite really was reverting to being a teenager but loving it. How fickle she was, one minute swamped in memories, the next racing to make new ones.

Arriving in a taxi, his long legged presence, his manliness, filled the room as they reached out for each other. The next hour they explored each other's bodies, noting any small scars, his skin young and soft but his body strong, wide shoulders tapering to a slim waist and joining together perfectly. Marguerite felt lost but removed from any worries or hesitation as they continued until they were sated.

Footsteps could be heard as Rodrigo snatched his clothing and fled. Marguerite was scantily clad but covered, feeling flushed and eyes dreamy, but soon filling with sheer panic upon realisation that the game was over. Roly appeared, his cold stare terrifying as his hands pressed hard on her shoulders, she knew she smelt different, expensive perfume disguising the worst, she felt mortified as all his pent up stuffiness was released on her. Years of restraint, keeping control, she abandoned herself to her fate, her body limp but Rodrigo suddenly appeared, a man possessed, as he pulled Roly from her and at the sudden release she fell, hitting her face on the side of the cabinet.

Flailing fists, both men became a blur knocking the glass coffee table turning it on its side as a cascade of splinters erupted in a frenzied froth. Marguerite watched, barely focusing, losing herself into darkness, only vaguely aware of the two men covered in blood as they took the fight outside. Rodrigo held his hands up, he was the younger man, Roly was strong with anger but he was much older so he knew he had to stop it.

Marguerite was hurt, Rodrigo gate crashed her life knowing she was married, he should have resisted, been the noble one and shown respect towards an older woman, but he hadn't. He had taken what he wanted, sensing his power over the woman he had fallen in love with almost instantly, he believed in fate and this had brought it all out in to the open.

Roly hadn't caught them as such, but he had made judgement as the signs were there, they were alone in the house, what innocent reason could have brought them there? This man was trying to take his wife and he knew it. Roly could kill him, and vice versa, but Rodrigo looked at Roly, seeing him as old and dejected, a measure of sympathy briefly replaced by hate. Marguerite was lying still on the floor amidst fragments of glass, Roly was red faced and perspiring heavily as he yelled "get out you chancer!"

Rodrigo fell silent, less of a threat, knowing he was beaten. It was this man's house, he was the one who had to leave and reluctantly did so as he glanced back to see Marguerite get up from the floor. He knew she was alive and for now he had to be satisfied with that, but in a menacing tone said to Roly "If you touch her again, I'll have you" and with that, he strode purposefully away, not calling a taxi but just walking, wondering if he would ever see her again or would this idiot Roly make a last chance attempt to save his marriage.

Roly, having established his wife was not seriously hurt, couldn't trust his self with her and didn't want to know if what he suspected had taken place. He knew it wasn't innocent but as its full extent was not confirmed, he said nothing to her, couldn't, he wanted to leave as usual but his daughters had just arrived home so he was trapped. The look of abject horror on four faces was clear his daughters were with two boys he didn't know.

Beattie flew at him, beating her fists on his chest as she screamed at him "Monster!"

Marguerite, still slipping into darkness for what could have been minutes, an hour, she didn't know but a wet cloth was mopping her face. Beattie put a blanket over her and Marguerite was in shock as she questioned why she was being so kind and if she knew the extent of her betrayal. She loved all her children unconditionally, but with the children love came with conditions. The boys had left she was told when she was again coherent and conscious of her surroundings. Roly had also left and nothing he could say would justify his behaviour. Had their dad ever hit her? The girls asked, white faced.

"No" Marguerite shook her head. "Tonight was just an accident that shouldn't have happened and violence is not the answer in any situation, it was just an act of desperation."

Her daughters sat either side of her, each holding one of her shaky hands. Marguerite felt unwell as the lump on the side of her face swelled the bruise blue at this stage but not wanting to be checked by a doctor, knowing she could have concussion, but the thought of having the doctor look and confirm it to her she couldn't bear. She wanted no sympathy or pity from any outside source. Roly hadn't contacted her. Surely he cared at least at some level but she knew he would not say sorry. He had been shamed and behaved like an animal but emotion had finally surfaced which he possibly had struggled to keep hidden, avoiding conflict perhaps. He knew that this was how he would behave and he hated anything to disturb his position as master of his house. How he appeared to his work colleagues, friends, acquaintances, that was what mattered but he was now diminished and he couldn't cope with her having brought him to shame. Marguerite had taken away the respect of his children and they would take her side rightly, no child accepts ill treatment of their mother.

Rodrigo sent endless messages so that she knew he was thinking of her but the enormity of her straying and the proportions of its consequences now felt doomed, all the joy she felt before diminished.

Maisie had suspected this, seen how her mother had changed but couldn't take on her being with this man that was undeniably attractive, but it all felt wrong and dangerous, spreading out affecting each of them in different ways as her dad too became someone she didn't know. Maisie understood love was complicated, irresistible, but her mother being caught in this situation she could never have foreseen. She now noticed how shallow she was herself, flitting from Mitac who she loved, or was that just lust moving seamlessly to Greg who excited her in a different way, danger surrounding him. Was that what she and other girls wanted, to be permanently on a high? It seemed her mother was caught in this turmoil with age providing no barrier. Considering last night's activities, a pang of nostalgia pulled uncomfortably as she herself longed for excitement and thrills, but it tired you and she too felt burnt out as she struggled to make some sort of sense of what was happening at the Chevelly household. What next? She wondered. Her mother had been hurt by their father undeniably, but she couldn't take it on at all. He was so righteous, so law abiding, but he was not immune to outside forces that threatened them and one bad choice lead to more and then you were lost. There wasn't a safe place to be right now.

She thought of Greg and his association with drugs and her involvement with them now too. She and Greg had laughed, listened to loud music in the garden with people that Greg knew but she didn't and later taking the party to her room just the two of them. She knew it was wrong but she enjoyed it, not the repercussions that followed however.

CHAPTER 23

Maisie's phone rang; it was a very agitated Greg saying that he desperately needed her help as he had just received a text message saying the money he owed was now due with interest.

"How much"? She asked.

"A grand" he replied.

Maisie was horrified, how was she supposed to help with that kind of money when she didn't have her own cash? He knew that, as she had told him before, but she repeated the information anyway.

Greg laughed nastily "You are joking aren't you? You go to a posh college and live in an amazing house yet you have got no money?"

"The family has money Greg, not me" Maisie answered. "And why do I have to help you? It's nothing to do with me"

"It is, I am your boyfriend and you smoked it with me"

"I had a few spliffs with you and now I have to help you pay £1000? I don't think so Greg".

Maisie was getting annoyed now, what was she doing messing with him? Allowing herself to be introduced in to this seedier life, sleeping with him and taking risks, bringing his dodgy friends into their garden and causing the neighbours to complain. Before he arrived in her life they had been a respected family in the community, but she wasn't too bothered about that as such, however she wasn't about to ask her mother for money to pay off her boyfriend's drug debt. She wouldn't be sympathetic and would ask why Greg couldn't go to his own family, who Maisie already knew he wouldn't dare ask, yet he had dared to ask hers.

"If you cared for me Greg, you wouldn't bring this to my door".

Greg sounded close to tears now and having failed to get Maisie on side he hung up the phone.

Greg didn't care about Maisie's reputation, or her families, and showed little respect to others. His little brother however was different and he at least acted respectfully, appeared to like her mother and always spoke to her as she felt she deserved to be spoken to and treated Beattie like she was precious.

Beattie was a looker and together she and Mace looked surreal. He, like Beattie, seemed to be loved by all. Not for their looks but for the happiness that they projected, people liked happy people, it was infectious. But isn't it easy to be nice when you are beautiful?

Maisie and Greg had alternating sides to their personalities; they suited at that level but not in much else. She was clever and he was reasonably bright in a practical way, but not smart enough to refuse drugs, especially those he couldn't afford to pay for and he enjoyed drinking too much. Really, what was she doing with him? She was clever she was told, but she was all too easily pulled in. Her thoughts then drifted to her other love interest.

Mitac, now at home in Romania, was abandoned by Maisie and with no messages coming through he knew nothing about her life now. He wanted to return to his studies but without her it didn't have much appeal anymore, despite his previous determination to succeed no matter what obstacles arose.

He could try to get back to his studies and to her, Maisie would expect it, and he didn't blame her for moving on as he knew how much attention she needed. She was only sixteen, but in his country young women were often married by then, no careers. Though of course the occasional Romanian girl tried to break the mould, but it was difficult in a very male-dominated culture.

Back in Scotland however, Rodrigo was becoming increasingly anxious with Marguerites prolonged silence and, inventing scenarios in his head, he could not wait any longer. He would have to take his chances and go to the house, hoping of course that she would be pleased to see him and that her horrible husband would not be there. Rodrigo called a taxi. A walk, though not that far, would detain him and he was far too impatient now.

On arrival, he immediately noticed that the front garden was unruly and the once pristine white picket fences were now greying. He could change that, he was indispensable and had time to give willingly and he would give it for free, but his wandering thoughts were stopped suddenly as he heard Marguerites voice. She was in the garden, had seen him approaching and upon doing so yelled a hasty goodbye to whom she was talking to and began running towards him, her arms open wide. His fears diminished immediately as his long arms caught around her slim waist where she fitted perfectly. To say she looked happy would have been a drastic underestimation as her reaction to his arrival was like an excited teenager no less, bounding across into his arms. Marguerite was clearly grateful that he had made this decision and neither could resist each other now. The lovemaking was frenzied and primal, over quickly, not wanting to get caught and leaving them feeling deeper in love, or lust, neither could be sure which.

Later on Marguerite considered all the bills; Utilities, insurance, mobile phones, which the boys didn't have yet of course. She didn't think Roly would want to pay for them, much as he depended on his own, he would likely see it as punishment for them all to be deprived of this luxury.

She hadn't needed a credit card before but had managed to get one easily now, she would only be able to pay the minimum monthly repayments but it resolved the issue for the time being so the girls could keep using their phones. Roly still paid for the water, electricity and gas and, for now, gave her enough money to buy food. She was getting clever at budgeting, using non-branded goods; the box was just a container anyway when the contents were the same. Some things however really did taste better if they cost more but it wasn't important right now and if the children did notice the difference, a sharp look from their mother would render any complaint benign.

Marguerite was thin now, not slim. She could wear tiny clothes and she looked good in them, but she knew any thinner and she would be just a bag of bones. She was eating but the stress and worry was rapidly burning the calories, so she had started to eat chocolate because it was cheap and halted the weight loss.

People, in what was a very small village, had once admired the family but now they all talked in whispers about them as though they were outsiders that no longer fit in to their idealistic box. If they noticed a difference in how Marguerite looked, they didn't comment or ask why, nor did they enquire about Roly, who was rarely seen in the village anymore, his absence going seemingly unnoticed.

Greg had succeeded in working his way back into the house. Despite being told to leave that night, he had been supportive when Marguerite had been hurt so she had decided to give him a second chance. Maisie thanked her for it, but it would have been better in many ways if she had kept a hold on that ban, as the strangers now entering the house on a daily basis were increasing in numbers, always disappearing upstairs or into the garden. The house however was filled with life and that part she savoured, sometimes she was pulled into the party where the strange smell wafted, but she chose to ignore it as long as it was outside, the Scottish air diluting it as she watched and even joined in with the dancing. She quite liked rap, which was the current favourite, the words were brutal and true to life but the atmosphere was relaxed and to have the garden utilised was great. She had always felt that, as a family before, they hadn't made the most of it with other family members and friends. Roly had been all for keeping them isolated, perhaps he had been scared that something or someone would upset his life had he dared to let anyone else enter? He hadn't been wrong.

Rodrigo was closer in age to these people in comparison to Marguerite, but he and she weren't noticeable, they were just part of the crowd. She always made sure the boys were tucked away in their beds and they usually slept through it all without disturbance, keeping their windows firmly shut, she wasn't putting them at risk and felt justified in having some fun for once. It seemed such a long time ago now, when they were a proper family, enjoying the fruits of Roly's ambition. She would probably prefer that the children didn't have these types of friends, but they had been so restrained that it seemed unfair to continue where Roly had left off, they should be free to choose their friends and learn from experience. She recalled how compelled she had been in her youth to go against the rules, funny how she had become a prisoner to them all after all. She thought of their wonderful holidays, but it had become hazy, as though they had never happened. It was the only time the family had had fun together, when Roly was on holiday he relaxed and could be considered good company, but as soon as they were home again things went back to the way they had always been.

Maisie had again been asked for money by Greg, and maybe yes, she was marginally involved by association, but she didn't have her own access to money or a need to have it, as she told Greg yet again. He wasn't pleased, didn't she realise that he was in danger? Scare-mongering she had declared was all it was, and yes, he was scared.

Honestly, how wealthy did he think they were? Maisie chose not to give it much thought, it was for Greg to work out, and when she had dared to suggest he ask his father he had said that he was very strict and would be beyond unpleasant. Fathers, how useful were they? Not very, it seemed. She felt irritated, thinking that surely she and Greg should be able to go to their fathers and tell them the truth or ask for help. Fortunately for her she had her mother and she knew she would support them all, regardless of deed.

CHAPTER 24

At college the next day, without warning, Mitac had appeared. Maisie felt the attraction briefly but then it subsided and she questioned herself as the tutor's voice became audible then distant as she battled her loyalty with Greg, who was currently a problem but was still her boyfriend. She was too impatient, hadn't allowed herself to settle before embarking on a new relationship. The class ended but she didn't have a clue what the topic was or had been, nor had she asked any questions. It was probably noticeable she wasn't listening but ultimately she was the one who missed out if she didn't listen or take notes, she would have to check with a friend to get updates.

Mitac had tears in his eyes; honestly it was never right was it? All Maisie wanted was to see some softness in her father, but he actively disliked it in any of her boyfriends. Maisie however appreciated how much they cared, or pretended to, but tears? No, she didn't like that, it made her feel guilty and she couldn't cope so she ran, like her father possibly, not wanting to face the truth. Mitac just watched her, rooted to the spot, did she love him? Did she love Greg? She felt she knew nothing, was just playing a long. Her father had left and was living in a flat in town now, but her mother was living the dream with a younger man. She knew it was all wrong but she longed for what they had. Hot tears splashed onto her cheeks, her nose dripping as she sprinted with her blonde ringlets whipping her face. She could barely see where she was going, but her feet knew the route to the park and she eventually collapsed hidden within a circle of trees and with no food or drink, she turned her phone to silent.

Nobody had heard from Maisie, it was pitch black outside now and someone was at the door, not Maisie as she had a key, though sometimes couldn't find it. It was Mitac. Marguerite was momentarily shocked, hadn't really considered him real having never met him. He was of course, but belonged in Maisie's college life, not here on her doorstep, not a part of the family's daily lives. Perhaps if Roly had been friendlier Maisie would have brought him home. He was very dark, black, unruly hair; his eyes just as dark with thick lashes that were just as beautiful as he was. He was dressed casually, in jeans and a woollen jumper he was a very desirable young man. Greg was English but this man was exotic, where was her daughter? Mitac, still on the doorstep, was talking so fast it was difficult to understand him with his strong accent.

"Come in" Marguerite said, smiling at him as he looked so anxious. She took him through to the kitchen and offered him a coffee but he shook his head, clearly still in a hurry to get his words out.

"I've upset her. She didn't believe me when I said I would come back to her, but I had things to sort, you know, at home" he smiled quickly, apologetically, and she felt his pain, aware of the fragility of human nature. Age gave wisdom but despite that, it was not always acted on. They considered a call to the police but Marguerite felt it too ridiculous as Maisie was nearly 17, not 6, and therefore quite entitled to be out after dark and even turn her phone off, but she never did that so it was a cause for concern.

The door slammed suddenly, alerting them towards the front door as Maisie appeared, and startled to see Mitac, the very person she had run from. She checked her appearance quickly in the mirror, causing them both to smile, still acting vain in the most desperate situations but she looked a mess, her hair a mass of knotted ringlets and mascara streaked on her cheeks.

Maisie had gone straight into a new relationship, not even considering that she had slept with two men a few weeks apart. She felt like a tart, in this situation nobody knew about, but it would be resolved now. Her stomach felt uneasy as she put on a straight face but it fooled no one.

"I'm fine, sorry and hello Mitac, why are you at my house? Still, lovely to see you" she declared. What was she, the lead role in a film? But her mother looked relieved, glad to have her eldest daughter back in the nest.

Marguerite approved of a boy with principles, Greg was a danger to them all bringing drugs and alcohol into the house. She of course knew it was out there but didn't want it in her home. Mitac had done what he needed to do and shook Marguerite's hand as his eyes beseechingly turned to Maisie, begging for a crumb to be offered, but none was forthcoming.

"I'm sorry for everything" he said to Maisie as he left "See you at college".

Maisie knew she was the one that should be sorry, she had been impatient and unkind, inconsiderate of others feelings, realising she might be more like her father than she had first thought. She felt worthless now, couldn't even bring herself to talk to her mother, she was wiped out and had said as much but Marguerite understood this, so a conversation regarding that evening didn't take place until much later.

A few weeks passed but nothing to note happened, until one morning Marguerite went out to the driveway to take the boys on their usual school run, where was her car? Startled briefly, she considered maybe it was in the garage, but she rarely did that and the MOT wasn't due. No, it was gone, it must have been stolen. She still had to get the boys to school but she felt flummoxed as she called the police and they knew who she was immediately, which was embarrassing.

"Stolen"? The voice said at the other end of the phone "Oh dear".

Hardly an adequate response to such an event in the village, a rare event that she was sure would be a likely cause for excitement at the local police station despite the officer's uninterested tone. But wasn't her family causing enough excitement for the local police lately? Someone would apparently be sent to call at her house later that morning so Marguerite ordered a taxi for the boys. Neither had really taken in that their mother's car had been stolen and the implications of it so were thrilled at what seemed to be a treat for them.

Maisie didn't want to go to college, said she wanted to stay with her mother, but Marguerite insisted she was fine and that Maisie mustn't miss her studies, knowing that Maisie would opt out of going at the slightest excuse. Mitac was of course in her class and she had to face him every day, but we all have to face the consequences of our actions and running away was not to be an option made easy for her in this case, though it is often the most chosen.

Maisie accepted her fate and got in the taxi with the boys, said she would walk home, it wasn't that far. Beattie walked regularly, being the keener one on maintaining physical fitness, whereas Maisie was always running late so took the easier and quicker option.

So here Marguerite was again with the police. They asked lots of questions, of which she had no answers for. Had she left the key in the ignition? Of course not, she had patiently replied, not really quite believing that she was even having this conversation as she put the car key down on the table. It was a Scottish village where nobody even considered theft a possibility, but the officers assured her they would call if they had any news, so now she had no car.

Later in the evening she received a call. Her car had been found, burnt out and left abandoned but with no idea as to who could have done it, did she have any suggestions?

Maisie, after a stressful day at college, sat with her mother at the kitchen table, both were equally puzzled. Greg called again, said he needed to speak with her urgently and her mother said they could sit in the garden but she was angry and not pleased with the continuing contact between the two of them. She hadn't minded initially, saw it as a distraction from Mitac, but now he was back and she felt it was going to blow up in all their faces. Maisie was too quick to fall in love, or to think she was, but who was she to say that? 30 seconds, perhaps a minute tops and she was hooked on Rodrigo.

It transpired that Greg had been threatened as he hadn't paid the money that was still owed, but was this related to Maisie's mum's car? He had said he wasn't sure but suspected it, but they couldn't tell the police as it would put him in more danger. Was this paranoia genuine or just an effect of the drugs? The interest was being added daily now and he mentioned an even bigger amount of money than before.

Later that night everyone was sleeping when a bright light shining in the garden directly below the balcony woke Marguerite. She crept out of bed and pulled herself across the floor on her stomach to the balcony, so as not to be noticed. Oh how her life was changing, she felt as though she was in a movie now, but she couldn't see anyone and the light had quickly extinguished. She knew she hadn't imagined it, but wasn't about to prowl around the garden at this hour, so she resolved herself back to bed, alert but eventually falling back to sleep.

The next morning she went out onto the balcony to find an array of bits of wood spread out across the garden, the boys den had been destroyed. It was a big garden so any noise could go unnoticed, and had. But who was doing this? Someone clearly didn't like them, but who? Marguerite knew little about drugs but knew this must be related, involving someone in the house. Maisie and Beattie, they both had been allowed by her to associate with less than suitable friends and acquaintances, but to destroy the den and punish two innocent boys? This was a warning.

Maisie, again confused, her thoughts scattered as her mother informed her about the den that was now lying in bits. The boys were devastated. It was a subtle warning of worse to come. Maisie had started her period this morning so one weight had been removed that no one new about, but she saw how her life could have quickly become so complicated. One wrong choice, a careless action, if only she could just focus on what was important! Her studies, that she had once been so excited about, going to college and the thought of achieving the excellence she knew she was destined, but the thought was one thing and the work and dedication involved to obtain the end result was another. She hadn't bargained for Mitac, it was a female dominated course that she thought was unlikely to meet a boy on but she hadn't been able to resist and was careless to birth control, hadn't been advised much on the subject. But she should have been attentive to this as obviously she would ultimately be the one to pay the price. She despised girls who ended up with babies at a young age, thought them ignorant, this was the 21st century, contraceptives were available to all in varying forms, including condoms for men. She almost laughed at the thought of this, how many men took that responsibility? Perhaps only a select few that were scared of STD's but the rest likely considered it should be the woman's problem if they fell pregnant. She was in agreement partly, as they were the ones to carry and give birth and ultimately have a child to consider, even into adulthood, but it was a serious thing that wasn't to be taken lightly. Many probably thought of it as a way to get their man to commit, a misplaced ideal as it didn't hold a couple together if the man didn't want to be held.

Now Maisie was sleeping with no one, she couldn't deal with Greg and no longer actually liked him as he had betrayed her and her family. Perhaps not deliberately, but her lack of judgement had brought trouble to her home, having taken what she wanted and letting go at the first sign of trouble, her idea of love was false.

The police were watching the house now and she felt nostalgic for their previous safety, but her father had shown a nasty side that she had always suspected he had. Did she have that side too? Mum didn't really have sides, she was what you see is what you get, but she was vulnerable and needed to be loved properly. Maisie didn't actually know how she expected to be loved, she thought she needed an all-consuming love, yet she flicked it off so easily herself.

Mitac was too nice for her, looking at her with those soulful eyes that begged for her attention and deep down she knew she didn't want them to turn elsewhere. There were so many girls, but he seemed to only be aware of her. He knew how to love properly, but she was a disaster zone and she had hurt him but not intentionally. She knew going to his family was a normal thing to do but had been selfish, jealous and untrusting, but she didn't know his family or their culture and she couldn't wait for anything. She was the loser really but she didn't want to admit it or start again with him, knowing that more of the same would follow. He deserved better.

Roly hadn't been to the house, he wasn't allowed, had been told he was to stay away until his case was heard. So he knew nothing of the events that were now unfolding at the house, but what could he say or do? He still had his work, but that gave him little satisfaction now. He needed to find some other outlet, someone perhaps as he felt lonely, but he didn't feel ready for that yet and what did he have to offer? He always liked his own company before. So much so that he continually sought it out when he was in his own home, knowing his family were there should he want to engage with them, but now he didn't even have that to fall back on and he just felt alone.

CHAPTER 25

Marguerite knew the police wouldn't watch the house 24/7, but she regularly saw from her balcony a single police car that would periodically pass by slowly at random times throughout the day and night. She pondered on the thought of the neighbours seeing the vehicle and linking it to the Chevelly house, but did she care? Her mind was full of enough problems already, and she was desperately looking for a solution to all of them.

The boys were of course still upset about the den.

"Was it the wind, mummy"? They had asked her.

She had said yes and went along with it, that was easier than explaining the truth and easier for them to understand. But now they were excited with the idea of rebuilding it so, without thinking, she called Rodrigo.

He sounded relieved to hear her voice and she found herself smiling again and despite everything, began to feel a little more optimistic. Rodrigo was as excited as the boys at the prospect of helping them all to rebuild the den and it meant they could spend more time together too. The boys just accepted him as a friend as far as their mother was concerned. At their age they didn't yet question or look for details, in a year or two that would likely change, but for now Marguerite was grateful for their innocence. With this in mind, she resolved herself to remain calm and just believe that all would work out eventually.

Upstairs in her bedroom, Maisie was unable to resist calling Greg. She needed to know if he was the reason for this sudden vendetta against her family.

"Not directly" he said. But yes, he had received further demands for the money. Maisie asked again why this was now something for her family to be punished for and Greg was again angry at her dismissal of any involvement in what was owed, asking why she couldn't help him, claiming she must not love him. But what did he know of love? He was emotionally blackmailing her now. All because she was the daughter of a rich man, which was an exaggeration. Yes they were well off, comfortably so, but not rich. Nor was Maisie in a position where she could just get hold of a large sum of cash without a valid explanation for why she needed it and no, as she had told him countless times now, she didn't have any of her own. She was only given money when she needed it and just for small things, such as her lunch at college and maybe a few pounds if she wanted to go out for an evening with her friends. There was no point in asking why he had got himself into this situation, he had obviously been caught out, dependent on a drug that had lead him to partake in others more potent and the cost had just accumulated. He didn't foresee this outcome of course, but the dealer must have picked up on that her family had money and that was the reason for the family becoming a target, it wasn't personal. But it was, very personal. Greg was desperate now, why wasn't she prepared to do anything for him and if not for him, for the protection of her family?

Did that level of love even exist? Maisie considered the notion and quickly concluded that clearly it did not, even between her parents who had been together for years. She saw it now; her father lavished luxuries on her mother and expected her to be in his control in return. Almost like a slave, as oppose to being valued as a person that he needed to protect and support when there were problems with the children or life in general, or if she just wanted some reassurance. Was that not the basic foundations of a marriage? Even now after everything, she thought, surely her father should be fighting to get her mother back? But she knew he just wasn't that kind of man, he wouldn't risk his pride for the possibility of making a fool of himself.

Maisie had poor taste in men. Mitac the foreigner, who was a good man but he was from a poor country and with a different culture to her own and now Greg, a drug addict. Perhaps her father had been right about something, this connection had brought devastation.

She told Greg that the money was his problem, not hers and not her families and ended the call, but somehow she knew this was all partly down to her naiveté, and without her father there anymore she was vulnerable and open to exploitation.

Suddenly, she recalled seeing a youngish man in the town centre, a bit rough but had an air about him, acted as though he was friendly but something seemed off. She had seen him mingling with the local teenagers, heard him encouraging them to dabble in something from inside a small plastic bag that was supposedly fun and free. It was a quiet town, so a chance of something different was an attraction to well-brought-up children that were looking for rebellion and longing for a bit of excitement, they were an easy target. She thought of herself and Beattie, with all their advantages and privileges, still preferring to get involved in the seedier side of life. Her father's words echoed in her head now; 'be selective, don't mix with the low lives' but it was such a broad generalisation as he branded so many people with that label, all those that were less successful than himself. Now look at them all. Her thoughts turned then to Mitac, he was from a poor background but he had a hunger for success at the exclusion of all else. Perhaps it was unhealthy to have too much too easily, it dulled ambition and took away motivation. She felt sick as she considered how she had rejected him, but really it was better to stick with your own class and nationality. Mixed race couples were rare in Scotland so perhaps she had been narrow-minded, but the realisation was dawning on her now.

The drugs were given on tick not free and if you couldn't pay, the debt grew and continued to do so until it was paid off, it was never forgotten. Maisie had allowed this to be brought into the Chevelly house and now, her mother who had nothing to do with drugs, was waiting for the next instruction. They knew it wouldn't be over until the debt was paid and somehow Marguerite would have to resolve this as with Roly gone, there was nothing and no one to protect them. The door was open to anyone who asked to be invited in and even to those that didn't.

Marguerite was outside, enjoying the garden as she always did, but was startled by the sudden appearance of a dark-haired youth that had just assumed it was acceptable to walk straight through her back gate. She had always felt safe in her home and garden before, but now she felt vulnerable, she was alone and it was strange there without a man in situ. She felt different, free but without an anchor.

The man was not unattractive, but he had a sinister air surrounding him. He was wearing a sleeveless tee shirt and his arms were covered in tattoos, he looked familiar and she immediately recalled that he had come to her door previously, asking for money and wanting to see Greg.

"Right, business" he barked. "Your daughter, blonde, Greg's girl"

Marguerite informed him that she wasn't his girl anymore and, acting more naïve than she was, asked if this was about the night her house had an overpowering smell wafting through the rooms.

"These things have to be paid for and Greg still owes me money" he said nastily, by way of an answer.

Had Maisie been involved in more than just participating in smoking? How had this now been made her problem? But acutely it had; the car the den, why not have sold the car? Too complicated and traceable, this was the way to frighten people. A thousand pound for what Marguerite thought. Likely noticing her shocked expression, the man explained.

"He's had other things on tick, other types of drugs. More expensive ones"

Marguerite couldn't really get her head around the conversation or where it was going, but she knew it was only going to get worse, unless she paid. Whether she should be involved or not was no longer relevant, this man was in her garden and knew where she lived, had already destroyed her car and destroyed the boys' den, what would be next, the house? She thought of her patrolling policeman, where was he now? He wouldn't be able to see what was happening in the garden she supposed, she was trapped.

At that moment, the man began to run. Her sixth sense must have alerted him as she looked up in surprise to see her patrolling policeman strolling across the garden towards her. She had been fumbling around in her pocket for her phone and in doing so had managed to redial the last call she had made to the police.

The man dodged past the policeman as he tried to lunge for him but missed and continued towards the gate but he was too quick, obviously used to dodging the law and managing to disappear. The policeman tried to catch up but it was hopeless, so he returned to Marguerite. She offered him a hot drink, she needed one herself, dazed and in shock at the continuing domino effect that was her life. He politely refused and proceeded to talk in to his radio, he had ear phones in, always connected, it would have been almost comical had it have been under different circumstances. He was talking seriously, with an obvious edge of excitement to his voice, as he alerted the local cop cars by giving a brief description of the man in question. He hadn't seen his face so Marguerite relayed the details; very dark hair, about 25 years old, around 5 foot 8 in height with black eyes or as near as, pasty skin that clearly didn't get enough daylight, vest top and lots of tattoos.

The police man concluded that he would increase the surveillance on the house but thought it unlikely the man would act again anytime soon, if ever, but if Marguerite was to pay she would likely find herself trapped in a never ending cycle. But what if she didn't and someone got hurt? Greg could be beaten up or worse and she didn't want that, he was just young and foolish and he needed help. Money was not useful if it couldn't be used in a proactive way and she hated that she was in this position, but she chose to wait for instruction, her previous ambience of peace destroyed as she looked anxiously out to the garden to rescue her. This time it failed. She had just needed a distraction that was all. Everything was really taking its toll now, destruction taking hold, its fingers twisting, latching on and spreading. Nothing was ever just about you, actions taken had an effect on all those closely connected, branching out further to friends and other connections and introducing outside elements that had never even been thought of. Finding herself involved with drugs, burnt out cars, this was a life so outside of her vision, out of her control. She really hadn't been grateful enough, she had been lucky, fantastic holidays she had been fortunate enough to enjoy, a lovely family, everything one could possibly want. Maybe she didn't have that extra emotional support that she craved, but how little she and probably many others really appreciated the safety and security of a home and a family. Tears fell heavily down her face as she found herself struggling to breathe but still lit a cigarette, the worst thing to do perhaps, but it calmed her as she stopped crying and redirected her thoughts.

She could pay, she had a credit card, she knew she shouldn't and had been advised against it but this was a real situation and if she didn't they could add more interest, continue the threats, someone could get hurt. The situation was in her hands now, not knowing what she was waiting for, but knowing she would likely find out soon enough.

CHAPTER 26

Taxis were of course expensive and Marguerite had had to use her credit card to pay for yet another to bring the boys back from her parents. Rodrigo had also appeared in one, but at least he paid for his there and then, whereas she was borrowing the money. Just as well she had a very high credit limit, but obviously interest accrued and she wasn't able to pay it off in full. She had also got a store card recently as Maisie and Beattie had declared that their wardrobes were behind the fashion of the day so she had indulged them and they spent a few hours laughing and trying on clothes, most of which she ended up purchasing. She also brought some clothes for herself as she needed them; hers hung off her now as she had dropped at least a couple of dress sizes. She looked almost ethereal and fragile, but she couldn't afford to be, she needed to be strong. She wanted to dress up for Rodrigo and she looked young and girly dressed in a sheer summer dress. It was quite short and her legs were so slim that they stuck out at the bottom like two sticks, but they were shapely. She had brought some pretty sandals to go with it, they had cost a lot, but the look in Rodrigo's eyes later when he saw her would be her reward. For the boys she had brought shorts and T-shirts from the store next door, The Young Scene. They were similar to look at, both with lots of dark hair, Maurice's slightly lighter than Frankie's, both with baby noses, though Frankie's was sharper, and both with wide smiles, but the main feature that set them apart was their eyes. Frankie's were very dark brown like Marguerite's, Maurice's light blue like Roly's, however his held a hard expression but Maurice's were soft.

Hyped with the anticipation of the day's activities, the den was taking shape, previously built over a long period of time but now it was to be built in a day. Casual in a pair of old denim jeans ripped at the knees, muscled arms on show, Rodrigo was as excited as them with a hammer and nails, happy just to be with them all. Marguerite watched while they set straight in to the task at hand, there were lots of twigs and branches, they had a wonderful time, and a few hours later the den stood proud with the boys inside exhausted, covered in scratches and streaks of dirt. Once everyone had cleaned themselves up, the girls joined them for dinner; all of them eating a mixture of leftovers scraped together that somehow resulted as something edible and then trooping into the lounge to watch TV with huge bowls of ice cream. They were watching a film and for the first time in a while they all felt like a family again, Rodrigo slipping into Roly's place, he fit just somehow. The boys adored him and the girls accepted him as he made their mother happy.

Later that evening they left Marguerite and Rodrigo alone, the girls went to chat with friends in their rooms and the boys went to their rooms to sleep after their busy day. She didn't think the children would care much what she was doing with Rodrigo now with their father gone, so they had made love, the sheer dress slipping off easily, the patio doors left wide open. With Rodrigo, she just felt happy. She was a sucker for love, gave in to it and allowed it to take her beyond herself where she felt she was truly alive. A life without him seemed impossible now.

Rodrigo left in the early hours. Marguerite was reluctant to wash away their union but never the less she showered and dressed simply, ready to start another day. Their transport arrived, she was the taxi man's best friend now, said he was fortunate to have made her acquaintance and of course she knew why. But she had no choice as the insurance company hadn't paid out for the car. They had offered her a courtesy car but Marguerite refused to fear a reprisal, it was better to wait without a car for a little longer.

The police officers predictions had unfortunately turned out to be way off and Marguerites unwelcome visitor wasted no time in striking again. This time what happened was unthinkable, Marguerite should just have paid him.

At the school, Marguerite sat in the taxi waiting for the boys to appear like usual, but this time, they didn't. It crossed her mind that maybe Roly could have collected them, but he rarely if ever did that and he wouldn't risk jeopardising his restraining order. She got out of the taxi, asking her new 'friend' to wait for her to return. Were the boys being kept in and if so why? She went straight to the headmistress's office, the headmistress looked surprised and then guilty, obviously realising now that she had just made a huge mistake. She told Marguerite the boys had been collected early by an uncle. This couldn't be happening. They did have an uncle, but he wouldn't have collected the children from school, certainly not without telling her. She stared angrily at the headmistress, accused her of incompetence. How dare she send her children off with a stranger? She tried to plead with Marguerite, said the boys appeared to know him and apparently she had been delayed.

"But you didn't check with me before letting them go. You know I would have called to tell you if there was a change of arrangements"!

Marguerite accepted that this was a sleepy Scottish village and these things that were happening just didn't happen here, but it had and it was happening now, to her. She would have to call the police again. She let it ring until finally it was picked up on the other end.

A female voice spoke. "Yes, how can we help"?

"It's Marguerite Chevelly. My sons have been kidnapped"

It sounded unbelievable even to her. The response was steely "kidnapped"? What was going on with this woman? One thing had followed another and now her children had been kidnapped. Marguerite had to slow herself as she described to the officer how the boys looked and relayed a hasty description from the headmistress of the stand in uncle. She said he had been immaculate, polite and respectable, which didn't sound anything like her visitor, no one would have handed over the care of children to him. The headmistress was distressed but Marguerite remained vehement in telling her that she of all people should have adhered to the rules which are put in place to protect them and this was outright unacceptable. The headmistress accepted that the usual school policy had not been administered, but it had just seemed so genuine and all she could do was apologise and pleaded with Marguerite to let her know as soon as the children were back with her. The police would be calling to the house again shortly, it was most unpleasant, and apparently during the headmistress's time at the school, this had never happened before.

Back in the taxi without the boys, the taxi man looked at her oddly, enquired if something was wrong, but she just said that the boys had detention.

He chuckled. "Little horrors! So are you in need of a taxi again later"?

"No, I shall walk, it's a nice afternoon"

He looked at her strangely then and she realised she had just said it without even taking in her surroundings as it wasn't nice at all it was raining. He must have suspected something, undoubtedly not anything close to what had actually happened.

Marguerite was absolutely mortified. She couldn't think who would have collected them that could have been seen as acceptable by the boys. Nobody other than herself or Roly of course, or the girls possibly, but then the boys had easily accepted all the changes recently, this probably just seemed like another adventure to them. She could sort of understand how the Head Mistress had accepted the story. It was a Scottish village where nothing bad ever happened, but obviously that was no longer true.

Back at home, Marguerite waited for the officer to visit when she explained everything that had happened yet again. Obviously she secretly knew why it had happened, but didn't reveal this, expecting instruction of what she should do next. Greg had called the house, desperate and crying, saying she must please pay them. He wasn't heartless and was terrified, for himself and for the boys for all of them in fact. The debt had been raised now to £1500, along with a demand for no police involvement. Could she get that kind of money? It would take time, time which she didn't have. She had savings but you couldn't just draw out that amount of money straight away. At the realisation of this, she panicked briefly but then calmed herself, remembering she had been told that the boys had been happy to go with this man and were probably innocently enjoying a meal at McDonald's.

Finally, the phone rang; a withheld number. A time had been arranged at a much later hour to meet, outside an abandoned house near the park. She had clear instructions to be alone and was told that after the boys had been sent outside, she was to place an envelope containing the money on the doorstep. She could have told the police and possibly caught them red-handed, but she knew and likely so would they that she wouldn't risk jeopardising the safety of her boys. They were out of her care now and any wrong move could change the mind-set of the kidnapper.

Her parents had rescued her by coming up with the money. They could not possibly even begin to understand the situation that their daughter had now found herself in. They were surprised, but not overly so, she couldn't remember the last time she was with them alone. They had shown concern and their worried faces unnerved her as she longed to dispel her fears; scream, rage, weep, but she didn't want to burden them and, truthfully, to reveal the extent of how far she was now from her previously comfortable life, she would just look like a fool. They said they could help, but her father had to go to the bank as they didn't have that much cash sitting around, but would give her an extra £500 on top of the £1500. While her father was gone, she and her mother chatted about inconsequential things. She knew her mother could see right through the falseness, but she was like her in as much as she never pushed for information. It was to be given freely or not at all.

She had no car of course, so yet again she had had to call her taxi man to take her to and from her parents. She felt reluctant to involve him at this point because he could start to be suspicious and ask questions, but it was a taxi fare and he had agreed to wait round the corner while she was inside her parent's house. She arranged the taxi for later as well. He had asked after the boys and she had said she would just be collecting them from an uncle. That was plausible and partially true. She felt the boys were fine, but knew they wouldn't be truly happy until they were back with her again.

She suddenly noticed her mother watching her intently, she knew what she could see and would be thinking, her daughter now virtually a bag of bones. Did she suspect that Marguerite had another man? One day she would tell her mother, but today she had her sons to worry about and truthfully, she was petrified but now was not the time for offloading all of her burdens. They seemed to be growing daily now and it was becoming very difficult, but hadn't she always dealt with everything alone? Of course this was at another level however. Her father returned with the money and she left, thanking them both and promising to repay it as soon as she could.

Marguerite dressed in black for the meeting, thought it seemed appropriate, and the taxi man was again waiting in a side road round the corner. Her heart was thumping and she was nervous, but everything went as planned. The front door opened but she couldn't see in clearly, she noted a figure that was tall and slim, the shadowy outlines of a man in the dark hallway. Two sudden bursts of colour ran out, her boys, chatting excitedly but looking bewildered. They asked why she wouldn't come in and watched in confusion as she placed an envelope on the doorstep.

"Please don't ask" she said anxiously.

She wanted to run but forced herself to keep a steady pace and with one boy on each side, she held their hands tightly. They talked across her, to each other and also to her, but she couldn't listen, she couldn't relax. They all got into the taxi but she didn't hug them until they were back at the house, at which point she was on the brink of tears and desperately squeezed them both tight.

Maurice complained she was hurting him, looking at her with his usual heightened level of sensitivity.

"We're alright Mum. Did you miss us that much"?

That was the undoing of her and the tears fell.

"Silly mummy" he said as he hugged her tight, his arms fitting comfortably around her now that she was so thin.

Much later, Marguerite sat out on her balcony, staring out into the darkness. Just the odd bursts of light could be seen from the nearby houses as she lit a cigarette, she was alone now. Her boys were so precious and she was so grateful that they had come to no harm; she was frightened and could only hope that it was the end of this now. They had their money and she had her boys.

CHAPTER 27

Marguerite had to inform the police that she had gotten the boys back, which could go either way. She would have preferred to keep them out of the equation but they had said that it could not be left, so she decided to give them the most minimal information possible and take the boys back to her parents just in case. She told them a lie of course, just a white one, that the school was being refurbished. Normally she preferred the truth but it was so unbelievable that they probably wouldn't believe her even if she told them and it was for their protection. The taxi driver was of course overjoyed at all the additional business, said they were like partners in crime, she laughed at the irony of how close to the truth that was and she was glad of the additional £500 her parents had given. The taxi runs had cost £100 over the last couple of days, money certainly served its purpose, but arguably the fact that she was considered wealthy was the reason she was in this situation. Too little, too much, it was always an issue. She hoped she could return the money one day to her parents, she knew they wouldn't really want her to give it back but was sure they would appreciate the offer. They were obviously bewildered but happy to have the boys to stay, it was tiring for them but they did their best to keep the boys happy and entertained. Again, the boys not really understanding much were having a great time without knowing the reasons, just accepting what they were told.

The police reluctantly accepted her story and closed the case, but the school would still be getting a visit and the headmistress was in danger of losing her long-held respectable position, another victim of the saga that was now Marguerite's life. Maisie had told

Greg not to contact her ever again, she hated him for what he had done to her family, intentionally or not, they were over but Beattie was still seeing Mace. He was so different to Greg but was still a connection and Maisie had discussed her concern of this with Beattie, but Beattie refused to break it off, stating that Mace was innocent and his brothers bad deeds were not his own. Maisie hoped that Greg would accept that he had to leave her family alone, but knew he would be beyond angry that Mace was still allowed to be a part of their lives. He had been mortified at what he had caused and beyond apologetic, but it didn't matter now, Maisie had to make sure it couldn't ever happen again.

Red-faced and angry, Maisie joined Marguerite at the kitchen table. They talked but she was past being rational, her mother was in bits and Maisie now knew she had had to borrow the money from her grandparents. The money could have been used for more important things, though of course it had gotten them out of a nasty situation, but really she had no idea how much it cost to sustain a house and the lifestyle they had become accustomed to. She knew her mother couldn't ask her father, not now, and there had been no offer from Greg to pay her back either, even over a period of time, but really they were better off severing the connection altogether. He, who was in a terrible state now, was only young and had just been careless. Maisie, who had thought her parents would be past the stage of acting without thought, could see now that they were not as they were still effectively squabbling like children. It was ridiculous; surely they could just behave like adults? The examples both of them had set before they separated now seriously flawed. She felt numb. Greg had to be in the past, Mitac too, and college was almost impossible with every area of her life seemingly falling apart, the domino effect was relentless. She stayed sat with her mother, not talking much but just feeling the need for company instead of going to her room, scared of being alone with her own thoughts.

Marguerite received a message from Roly, asking after Frankie and Maurice. He knew he couldn't come to the house but surely he could have some time with his sons? Marguerite was concerned that in their innocence they would reveal things she wouldn't want him to know so instead she turned on him, feeling vulnerable and worn down by the surreal events that had endangered their sons.

"You're a coward Roly" she messaged, feeling sure he would almost taste her icy tone.

Even if she did partially deserve what had happened, she was angry at him for so many things, why target the boys? He hadn't even asked about the girls, she supposed this was because they were less likely to be a source of information and she knew he would ask questions, want to know why they weren't in school. Marguerite had heard from the police and the school that the headmistress had been removed from her post. This was to be temporary but may become permanent, it hadn't yet been decided. The deputy head was in charge for now but Marguerite felt she could no longer trust the school. There were others in the area but the boys were used to this one, had made friends there and though they had seemingly been happy to accept any changes up to this point, changing schools could prove quite difficult.

Beattie had been equally disgusted with Greg and she too was concerned with the turn of events in their lives, knowing she was taking risks too. Mace was nice, kind and polite, but nevertheless he was Greg's brother and a link they definitely didn't need but he had done nothing wrong to deserve being banished from her life and the house.

Maisie was of course single now and angry at herself for her own stupidity, but she couldn't deal with Mitac even if Greg was out of the picture. She felt disorientated and upset, missing her brothers who were away from the family again and, even though he probably didn't deserve it, she missed her father. If only he had paid attention to her mother more, all of them even, this could have been avoided.

Of course, they had all benefited from the house, nice clothes, holidays, but Maisie knew how important looking after a person's emotional wellbeing was and she was subsequently drawn to boys who she thought might offer her that. Still, it was done now. What next? Where would their lives lead them? To a new house maybe? She didn't know but for now they were still in the family home so she decided not to concern herself with what might happen as even if it did, it could take years.

Roly had pleaded a little with Marguerite, claiming he wasn't himself and he clearly struggled with this admission, which she knew must have choked him. Marguerite understood he had been fuelled by jealousy but now he had a court case to deal with which was in a week's time. Roly didn't know the boys were at her parents, he should have contact really, but she didn't trust him now that he had revealed a nasty side. She hadn't met with Rodrigo again recently either, she needed to sort things properly and couldn't maintain the house without financial support. She wondered if anyone considered, when they chose to marry, what they would do if it all went wrong. Especially in the case of a woman that didn't have a lucrative career to support herself, forever reliant on a man that could pull the plug and use manipulation to his advantage. Was her affair worth it? Rodrigo couldn't support her, he could barely support himself. There was no certainty of anything, but then hadn't that been what she hadn't liked about the way things were before? Surely their lust would soon burn out with the mundane problems, money issues and general daily worries, but she accepted now that hers and Roly's marriage had failed.

She needed to get out of the house; the walls were closing in on her. She had no car and the taxis were using up what little money she had left. The insurance company had said the cheque would be with her soon and she had decided she would risk buying another car. The debt had been paid now but the man was yet to be found, probably too smart to get caught and she couldn't actually prove that she knew the man who was responsible anyway. She would get a run about, a reliable car, but not a BMW and with her debts rising daily, she called the taxi man, a direct number now. Would he miss her? Unlikely she thought, just the money, but he was a nice man, jovial, taking life as it came. She was going to her café. She needed a focus, a job, perhaps just part-time as she couldn't spend the rest of her life only maintaining the house. The girls needed her less now in some ways, more in others, but the boys of course needed her to make sure they had clean clothes, lunch boxes filled, shoelaces tied, the daily ritual. She knew she should just insist they learn to do it themselves, or perhaps she should just get them the shoes with Velcro straps that most of the other children wore. She felt ashamed of what she had caused and felt guilty now that she hadn't even given her boys the courtesy of telling them the truth.

At the cafe her usual table was free. It was getting cold outside now, the Scottish breeze more forceful but as usual she relished it as she ordered her coffee and lit a cigarette. She brought a paper, something she never did, and turned to the jobs page, it was full. What could she do? Something challenging she thought, but could she cope? She would have to push herself; she hadn't worked for 17 years. She noticed an advert for the haberdashery shop close by, just a few hours a day and feeling a bit more positive she circled the ad, she could call them now. The shop was not so far from the café. Finishing her coffee and cigarette she dialled the number and, after advising them of her current location, an interview was arranged immediately. She sprayed herself liberally with the expensive perfume she kept in her handbag for emergencies; she was dressed casually but looked smart enough.

The shops doorbell tinkled as she entered and Marguerite quickly took in her surroundings. The shop was crammed full with tubes of multi coloured materials that leaned against every bit of wall space, swatches lined the counter top and shelves were filled with jars of buttons of all sizes and rolls of all kinds of thread, the place felt cosy and welcomed her like an old friend.

A mature lady, possibly as old as 70, stepped forward to greet her and she was led to the back of the shop for a chat, hardly an interview, conducted in a small kitchen where brightly coloured cups hung from the walls on plastic hooks. The lady introduced herself as Enid, she was a widow and she owned the shop. Enid explained to Marguerite that she was getting a bit tired these days, she needed a bit of free time to visit family and just enjoy some kind of retirement, but she didn't want to sell the shop as she enjoyed it. Marguerite felt she could easily work there, it didn't appear to be a too taxing job, but she would have to hurry up and get a car as the taxis would use up most of the earnings. This was as much about a distraction as it was about money. Following the conversation, a start date was agreed and working hours set to be from ten until two on week days.

"I think you will fit in nicely here" she said to Marguerite, as she left feeling pleased with herself. This was a step towards a better future where she could begin to become self-sufficient.

Marguerite felt she needed to tell someone her good news, it was late in the day when she got back, but she was pleased to find Beattie in the kitchen making a snack. That was something they all did now as a real meal had become a special occasion these days. Beattie was surprised but happy for her mother.

"That's great mum"! She exclaimed as Marguerite described the shop to her daughter. "I can see you there" Beattie grinned.

It wouldn't affect the girls or the boys, Marguerite informed her, suddenly feeling almost guilty for doing something for herself. She would still be there in the morning to take the boys to school, which Beattie said she shouldn't change, confirming what Marguerite had thought already that they had been through enough changes recently. The headmistress had gone now, the decision made that she should be dismissed, but Marguerite worried that the boys might be treated differently because of what happened.

"I don't know mum" Beattie said "Maybe a fresh start could be beneficial" and they bandied about thoughts and ideas, concluding that a new school probably should be sourced after all. It was nice to be chatting with her daughter, Marguerite thought. Beattie had gone astray for a while but was back on an even keel, she was still with Mace but had almost finished at senior school and was soon to be moving on to college, to new horizons. Maisie was Marguerites main concern now, the girl was so nervy and didn't look well and Marguerite knew she must have a proper conversation with her soon, but Maisie was being uncommunicative, spending hours alone in her room. No sound giving anything away. What was she doing up there? Sitting and staring at a blank wall torturing herself she supposed, and Marguerite knew to keep her distance during this black mood episode until it lifted. She didn't know how else to deal with it and this could go on for day's even weeks, but Marguerite would wait it out. She had lots to keep herself busy, such as finding a new car, sorting a new school for the boys, a college for Beattie and a new job to start, not to mention thinking how she and Rodrigo could finally properly be together. She didn't want to flaunt him, conscious of the fact that Maisie was now the only one without a boyfriend, though she still had Mitac attempting to pursue her and Greg too, but that would cause Maisie to feel excluded so they all danced around her, but hadn't they always? Honestly, this was how women failed, by not feeling complete without a man. Of course it was natural to be a part of a pair but who you chose to be your other half was a serious decision and wrong choices brought heartbreak. Maisie's heart was battered a bit now but Marguerite was sure she wouldn't be alone long more's the pity as she always rushed in. Hopefully she had learnt something now and would be less likely to jump in to a new relationship with the next man she met.

Marguerite had found a school in the village for the boys and it was so close by that they could walk, she knew she needed to let go of the reigns on them a little. Frankie only had one more year then he would be a senior, they would have to learn to be separate. She knew Roly would not be impressed; the school was 'behind the times and no good for his children' she recalled him saying years ago when they had considered it before for the girls and as usual Roly had had the last word. This time she decided for herself that this was what was best for the boys and she called to arrange a viewing.

Strolling through the village, Marguerite enjoyed the colder air, it signalled winter was approaching. The school was warm and the walls bright from the artwork, it felt right. She knew Maurice would love it, Frankie would be more critical, but he would accept her decision. The school had a headmaster, which was unusual as women were more commonly selected for the role, perhaps because they appeared more in touch with the children. The headmaster was plump and had a beaming smile, said how wonderful it was that her sons were going to be joining the school. He didn't ask the reason for the move, Marguerite likely giving off signals of not wanting to disclose their personal details. The boys could start next week; luckily they had a few spaces now as some children had recently left due to moving away. She could tick this to do off the list she thought happily as she hurried home, it was bitterly cold now.

Later on Marguerite discussed college with Beattie, Maisie's college offered a course in fashion design so the two girls would be able to walk together. It was quite a long walk, but Maisie was nearly 17 so she could learn to drive now. Roly would likely have considered getting her a car, had things been as before, but he had the expense of his own flat now on top of everything else. However, he might think of it as a way to get back some respect from his daughter. His hearing was just a week away now. Following that Marguerite would be starting her new job, aware then of the outcome, pieces slotting in nicely for the time being unlike before.

At college, Maisie had been summoned. The head of her course, who also oversaw other courses, wanted to speak to her with urgency and the other students stared at her as she left the classroom. She almost tripped over from the anxiety, wearing too high heels that were foolish really for everyday wear and in the office she was being looked at, assessed. Maisie knew that she didn't look like a serious student. Her hair was very long, which had taken all of her life not cutting it, each ringlet forming corkscrews that shortened it by half of its length. Today, her hair was loose and untamed which was representative of her current state of mind, her looks and dress sense perhaps deceiving of her actual capability. She was invited to sit down and waited nervously for the show down to begin.

"What's been going on recently Maisie? Your work has gotten poor, but you had started out as such a promising student" he said as he gave her a little smile, suddenly seeing her dad in his disappointed scorn she responded immediately.

"Family problems sir"

She was sure he knew that it could be that, but probably assumed it was more likely man trouble, as he was acutely aware of the tension between her and the token Romanian in the class who had unexpectedly become an excellent student. The head continued on and Maisie grasped that she was to concentrate and try her best to catch up and said he would talk with her again soon, giving her no opportunity to say anything more. She nodded in acknowledgement and left, accepting that everything he had said had been right, she must regain focus. But how could she concentrate properly with Mitac still in her class? She knew he wouldn't leave, he already had his life planned out, he was going to get a great job, just needed to convince a Scottish girl that a Romanian was a suitable partner and he would press on undeterred, residual feelings left fermenting.

Maisie sat at the back of the room on her return, thinking that perhaps it would have been better at the front so she couldn't see Mitac without turning around. But wouldn't it have been worse to feel his eyes burning into the back of her? She knew they wouldn't be. His eyes would be focussed on his work as always. But for her, wherever she sat, she was acutely aware of him and she didn't know how to ignore it.

CHAPTER 28

Marguerite, now with renewed energy, was in the garden pulling out weeds. The grass was long, too much for the lawnmower, it would have to be cut down a bit first. The garden was no longer the colourful haven that it had been before. In summer, even in autumn, it retained itself with orange and yellow leaves, but now it was closing down for winter.

The boys were due to start their new school soon and Marguerite really wanted to go to her parents to visit but she still felt she shouldn't tell them anything yet. Perhaps she should? Maybe it would help give her clarity. But Marguerite didn't want to go over old ground and she would have to find a car first, she couldn't afford another taxi, so she called the local garage to enquire about a car she had seen in the paper. It wasn't her ideal choice, a people carrier, but it was practical and a good price. Was it still available? They told her it was, so she began to ask all what she thought were the usual appropriate questions, what was the mileage and were there any faults, did it have MOT and tax? She knew they would be surprised that 'Mrs Chevelly' was buying a car from them and not from a main dealer in the town, but she decided to go and see the car for herself and any others they had to offer.

After a short walk Marguerite arrived at the garage, there wasn't much room on the show court so there weren't many cars to look at but to look anywhere else meant paying for transport. They had claimed they could source another if she was looking for something more specific, but Marguerite decided that the one she had first enquired about was fine and tomorrow morning she would return to test drive it and if satisfied, buy the car. This was a first for her and she felt pleased with herself, suddenly feeling as though there was nothing she couldn't do or achieve.

The next day, Marguerite arrived early. A couple of youngish men were already busy working, but one of them stopped what he was doing and came to greet her.

Enthusiastically he showed her the car, singing its merits and clearly eager for a sale. Visibly the car looked good it was very clean, no scratches, and had just been serviced as all the cars were, just right for her family. It wasn't what she was used to, it was a bus, and when she got in she sat high, but it was suitable for her family and it was time for something different so she agreed on a price.

Satisfied with her purchase, she went to collect the boys from her parents, getting used to the car as she drove. She had called them first of course, giving them a chance to get ready and pack their belongings, and by the time she arrived she was handling the car without a problem. The boys were beyond excited to see her, they weren't used to spending so much time away from home, and much as they enjoyed staying with their grandparents they missed the comfort of their own home. They hugged Marguerite and then sat as close as possible to her while she tried to have a proper conversation with her parents. They were delighted she had a job but secretly thought she had more than enough to do already now as a single mother. She hadn't told them the whole truth, which had became commonplace now, as she lied about her old car being faulty, an unlikely story as a BMW rarely went wrong. The boys didn't really know what had gone on before they quite happily went in the taxis, so there was no one to suggest her story was anything different.

On the way back home, Marguerite felt it was time to ask them a bit more about what had happened that day when they had got taken from the school. Maurice said the man was their father's brother, whom they hadn't met, and went on to ask why he hadn't been to the house before, didn't Dad like him? So, an estranged brother of Roly's, of course he wasn't that at all, but the boys and the headmistress had believed him. She left it there, didn't want to think any more about what had happened, it was done now. Instead, she told them about their new school and was relieved that they seemed just as pleased about it as she was, had their life been that dull before? The school meant new uniforms, more expense, but she decided to get them today and afterwards they went to her café. The boys pushed the door open, the smell of coffee and a concoction of indeterminate smells overwhelmed the senses as they asked for hot chocolates and Marguerite ordered her usual cappuccino. She left the boys chatting, working their way through delicious door stop sandwiches, and went outside for a cigarette, her table of course available as it was too cold for anyone to sit outside today.

Unbelievably just at that moment Rodrigo walked by, they embraced quickly and she couldn't resist inviting him to the house later. He was visibly relieved, hating the communication silences between their meetings and he, unlike her, did not have lots to do. He had his work and his friends, but nothing pressing that he wouldn't drop to be with her.

Back at home the boys were fired up at the idea of something new and were full of chat with their sisters as they all congregated in the lounge, the TV in the background barely audible over the babble. Marguerite felt she had turned a corner now, open to the unexpected but always on the alert for anything that may yet again change the course of their lives. Complacency and predictability were no longer, but she was feeling more alive and ready and able to face any future challenges and she decided that today was the start of a better life, one that was in her control.

The boys started at the new school. They were a little nervous but they had each other which as always doubled their confidence. Marguerite had half an hour now, if that, to prepare for her new job. She dressed smart, a gorgeous silk shirt in powder blue wasn't her best colour but it was expensive and it went well with a charcoal grey pencil skirt. Her shoes were black courts with a little bow and they were comfortable, as was all of her footwear, expensive often assured a good fit that ultimately paid for themselves in their longevity. Finally she pulled on her jacket which was a grey cord and wrapped a small scarf around her neck, it was pale grey littered with sprigs of flowers to take away the plainness. Happy with the result she was soon in her car and on her way.

The car drove well, it suited her needs and cost much less than what she had received from the insurance company for the BMW, so she been able to add the difference to her savings. The car got her to her destination, maybe not as smoothly but it got her there, and she found somewhere to park. Arriving at the shop she took a deep breath as she opened the door to another new beginning.

The shop was smart, smelt fresh and clean, and Marguerite couldn't help but wonder if Enid kept it like that or employed a cleaner, but thought that doubtful as she still appeared healthy and able enough herself. Enid appeared delighted with her new employee, exclaiming she looked so efficient and was a credit to the surroundings as she chatted about where things were and how to use the till. She then said she would be leaving her for a few hours, but if there were any problems not to hesitate to call and writing her number on a post it note she bundled out of the shop to relish a little time away.

Marguerite couldn't quite believe that she was actually working, what would Roly really think of her now she wondered, what would he make of her handling everything without him? He thought himself so vital to them and he had been in many ways, but the house could be sold and she would manage without his financial support. Despite all that had happened, she felt a sudden wave of sadness. She accepted now that the relationship they had should have been improved upon much sooner and she felt some level of responsibility for accepting the things she didn't like instead of speaking up about them but he too was guilty, for not taking as much notice of them as he should have. When they had been on holidays they had all been together of course, but 2 weeks out of the year was hardly enough. What was it that had really tipped her to the point of no return though? At night when she couldn't sleep she often spent hours going over the finer details of when the marriage had started to decline. Primarily it was his lack of acceptance with Maisie, not realising she was difficult and had issues but he had shown no sympathy for it. On occasion Marguerite had seen Maisie almost begging for understanding from him, longing to introduce her boyfriend and she had said as much to her mother, but Marguerite had been cowardly herself and not pushed for it. She knew that a respectable Scot might have been seen to Roly as acceptable, but a soulful sensitive Romanian, he would just have put on his usual smirk and that would have said it all. She was too young for a serious boyfriend, should be concentrating on her college education and then a career first as far as he was concerned. Marguerite decided then that Roly would probably laugh, and not in a nice way, at her own career choice. He would consider she had aimed herself too low.

The shop bell tinkled, a customer arriving disrupting her thoughts as she jumped in to her new role, role number six or was it seven? Number six being herself now. The customer was looking for some material to cover a chair and Marguerite felt proud of herself having discovered a yellow and blue tartan that pleased the elegant lady. She then found some matching thread, sapphire blue and primula yellow, and placed them in a bag for her first customer. She made herself a coffee in a bright red mug to celebrate, not champagne which was of course not appropriate even if she could, and more customers arrived sporadically. One brought some red and white gingham for a tablecloth and another brought blue velvet for some cushions. It was a specialist market and the shop stocked numerous textures and colours with all purchases placed in a haberdashery delights bag.

After what seemed like no time at all, Enid returned laden with purchases saying she had had a super time, as she grinned at Marguerite and said again how happy she was that she had found such a suitable addition to the shop. She declared that she already knew she was going to fit in just perfectly and Marguerite bustled with pride.

CHAPTER 29

Roly deemed his newly enforced lifestyle painful now. He missed his home and the fact that he was no longer in it with his children. Did he miss Marguerite? He couldn't even bear to think of her, she had hurt him so badly and destroyed the fabric of their lives and here he was ousted out.

Today was the day of the court hearing. Roly dressed in a tailored navy suit that was smartly matched with a crisp white shirt, a dark blue tie with thin pale blue stripes, silk and black lace-up shoes so shiny you could see yourself in them. He had had a haircut, not too short, Marguerites words echoing in his ears, she hadn't liked his hair short, said it didn't suit him, but long hair looked scruffy. He couldn't look less like a wife beater if he tried, but then how did they look? Perhaps those that were assumed to look as such were in fact most likely not to be the ones who abused their wives. All criminals came in different forms, conmen usually charismatic and intelligent the outside not representative of the inside.

Roly arrived at the court, not really quite believing that he was actually there, as he parked his expensive car and walked purposefully in to the large building, inside it smelt strongly of polish. He had to sign in and was asked to empty his pockets, small change, a key and not much else clattered into the bowl. He found a seat amongst the rows of plastic chairs that were bolted to the floor and he sat straight-backed and tense with his knuckles clenched and white, gripping on to the edge of the chair. It was sometime before he was called. He entered the court and a short statement was read out where he was referred to as Mr Chevelly. The female Judge observed him quickly and then looked again, seemingly deeper this time, weighing him up, seeing in front of her a respectable businessman accused of being violent towards his wife, they really came in all shapes and sizes she thought.

"Mr Chevelly, please tell us in your own words what happened the night in question"

Roly began to speak quickly, then stopped and slowed himself, making sure to pronounce each word with clarity but realising upon vocalisation of the story that it just sounded lame and inexcusable. I'm sorry, he added at the end. But was he? Yes, sorry he had brought this low of a slur on his character certainly, it was embarrassing as hell. It was over quickly and he was informed that he could now make arrangements with the consent of his wife, and of course his daughters if they felt the need to speak with him, the younger children could have their say too. He was free now to leave the court room, but he couldn't return to his flat it depressed him, he felt humiliated and unable to face his children and even less able to face or speak with Marguerite. He knew she would expect to hear something from him, she knew today was the hearing and the possible removal of the charge which had indeed been lifted, so he could now see his children again. The boys didn't have mobiles so to talk to them he would need to call the house phone, thereby possibly having to speak to Marguerite, who he knew would most likely answer. He considered the girls, thought Beattie would possibly be more sympathetic but then dismissed the idea as she too would likely be unable to forgive his behaviour towards her mother. Maisie had a dark side, he had obviously noticed but preferred to ignore it, thinking that perhaps she would relate better to the situation as she was older, but she wasn't wiser, far from it. Regardless, he decided it was right to speak with his firstborn child first, and he found himself shaking uncontrollably as he dialled her number.

"Daddy...."? A childish term for a 17 year old, Maisie answered almost straight away, her voice representative of shock that it was her he had chosen to contact first after all this time.

She knew he had been told there was to be no physical contact, but to not even at least have messaged? His silence confirmed his crime.

"Maisie" he said, his voice soft unlike his usual stern tone "How are you"? He asked.

"Alive" she replied, as always the drama queen.

Roly went on to suggest that he could meet with her and Beattie, she said she didn't know if Beattie would agree to it but would ask and he knew he had to be satisfied with that. A very stilted conversation followed; yes she was doing well at college, another lie, but hadn't they all always sugar coated everything for him.

Maisie was still shaking when the conversation ended, the sound of her father's voice invading into her consciousness, and she called Beattie straight away to update her but said little over the phone and instead arranged to meet her in the park so they could talk without anybody listening.

She and Beattie, each arriving on foot, sat together on a gnarled old bench dedicated to someone unknown to them. The park was often chosen as a place to sit and think enjoying the anonymity it afforded. Clusters of trees that had stood for hundreds of years surrounded them, the air was sharp, winter was almost here, the clouds were full and heavy and it was dismal which matched their moods. The trees had shed most of their leaves and a few were blowing in circles now around their feet, both girls dressed in quality warm clothes, their matching genuine Ugg boots keeping the cold out.

Do you miss Dad? Maisie asked Beattie. Her answer was that she didn't know, said it had been easier without him as they could do as they liked now and mum barely noticed anything anymore what with her work, the house, Rodrigo and the boys. They all seemed happier without the strained atmosphere. The girls had grown quite fond of Rodrigo, liked how he was with their mother and the boys, and as bizarre as it was Marguerite seemed to be looking younger and more beautiful every day. She was glowing. Love did that she said, it lit you up from within and they couldn't begrudge her that, whatever form it took.

Did they want to meet with their father or was it too soon? They knew he could ask uncomfortable questions, but he had served his punishment with the charge now. They decided to think it over, debated if they should speak to their mother about it, but decided it should be solely their decision. They were pulled by their loyalty to Marguerite but felt profoundly sad, a free reign for them had afforded some good benefits but it had also lead them astray and the consequences had been bad. Beattie had found Mace, but she was only 15 and she was so talented, Maisie felt Beattie was much less likely to be side tracked from her destiny by a boy. A fashion designer was what she aspired to, but love was always a great pull for women and their mother had proven that. Men it seemed could have everything, not their fault they couldn't give birth of course, but they could make more of an effort to engage themselves with their family. Perhaps other fathers were different? It wasn't really something Maisie had ever discussed with her friends, they mostly just talked about boys, clothes and a little about college.

Maisie consciously avoided her mother that evening. Marguerite noticed but thought little of it, her own mind preoccupied with what Roly would do now the charge had been removed. She was sure he wouldn't just let her keep the house but would undoubtedly prefer her to continue with the children's care and needs. She thought he would find some way to hurt her, knew he would be reeling from the humiliation that he had suffered and would do something about it, but what? The court order had given her time to continue as before without him, but what were her rights? She didn't know and she felt agitated and on edge about it, knowing she was going to have to find out.

Roly didn't want to stay in the flat anymore. He had a house after all and it was large, perhaps he and Marguerite could both live in it separately though he knew that would be hell. Was that man living there now too? He didn't think Marguerite would have allowed that, but for her it would have been perfect, easy, if he never returned there. No, he wanted her to suffer but he wasn't quite sure how to go about it. He could request custody of the children, but obviously the boys needed their mother. Perhaps he could arrange an Au pair or a nanny to take them to school and help look after them? But an affair was not a crime as such. Yes, it broke the vows of marriage which she had always taken seriously before as did he, and now they were separated but the house was theirs together and they were still married. He knew that legally she would be entitled to half the house and the children would choose her over him without doubt, so what could he or should he do? His daughters hadn't got back to him yet about his suggestion to meet. Didn't want to go against their mother, their mainstay, he assumed.

Maisie thought she could continue saying nothing but soon failed, her mother looked at her and clearly knew that something was wrong and she, feeling confused with mixed feelings, couldn't resist the words tumbling out. Maisie spoke so fast that she had to repeat herself so her mother could understand and Beattie overheard and joined them so together they discussed for and against. Marguerite, being generous and philosophical, said it was a good idea to keep their father on side and maintain contact as if they cut him off he could turn nasty, and then what?

Later that evening Roly received a message saying the girls had agreed to meet so he immediately took a few hours off work, noting how easy it had been to do that and always would have been really. He worked the 9 to 5 hours now which gave him the free time but he didn't actually want it.

Sitting in a café he had chosen, a favourite of his, Roly looked up at his girls as they arrived. Maisie's white blonde hair, the ringlets splaying out from beneath a blue beanie and Beattie, no hat, her abundant thick dark hair enough to keep her warm. They looked perfect he thought, untouched on the outside, but inside who knew? Had he ever really considered the inside of a person? The girls were hesitant on whether to hug him at first, but when they did the smell of expensive perfume and shampoo overwhelmed him and he found tears suddenly blurring his vision, he dismissed the cause as the wind, it was biting today. The girls noted that he still looked like their dad, but different, sad, as opposed to their mother who was positively bursting with love for Rodrigo, the man that had stolen her from their father. He had been careless, left her unattended for too long, and now he was paying for it big time.

The café, Roly visited regularly he said, was cosy and old fashioned, the lighting so low it was almost dark inside. Oil lamps gave off an odd smell but a warm glow as they all sat on comfortable arm chairs, it was an emotional experience. He wondered why he hadn't thought to take his girls out for a drink or something before or his boys to the park. Too little too late, he knew that now. The girls related sparsely a few things, both nursing mugs of hot chocolate in their hands, saying very little and almost nothing about their mother, only that she looked fabulous now, a bit thin but she had gotten a job. He hadn't known that but sensibly decided not to comment on it. He felt surplus to their lives now, a bitter taste forming in his mouth but he didn't want to punish them, his children, but he felt a real envy of the devotion to their mother, so deserved in fairness as she was always there for them. He knew they would not turn against her no matter what, so it was for him now to find his own way into their hearts but he had no idea where to start. He was aware that they were looking at him, expecting something, but he had nothing to give, didn't know what to say for fear of saying something wrong, so they remained sat in awkward silence for a few minutes more.

They didn't arrange another meeting he couldn't bear the disappointment in his daughter's eyes. His sons would possibly be easier but he doubted it, they too had their mother who was there for them and he couldn't have felt worse. He hadn't been able to visit his children but they clearly were not suffering without him, the girls looked happy, well and relaxed, somehow the strain had appeared to have been lifted from them but it had fallen on him like a ton of bricks. They probably wouldn't care about the lack of holidays, not yet anyway, and Marguerite would most likely make that happen in time, she could possibly move on again from the young man to a man who had money, but he doubted that too. Love was riches to Marguerite and he had loved her in his own way but not in her way, the way she had wanted, and now he felt like a very stupid careless man that was full of regret.

CHAPTER 30

Marguerite was at home, the boys watching TV quietly, aware of their mothers need to just sit. She did so whilst offering them a helpless smile every now and then which they returned with a grin, as always oblivious. The girls returned, a rush of cold air accompanying them, their coats removed and flung on the back of chairs but their feet still encased in Ugg boots as they joined her and the boys.

'No shoes in the house'! She could hear Roly say. She felt sick, hated that she now thought of him in this way when once they had been everything to each other.

Marguerite listened as Maisie and Beattie talked over each other about the meeting with their father, but she got the gist of it, he was sad. Her stomach lurched, tears falling silently unchecked, the boys too engrossed in an exciting part of the film to notice, the girls infected by the day. She grieved for the loss of a life that had so callously been destroyed through a lack of emotional support that should have been fundamental really. It begun just as a hairline crack, but it had been pushed, building strength relentlessly as the tottering walls of the Chevelly house threatened to fall and had now crashed. For all the freedom they felt they had, Roly had spoilt them all with possessions and holidays, her and the girls, the boys too had the best of everything; the latest fashions, toys, but really they needed and asked for nothing, they were at their happiest just playing in the garden. Of course when they grew older they would want more, but for now they would most likely just enjoy a more simple life, which was a quality perhaps they had all needed. They were disorientated but accepted this new way of life, what was in store for them all now? Marguerite pondered, as she and the girls turned towards the TV hearing nothing at all.

The next day a subdued atmosphere was present in the house. Maisie and Beattie were feeling unsure of their next steps, feeling guilty through loyalty to their mother and not wanting to cut all contact with their father. Marguerite would never suggest or expect that. If they felt uncomfortable with Roly and couldn't talk freely that was for them to figure out, so she told the girls they must decide for themselves what to do. Maisie, who usually acted without thought, couldn't conclude but Beattie felt she couldn't forgive him, he was diminished in her eyes and she had decided it was for him to find a way back to her now. The boys had been hurt too that their father hadn't asked to meet with them but seen the girls, didn't he care about them?

Marguerite too felt torn, should a person be judged on one mistake at the expense of any previous good? It was unfortunate that one bad act had had the ability to wipe out everything else, he had done his best he would say, he had kept them all in a lifestyle they had all enjoyed. His inability to connect emotionally was just a part of the person he was and always had been, but now he would have to accept that it wasn't possible to go back, Marguerite had already moved on. She didn't know what her future held now but had seen what she thought would have been her future with Roly, much of the same she assumed, just living out her days with her husband. She hadn't liked what she saw, felt a predictable routine was no longer the life for her, she liked that her future was uncertain now and full of possibilities, she had a job again and she savoured the unpredictability. Roly on the other hand felt safe within it, he needed it, and in time he would likely meet someone right for him and that kind of life. He and Marguerite had been right for each other at the start but they had grown apart and Marguerite was not prepared to adapt and lose herself in the process any longer.

She focussed back on her youngest son, now wide-eyed and questioning, told Maurice that everything would be fine and she was rewarded with his usual grin in response. Of course the boys missed their dad in some ways, she reassured them that he would be missing them too, but perhaps he didn't know what to do at the moment much like the rest of them. He had still been present throughout their lives up until now, even if only in the background. Frankie took himself up to his room, no chat tonight, so Marguerite said goodnight to him and closed his bedroom door. The boys often just went along with things unmoved but Maurice was a bit confused from all the whispering and then crying tonight, so she went with him and waited until he was asleep. She tousled his hair, it was babyish and curling on his collar, his pyjamas blue and covered in trains, the boys needed new clothes really. Frankie had grown rapidly recently, as boys do in sudden spurts and much of Maurice's clothes were too childish for him now. She would have to take them shopping when funds allowed, perhaps when she got her first pay check from the shop. Maurice snuggled under his duvet, just the top of his head showing, and soon snuffles could be heard, he was asleep. Tears never far away rested on the inner rims of her eyes as she shut the door quietly, the girls already in their rooms deciding they needed to be alone. She thought of Maisie's room always awash with the smells of perfume, Beattie's with mountains of clothes piled all over the floor, the clothes all mixed, representative of the colourful character that Beattie was. Apparently she could always find what she was looking for and she had told her mother that when Marguerite had suggested she hang them up in her wardrobe.

In her own bedroom now, Marguerite ventured out onto the balcony, she decided an early night would be good. Returning briefly to the room, she put on a thick cardigan that had cigarettes in the pocket and, looking out into the blackness, smoke billowing around her, she allowed the tears to fall again. It was therapeutic, her children on her mind, what had she done? The boy's were dependant on her to keep their lives secure as she always had done, the girls immersed in their phones, any sign of any rules gone out the window now she thought, as she puffed intermittently on her cigarette.

She had expected a call from Roly, a message or even a solicitor's letter, none of which had arrived. She felt it was important the boys be reassured that their father hadn't given up on them and the old Marguerite resurfaced briefly, compliance a hard habit to break. Surely it couldn't do her any harm to be seen as being reasonable she thought, so she messaged him briefly. She told him the boys were hurt that he had seen the girls but not them, and a message in reply appeared on her phone shortly after. Roly said he had been stuck in his routine, waiting until his work was done before he dealt with any more unrelated issues. He suggested Saturday morning and alarm bells rang in her head, she didn't want him to come to the house, he would notice her car, want to know why she had got rid of the BMW. To say she needed the money would be a mistake, he knew how much the BMW was worth and he could take that as an opportunity to give her less money. She replied to him, asking when and where, assuming Roly would probably be suspicious but she hoped he wouldn't start asking questions now. He named the cafe where the girls had met him and she thought that surely he could have thought of a better venue for two young boys, minor details she surmised relieved that the house had been avoided as she got in to bed, falling asleep quickly.

Marguerite tried to make a point of talking to each boy separately every day. They were so often talked to together, referred to as the boys, not Frankie or Maurice. So the next morning she told them individually that she had received a message from Roly, Frankie couldn't hide that he was pleased he was going to see his father but Maurice was more aware of people's feelings, especially his mother's, but his only concern was that she wouldn't like it. She assured him it was fine.

Saturday morning came around fast. Roly was jittery, he hadn't seen the boys for months, but when the heavy door of the cafe opened he leapt on to his feet finding himself wanting to hug them, but quickly pulled back not wanting to scare them. He wasn't a touchy feely person normally so a pat on the head was all he managed. He was smiling but the boys could tell it was forced and they looked around, spotted a large chair and both ran to huddle together in it. Roly smiled again as he sat on the chair opposite, this time the boys found it genuine, and they visibly relaxed with big smiles on their faces. They sensed the awkwardness but immediately launched into voicing everything that popped into their heads, uncensored. Roly listened and watched their animated faces, hardly understanding any of it, something about an uncle they had never met, asked why hadn't he been to the house? The uncle was his brother apparently. Confused, Roly continued to listen, thinking perhaps it would become clear as they continued. The den had been destroyed by the wind and, in their innocence, said that Mummies friend had rebuilt it with them. A lump rose in his throat, there were questions that needed answers, but this was definitely not the time so he managed to maintain his smile and contain his emotions, hadn't he been an expert at this? Refusing to feel, living his life on his own terms, problem free.

Marguerite stayed close by for the duration of the meeting. She hadn't suggested topics of conversation to the boys, that would have been ridiculous and they should be able to talk freely in the way that children do, but she was concerned they could give away information, not realising it was sacred and better left unsaid.

A couple of torturous hours passed before a text alerted her to collect the boys and she rushed to wait a few feet away from the café entrance as her two boys emerged almost immediately, running straight to her side. They hurried back to the car, none of them wanting Roly to follow. The boys were quiet and she caught Maurice absently chewing his fingernails, Frankie wrapping his too-long hair around his fingers, both clearly suffering in their own way. Marguerite tried to keep a semblance of normality, tried to keep them safe, but the domino effect was relentless and it was far from over. Choices were always just that, you turn left or right but you ultimately made the decision. Marguerite awaited retribution from Roly regarding the pieces of information the boys had given him, he would likely hide away to begin with, gather his thoughts and then regroup. But she knew him, no misdeed was forgiven, they were always paid for and this would be no different.

CHAPTER 31

At college Maisie continued to see Mitac daily, of course being in the same class it was unavoidable and he constantly begged her to talk. What about? She would often ask, thinking it had all been said already and there was no point in keep going over painful ground, but today she relented.

It was a balmy day, surprisingly warm considering the time of year that it was, but she felt in a strange mood and couldn't understand, yet partly did, why Mitac wouldn't just accept the situation when it was in her opinion him that had caused the problem by not putting her first. Apportioning most of the blame to him was easier but deep down she knew it was her reluctance to wait and not being understanding enough of his family and culture that had broken it. They started to walk, side by side but not touching, but who should be waiting at the gates?

Maisie tried to pretend she hadn't seen him, his grey eyes beseeching her as she felt a flicker of guilt but, again it had been him that was the cause of her having to end the relationship. Of course he hadn't deliberately caused the problem but it didn't matter now, he was bad news and she had only just told him again last night that there was nothing more to say and the relationship was irreparable. Secretly however, Maisie enjoyed this attention now from the two men, getting a sadistic pleasure from hurting them when she felt they had hurt her first. But Greg looked visibly pained now as he called after her but Maisie continued to ignore him, still walking with Mitac. He must have thought perhaps she hadn't heard him as he began to shout louder and people were staring now, as he desperately urged her to forgive him and confirm that she was still his, he was more than sorry.

"I'm not yours anymore Greg, just go away you evil shit!"

Alarmed by Maisie's tone and sudden change of mood, Mitac tried to hurry her along by pulling her behind him, slowly widening the gap between them both and Greg who, feeling his temperature rising persisted a little longer, but soon backed off. He had decided that perhaps starting a fight now with the man she was walking with probably wasn't the way back to her but who the hell was this idiot? He thought. He hated foreign men, always muscling in on other people's women with their lies and promises. This one looked particularly pathetic pulling Maisie along but he noted he was tall and well built. This was not a factor to deter Greg however who, despite his size, could fight and win against most men through pure determination alone. He considered then that maybe Maisie would have enjoyed the two men fighting over her. Perhaps he would get the chance another time.

Maisie and Mitac reached the park, just the two of them, and Maisie chose one of the many benches to sit on as she briefly told Mitac about Greg, dismissing it lightly. She had felt strongly at first, but then didn't she always, soon leaving at the first sign of anything less than total devotion to her. But Greg really had caused too much trouble, he had even endangered her family and Mitac understood that that was unforgivable. Either way, Mitac was of course pleased that she was free again whatever the reason for it, and he thought that she might now understand his situation better as she too was clearly devoted to her own family. But what he didn't know was that inside Maisie was complicated and she didn't understand herself, let alone expect anyone else to, but she wished she had someone that could. Ultimately aren't we all looking for someone who understands us, someone capable of loving us at our best yet still loving us at our worst? Right now Maisie trusted no man, they all let you down. Maybe not straight away but eventually they all did, even her father it seemed.

Back at the college gates Greg had disappeared, in search of a joint no doubt but he needed a new supplier now. He had been surprised at its availability in the Scottish town, but he supposed that in most places there was likely to be someone prepared to sell it and even more people prepared to buy it.

Maisie's conversation with Mitac hadn't made her want to try again with him. She was all over the place at the moment, but he had been disappointed that they had gone their separate ways after the park. They would have been better to not have returned to what had been done, Maisie was right that talking more in these situations didn't change anything.

The next day at college Maisie felt bored and the class did nothing to change that as they were discussing the history of textiles today. Mitac even seemed distracted for once and she knew he wouldn't wait indefinitely, would likely find another girlfriend soon but she knew that her relationship with him wouldn't have been her lifelong one as she was still at the experimental age. But the idea of him moving on didn't please her either, deep down she quite liked him hovering and pleading for her attention. At that moment she caught him glance at her, as if he knew what she was thinking, and mesmerised she looked in to his soulful dark eyes for a second, then turned away to look down at her blank notebook. Attempting to tune into the teacher's voice she wrote a word or two on the paper thinking they could be useful later, she was expected to write an essay of what was discussed today but she wasn't too concerned as she could always google the subject, there was always a way. She was going to walk home again today, she needed some air but it was very cold as she walked through the gates, but feeling the wind bite satisfied her as she was warmly dressed and she put on reactor sunglasses to stop her eyes watering.

Beattie was still seeing Mace but a new boy; youngish yet more mature than Mace had recently been appearing in places she frequented with friends. Greg too popped up from time to time, still harping on about Maisie, but Beattie knew she had been right to cut contact with him. He was an idiot, but the incident was not referred to again as Beattie preferred not to consider the possible outcome, had her mother not been able to raise the cash.

The boys had met with their father now, but he had not attempted to meet with her or Maisie again since the last time. She felt so disappointed with him for letting go of them all without a fight, but she understood the situation was delicate and that her father must be feeling humiliated, but she mostly blamed him for not taking better care of her mother. Now Christmas was approaching, the first that would not be spent as a nuclear family and it felt very odd. Christmas tended to be one of the only times Roly seemed to soften a little and his participation was actually a bit of fun, but how would it be this year? Her mother would undoubtedly want Rodrigo at the table for dinner, but Maisie was without a boyfriend now, so Beattie knew she would not be happy with her mother with Rodrigo, herself with Mace and Maisie alone. Her mood would ruin Christmas and make it harder than it was already, Beattie knew her sister well, or was it possible that all the change in their lives would make her a little more sensible? She doubted it.

Following meeting with his sons, Roly had thought long into the night; going over what they had said about how the den had been destroyed by the wind. He knew the Scottish elements could be fierce but he couldn't think of a time earlier in the year when the weather could have been bad enough to cause it. The boys had apparently changed school too, but he hadn't been told and Marguerite wasn't going to tell him anything that might put her in a bad light. The boys had also mentioned an uncle that had collected them from school one day. He had a brother, but he knew he would not have done that, they weren't in contact much and he hadn't yet been made aware of the seriousness of the fallout of his brothers' marriage, not by him anyway and he was sure Marguerite wouldn't have informed him. He would genuinely be taken aback. Roly was so successful with his highly paid job, a fabulous home and his wife well-kept and a presumably faithful kind of person, but there was much more to it than what was seen on the surface. His brother, in a rare moment, had once said he thought Roly to be a 'lucky bugger'! At the time Roly had felt particularly smug at this comment, but there wasn't much left to feel like that about now. So, who was this man and why were the boys now at that village school? The boys hadn't named it specifically, but Maurice had described it so perfectly that Roly was sure they were there and he wasn't pleased, the boys would not be turned into young men at a provincial school. They were babied too much by Marguerite and he noted he would now have to approach his wife to have it out with her and fill in the gaps, have a civilised conversation before he could even consider a reprimand from her would be forthcoming. He pulled out his phone and sent a precise message before he had a chance to change his mind, a message which he knew she would not ignore.

Beattie had been spending much of her time still considering Christmas, but before that it was her birthday, it was a week away now and she would be turning sixteen. She had mentioned it to her mother, who obviously wouldn't have forgotten, and would almost certainly be trying to think what she could possibly buy for a girl that already had everything and what she could do for it. It was so cold in Scotland now that outside activities could be a risk, but she liked the weather providing you were dressed for it and she thought a barbecue could be fun. Maybe a low alcohol punch and possibly toffee apples, a theme was forming.

Beattie and Maisie talked into the night, in Maisie's room where they could concentrate without the untidiness of Beattie's, which was the usual topic of discussion they were distracted by if Maisie was to go in there. Most of their friends were mutual, apart from a select couple of girls in Maisie's class that she wanted to invite, and Beattie wanted just to invite everyone as she found that with her birthday being so close to Christmas most people were too busy being involved in Christmas festivities, so better to over invite.

Meanwhile that evening, Marguerite found herself having to go to her husband's café. They had that in common she noted, that they both liked expensive coffee in comfortable atmospheric surroundings. She had dressed with care that evening, recognising that she looked almost skeletal now and that he would be shocked to see her looking so fragile. She didn't want to appear so, so she decided on some smart black tailored trousers and a huge red fluffy jumper that made her look less thin. Her hair was loose and a bit unruly, but her make up gave her an overall polished look and she chose a long camel coat to put on over the ensemble and some boots with a small heel. It wasn't a perfectly harmonised match, but she thought she looked well enough, hoping he wouldn't notice the underlying gauntness.

Roly's first thought when she arrived, bundled in a huge coat ready for the Antarctic, was that it didn't disguise her fragility in the way she had hoped at all. Her eyes were huge within a gaunt face, cheeks highlighted with blusher and a dash of red lipstick on her lips, which she never usually wore, was stark against her transparent pale skin and she looked ethereal. Roly was shocked, thought she looked beautiful but like a delicate porcelain doll that could shatter at any moment. Her manner was forced, hard, and he knew he didn't look good, he too undercover in his immaculate suit and coat, his face lined with black shadows like bruises under his eyes. She offered a hello, looking stern at first but then terrified as her face clearly represented her pain but he was resolved and couldn't afford to soften, she had taken everything from him but he knew he wasn't innocent and the collapse of marriage was down to the two of them. He felt he had done everything right, never envisaged this happening, believing so much in his own self-satisfaction that it would not cause her to look outside of the house for alternative attention. In his naivety he had presumed she would not have had the opportunity but evidently now he saw that it could in fact happen anywhere and to anyone, even him. Now he longed for what he had had before but taken for granted and this moment was his opportunity to find out what had been going on since he left and he didn't want to waste it. Hastily, he relayed his conversation with the boys to Marguerite as she pulled her coat tighter for ineffective protection. It was warm in the café but she showed no signs of removing the coat or staying long, so she went over in her head her responses to his questions, utilising the little time she had as he ordered two coffees. He knew that much wouldn't have changed, they had both always enjoyed a good coffee, her even more so than him. Marguerite smiled weakly as she picked up a large cappuccino and sipped it, her eyes large and luminous in her thin face as Roly noted that she didn't appear to look like someone that was helplessly in love, had that gone wrong already? The boys had told him of a man helping them rebuild the den, but that was earlier in the year, had she wrecked their lives for a fling? He didn't think that was her style, it was serious it had to be, but he couldn't bear to think of it. He was awash with all the emotions he had desperately fought to hide and even now couldn't pinpoint which, but it was anger mostly. He was the provider and financially she had contributed very little, but he had overlooked the fact that without her taking care of the family his career wouldn't have been so successful, but she was not to win. She was barely held together now, lacking in substance, and for a second he was horrified at the results of his coldness sat in front of him but he couldn't let it go, he needed to know.

Marguerite wasn't a natural liar and she faltered as she spoke but said the school was closer to the house and no, she didn't know who the fictitious uncle was. Her expression was closed, he could get nothing from her and he felt defeated and deflated that he had found out nothing, not knowing what more he could do or say. He knew his children would not take his side, there had been too many years passed now of him not listening and taking the time to get to know them, they were Marguerite's children through and through and he knew their loyalty would remain with her. But suddenly, one last glimmer of hope surfaced as he remembered Beattie had a birthday approaching, her sixteenth, that was his chance to get in the house. He couldn't be denied access that day.

On Beattie's birthday a message, amongst many others from friends, arrived from her father. He said he would give her a call soon to arrange a time and place that he could give her a birthday gift, so he wouldn't be expected to turn up at the house today now. Not that she thought he would anyway as she hadn't heard from him for a while but it gave her a lift that he had been in contact and, as angry as she felt, he was still her father.

The party was going to be fun, and most had surprisingly accepted her invite, so it promised to be a good night. She would wear the large hoop earrings studded with diamonds that had been a gift from her mother, her outfit planned, which was unusual for her as it was often her way to decide on the spur of the moment, throwing together items with skill. But that evening she wore skin tight jeans and an even tighter cashmere jumper in pale green, a silk puffer jacket in deep brown and long leather boots that stopped above the knee. She was feeling good. Turning sixteen opened doors and she were well on her way, school was finished until the New Year and the holidays had started. Rodrigo was setting up the barbecue now and Mace would be arriving later, she didn't know about Greg but it was the season of goodwill, even though it was hard to find any to send his way but she left it to Maisie to decide. The mood was set, music playing quietly ready to be pumped up later. The neighbours, barely knowing the Chevelley family now, had been informed and would just have to tolerate a bit of noise. Children grew and became a problem, even the Chevelley children apparently. By 8 o clock a few people were meandering, the patio doors open and glasses, plates, cutlery and serviettes set aside neatly. An array of scented candles were lit but out of harm's way, placed strategically where they couldn't be knocked down or blown out and the aroma of cranberries filled the air, the Christmas tree in the corner. Beattie didn't foresee any trouble and considered briefly that if her father had been there it would have been a guarantee. The guest list would have been vetted, a look from him upon suggestion of certain people an immediate deterrent, though he looked less scary nowadays. Marguerite was in the lounge with Rodrigo, two starry-eyed lovers, who could begrudge her or him.

Both Maisie's admirers were here and Beattie hoped they wouldn't kick off on her birthday. It was so like Maisie to not even consider that this could happen but Maisie assured her that they wouldn't dare, but she knew that drunken people easily turned. The air was mellow, it was a cold night, but it was calm with a possibility of snow which would make it even more memorable. Maisie was bouncing between her two men, dressed in a white coat that was trimmed with fur she looked like a film star but Beattie didn't feel outdone. They were so different, rarely liked the same boys, so there was no rivalry of that kind between them. She watched as Mitac moved in closer to Maisie, chancing his luck, but Greg was close by looking put out. Beattie hoped that he would remember he was only there tonight because she had allowed it. Maisie had wanted to invite him and he was her boyfriend's brother after all. Suddenly side tracked by the other people, she noticed two boys at one of the tables on the terrace. It was nine now and the garden was full, she didn't recognise some of the guests but she liked new people. Her attention diverted to a stocky guy that was sat at the table looking as though he owned the place. Beattie felt a flicker of interest, he was all man, but what did she know? She was only sixteen but felt more aware of the opposite sex now than usual. Mace was gorgeous and gentle, but he looked like a baby compared to this other man. Another guy that she didn't recognise was sat next to him, what were they talking about? It didn't matter. She made herself busy flitting about talking to her friends as an odd smell filled her nose but she was immediately distracted by a horrifyingly familiar voice. It was her father.

She panicked, this was not good, her party was about to be ruined. Everybody had drinks, mostly wine and her mother had agreed to a low alcohol punch and there were the toffee apples, childish but popular. The barbecue was thankfully now being overseen by Maisie and Greg, who had wormed his way around to her as Maisie was a little drunk now but in an amicable mood. There no sign of Mitac but she was sure he was around somewhere, Maisie liked to have a following. She called out to Maisie, who too had become aware of their fathers presence, and immediately rushed off to find her mother who bundled Rodrigo out of the room upstairs to hide. Her father would go insane at the drinks, drugs, friends that were barely so, and worse, there was dealing going on in the garden but Greg had said it was not a good idea to get on the wrong side of the guy doing it as he, amongst others, had turned up at the party uninvited. If Roly caught on that there were drug dealers at his daughters party he would surely cast the blame at her mother, but Marguerite didn't even know the man was there or what he was doing as she had stayed in the lounge with Rodrigo, barely aware of anything that was going on outside.

The scene was set now and they would have to play it out, the possibility that Roly might appear hadn't even crossed their minds and it was too late to do anything about it now. The music was too loud, but was that a crime? Maisie returned to the garden, alerting her friends to empty their glasses quickly, it was only punch and she was eighteen but some of Beattie's friends were too young to be drinking it and her father would be furious at her mother, thinking she had completely lost control by allowing this. The punch was very weak but even so it was another weapon for him to use against her so the girls rapidly attempted to conceal the evidence. Then Marguerite sheepishly appeared, a shawl wrapped around her and everyone turned to look at her but at that moment, as if to save them all, it started to snow.

It was spectacular, everyone began jumping around with excitement and Beattie took that chance to whisk her father away to the kitchen, before he could take in the scene, giving everyone time to get rid of anything suspicious. It seemed as though the party would be saved. Marguerite entered the kitchen to light birthday candles on a cake, Maisie noticing the look she gave to her father now, daring him to spoil Beattie's birthday. She was sure that he wasn't there to cause trouble, attempting to build bridges not to knock them down.

Roly considered that Rodrigo was possibly somewhere in the house, but for now he was not in the kitchen or in his line of sight, so he decided to let the thought go and just be nice. Unbelievably, he had brought Beattie a necklace 'To my Daughter on her 16th' and Beattie was choked up as he had never given her this kind of a gift before and she couldn't have felt happier.

Back outside it was snowing so much now that most of the guests had left leaving only Maisie and Mace, Greg and Mitac and a couple of her best friends from school. They moved into the candlelit lounge, it was so Christmassy, and with Roly there it seemed complete. They had all thankfully decided to think of Beattie and put their personal feelings aside today as the boys came downstairs for the cake. They had been in the garden much earlier but gone upstairs to play, it was the perfect birthday. Beattie's party had changed from the direction it could have taken, but that was probably a good thing.

Roly felt some measure of happiness but privately wondered who the boys were at the party. There was no sign of any attachment to his daughters, so they must just be friends he hadn't seen before, but little did he know. Marguerite looked relieved and gave him a thankful glance, was he that much of an ogre? He realised then that they all seemed so grateful for any small kindness they were offered from him as they all sang Happy Birthday to Beattie, the boys overjoyed at all the family being together again. Roly left after an hour, not wanting to risk any upset by overstaying his welcome, and the girls hugged him, the boys too. Marguerite just stood there, looking so less of herself. What had he done to her really? It was his fault and he knew that deep down, as he slipped out in much the same way as he had arrived. The garden was a brilliant white, Christmas was approaching, but he knew that this year he would have to be alone. Of course he had his family but his parents were often neglected by him, his brother even more so, he didn't deserve their sympathy. Instead he resolved that he would just call his children individually on Christmas day, hoping it would be a start in the right direction.

The next day was the start of the holidays for the children but Marguerite still had work. The girls were watching out for the boys but they needed little supervision, too engrossed in the snow which had covered the garden last night and later disappearing in to the den. It was warm inside despite the cold as it was insulated. The roads were a little treacherous but Marguerite was used to the snow now and just drove very slowly to the shop, knowing they would still have customers as it was the festive season and the haberdashery delight had some nice sewing boxes and gift sets incorporating the basics that were popular, as were the pincushions, unusual but traditional. Enid had bought Christmas decorated bags and was offering the service of gift wrapping this year which was all classy and expensive, materials always sold at any time of the year. Marguerite was so relieved that the party had been a success, Roly behaved well and they had all enjoyed a reprieve from the battle. Had Roly been more like how he was last night on other occasions maybe things could have been different now, but he hadn't and people didn't change, they always reverted back to themselves. In her case, it had taken years, but she felt now that she was finally her true self again.

CHAPTER 32

The day passed slowly at Haberdashery delights. A few customers shook off the snow as they searched the shop until they could find all the gifts that they had not yet managed to find, anxious to get their presents all sorted and gift-wrapped so they could just look forward to Christmas. The night before, Marguerite had gone upstairs as soon as she could but the children however were reluctant for the evening to be over. She found Rodrigo sleeping and wondered how long he would want to stay involved in her complicated life. He was young with no commitments so he could do anything. She lay next to him and immediately his arm slid across her, she felt warmed by the gesture, he was so affectionate and she needed someone who was both physical and attentive. Rodrigo was so in tune with her, it felt unusual to have someone so focused just on her and she felt peaceful as she got as close as she could. In the morning she relished the love making, it was decadent and nothing could make her regret feeling truly happy and cherished.

Finally it was time to shut the shop. It was pretty straightforward, just making sure the shop was tidy and locking the door behind her when she left. Marguerite had a bundle of cash from the till which she took to the bank, she walked there as it was not too far down the road and it was quiet so nobody noticed her. Returning she found the car covered in fresh snow, it was dark inside as she rummaged for the ice scraper but fortunately she had recently brought one. When her car had been stolen and then destroyed she had lost all her accessories and music CDs. She had even brought blankets for this car, they were rarely needed in the BMW as it had an effective heating system that instantly cleared the windows and warmed the car, but this car was much older and not so efficient but it got her where she wanted to go. She pushed the last of the snow off the top of the car whilst leaving the engine running, it was a precarious drive and she knew the route but the car was slipping and sliding as she hadn't put snow chains on her car. She noted that that was something she must organise as soon as possible, but for now she succeeded in getting onto the road home. It was difficult but she crawled along hoping that conditions would improve, though it was unlikely. Scottish winters were fierce and it was mentally exhausting driving in this weather, especially without snow chains and she knew it was not a good idea.

Delicious aromas hit her as she walked through the front door. Excited voices could be heard as she followed them to the kitchen to find that the table was already set. The boys were seated, the girls and Rodrigo busying about, as fresh bread was placed on the table and a jug of fruit juice. Marguerite felt overwhelmed by the change in her family as she smiled with her eyes full of unshed tears. It didn't get much better than this, this was what she always wanted, music playing softly in the back background. Rodrigo was young but that endeared him to her children as they could relate to him and him to them, he wasn't a replacement for their father but an addition, simply slotting into the areas where Roly had failed. They were all laughing and chatting through-out the meal and the dinner was excellent, Rodrigo had prepared it with the girls assisting. He was an inventive cook and Marguerite felt she could get used to this. So far it felt good and right so she decided to risk letting Rodrigo stay, it was a large house and she thought why deny her this happiness. She put it to him and was immediately rewarded with the laziest smile, his eyes dancing as he declared that he would let his room go, his voice raised high with excitement. Marguerite thought that he should perhaps keep his room, but she supposed that to pay for a room that he wasn't using was wasteful but could protect them just in case. In case of what exactly she didn't know as they were a couple now, rightly or wrongly, was it wrong to be together? She questioned herself but then reasoned that it was her house as well as her husband's, even though she knew Roly would be outraged. She and Roly had been together a long time, but he didn't need to know and for now she felt she didn't care, let him do his worst, Rodrigo could always find another room if necessary. Should she even feel any sympathy? A concoction of messed up thoughts were rising, but she felt she was being tested in life now by being given what she wanted and it had been hard, but was the worst over?

The morning after a perfect night, Marguerite rolled away from Rodrigo's arms as he lazily opened one eye. He engaged in smoking cannabis on occasion, hence the laid-back attitude, so she was effectively a passive smoker just by being in the vicinity of it. She kept her distance but it hung around. She could understand the qualities but knew there was always a price to pay in any type of addiction. She, so disciplined and not needing or wanting anything to add to her mood which was fixed on a high at the moment, she would find ways to raise her mood safely. Arguably she was far from safe at the moment, risking her security for what could just be a fling, but still she had taken this direction and ran with it, how far could she fall? She felt both safe in his arms yet unsafe, fearing his loss at any time.

Rodrigo was fully awake now but reluctant to leave the sheer luxury of the bed in the en suite bedroom that had been inspired by her husband. But it hadn't been enough had it, enough to keep his woman? Now Rodrigo had taken his place in their bed, in their house and in to the heart of her family.

Maisie had decided not to invite either of her love interests on Christmas Day. Marguerite thought she might regret it as she would likely feel envious of her mother with her boyfriend, but Beattie had not invited Mace either. She said she wanted Christmas to be happy, it was hard enough already with it being the first without their father. She told Maisie that doing this was her contribution to the day and Maisie had grinned with satisfaction, saying they didn't need men to enjoy themselves, but she pondered over where Mitac would go as he hadn't any family here. Beattie considered how the day would be without Roly and decided she was going to dress with care, careless to colour coordination as usual, but it was Christmas so it was to be recognised. The house, which they had all had a hand in decorating, was truly alive with a mass of garish decorations. The tree was adorned by a free theme and the boys enjoyed their efforts not being rectified, even though it was dramatically lopsided with too many balls on one side and patches where there were none at all, but it represented their new less than perfect life.

The day Roly had dreaded was here, but he considered that perhaps everyone should spend at least one Christmas Day alone, and a lot of people did. He thought then of the homeless, which weren't a train of thought he had given much thought to before. He wasn't homeless, in that he still had a roof over his head, but it didn't feel like a home and the flat did not indicate Christmas, other than a few cards from work colleagues. His family; his parents and his brother had messaged him yesterday but they would now likely be enjoying their day without him, he assumed he would not have been a welcome guest in his present situation even though they hadn't said specifically. They had rarely gone as a family on a regular day of the week but on Boxing Day they would visit either her parents or his and the day after that would be for the other set of parents. Christmas Day was always a day spent at home with just him, his wife and the children as he let himself soften a little and play games which he secretly hated but made himself available. He would assist with the Christmas dinner, trying hard not to criticise or mention the chaos which was how his wife operated within in the kitchen, as he set the table with table mats, glasses, condiments and serviettes placed perfectly, his standards high. He thought of each of them now and one by one he called his children, his gift to himself. They had not sent him gifts and he had not to them. He would have a delayed Christmas and possibly get them all together in his flat.

Roly's conversation with Maisie was stilted and he fought with the intense feeling of regret as he wished her a happy day. She was quiet, carefully considering the responses in which she settled on. "Don't drink too much" he said to her as he ended the call. Next Beattie, who chatted about inconsequential things, not wanting to face the elephant in the room, "Let's arrange a get together soon" were her closing words. The boys were the opposite of the girls, hyped with excitement regardless of his absence, which was commonplace for them when Roly had been living there and now they probably barely noticed he wasn't. Roly didn't ask them too much, he didn't want to know too much as this was already a difficult day but at least he was talking to his children. He didn't speak to Marguerite or wish his wife anything and she didn't message him again either, also not waiting to acknowledge the unexpected situation that he and all of them were in this year.

Marguerite couldn't believe the past week had passed without anything untoward. Roly was collecting all of the children tomorrow in his sports car, rarely used other than for work and his own pleasure, so it accommodated very tightly all the children. Rodrigo had gone out before Roly's arrival so Marguerite began tidying his belongings away in a box at the foot of the wardrobe, leaving nothing to chance as Roly could be capable of anything. She didn't need to speak to Roly, the children would hear his car and just go out, and it happened just like that. Now Marguerite was alone, a situation she was rarely in. If she was home from work Rodrigo would juggle his work to be there, how different he was to Roly, but he had it all to gain, didn't he? A ready-made home and a family belonging to another man, but Marguerite was beginning to care less, choosing to savour the time, her memories now bitter sweet.

On the ride in their father's car the boys were in their element, sounding expletives at every roar of the engine and Roly felt their excitement, seeing the car through their eyes. The girls remained quiet, letting the boys take centre stage. After a short time they arrived at a modern building, Roly had to put in a code to enter and they went in, calling for the lift as it was four floors up. The lift doors opened on reaching the right level and they all followed their father down the long hall. The hall was carpeted and smelt new, it was lit as it had only one window which couldn't be opened. It was like they were in a hotel until they came to the door of his apartment, which he opened and he sensed they're hesitance as he showed them into the lounge. Maisie was carrying a bag full of gifts that they had all taken their time choosing, or someone had. What did they think of the flat? Roly wondered as blank faces looked at him, it wasn't a home it was clinical; straight lines, black furniture with metal legs that you wouldn't want to catch your selves on. Still, that wasn't going to happen as they all sat like upright soldiers, it felt strange, the boys squashed together into what was the most comfortable chair. It had a low back but for them they were just about small enough to lean against it with a measure of comfort not afforded to an adult. Roly switched on some background music, feeling awkward by the silence, and it helped a little as the girls started talking together and Beattie allowed Maisie to take the lead which was a good move. They didn't want to talk about Christmas so it was hard to find a suitable topic but the boys broke the ice by admiring the huge TV. They had a large TV at home, but this one overtook the whole wall. Roly turned it on and pressed a few buttons, the room starting to come alive as he switched to the latest Superman movie which competed against the background music. The boys settled more into the chair and Roly gave them both snacks; crisps and some bottles of soft drink, and they were soon lost in the film, forgetting about the gifts. The girls, glad to have something to do other than talk, gave Roly a pile of perfectly wrapped gifts. Maisie had wrapped them, which Beattie informed him, as she could barely recall what the gifts from her even were now. Her gifts to everyone just fell out with minimum effort, whereas Maisie's looked too good to open. A swell of emotions attacked him. Would it be so bad if he voiced it, it would likely make them laugh and show he cared, that he was sorry, but it was hard for him and he had to satisfy himself with that. He really didn't want to have caused any disharmony though it was far too late to change it.

The gifts were mostly practical and some a little indulgent, his favourite aftershave, Marguerite must have told them about that and the same with the silk ties. He had gifts for them, large boxes expertly wrapped by a shop, the first boxes revealing for Maisie a beauty box for a blonde girl, for Beattie a beauty box for a brunette, Frankie a state of the art CD player with a radio and Maurice a compact TV/DVD player in one that could be used anywhere. Both the boys gifts could be played in the den with batteries, but his sons were not technical as they still enjoyed the outside adventures, for a while yet at least.

Once the gifts had all been unwrapped, a takeaway was ordered and the room took on a new ambience. Roly felt satisfied in that his day with the children was a success and he was grateful for it, starting to appreciate what he had and could have again. He knew it wouldn't be in the same way as before, but he now felt a little of the previous bitterness leave him.

CHAPTER 33

It was now the start of another year and everyone had their own resolutions, Marguerites simply just to continue with her job and keeping everything going. Maisie was keen to get back on track with college but she doubted that she could, the school had written now to say that they weren't sure if there was any point in her continuing the course as she spent most of her time dreaming at her desk, staring out the window and not listening or taking notes. Without her father continually reminding her that her education was her future, she seemed to have decided that it wasn't. Maisie was like a butterfly, flitting aimlessly through the day, a destination undefined. Beattie however was already counting down the days until the next holidays when she would be free to begin her life as a fashion designer. Two years of study preceded it but Beattie was already skilled enough and selling her creations, she just needed the credibility of a certificate but her work spoke for her. The boys were too young to have New Year resolutions, The New Year was just that to them.

Roly was quiet, not a good sign, what did he have planned for the upcoming year? It would be a vastly different one for him in comparison to any prior, but the girls had said he had mellowed. Unlikely Marguerite thought, he was a snake changing his skin to suit his needs.

The village people were now gossiping about the Chevelly's, they were no longer respected, but Marguerite cared little for that as she would prefer them to admire her for reasons other than wealth, and what business was it of theirs anyway? She had casual friends but she wasn't one to need female friendships. She had her mother but she didn't ask her for advice or tell her anything much either, she would speak to her daughters if she wanted to talk but advice, they were not really experienced enough to give. Instead Marguerite would mull over things and reach her own conclusions in the way that she always had, she felt she was self-sufficient but had bowed down a little when she was with Roly, perhaps a lot really for a quiet life that she now knew she hated. She had called herself up on so many things recently that she thought could possibly have improved her marriage but she was happier now than she had been for a long time, even if it was edged with fear. She knew already that nothing should be taken for granted and Roly had found that out the hard way, now living in a small flat alone, punishment painstakingly received.

Rodrigo was in a mess at work. He was rushing his delivery rounds now trying to remember to get signatures, which he had missed on a few occasions, and received a final warning for it. His family had messaged and called him over Christmas asking where he was, what he was doing and had he just forgotten them all? They guessed that a woman must be involved but to the exclusion of all else? They wouldn't understand why he wasn't working his way through all the young local girls instead. He thought Marguerite was class however, felt he had done well, but worried himself that she could tire of him and one day replace him with another man that was richer and better looking. At the moment this seemed impossible as they were so in love, but was it just lust? Every afternoon they were able to indulge themselves anywhere in the house, nowhere was taboo until the family were back from school and college, and he couldn't be happier when he was there, but when he was alone he was in a continual state of anxiety that was un-natural to him. He was so laid back by nature but now he felt nothing else mattered but Marguerite, he didn't even need to keep his job really but she was out of the house for a few hours a day at the shop so he needed that time to be filled.

It wouldn't have been difficult for him to find other things to do but he needed at least some mental distraction and stability so he tried to keep it going for now.

In the shop Marguerite was not pushed either, she saw it as an income not a career, and she was a victim to the syndrome that most women always fell to, being either obsessed or possessed by a man. She had the boys still needing her but they asked little of her now, as always content in each other's company. When Frankie moves to senior school this closeness could be threatened but they would always be best friends and she was sure of that.

Maisie too was in an anxious state without a boyfriend, this couldn't last it was unnatural to her. Mitac had given up approaching her now, expecting perhaps that Maisie could then turn to him, which was a possibility as you could never be sure what Maisie would do if it suited her in the moment. Greg was still hanging around outside the college, hankering after her most days, risking his job to be there. What was his job? No one was really sure, but love seemed to have made a mess of them all.

Beattie was restless as usual, school now mind numbingly boring for her, she was ready to leave and her school friends shared this impatience. She thought a lot of Mace but had lately become more aware of this blonde boy. He was surely bad news as she knew that he hung around with dubious characters, he had been at her party but with the arrival of her father she hadn't had a chance to find out why. So many of her friends had been talking to them, another mystery, but drugs were most likely to have been the subject of discussion. She hadn't heard enough to be sure, like who had set fire to her mother's car or who had kidnapped the boys from school, still gaps that needed to be filled. When the school bell deigned to ring, she and her best friend decided to go to the local Café. Beattie hoped the two boys might be there today but they weren't and she was disappointed so decided to leave. The girls lived opposite ends of the village so Beattie walked home alone, but on the way back she spotted him, suddenly feeling her heart tremor. Was she becoming like Maisie? She was always on the alert for male attention. Beattie was in a hurry, as was he but he gave her his ice blue stare and she shook herself. Don't go there Beattie, he's trouble, but it gave her a release from the mundanity of school and she felt happier immediately, more herself. As she approached the house she found her key in her pocket, keen to get inside, and she was immediately welcomed with warmth and delicious aromas. Rodrigo cooked for them all, he was an asset. Her mother's cooking was just about edible but rarely anything more than just something simple to keep hunger at bay. She thought they would all probably get fat now, with Rodrigo serving calorific dinners and sometimes desserts too and if not they would take ice cream in to the lounge. Huge bowls filled their laps as they would all sit together to watch a film and chat together for a few hours before they dispersed, on to their own exploits. It was idyllic, her mother always lit from the inside, and Beattie was happy for her despite everything. The house felt more relaxed now with everyone unrestrained and they spent more time together.

Mace called round that evening. He was wearing drainpipe black jeans and a skin tight white turtleneck jumper that showed off his toned physique. His trainer's, always pristine, he was so clean and smelt delicious, he was beautiful. Beattie cared for him and not just for his beauty as he was nice too, which was rare in a boy to have both qualities. He had stayed in Scotland because of her but he had to get back to his old life, if only just to tie up a few loose ends, but he saw his future with Beattie and decided to tell her as much. His eyes stared deep into hers they were deep brown but not as dark as Beattie's, as he looked at her with admiration. They really were an eye catching couple and when they went out together people's heads turned to admire them, envious of their good looks. She knew he would be back with her again soon but she would miss him and he hugged her then, stroking her back and pulling her long silky hair through his fingers. Beattie was surprised at this news as they were only 16, too young really she thought for a serious relationship, though she knew that age had nothing to do with it as far as love was concerned. She found herself thinking of the blonde boy, still didn't even know his name, Mace was a catch but was he really the one already? Well she would soon find out and she knew he would return to her as her power over boys had always reassured her. Mace was the best looking she had met to date, but it was more than just looks as she thought then of her parents. Her father had given Marguerite everything she could ever ask for materialistically but he no longer owned her heart, sent her pulses racing in the way Rodrigo had. Beattie had discussed this with her mother and she could understand now that nothing could compare to that feeling. Her poor father to not have realised sooner his wife's values, he had been careless and smug, but it never did well to think that someone would never leave you. Beattie was at the age now where life was offering her so much, did she just want a boy? Beattie wanted success and power, was she about to risk that and throw it all away for Mace? She hoped now that her sensible side would prevail.

CHAPTER 34

Roly was keeping a low profile. It was a new year and he knew he should be making decisions, preparing for a divorce, but it was so final as then there was no way back. He considered then that perhaps he hadn't ever been the way his wife wanted, had always known that he had been forcing her to be a puppet to him, a necessity to his career and sustaining the needs of his children. He had noticed signs of indignation in her but swept them away, never expecting retaliation, yet always knew she was more than he had let her be. He had weighed her down with guilt by always allowing her free reign with his money, but now she had decided that that alone was not enough and he regretted it deeply. Marguerite was still in the house with his children, him managing in the flat but he missed the garden and the comfort of not having to think of meals. But did he miss her for herself? He could force her out if he wanted to he had the ammunition, several things he could use, but he himself had now been tainted as a wife beater though it had been an accident. But he had still attacked her, hoping to shake her to her senses, and if that man hadn't come to her rescue he could perhaps have really hurt her. Had she been hurt when she fell? He wasn't sure but he felt helpless now knowing he couldn't manipulate her any more. He recalled that she had remained limp in his hold, allowing anything of him, and she couldn't fight back as she was too weak, so thin and so frail. He accepted now that he likely wouldn't be considered safe to be in charge of the children and they would only fight to stay with Marguerite anyway. He wanted the house but it was too big for him alone and he wouldn't want to rattle around each room that was full of only memories now, but he had worked so hard for it and he wanted badly to have that superior status back. Perhaps he could get past the nostalgia and redecorate? The house could be re-mortgaged and he would pay off Marguerite, allowing her to take the children and get something smaller, plenty of families managed this way but it was a flimsy idea. He decided he would have to pay another surprise visit, considering himself over the worst now. He needed to face what was going on at the house, resentment building as he brooded over how badly things were stacked up against him now, his huge TV on for background noise so he felt less alone. It was odd how he had liked to be alone before, but only when he had chosen it and he felt charged and ready to push him-self to the limit now.

The next day Roly arrived at the house, his family could be heard inside as he viewed the place critically. The patio doors were open, even in the winter as it was a rare warm day, but he decided to start in the right way and rang the doorbell of his own house. It took a while before the door opened and it was Maurice that stood there.

"Daddy"!

Maurice looked taken aback as he ran ahead to the lounge and Roly followed him.

"Everyone, it's Daddy"!"

Maurice announced as faces stared back at Roly that suggested he was not welcome there. The room looked lived in and Marguerite gave him a glimmer of a smile but looked quizzical and ill-prepared. Where was the man hiding, or was he not there today? He planned to go to the bedroom and check it out, find evidence. It would be there if anywhere.

"I'm here to collect my shirts" he declared lamely. He could replace them and he knew Marguerite would be thinking that as she panicked, knowing Rodrigo's now hung side-by-side to Roly's. Roly could feel her mind mentally going over the giveaway signs as Marguerite told Maisie to go and retrieve her father's shirts, a last ditch attempt to prevent Roly from going up there. But her efforts were in vain as Roly had already decided that this was just an excuse for him to check for other things and he could sense Marguerite knew now that the game was up. Beattie, immediately picking up on what was to come, urged the boys away from the situation with the first thought that came in to her head.

"Come on boys" she said. "Let's play hide and seek"!

Random, Roly thought, the boys were too old for that, but they agreed and ran off to hide together with Maisie following them, not a sound could be heard as he and Marguerite were left alone.

Roly spoke first, taking control "Right Marguerite, that man is clearly living here"!

It was a statement and not a question and Marguerite didn't confirm or deny it, but she knew they couldn't continue like this, they needed something to bring it all to a conclusion. Roly went ahead upstairs to the bedroom and opened the wardrobe to find that his shirts were still there where he had left them and some spare suit trousers, not noticing Rodrigo's next to them. In the bathroom, he observed all Marguerites toiletries but there was nothing at all to suggest a man had been in there. He looked around the bedroom again, Marguerite's things were there and it wasn't very tidy, it looked how he would have expected her room to be, and he went back downstairs defeated.

"Clever" he said to Marguerite as she relaxed a little. "I know I can't prove it now, but I shall and that BOY has no right to be living in my house"!

"OUR house" Marguerite countered back as Roly looked annoyed. In the eyes of the law, yes, the house belonged to both of them and he knew that the law would likely consider that she as the mother should have the house, but he wasn't going to allow that to happen. He didn't consider that Marguerite was behind his success, leaving him to pursue his career without interruption, and he decided to leave before his other side surfaced as he thought of his wife and that common man, it made him sick, he hadn't accepted it at all it seemed.

"I'll be in touch again" he informed Marguerite, leaving the date and time open to speculation as she remained sat on the chair motionless, staring out at him as though she didn't know him anymore at all as he left the house. It was bizarre how you could be everything to someone and then suddenly nothing at all she thought.

That night Marguerite chose not to discuss what had just happened, the children were all likely listening throughout and had probably heard it all anyway as no questions were asked.

At the college, Maisie was acutely aware of Greg's time wasting and decided today to acknowledge it.

"Shouldn't you be at work" she asked him, when he was found yet again to be waiting at the college gates. He explained to her that he was in no fit state to work and she felt some measure of sympathy. She always had the ability to relate to situations of the mind getting the better of you, sometimes rendering you useless for normal life. She also kind of liked his persistence and as he spotted some warmth in her, he pushed his daily request just to walk her home and this time she gave in. As he smiled she felt a fraction of her original desire for him as he quickly took the opportunity to take her hand in his, his hand felt warm despite the cold but Maisie could feel the roughness, they were a real man's hands, not soft and cared for and she hated that. She supposed that he was likely only there for sex, she wasn't stupid, but he could get it elsewhere he was popular enough. But he seemed to only want her and she liked that he, unlike her, didn't give up easily if he wanted something or someone. He had persisted through her resistance and it was catching, his enthusiasm, and she hadn't had sex for too long, still hadn't looked into getting herself protected either but this was a walk and a chat, nothing more intended.

It was dark already, still winter and freezing, but as a Scot you were used to it. On reaching the park Greg suddenly pushed her against a tree, pushing home his advantage, the park was empty and she gave in wanting to be close to him in that fleeting moment. He felt hot and her body welcomed him, it was over quickly but it satisfied them both, him pulling out just before the climax like he had done before on occasion. He probably didn't want to impregnate her, boys just got so carried away that sometimes it happened and you were left to wonder for a few weeks before a period came. A small part of you visualising the possible result, a cute little baby with his eyes and her nose, but she was no fool. The devotion required to that red squalling infant was 24/7 and she was too selfish to want that. Greg looked victorious but Maisie was annoyed with herself but not sorry, once you had sex once you wanted it more, it was natural and vital. Libidos varied and so did attraction but she did fancy Greg at least.

Greg was at the gates most days after that and they fell back into some kind of a relationship. Maisie was cross with herself, why had she gotten back with Greg? He hadn't meant any of what happened before but it had, but for now she allowed those memories to be repressed. She didn't dare suggest he go to the house, her mother would not forget so easily, but she couldn't resist the sex. Even though she still hankered for Mitac she resisted him as she had Greg to satisfy that need in her now and Mitac had finally cut her off. It wasn't easy for him to have Maisie so close, knowing she was now pursuing her interest in Greg again, who was English and more likely to be accepted by her family. Maisie had told him before that he had ruined his chances, and he knew a bit of what had happened but he hadn't really been listening properly and not understood that money was the defining cause. Greg had no doubt noticed that Mitac was the nicer person, but nice people were always the losers and he knew a foreigner had no chance of acceptance in Maisie's family.

Maisie had been unwell lately, some sort of bug and she didn't feel well enough to be at college but she didn't want to stay at home. Marguerite was at work until early afternoon and then Rodrigo was there, it was too much, and she envied her mother. How wonderful to be in love and be loved back in return with equal measure.

Beattie was now without Mace most of the time, though still his girlfriend and he kept messaging enough to assure her that she was still his girl. He was amusing and light-hearted and she messaged him too, though making him wait for a reply sometimes as she knew not to make herself too available. Instead, she kept busy spending a lot of her time out with various friends and the blonde boy, Zachary that was his name she had finally discovered, was growing on her like a nasty rash and he was just that. But she felt an attraction to him, as you do to things you shouldn't have or take, and she had dared to dabble in light drugs, of which she believed she was in control of. A totally naive perception as alcohol was effective too in mellowing the resolve to keep in control of it. She knew she shouldn't, but she was young and at the experimental stage of her life. Mace had smoked cannabis but only intermittently, Greg however was full on and even Rodrigo smoked it. Marguerite of course was always on her pedestal, accepting of others weaknesses but she liked to be in control or at least think she was. Beattie laughed at this as her mother couldn't be less in control if she tried. Her daughters were running amok but the boys luckily were easy to deal with, just needed feeding, the rest of the time they were outside or in each other's respective rooms.

Maisie and Beattie were in a local restaurant now, they didn't often go out just the two of them but they wanted to talk outside the house instead of skulking in their rooms. Roly had apparently said to Maisie that he would consider getting her a car and pay for driving lessons. Beattie hadn't been surprised really, throwing money at them instead of time and attention was his way.

"He doesn't ask me much, like, have I got a boyfriend"? Maisie said to her sister. "Do you think he just thinks we are not interested in boys yet"?

Beattie shook her head "I think he just doesn't want to know about anything that might cause trouble"

Maisie gave Beattie a helpless look "How do you think I seem at the moment"?

Beattie's quizzical chocolate eyes looked at her critically. "Truthfully, you look fantastic Maisie, kind of glowing"!

Maisie gulped as a rush of sickness enfolded her.

"But I've had this stupid bug for ages now, sometimes it goes and I feel a bit odd, but..."

Beattie suddenly looked horrified, Maisie's implication dawning on her.

"You are joking aren't you"?

Maisie looked shame faced for a moment.

"You idiot Maisie, it's a bug that's all, you look fine, really" Beattie told her.

"Yeah, of course it is just that, I'm just overthinking it"

Beattie then went on to tell Maisie about Zachary and Maisie welcomed the turn in conversation, but it was Maisie's turn now to look horrified.

"Surely you aren't hanging around with that boy Beattie, he was probably the one involved in the kidnapping"!

Beattie was shocked at this new piece of information but insisted that Maisie must be mistaken as there was no proof so Zachary couldn't have been involved. Maisie, sensing Beattie's unease, decided to retract the conviction.

"No, you're probably right" she said, knowing that he still could have been. Was Beattie falling prey to the fatal attraction that she had once considered herself to be above?

Roly had sent a letter to Marguerite, handwritten so quaint, that mostly reflected that he hated that their marriage was over just that, like it meant nothing to her. He knew he had to accept that they both wanted a different kind of life not that he hadn't liked his old one, but he had refused to get to know her properly by preferring for everyone generally to be what he wanted them to be rather than who they were. All of that was omitted throughout the letter but Marguerite could imagine Roly as he was writing it, saying to himself in his head that this was really his chance to tell the truth about his feelings, but of course he still stood apart from that. Should they separate? They already were as far as she was concerned which would ultimately lead to a divorce, that much was clear. As for the house, he would look into buying her out if he could, but he needed confirmation from her and she reflected again about the situation, had Roly ever truly cared for them at all? It hadn't felt like it as Marguerite read the letter several times over in case she had missed something. If he had that kind of money, half of that would be hers, she should have a solicitor. She had some savings that were hers alone but she was reluctant to start something that she didn't have the finances to sustain. Roly would surely have his way. He was aware of his rights and knew a lot about the law. An advantage he had over her as she was foggy about it, but knew she was entitled to half of his assets and possibly the house as well whilst the children were at school or in college. She knew she was ultimately the one who had broken the vows of their marriage, though she didn't consider she had, but she had ended it and no matter how she looked at it the law would not justify her actions. The law wasn't about feeling, it was about money. But she was happy in the house now appreciating finally what she actually had and what was missing, the puzzle was complete and Rodrigo had filled the missing piece. She would miss the garden most about the house, but a line had to be drawn. She considered Rodrigo could leave her, be lured away, but it didn't seem likely as they were still so engrossed in each other. Could it get more intense? The breath was knocked out of her daily by the strength of the connection and it was painful by definition, but to feel like that if only once in your life was ultimate.

CHAPTER 35

Outside the house Maisie was sitting on the patio, bundled in her fur trimmed coat, she looked like Madonna. Beattie was watching her from the open door, she wondered if her sister realised she looked so beautiful, so peaceful. But what was to follow was far from peaceful, it was going to be hell for them all as Maisie sat with her hands laid folded across her stomach. Beattie was on a quest for information she was not interested in fiction, liked only facts and she knew now what Maisie must also know but was too scared to voice. She decided to let Maisie work it all out for herself, but how was their mother going to feel about it? She was sure it would be very different to how her father would react. He would probably accuse her mother she thought, tell her she had been selfishly indulging herself and taken her eye off the ball. But she knew her mother lived in a constant state of fear of her happiness being snatched away and her father still hadn't contacted her again, suggesting that perhaps he had learnt nothing at all.

At college Mitac was watching Maisie again, overwhelmed by a mixture of sadness and anger, tortured that Maisie had chosen Greg who had fought harder for her attention when he had given up. His plans of his future with a Scottish girl and a career he could uphold as an example to his family and friends had not been a success and now he felt like a failure. She was keeping a secret, he could tell, as she was distant again with her notebook untouched on the table and the teacher's voice not registering with her, or with him. Mitac wasn't coping well. He wanted a career, but he wanted her too and he was from such a volatile race, yet he had given in easily thinking he had done all he could, but in doing so had allowed another man to take her from him and secure her. To him she was a goddess, now untouchable in another man's possession. Suddenly he knew what she hadn't said, he had seen his female cousins grow fat and dreamy he knew all the signs.

After college he saw her leave linking arms with Greg who had been at the gates again waiting, his anger was reaching dangerous levels now and he needed an outlet for it but he knew that risked deportation. He decided to hang around outside Maisie's house but catching a glimpse of her at the window only further fuelled his rage and this time he gave reign to it. He was holding a bag of rocks and one by one they reached the target. He was some distance from the house but able to get a good shot, feeling satisfied when he heard a smash as the window finally succumbed and shattered. He hadn't intended to throw them really, so why had he brought them? His anger now spent, he quickly found a row of hedges and pushed himself into a gap underneath. He let the tears fall as he lay there, feeling his heart shatter like the window, as he moved further back on hearing voices in the garden. Maisie's family were investigating outside the house and Mitac suddenly felt an overwhelming sense of shame, as well as loneliness. Who could he even talk to? He knew only of his one friend Eduardo but he would only call him a fool.

The Scottish girls don't marry boys like us, they just play and we have to play them back, that way we both have our fun, he later told Mitac when he had appeared on his doorstep in a dejected state. Eduardo hugged him in the way that Europeans do and let him cry it out, he felt sad for him but reminded him that he was a Romanian. They didn't get the girl, especially not a rich one, it could only ever be for fun and ultimately they suffered the heartbreak.

Marguerite was sat with her girls at the kitchen table to talk about the window incident. Maisie assured her it was nothing to do with

Greg as she started to weep uncontrollably, it was clear to Marguerite now that her daughter was pregnant as she got up to stroke her blonde ringlets. An image of Mitac materialised, no chance for him now she knew, what a mess.

"Maisie, do you love Greg"? Marguerite asked her gently.

Maisie nodded "I think so, I need him"

But was that really the same? Needing and wanting were two completely different things. But she wanted the baby that much was certain and Maisie was glad that her maternal instincts were emerging now, as she was thinking of how to protect herself and her unborn baby. She hadn't voiced that she thought the window could have been a result of Mitac's anger and it had already been boarded up straight away by Rodrigo.

Beattie was relieved the pregnancy had now been confirmed. A new life was going to join them, and she was surprisingly excited even though Maisie had upstaged them all, as she always claimed she would but Beattie was thrilled that she was going to be an Auntie at 16. She knew her father would not be there when his grandchild arrived and his handling of the situation would be something none of them would ever be able to forget. On receiving the news he had cut Maisie off completely from his life, he was too disappointed and not able to deal with it. He had called her a fool and labelled Marguerite a useless mother, who had retaliated by pointing out that he too was useless and wasn't a father to the children in any shape or form that mattered, as she slammed the phone down.

Maisie returned to college but found that Mitac was no longer there, had he left? He had always protested that nothing would stop his success but it seemed her return to Greg had been too much for him to bear. Eduardo had come to sit with Maisie during the lunch break, and for a moment she thought he was going to hit on her, but he only wanted to blame her for Mitac's misery. He told her she had broken his heart and he called her a bitch. Maisie was hurt that he thought that of her but she wasn't about to tell him her news, he probably already knew it was obvious, as she noted her hands that were folded across her stomach again. She had someone else to think about now and she told him as much. She wasn't responsible for Mitac's heartbreak, it had been his choice to give up on her, but in solidarity to his friend Eduardo told her that men actually have hearts too, his accent thick. Maisie wondered if he really understood the pain of heartbreak, he was such a player himself and as such you didn't get hurt.

A few weeks later a message arrived to Maisie; Mitac was leaving Scotland to find a job back home in Romania. He said he had tried here but failed and his family needed him, but he didn't say anything more about his feelings, likely knowing that Eduardo had already told her. But Maisie needed to look after herself now and grow up, her childhood fantasies were over. She had explained to Eduardo that her life was just too complicated, but she wasn't a bad person or trying to hurt anyone. Maisie was so young really and now she had a child to consider, thanks to a man not taking responsibility and her naivety in not protecting herself. After their conversation that day, Eduardo had surprisingly become a loyal friend to her, defending Maisie when snide remarks were voiced, but she would not be able to complete the college course now, maybe in the future she could return. Motherhood was her future now, as she wondered about how the baby would look. Like her and Greg presumably, but sometimes genetics played games, she herself had blonde ringlets that were a throwback but it was interesting to fantasize. She wasn't unhappy with the idea of being a mother, babies were cute, but your own was a real gift her mother had always said, a gift of the most precious kind.

CHAPTER 36

Maisie was thankfully feeling a lot better. The sickness that she, at its worst, had refused to think was anything but a bug was finally subsiding. Wearing clothes that disguised her tiny bump; longline jackets, loose-fitting full-legged trousers, high quality oversized shirts and sensible shoes adorned with flowers and butterflies, she felt quite the fashion guru. She wanted to leave college with the option to return after the birth and she was feeling focused, but the hormones were taking control, making her thoughts hazy and her body even more so.

Beattie, ever observant of everything, watched as her sister's abrasive personality softened but she found herself missing Maisie's attitudes and unpredictable moods. They had been annoying but it was Maisie, this Maisie was vague and Beattie felt as though she had lost an ally now. Her mother was already a slave to her own hormones, namely Rodrigo, was she the only one with any common sense left? She thought her father an idiot too for not wanting to support her sister in such an important stage of her life, but the boys had accepted everything and continued as usual with their childhood with no concerns, just enjoying the different people popping in and out of their lives and the extra attention from Roly all of a sudden.

Greg was in the house at every opportunity, puffed out with pride at the thought of being a father and having secured Maisie as the mother. He had gotten a new job now that paid more than the last, but did he honestly think he could keep Maisie in the style she was accustomed to? As a family they all had less money now without Roly, but Marguerite always seemed to be able to get it.

Beattie knew Marguerite had credit cards and that she didn't care if she paid the money back, everything would sort itself out was what she told herself.

Greg was becoming irritating. To Beattie men always seemed to give too little or too much of them and Greg seemed to be living up to the extremes. He was not the potential son-in-law their father would have wanted either, but a normal father would have gone berserk and insisted on marriage after impregnating his daughter, but not theirs. He had no curiosity regarding the father of his grandchild and to him, ignoring his daughter and the baby would mean it simply didn't exist as a pregnant 17-year-old daughter was not for the likes of him.

Marguerite on the other hand was thrilled, but should she be? He daughter now eternally linked with Greg who was a druggie, though apparently reformed, but these things didn't often just go away, but who was she to judge? Her mother liked to see the good in everyone but where had that got her? Beattie liked Rodrigo but he was a stone around her mother's neck, someone else to care for, when what she really needed was someone that could support her both financially and emotionally. Rodrigo was better than Roly had been with the emotional side of things, but he had nothing to offer on the financial side. Marguerite was foolish at times and she was too soft, considering that to be more important, but right now despite her job she still had to be dependent on Roly for money, both of them effectively supporting her needs. Beattie considered then that her mother had messed it all up. Her mother had rejected her father first and he understandably hadn't taken too kindly to it, the boys now the only reason he was continuing to financially support them. But was he succeeding in getting the boys on his side? She couldn't think that he would want the responsibility of having her brothers full time, he was playing nice Daddy by taking them out and buying things, but Marguerite was ultimately their rock. She was a bit shaky nowadays but she would always protect them with all that she had left in her when it mattered. He really was just the biggest fool to have allowed his self to lose her Marguerite, who had given all of herself to be responsible for all of their happiness. But Beattie wasn't stupid she knew they were all capable of making their own choices, even bad ones which they could withdraw from with willpower and now even she was finding herself getting sucked in to it all. Zachary was a challenge that should be ignored, but would she have the good sense to resist?

CHAPTER 37

Rodrigo had been a bit taken aback by the news that he was now partner to a grandmother to be, but Marguerites excitement had warmed him. She was still his but he knew that another person; a grandchild, would also be in need of her love. Love is infinite it doesn't run out, she had reassured him and they were as close as ever, falling into their lives together naturally. Marguerite hadn't met his family yet and Rodrigo was not proud of this, but Marguerite had many times speculated over how they felt about the relationship. Especially his mother who was probably close to her age, who wanted that for their son? Rodrigo had decided that he didn't want to mix his family with hers as it could spoil it, they wouldn't approve of Marguerite. Her family didn't approve of Rodrigo either really but they genuinely liked him and he had been accepted for their mother's sake. Rodrigo had told his family that he had a woman but they didn't approve of her situation; married, though separated with four children, was he completely deranged settling for an older woman with baggage when he could be out having fun with someone his own age? But they had sort of understood the idea of the older woman fantasy, though he hadn't actually shared that with anyone, and had just said that one day he would take Marguerite to meet his mother. She was quite stern on the outside but a genuinely nice person on the inside and would surely only want to see that Rodrigo was happy with his choice.

Marguerite wondered if the meeting would ever happen, it was early days and the fewer people involved the better, but she didn't care what people thought and she now had a Grandchild to look forward to, another new role number eight as Grandmother. She had expected Grandchildren to arrive at some point but hadn't expected one so soon and could never have envisaged the time ahead to be with so many complications, but she would be there for Maisie. Once again, her husband couldn't accept that things happened unplanned. A daughter with a child at 17 was not for him, but he would be the loser again as he had rejected Maisie and now Beattie had abandoned him because of it. The boys however seemed ever oblivious to all the conflict, their innocence protecting them.

Roly could barely even consider that this had happened, he too had let go of the reins. The family had always been in his control and played by his rules when he was there, but his denying any association with any boyfriends that his girls must have had was just ignorant. He had thought that Maisie was the intelligent child that he knew her to be, not stupid enough to get pregnant in the 21st century, but perhaps he had just refused to accept that Maisie and Beattie were young and very attractive women now, of course they were going to get male attention. Expecting a baby, he knew how it happened, was his wife living out her own fairy tale and not watching over the children? Roly knew that couldn't be altogether true, but with her guard down Marguerite hadn't seen what was going on so the blame was now at her door. He had refused to consider his part in it that he too had failed as a father and he was in turmoil with himself now that his daughter was going to be a mother soon, yet hadn't even acknowledged the babies existence. He just couldn't and he was devastated that nothing he had tried to teach the children seemed to have registered. The boys had mentioned to him that Maisie was getting fat, they knew of course, and asked did he like the idea of being a Grandad? But he didn't reply, just smirked and skipped the subject effortlessly by distracting the boys again with something on the TV.

Roly wanted to start the proceedings to sell the house. He was alright in the flat but it was rented and therefore a waste of valuable funds and he couldn't afford another house without selling, but for now he was passing time by enjoying his motorbike which he had recently purchased. The boys had been gobsmacked when he had shown it to them and he smiled as he recalled their faces with wide eyes, they hadn't thought of their father as being someone interested in bikes. He had been to a bike club a few times and there were a few female bikers, but because he was so out of the game now he didn't know how to approach women with a view to date. There was this one lady who seemed to like him but it felt odd, he had been with his wife for so long that it felt disloyal, but she clearly hadn't thought of it like that. Marguerite was blissfully happy apparently, the boys had said that she was always in a good mood. But hadn't she always been, not ever allowing any negativity into their lives? He could have tried harder but it was too late now, there was nothing nice left on her side now or his, only anger at his own stupidity and rage at Marguerite who he now thought of as ungrateful. He found himself thinking again of the woman at the bike club. He thought she looked as though she could be interested in him, they had caught each other's eye on occasion, and she liked bikes so that was a shared interest. Maybe he could ask her for a drink when he felt ready? He didn't have much of himself to offer her, he was a shell of himself now, but he hoped she would say yes.

Beattie had only a few weeks now until she finished school and then her college life could begin. Maisie wouldn't be there as she would be leaving at the start of the holidays and then they would all be at home awaiting the birth. Beattie relished the idea of the freedom she would have, her mother being preoccupied with Maisie meant that she would barely notice what Beattie was doing. Perhaps that was an unfair assumption to make as she knew she would still be noticed, but Marguerite was trying to take a more modern approach in thinking that her daughters needed to experiment with life. The result of which was now a new family member. Beattie was still Mace's girlfriend and he often messaged her in a jokey manner, nothing serious and no undying love promises or how much he missed her either. So she replied equally casually, it was less demanding than an overeager boyfriend, but it was a little annoying. Really girls were never satisfied, was it any wonder men lost the plot? They didn't have a clue what women wanted. Mace knew he was considered good-looking but he didn't really see himself as anything special, he wasn't popular he told Beattie. Said that maybe he wasn't nasty enough as girls often preferred the bad boys, his eyes would have been filled with amusement as he typed that. Beattie pondered the idea and a trickle of excitement leaked as she thought of Zachary, he was a cold fish, always acknowledging her presence with a stare but hadn't shown any real signs of taking it further.

CHAPTER 38

The summer was warm but not unpleasantly hot, in Scotland there was always a breeze. Maisie's neat little bump had expanded and her cheeks were rosy as she sat in the shade, indulging in a past interest of reading. Beattie had researched, considering only facts to be important, about all baby-related issues. Having a baby was an everyday occurrence, but each girl acted as though she was the first and it was a first for Maisie as a Mother, Beattie as an Auntie, the boys' as Uncles and Marguerite and Roly as Grandparents, even though he was still choosing to deny the fact.

Marguerite had been working today and came home with offcuts for Beattie to use to make clothes. It showed Beattie that she had been on her mind and her happiness and well-being was still taken in to consideration. Marguerite had always tried to remain fair in dividing her attention with all of her children, giving it when it was needed.

The house was big but it didn't have a fifth bedroom, so it had been decided that Maisie and the baby would use the study at night, it was bigger so it would be easier, so Maisie and Greg had begun to make room for a crib. Greg had also assisted Marguerite in packing away what was left of Roly's belongings that were now covered in dust. Her bedroom and the study hadn't been properly cleaned since Roly had left, and the boxes were put in the loft should he ever need them. Obviously most of it was useless to him now, as Roly hadn't taken any of it, but his flat was minimalist and wouldn't lend itself to clutter. It was fun to think of a theme for the study, that was now the nursery. Greg had decorated it pale yellow as he and Maisie had chosen not to find out the sex, and it was clean and empty now for when the baby was ready to move into it a few months later. Greg wanted to move into the room with them, he was there most of the time anyway he had said, but Maisie held out. When the baby arrived she would need him, and he was so enthusiastic and keen to be the best father, but they could get a place of their own soon so they could just stay as they were. They had a nursery now so there was no rush, but Maisie couldn't really envisage herself out of the house, it was all she knew. Instead she let Greg ramble on just nodding her head, not in agreement, but it was easier than a confrontation. She was preparing herself just for the baby, oblivious to anyone else's needs, and was savouring the time she had left with her being the only occupant in the room.

Beattie was kind to Maisie, always bringing her cold drinks and snacks as she was constantly hungry, and the days passed aimlessly. The boys had returned home and they and Rodrigo were playing football in the garden now, a pole with a net had also been added for basketball and an outdoor Jacuzzi for their own pleasure. Again, Marguerite had somehow found the money for this, but everyone was enjoying the reprieve that this baby had given them, Roly as ever remaining absent.

In the last few weeks before the birth of her Grandchild, Marguerite had taken some leave from work, wanting to be close to her family. She had neglected Rodrigo a little but he seemed to understand, as always being in tune with her, and he occupied the boys after school. They really cared for him and found he was such fun but he didn't buy them gifts. Sometimes he would find them lolly pops or a bag of sweets in his pocket, as a cannabis smoker he was always craving them, but he was generous and gave what he had readily and freely. Rodrigo helped in the garden and continued to cook for them all he was a good person and cared for them all in different ways. He was wonderful even to Maisie, looking forward to the baby as the Step-Grandad that he considered himself to be. Marguerite had seen him share the odd joint with Beattie, she didn't like that Beattie was partaking in this now too, but Beattie was so disciplined and would surely stop if it became a problem so she pretended not to notice. Greg had become agitated and restless now with waiting to start his new life with Maisie when the baby was here, so he often joined Beattie and Rodrigo to smoke, despite previously saying he was reformed.

Mace had returned briefly for a holiday, he had work back home now, but he wanted to be a part of what was going on at the Chevelly house. He hadn't voiced it but he was missing Beattie, but he was smart as he knew that she didn't like possessiveness and she valued her freedom. Their relationship was being held together loosely now, but his company was appreciated as he was always in a good mood which softened Beattie's heart. This was the life that suited her, in the hub of her family with a man at her side who understood her and was there to help and comfort her. Any doubts about the future she had stored away, choosing now just to enjoy this important stage of their lives. Roly had decided that he would wait until the baby was born before doing anything about the house, he wasn't that evil.

A few weeks later, late into the night, Maisie called out urgently to anyone that could hear her. She was experiencing intense pains now and having trouble breathing. The baby was big now, as was she, her ankles were swollen and her face had ballooned and her eyes bright but sinking into fat, her hair long with the ringlets forming a perfect halo of gold that had darkened during the pregnancy. It had become difficult now for Marguerite not to consider the impact that the birth could have on her personally. Maisie was still so young would it be left down to her to care for him or her? She feared that this could happen once the novelty had worn off as she recalled how hard she herself had found the sleepless nights, but she had been much older than Maisie. Maybe being young was an advantage? And there were many hands to help her.

Maisie was grabbing her mother's hand now for strength as she and Greg struggled to get Maisie out to the car. Beattie and Rodrigo had been alerted to the situation so they couldn't get back to sleep now, but had said they would instead listen out for the boys who were to be left to sleep through, but they had already heard the car leave and wanted to be with Rodrigo and Beattie. Mace was also there again and he too had been woken, so Beattie decided to put on a film, but nobody could pay attention to it. The suspense now at unbearable levels, they all sat bonded tightly together.

Marguerite was outside the delivery room as Greg had insisted he and Maisie should do this together. She didn't mind as she thought that actually watching her daughter give birth would be harrowing, though exciting, but she stepped back and said she would wait there in case she was needed.

Marguerite was the first to receive the news, a boy! 7 lb 11oz. Greg was ecstatic, tears cascading freely as he hugged Marguerite and she returned the gesture with equal emotion, both of them overwhelmed. She considered then that this was a moment she should have been sharing with her husband, he wouldn't have been like this, but she could see that Greg genuinely loved her daughter. He held Marguerite's hand tightly as they went in to the delivery room where Maisie was, now looking more herself as the nurse made her presentable, and a tiny baby boy peeked out from a tightly wrapped blue blanket on her chest. His little face was all that was visible and it was perfectly rounded with his eyes blue, a broad nose and a small bright red mouth. Colm was his name they informed her, as he peeked up at her and opened his mouth wide to let out a cry that echoed around them, he had arrived.

After a while Marguerite left Maisie, Greg and Colm. Greg could get home by himself he said, and Marguerite gave them the biggest smile. They were their own little family now; A Mother, Father and baby and she were a Grandmother, but she skipped like a little girl to her car to drive home, wanting to rush but needing to concentrate. Upon arriving home she burst into the house and ran in to the lounge, where she found empty glasses and packets of sweets littering the carpet and Beattie, Rodrigo, Mace, Maurice and Frankie sprawled out amongst it all, huddled together on cushions.

"Colm is here, he's so perfect"! She announced.

They all jumped to their feet, hugging each other and then all coming together in a group hug as Marguerite felt her heart could burst with joy.

The following day they awoke late, still all in the lounge, having fallen asleep at different times where they were. Suddenly Marguerite realised that she hadn't messaged her husband, it hadn't even occurred to her, he didn't deserve to know really as his coldness had reached new levels, but she sent him a message as it was the right thing to do. She didn't want anything to dispel the happy mood but this could not be spoilt, even Roly could not be so cruel as to not acknowledge the arrival of his own Grandson and would surely want to know his Daughter and the baby were well. However, she prepared herself for no response as she knew he would first consider all angles and come to a decision in his own time, unlike her who would act without thought. Another annoying trait as far as Roly was concerned.

Maisie was to remain in the hospital for a few days, as is the norm for a first-time mother, but unexpectedly seemed a natural and was soon competent at dealing with the baby, who was not so small at 7 lb 11 ounces and was robust. Greg was to and from the hospital regularly, bringing Maisie what she needed, the hospital supplying nappies and baby bath oils. He had a bicycle now that he had got from a friend, he was resourceful Marguerite noted, and his interest in his son and the well-being of her daughter consumed him as he wasn't afraid to show how much he cared. Marguerite liked that and was prepared to put aside the trouble he had unwittingly brought them all before, they were fine, he was the father of her Grandson and in that capacity a permanent part of all of their lives. Money was not a consideration, if was needed it would be found, and Frankie and Maurice only ever mentioned the incident with their uncle with excitement. They would ask Marguerite again, where was that Uncle? When they on occasion passed their old school in the car on route to somewhere else and had been reminded. Marguerite just fluffed over it each time, perhaps he would visit them Frankie had said, but she knew that wasn't going to happen. Sometimes the truth was not an option and it didn't matter, they didn't need to know.

Maisie and Greg looking impossibly proud on their arrival back at the house. Beattie, Rodrigo and the boys had decorated the lounge with balloons and a welcome banner and Maisie smiled as she held Colm close in a baby sling, she was slim again now but had lots of loose skin, but said that Colm was compensation enough for such a small sacrifice. Colm was asleep but had awoken to the sound of lots of excited voices and he was bundled around to each person but he accepted it. Just gazing up at each family member's face, he seemed a sociable baby as his tiny fingers curled around each person's hand. He was generous with his attention but when it got too much he let out a wail and everybody laughed as he was returned to Maisie, who held on to him possessively.

CHAPTER 39

R oly had taken a few days to act on the news and found he couldn't bring himself to congratulate his Daughter, but had decided on sending a message that again portrayed his disappointment. Did he want to meet his Grandson? He supposed it would be an opportunity for him to try and make good but he couldn't, not yet, maybe he would be able to come to terms with it one day but he knew to prolong it would be a mistake and would remove him even further from the family.

"Maisie…" he typed "This is not what I would have chosen for you, Motherhood as a teenager, but I have no choice other than to accept that you are now a Mother and perhaps in time you will understand the responsibility that that entails. I trust all is well. Dad"

He pressed send and Maisie immediately read the message on receipt, but didn't deem it worthy of a reply. She was too wrapped up in the joy of her new baby and, like her Mother, didn't want the intrusion of anyone to spoil anything. Colm was a delight, everything about him monopolised her, and she couldn't get enough of him. Maisie and Greg were bonded as parents for life, as were her Mother and Father, regardless of who they would choose to spend their lives with in the future if it wasn't each other. They were joined as parents of Colm and Marguerite and Roly as parents of Maisie, Beattie, Frankie and Maurice and now as Grandparents to Colm. She presumed that one day her Father would come around to it, but Maisie was not unaffected by the lack of interest he had shown, knowing that she had not lived up to his expectations and possibly never would, and that hurt. But she still had her Sister and Brothers, her Mother and

Greg and now her Son, so she was content, she felt as though her mood was going to be pink every day.

Beattie had been so caught up in the busy household that she hadn't had time to go back to the Cafe. Mace had left them now to go back to his work and she wished she could just settle, but who wanted to at 16, she was not ready and Mace wasn't either really. They liked each other a lot but it lacked a spark, she thought. And one day when she was out getting some nappies for Maisie from the convenience store, she glimpsed from behind a blonde boy that was approaching the exit. He was rangy, long legged, was it Zachary? The usual frisson was present. She hadn't bought anything yet but she would leave anyway just to find out, her heart beat quickening and her mouth going bone dry as he turned to look back, it was him. He had a pack of beers in his hand, his ice blue stare particularly cold, but then he caught her by surprise and smiled. Inside she wanted to scream with excitement, but she continued to walk on past and got ahead of him, trying to remain cool. She would have to go back for the nappies. Zachary called after her, she didn't know where she was going but she walked purposely as though she had a destination in mind.

"Hey"! He called again, as she turned and waved.

He was running to catch up with her now and she could barely breathe from the anxiety.

"Wanna beer"? He offered her and she took the cold can into her shaking hand.

"Cheers" she said, barely audibly.

Zachary seemed intent on walking with her and soon to her left was an open all hour's café, so she walked over to the one stray table that was left outside and they both sat down.

"Wanna smoke"? He said, lighting a joint.

Beattie was reluctant, knowing it would lower her defences. His hair was short and freshly cut, very blonde and so unlike Mace's, whose hair was so dark. Zachary looked intimidating, but the

164

attraction she felt was real as they sat at the table, him languishing with such confidence. Beattie, usually so cool, was unnerved and felt as though she should run but she knew something had already started now.

"Not today, I've got to go" she responded, getting up.

"Sure" Zachary said with a hint of disappointment. "See you around"?

Beattie knew she should ignore her feelings and not allow them to take hold, she had a choice. But despite that she continued visiting the supermarket, hoping to bump in to him again, picking up nappies if needed or a few luxury sweets for the boys and purposely walking past the Cafe where she and Zachary had sat. He wasn't there of course, but if deigned he would be one day, and she kept herself busy by keeping in contact with her old school friends, who were at college now or had started work. She thought she could sell her designs; she was always drawing and mixing colours and different textures, and Marguerite continued to bring home offcuts regularly, which she was allowed to buy cheap or have for free. She had plenty to do to keep her occupied yet Zachary was still there nagging at her relentlessly in her head and one evening, just wanting to be away from the domesticity of the house, Beattie called a few friends and they suggested going to a club. Well it wasn't really a club, more of a hang out with a bar, but there was music, and when they arrived there he was outside. Zachary caught sight of Beattie and opened his mouth to call her but she just went on inside pretending not to see him, her head held high. Shortly after he appeared at the bar looking a little angry.

"Beattie, are you ignoring me?" he asked.

But before she had a chance to respond he gave her a wide smile that softened him and her, as he put his arm loosely around her waist and pulled her towards him confidently. With his free hand he straightened out her face so that it was in line with his, his eyes were so blue; the colour of a clear summer's day sky, she was captivated, hating herself for it as his dry lips touched hers briefly.

"Beattie, have you got a boyfriend"? He asked sensing her hesitation, but Beattie didn't want to tell him that she had and thankfully he didn't wait to find out the answer.

"Want to hook up sometime"? He continued.

She felt herself losing her resolve, thinking she needed to at least spend some time with him and perhaps it would sort itself out. Maybe she would be able to pull herself back from him if he said or did anything she didn't like, he was already a drug dealer and she didn't like that, but evidently it wasn't enough to put her off. They arranged a day mid-week as he told her that he was busy at weekends, not with other girls but with work, was she delusional? She must be. But after a drink and a dance with her friends she went home floating, Mace interrupting her thoughts only briefly and then fading.

CHAPTER 40

The boys had returned home from their fortnightly visit to their Father, who now took them on exciting outings and still bought them expensive gifts. This impressed them, but Marguerite didn't feel threatened as she knew they could not be bought. The boys had told her that Roly now had a lady friend, not considering that it would upset her particularly as they had accepted her man friend. How would that change the dynamics now? It could work well and take the pressure off of her, but ultimately she knew that he would still do what was best for him, within the law or in some other way. The boys said that he looked a bit embarrassed when he had told them the news, and she laughed as she imagined him uncomfortable with relaying the information knowing it would reach its target of the girls and her. The girls also laughed, who would want to be his girlfriend? Maisie had spat out nastily, not meaning it in the way it had sounded, but still very hurt by her Father's actions towards her and Colm. Beattie said it felt odd to think of him with anyone but their Mother, but she wasn't that surprised as she thought men were helpless without a woman in their life.

The house was Marguerite's main worry now, it was bursting at the seams with Colm becoming more of a person by the day and beginning to show signs of a temper. With two volatile parents, he wasn't going to be an easy child, but genes also came through from past generations and could catch you unawares. He was amiable, with a shock of near white hair, as he charmed everyone with limitless smiles though out the day but kept them all up with his attention seeking screams at night. Roly was a fool not to get to know his Grandson during these important early stages, he wouldn't get that chance again with his own children so Colm was an opportunity to try again, to enjoy getting to know a child completely. But Roly hadn't changed and his pride still remained, standing in front of him unbreakable. Marguerite couldn't believe he didn't even want a photograph, that would make him real she supposed, but she couldn't understand the control as it was of no benefit to anyone and robbing him of all that was truly good.

Marguerite continued to be surprised by Maisie's devotion to her baby. She had become so absorbed and taken over by him, almost to the exclusion of all else, and Marguerite watched her now as Colm lay next to her on a blanket, his legs kicking and arms flailing. It filled her with joy, seeing Maisie so happy laughing at Colm gurgling, no concerns now for her lack of a career. Weren't women predictable? Babies kept us grounded and men kept us happy if we were lucky, for the time being occupied regardless until the facade faded and left you restless, as had happened for Marguerite.

Maisie viewed herself critically now in the full length freestanding mirror, her reflection of a Mother, she was curvaceous. The baby weight had rapidly fallen from her, but she wasn't as willowy and slim as she had been before. Her hair was longer now, a mass of incredible ringlets, and she had sometimes envied Beattie of her perfectly straight and much easier to maintain hair. They were so opposing in appearance, unlike some siblings who were like peas in a pod. The boys looked alike but retained their individuality with different colour eyes and different personalities to the other, Frankie being the more outgoing and Maurice the softer, quieter one.

Colm had been taking a nap but was now stirring, pulling at tufts of his fair hair that likely wouldn't change as both of his parents were blonde. His hands were growing chubby, as were his legs with dimples, and he was robust and healthy, his cry always breaking the peace of the early morning. Marguerite rushed off to the shower with a handful of clothes, loose fitting but expensive, they had made no sacrifices after Roly left. She still made sure that the children got all that they asked for as she had credit cards for everything and she worked. Greg was living at the house now and he was always up on time for work, bleary eyed but keen and uncomplaining, not seeing any problems and there were none. They were all being looked after by Marguerite who always managed somehow to pay for everything, not even asking for a contribution from Greg. Rodrigo also lived there for free, but he would contribute in his own way by keeping the car washed, continuing the cooking and working in the garden, always entertaining and taking care of the boys. But most importantly he kept Marguerite in high spirits and she was truly content, which was a rare state for anyone.

Maisie was settled in her pink phase, which could change to purple if overtired, but the black moods had thankfully become a thing of the past. Greg was relentless now in his quest to find a house just for him, Maisie and Colm. He wanted to support his family himself, a bit like Roly but not as Greg was so emotional, but Maisie liked that. They were a match in personality but a miss match in their hierarchy of class, but bonded together in genuine love for their Son.

Beattie couldn't understand herself nowadays, she had longed to get to college but now that she was there she found she had little to no interest in it. She had been designing her own clothes for years, experimenting with colours and fabrics, but she knew she had to perfect her craft and the foundation was necessary but tedious. Her thoughts often returned to Zachary, was she so different to Maisie? And thoughts of Mace hovered in the form of a guilty vision, as he regularly made the very long journey to Scotland which cost him a fortune, but he remained loyal to her. He would always be a part of her life as Colm's Uncle regardless of what happened between the two of them and that would make it harder if she got with another boy. She was fighting it, but she was too young to be worrying about staying with one person, she should just be out there. She felt suffocated, which was a notion that was understood by her Mother, who had been stifled for years and as a result was going back to her youth to relive it with a much younger partner. Beattie didn't want that to be her, in years to come wishing she had just done what she wanted. She didn't want to hurt Mace as he was the genuine article, but he deserved a girlfriend that would adore him. She knew she wasn't ready to settle with him, and Mace was much too young to be serious about anyone too. Marguerite had shifted some of that burden, but in doing so had increased it. Rodrigo was a very kind person and they would be lost without his help, he was a natural with the boys by always giving into their demands and Beattie liked watching how he was with Colm, he was fascinated by him. But wouldn't he want a child of his own one day? She knew her Mother was unlikely to want another child, hadn't she had enough of all that caring and sharing? And she had Colm now, a Grandson so not ultimately her responsibility, but Maisie was a child still herself so Marguerite assisted in supporting him, making sure he had the best clothes and toys, but she was a bit more careful as she thought that he should not be given into in the way she had all of her own children. The money was there and she often thought why not spend it? But she didn't buy much for herself and Greg didn't pay her any rent, or Rodrigo, she had made it easy for them.

Maisie was a surprisingly good Mother, but the baby had many helpers and he tolerated being passed around, finally expressing his feelings loudly to be returned to his Mother who would settle him again on his play mat where he would just kick and gurgle happily to himself. Too much, too little, nobody got it exactly right, and Beattie felt annoyed that she should have to explain any feelings she had to her family, but they were so closely knit that they noticed any small change in her behaviour. Greg would be annoyed she said to Maisie, who had agreed that if Beattie were to find another boyfriend Greg would think of her as disloyal, and if he knew who the object of her attention was he would think even less of her. He would say she was stupid and it would be the truth, but Zachary remained lodged uncomfortably in her thoughts.

Maisie's days were a marathon of tasks related to Colm, but she was endlessly fascinated with her Son and she was lucky as she didn't have a house to maintain or bills to pay. There was always someone prepared to give her a break if needed, so it was the perfect place for her as a young Mother to just enjoy her baby. Maisie thought Beattie was behaving a bit odd, always offering to go to the supermarket as though that was the height of her excitement now. Shouldn't she have that at college? But she said little about it, just mumbling that it was teaching her nothing she didn't already know. Maisie remembered herself being in class, distracted by Mitac, the syllabus not gripping her either. Beattie had Mace racing across the country visiting regularly but it wasn't every weekend, and she recalled now how she herself had strayed when Mitac had gone home to Romania, unable to wait it out.

Marguerite, with family life comfortable, was content. She had a man but there were things that still didn't add up from events before, like who was the drug dealer who appeared in her garden at Beattie's party? She knew that he knew Greg and that he was behind the kidnap of her sons, but as yet there hadn't been any evidence to actually prove it and therefore he couldn't be convicted. Furthermore, who had the man been that had taken the children? It was a serious crime but she had gotten the boys back in her care unharmed, she had thought they were safe at school but they hadn't been, and she knew that no matter how hard she worked at caring for her children and advising them, she had to let them be free to experiment and hope for the best. The car incident, the den, nothing had been found to incriminate, and she marvelled at how clever the criminal mind was.

Maisie felt different now, lazy and hormonal from the birth, but the darker moods stayed away. She didn't like to hand Colm over easily, only when she was tired, and at other times she was just being generous as everybody wanted to hold him and benefit from his smiles, comforting herself in that she had him to gaze at all day. She had no concerns now other than caring for her Son, and it took up all of her time as she didn't think of where she would go or what she would do in the future. Colm was all she needed now and being a Mother had settled her, she no longer felt continuously agitated as she was in the place she wanted to be. She sometimes found herself feeling bad that she and Greg had made no contribution to the household in monetary terms, but he was invaluable in his devotion to her and Colm, and Marguerite just waved it away if she was to mention it. So she continued just to pass her days sitting looking at Colm and his soft round face, his clear blue eyes looking unblinkingly at his Mother who was so much less of a child now. She was in a proper relationship with her own child, still living at home, but thought she and Greg should just stay there. They had no reason to leave and they needed the family, she was happy with them all being together. That was how it was in different cultures, everyone supporting each other. She thought of Mitac then, suddenly understanding what she hadn't before.

Beattie always dressed to catch the eyes of others, namely Zachary's, but if he noticed it didn't sway him. He was always involved in 'important' money making schemes with that other boy, who scrutinised her but turned a blind eye to it, neither of them considered a girlfriend a priority. Beattie supposed that they probably just used girls briefly to satisfy their needs, the idea of an actual girlfriend taboo to them. Beattie knew she shouldn't be there, she was better than this and should want better for herself and she had a great boyfriend already, so why jeopardise it? Mace was so cheerful, but behind that jovial front he could be easily hurt and Beattie didn't want to be the person to do that. But Zachary wasn't a problem of that kind yet, he didn't want to get involved with a rich spoilt girl and he thought her Father could be after him if he was to take anything further. He didn't know that her Father took little interest in his Daughters when they were in trouble, only liked when things were good, but he feared that an over-zealous father could cut short his freedom. Beattie decided to play him at his own game for now, she wouldn't be around, leave him to wonder.

The holidays were here again and the boys hadn't seemed too keen to go to their Grandparents this year, but Marguerite didn't want to disappoint her parents and the boys were growing less interested in just playing outside, climbing trees and other childlike pursuits. They had sustained their interest in the den, which now housed the Christmas gifts from the previous year that had been left untouched until now. Did she want them to go? She liked her family close. Things were different last year, she had been a mess, but it would be selfish of her to deprive her parents of something they looked forward to. A quick chat with the boys, explaining how disappointed the Grandparents would be if they didn't go, had struck a chord. Frankie, with a new maturity emerging as almost a senior and Maurice as ever not wanting to hurt or upset anyone, said they would go this time but maybe next year they would be too old for it. This suggestion amused Marguerite, you were never too old to be with your Grandparents, but she was glad she had taken them. Her parents had excitedly outlined some more grown up kind of activities for the boys this year, as of course they weren't little kids anymore, and the boys had beamed in agreeance as Marguerite left them feeling good that she had done the right thing. She was still that person.

Roly's plans were thwarted by another life, A Grandson to have been accommodated in his house. He didn't know or want to know the Father of the child, who he had actually unknowingly met the night that resulted in him being ousted out, a turning point in his life. He was also at Beattie's party, and Roly was certain he would be living there now, with his wife's man too. These facts were not confirmed to him, but the house was full to bursting now and he was beyond angry at Maisie throwing away her college education. But hadn't his wife done the same? She too had embraced motherhood to the exclusion of all else. He had tried to advise the children, keep them safe and give them the best of himself that he felt able. He knew that emotionally he had offered very little, but shouldn't everything else have been enough to counteract it? He had been rejected now and it sat badly with him, keeping him awake at night in his flat that was still clinical. He had added a few homely touches but it made little difference to him, he preferred minimal, but it was sterile and two of his children had already struck themselves off the visitors list. Maisie because he had rejected her and Beattie because she had rejected him, siding with her Sister and of course her Mother.

Beattie thought of her Father with a girlfriend now, was she some young airhead? Her Father hadn't been impressed with her Mother going for younger, so she doubted it and thought he was probably more likely to be with a sensible woman, of similar age and interests to him. She looked again at herself, now considering someone who was a villain; cold and not suitable at all for a girl like her, when she could easily have her pick from boys that were wealthy and educated, she was surely losing it. Beattie had heard about town that Zachary was to be feared, but knowing this changed nothing. She was going to a party Saturday but she wasn't expecting him to be there, his weekends were taken up with his sordid business, but on Saturday she dressed with care as she always did. Not set to intentionally outshine anyone or out of desire to be the best, or even look the best, it was her intention just to look untouchable and that was her protection. Mace hadn't been at the house for a while but kept in contact, and she tortured herself again over her lack of good sense. She hadn't acted on her feelings but knew she could one day be tempted by fate, she believed in that, but would it save her? But for now she was just excited to be going out as too much time at home made her restless.

CHAPTER 41

Beattie didn't make it to the party. On arrival to her friend's house she was surprised to find Zachary outside it, talking with some other boys, and she was whisked away by him without a chance to protest as he pulled her away possessively. Her heart thumped loudly in her chest, her mouth dry as she licked her lips, licking away her expensive pout so excessively that she thought she might choke. It had started to rain and horrifyingly her dress had become almost see through and she felt vulnerable, but his hand was holding hers tight. What was he doing, wasn't Saturday night his best night for business? But there was no escaping and electricity sparked between them as they found themselves taking cover under a tree. In the darkness their mouths met, sodden clothing sticking them together, as the kiss escalated rapidly, his hands on her back caressing her spine. She couldn't give out to him already she scolded herself mentally, as thoughts of her disloyalty to Mace made her pull away. Beattie was intoxicated by Zachary, felt inept, but this was not right even if she had been free to act on her impulses. The options available to her now echoed in her head, should she run? Zachary was agitated now, not understanding the problem, but the rain saved her as it was now torrential. He just shrugged as his eyes signalled acknowledgement that Beattie was not going to succumb to him, she was a classy girl. He kissed her again, this time with a surprising gentleness and he wrapped his coat around her as they both ran to the open all hour's café, a faint light in the distance.

A few minutes later they were inside, huddled together with two hot chocolates on order. But her treacherous heart betrayed her as later that evening they went back to Zachary's bedsit. It was surprisingly immaculate and the smell of scented candles filled the air as he rushed to light them, the mood was set, and this time it happened.

In the very early hours of the morning Marguerite heard the front door creak open, it needed some oil, and she listened as Beattie thundered up the stairs and slammed her bedroom door. She didn't attempt to go in and check on her, if Beattie wanted her Mother to know anything she would come to tell her herself when she was ready.

A few weeks later, everyone was up late. Colm didn't have a timetable to suit respectable hours but luckily for him, someone was always around to pander to him. Beattie appeared in the lounge to join Maisie and Marguerite, wrapped in a soft grey dressing gown, nursing a secret. Maisie, with Colm now sleeping with his head on her shoulder, rested a penetrating stare on her sister for it to be returned with a helpless look. Marguerite had picked up on the tension, but felt it decrease as Beattie just smiled at her sister and held out her arms for Colm. He stirred briefly but then snuggled into the softness of Beattie's dressing gown. How far they had all came. Marguerite now settled with Rodrigo, Maisie with Greg and their child, the boys in different schools now but as close as ever, growing more mature and accepting all of the changes effortlessly. Even Roly was in a relationship with this woman, a biker no less, she was a bit younger than him but not ridiculously so and it could be serious, Verity was her name. Beattie was involved with college but had been acting mysteriously lately, Maces absence noticeable, but nothing was said out loud.

It was Maisie that first picked up on the fact that Beattie seemed to be in a distant place. She thought that Beattie was starting to look a little in the way she had herself, in the early stages of her pregnancy, and she mentioned it to her Mother once Beattie had fallen back to sleep. It seemed that perhaps Marguerite was to be a Grandmother again sooner than she thought, the old saying be careful what you wish for resounded in her head.

CHAPTER 42

Marguerite recalled the day when Beattie had approached her with her news. She had looked so young, still a child herself like Maisie had been. Her huge chocolate brown eyes glistened with tears as her hands clasped together tightly, hardly baring to let go of the secret she had been guarding, until now. But Marguerite told her that she already knew. How? Beattie had asked in amazement. A Mother always knew when her child was troubled, but Maisie had been the one to point out the signs. Marguerite just patted Beattie's hands, noticing they were damp with perspiration. How would she, they even, tell Roly that Beattie too was now to become a young mother just like Maisie? She was sure his reaction this time would be more than just disappointment, he would be devastated.

Beattie hadn't even been in a relationship with the local bad boy, and she was more than annoyed at her lack of good sense to make sure she was protected. Zachary had backed off since the night in question, clearly he had gotten all that he had wanted, so Beattie decided not to tell him the result of it. She had presumed right, a girlfriend was a liability to Zachary, he only wanted a bit of fun and now her reputation was shot. Beattie felt overwhelmingly sad and rejected, but Marguerite jollied her along with her enthusiasm in that there was going to be another family member to join them all. She always loved and longed for a big family, seeing every new member as a bonus, and she assured Beattie that it would all be fine and she would make sure of it. She just smiled like it was everyday news, even though they both knew that it wasn't, but Beattie had a baby to consider now and that was far more important than the attitude and behaviour of Zachary. He was a part of their lives now but he was not likely to be an issue as he was unaware of his place in it, which left Beattie free to bring her own child up by herself. She found she quite liked that, slowly coming around to the idea of becoming a single Mother. Maisie had Greg and he at least tried to be working, hoping he could eventually move his family out of the house, but Beattie thought she would manage without her baby's Father.

Breaking the news to Roly, it had been difficult to find the right words, but Beattie had lost her patience in trying to soften the blow. What did it matter now? She considered. She and Maisie were both fallen women to him anyway, was it any surprise that Beattie had fallen too? He had just slammed the phone down no words were needed to signal his anticipated disgust.

Later a discussion between herself, Marguerite and Maisie led Beattie to decide that Zachary must also be told sooner rather than later and given the chance to do right by her and the baby, but he had been in total denial on hearing the news of his pending fatherhood. Any vestige of niceness in him was absent, as he dared to suggest Beattie was lying about him being the father.

"It ain't mine Beattie, don't come crawling to me, you are on your own"! He growled nastily, and she met his cold glare with a look of sheer hate.

"Who needs you Zachary, I have my family"!

"Yeah, no problem for you, money sorts everything"! He replied and walked away, the conversation over.

Beattie realised what she had felt for him before had just been fascination, a phase of youthful experimentation. She had told him, there was nothing more she could do, and as she walked home she thought about how Maisie was with Colm. Her sister who had been such a volatile person was now so calm and enjoying motherhood. Well she too would soon have her own baby, and feeling suddenly defiant and proud, she vowed to make the best of this wildcard which had landed at her side. Even without the support of her father or Zachary, she had the rest of her family, and that was all she needed for now.

A year later, they had weathered the storm and come through it all, but it had been difficult. Colm was now a toddler, full of fun and high spirits and Beattie had given birth to a beautiful baby girl. Grandchild number two for Marguerite. Bringing her roles to 7, role 5 still a remaining factor as Roly's wife as they were still separated but still not divorced, but the relationship he was in appeared to be serious now. He had been shamed again; both daughters' victims of teenage pregnancies and falling even further down the social scale as the family had once more become the source of local gossip. But he was not beyond reproach, and Marguerite would remind him of that should she get the opportunity, if he didn't try again to apportion the blame to her for it all.

The residents in the house equalled nine now, every area was over utilised and overcrowded but it was breathing, full of life. Beattie, a potential career girl who had had her wings temporarily clipped, hadn't taken to being a Mother in the way that Maisie had. Maisie was happy to lie down her pursuit of excitement and a career that she had barely held onto, in exchange for her first priority that was being a Mother but Beattie felt slightly robbed. Everything she had strived for appeared to have just been thrown up in to the air for now, but after sensible analysation it was concluded that new opportunities would arise later. Accepting that any thoughts and ideas would just have to be put aside for a time when Beattie was able to get herself through college. But unbeknownst to Beattie, an unexpected offer was coming her way sooner than she thought which would force her to think quickly and take a chance.

With the arrival of Maisie's baby, followed shortly after by the arrival of Beattie's, any move forward in divorce proceedings had again been halted and Roly had been unable to expect or ask for the house to be sold. Marguerite had been shocked and upset initially at the turn in events but had showed none of this to Beattie. Instead she reassured her daughter that nothing would stop her achieving her dreams, life was just unpredictable sometimes, as usual making light of what was serious. A new baby was a huge commitment and she knew that Beattie had great hopes to aspire to, but her dreams of being a fashion designer had been put on hold. Beattie was already successful in a small way, making unique outfits for friends but perhaps she could go it alone with her mother's help? Thoughts of a previous idea formed in Marguerite's mind, she had considered it before but now was it the time to bring it to fruition?

CHAPTER 43

Maisie and Beattie had had little to do with their father. He hadn't truly accepted Colm, but had acknowledged him grudgingly probably, as a birthday card had arrived on his first birthday signed 'from Grandad' which was a joke almost as he hadn't even begun to take the first steps to be one. Marguerite had initially thought that perhaps Verity had been behind it. She was nice, but quite strict, Frankie had told her after he and Maurice had been introduced. How dare she? Marguerite thought. The fact that Roly had another woman she didn't much care, but another woman being involved with her son's she hated, rationally reminding herself that no one could ever take her place with the boys.

Marguerite was in the garden now, looking back on the time before Elodie arrived. They had all had a hand in naming the baby as Beattie had wanted them all to be involved. She had said to each of them to think and choose a name to put on paper, and she would put all the names into a hat and, unless she hated it that would become the babies name, one for a boy and one for a girl. It had been a fun evening, they had music playing, drinks, snacks and they chatted and rejoiced. Nobody was fazed, all just thrilled about another baby and a playmate for Colm, even though he already had a houseful. Vaughn materialised for a boy, and Beattie liked it well enough, Elodie for a girl, she loved that, already hoping for a girl. They had Colm, so a girl who would keep the balance in the house would be perfect. A ready-made model for Beattie's line of children's clothes, girls gave more scope but either way, boy or girl, she felt accepting of her situation. It could even be the making of her, keep her away from the bad and admittedly some of the good, but it wouldn't stop her.

She, like Maisie, would have lots of on hand help and babysitters.

Now Elodie was here. Frankie, Marguerite's eldest boy, was now at seniors separated from Maurice who was still at juniors, but he had taken the step easily. Perhaps he had been a little pleased to not have to consider his brother and have the freedom to be with friends without him in tow, but when it came down to it he found that Maurice was still his best friend. The age gap was noticed less as they got older, and Frankie included Maurice in any activities that he could. Sensitive by nature Maurice did feel a bit unsupported without Frankie, but before long he would be joining him at seniors too. In the years before, every summer the boys had gone to their grandparents for a few weeks, but this had shortened to a few days or a weekend now as both had grown reluctant to be away from their home. Besides, the house felt incomplete without all of its members in residence, each person added something special.

Maisie, a turbulent teenager, was now approaching 20 and about to leave teenage years behind. Colm, now 18 months old, was walking and could say a few words but Maisie was concerned, shouldn't he be speaking more by now? He had walked late too, managing to get on two feet at the expected time, only to revert back to crawling.

The house and keeping it in order had become a battle they couldn't win and even Maisie, a clean freak, didn't criticise. Although her room with Greg and Colm, the study which had been converted to a nursery, was kept spotless and Colm himself was always clean, at least at the start of the day. Maisie was a great mother and had surprised everyone with her fierceness and protectiveness that she displayed and channelled, settling her hankering need to stretch her mind beyond her son. Marguerite didn't doubt that this would lay dormant for a while, at some point could raise its head, but she knew that she didn't need to be responsible for this child as

Maisie was coping admirably and of course, she had Greg who was a hands-on father.

At the shop Haberdashery Delights, where Marguerite had worked for two years now and was running almost entirely by herself, she handled all of the orders. She also handled all the cash, which she took nightly to the bank but was sure to vary the times she went, knowing that even sleepy villages had a criminal element, which she had personally dealt with in the past. She had gone straight to work after taking Maurice to school, Frankie now walking with friends to seniors. The shop opened at 9:30 now, which was half an hour later than before, so Enid the owner didn't have to open the shop and Marguerite could do it. Enid now only worked a couple of hours from two until four, also closing half an hour earlier than before so one hour of trading was lost. She would have liked Marguerite to have taken over completely, but Marguerite didn't feel ready yet as she disliked the idea of Maurice getting home by himself. Rodrigo had suggested he could collect him, but Marguerite refused as she had Beattie at home with Elodie too so she didn't want to be away more than she had to be. A year ago she had had the idea of her and Beattie taking over the shop, but then it had seemed too soon. Now Enid was still in good health, but was looking to retire, and she wanted the shop to go to Marguerite and had said that she would sell it to her at a reasonable price. Marguerite was taken aback, but the situation with the house hadn't been sorted and to find enough money to buy the shop had seemed impossible before, but now a plan was formulating. It was a good business and she could expand it with Beattie's help.

Beattie's hands had been full with the care of Elodie, but she still spent time on her designs and Elodie was very different from Colm in that she slept well, most nights in bed by 7 o'clock, which gave Beattie time to work. She was now working on a school uniform, an idea she had kept in her mind from when she was a pupil herself, that stage of her life now seeming a distant memory. Marguerite had observed her whilst endeavouring to find a way of buying the shop and furthering Beattie's career. She was extremely pushed, but her man Rodrigo kept the house reasonably maintained and cooked for them. On Sundays they would still have a lazy morning together, but then he would take himself off, no longer welded at the hip as much as they had been before. The urgency had subsided now that they were living together and secure in their relationship. So instead he would catch up with friends or family, to whom Marguerite still hadn't been introduced, but they no longer berated his choice as it was obvious to them now that it was permanent and he was content. He had a good life with her and her big family.

Marguerite hadn't told her parents too much, nor had she introduced Rodrigo to them either, as neither of them wanted to be criticised or told they were foolish. Words or comments suggesting that it wouldn't last, were not what they wanted to hear and time had strengthened their relationship. Even her husband, who had always been suspicious of the connection, knew his wife wouldn't give up easily. She had battled on with their marriage long after it no longer gave her satisfaction, but once the realisation had taken hold it hadn't taken much to sever it. She had met Rodrigo by pure chance, finding herself further dissatisfied with her life, feeling suppressed and unable to pursue her own interests as her family continually kept her busy. But later feeling increasingly redundant as the children grew and became more independent, engaged almost totally in their own lives and that was when her mind had wandered. That had been when she became involved with the much younger man.

The Chevelly family, that were once thought to be beyond reproach, had livened up the sleepy town and for a time kept the police occupied and the local gossips tongues wagging. But now nobody seemed surprised that Marguerite and Roly's second daughter was also having a baby so young and not married, it had barely raised an eyebrow. In Scotland it was considered that if you lived with someone, you were as good as married, and that was true in years gone by. But it suited Marguerite to believe it still was like that, older people still respected the idea but the younger ones didn't really care.

Beattie was in her bedroom, which now accommodated a cot in the corner. She was such a messy person. Before Elodie's birth she had tidied it well, but it was now a mess for different reasons, and bits of fabric and coloured threads clung to most areas of the carpet. She decided that on Sunday, when her mother was home and Rodrigo out in the afternoon, she would make good by hoovering it and have it ready for the next week while her mother entertained Elodie. She had the prototype for the school uniform ready now and was in the process of trying to get a school uniform retailer interested. She would need a school sanction, but if it was to be accepted she could be successful overnight.

Zachary had renewed his interest in her, now wanting to see the child she had claimed was his daughter. He had, had a few girlfriends since the fallout but none had lasted and he was still the local drug baron, but of course nobody could know that. Beattie thought Elodie should have the opportunity to know her father, despite his unsuitability and that he had treated her badly, and she indulged him by letting him spend a short time with her and Elodie in the park. It had become a regular thing now and seemed to have brought out a side in him that when shown, made him approachable. He was wonderful with Elodie, showering her with kisses and calling her his girl and Elodie was equally enamoured as she smiled and laughed out loud in his company. He had told Beattie that he was sorry for everything previously, that it wasn't easy for him to take on board, and he complimented her on how well cared for Elodie was. A sort of affection had surfaced between them, but she didn't want to further it as she had other plans now, but he was grateful that she was accommodating of him after his harsh treatment of her. One day, he had pressed a wad of notes into her hand.

"Yeah, I know you don't need it, but I want you to buy something for my girl" he told her.

Beattie put it into her handbag, said yes she would and thanked him. She hadn't had a chance to get to know him that well before, it had been over quickly, but she saw that kindness worked with him and they were linked now whether they liked it or not. It wasn't so bad, she could still bring Elodie up her way with no interference from him and it suited her.

Roly had done nothing regarding the house or the divorce, and the house was now home to his wife, his children, his grandson and now granddaughter, not to mention Colm's father and probably his wife's lover. To say he was devastated was putting it mildly. His girlfriend Verity had said he should attempt reconciliation with his daughters, meet his grandson and granddaughter as soon as possible. He had only told her when Elodie had been born and she was horrified that he had said nothing sooner. She wasn't impressed either when he had said that it was 'what happened when you don't watch your children', referring negatively to Marguerite. Roly had been surprised when Verity had responded by saying that he hadn't actually watched them at all and that surely he knew it was not something that could have been controlled, so it was a mistake not to be a part of their lives now. But he just couldn't accept the situation, said he wasn't like Marguerite who took on every shattering event and parked it on her shoulders which sounded like he had some respect remaining, but he was at a loss with his attitude and feelings. Verity had just asked what did it matter really in the scale of things, a baby was always a wonderful thing, a grandchild a blessing. Roly had never been particularly fond of babies, even his own but he was proud of his family, even though two of them had fallen now in his eyes. He was fond of Verity and glad of her company, but not always of her opinions even if she was right. He knew he would live to regret the loss and he felt curiosity and sadness now both in equal measures. He had not seen his daughter and grandson, or Beattie either. They supported each other, they didn't need him he told himself, but that was just another excuse. Marguerite was just too good as a mother and grandparent; he was less of her in every way. He continued paying the mortgage and council tax, adapting in that the house was too big just for him and possibly Verity, but without the sale of the house he wouldn't be able to buy anything much better than where he was currently living and to own something was always preferable to renting. Roly knew that if he left it much longer his children would barely remember him and his grandchildren wouldn't know who he was at all. He had been told of the arrival of Elodie and had been asked did he want to see her, but how could he when he had not even seen Colm yet? He couldn't even bring himself to send a message. The boys were still visiting him but not often, they were now taken up with other activities but he was grateful that they still wanted to see him although they preferred just to meet him by himself. They had told him that they still found it strange to have Verity around, so he limited the times they met with her but not entirely, because to omit her would possibly jeopardise the relationship and he would be unbearably lonely without her now.

The boys had received a mobile phone as gifts from their mother, who was as good as in charge of the shop now. She was progressing and seemed perfectly capable of maintaining her job and the family alone, but she wasn't able to cover all of the bills. These were paid by Roly in the form of maintenance for the boys, as by-law he no longer had to pay to support the girls.

Today was the boy's fortnightly visit, just at the flat this time. They asked their father did he want to look at photos of them all, but they didn't wait for a reply and Roly was immediately faced with a photo of Maisie. She looked truly amazing, a young woman now with a young man who visibly adored her, his arm circling her and their son Colm, who had lots of blonde hair and was smiling. They looked happy, had Maisie found her niche in life? A photo of Beattie followed and she was holding her small baby, another blonde child, presumably the father had been fair. She looked glamorous, dressed in an outfit she had apparently made herself and Roly became tearful. Maurice picked up on it straight away and patted his arm sympathetically.

"Do you miss them Dad, you could call round"?

It was all so simple to Maurice and in a way, it was, but Roly needed to let go of his anger and disappointment, he couldn't move on until he did. He couldn't bear to go to the house but the thought was there now and he would have to find a way to act on it. Maurice, whose phone had been turned off now so as not to show anymore photos, could see his father was trying to stay in control so he changed to other subjects and the moment passed.

Maisie was out in the garden with Beattie, the babies playing in their own way, Colm endlessly filling and emptying cups of water from a bowl, Elodie fascinated but too young to participate sat watching. Maisie and Beattie were in the shade just chatting, both with a glass of wine in their hand, as Maisie's phone pinged with a message and a few seconds later Beattie's did too. Maisie read her message out loud first. Hello it said, I think it's time I made the acquaintance of my grandson. I've seen a photo of you both, he didn't mention Greg, and would you like to meet in the coffee shop soon? They knew which one. Consider this and let me know soonest, Dad. Beattie read out her similar message, which of course named Elodie instead of Colm. They had already resigned themselves to their father's dismissal of them and their babies, so this was unexpected, but they were both very proud of their children and of course wanted to show them off and they, like their mother, had forgiveness within them. They decided not to reply immediately, he didn't deserve an instant answer or form of acceptance, as they gathered their babies and their thoughts. Both were pleased but felt jolted out of complacency, as not having to deal with their father had made their lives simpler.

Marguerite was told individually by each of her daughters that Roly had asked to meet them and the children, thinking perhaps he was finally realising the extent of his loss. The girls would meet him and she knew they would forgive him, a part of her she didn't feel she wanted to share anymore, but she didn't want to deprive the girls in any way or the grandchildren. Blood was blood.

CHAPTER 44

B eattie had settled now, finding herself accepting her current situation. She thought back to when she had been at school and how much she had disliked the uniform, thinking it dull, heavy and uncomfortable and she had decided then that she would one day design a modern-day uniform. It had been a tangible idea at the time, but now she would make it a reality, or she was certainly going to try. She wanted to design a uniform that pupils would be proud to wear, a uniform that gave room for some individuality, and she worked on her ideas whilst attending to her baby, who thankfully slept a lot. Getting herself back in to shape was also a priority, but she was ready to pursue the career she had always known was meant for her, now with Elodie at her side.

Beattie approached her old school and she wondered what her teachers would think of their former student, now a Mother with a baby girl. She arrived with Elodie and her portfolio, and the Headmistress was charmed by her baby who behaved impeccably, just smiling and gurgling away whilst Beattie demonstrated her work.

She had designed a loose-fitting skirt that was to be quite short, not the usual frumpy over the knee length the girls hated, and made with quality cotton polyester that was soft to the touch. The material of the current uniform clung to the skin unflatteringly, giving off sparks of electricity with every uncomfortable movement. But Beattie's new design would be made of hard-wearing, machine washable material that would look just as good a year down the line after being washed regularly, as it did at the time of purchase. It would be more expensive but it would pay for itself, and Beattie knew from the clothes in her own wardrobe that expensive clothes did just that. She also knew from experience that the girls always folded over the waistband to make the longer-length skirts shorter, so why not just make them shorter to begin with? She had also designed a relatively plain shirt, but in a choice of either blue or yellow, and a waistcoat which could be worn the whole year round keeping the arms free as blazers were uncomfortable and restrictive. The waistcoat was to be Scottish plaid, in blue and yellow, and she had a sample with her to demonstrate. Beattie had found inspiration for the design from an off-cut her mother had brought back from the shop. The socks were also blue or yellow to match and the overall look was stunning, complimented with soft Velcro strapped black leather shoes, and she even suggested an optional beret for the girls in either blue or yellow. For the boys, she had designed navy trousers in the same material, the shirts blue as she didn't think the boys would like yellow, but a tie in blue and yellow silk to subtly reflect the colours of the girl's uniform. The waistcoat was to be unisex, suitable for both the boys and the girls, and how about a butcher's cap for the boys? She added and raised a quizzical eyebrow at the Head Mistress who just smiled, amused, and Beattie laughed. Perhaps that was a step too far, maybe just a standard cap in navy would suffice?

The Head Mistress was impressed and surprised to find that she was actually taking it all very seriously. She had wanted to have her former student visit and show off her work, but hadn't been prepared to be convinced. She said the socks should be grey or white, not blue or yellow, but was happy with the rest and she considered Beattie who had always been a student that stood out. She was not a follower, and with such determination she had always felt that she would succeed, either in this or something else.

Sensing the headmistress was coming round to the idea, Beattie went on to explain how she would make her dream happen. She had it all so carefully planned out, she would of course need to find a company to make the clothes, but the number of orders would bring the prices down slightly to an affordable level. Beattie mentioned she was also working on a line of original outfits for children up to the age of five and currently making clothes for her friends and family in order to master and improve on her skills. Each outfit had turned out better than the last and she shared the photos of all her designs and final products in support of her credibility. Beattie's enthusiasm was infectious and the headmistress admired her tenacity, not doubting that she would succeed in all her endeavours. She didn't know what the governors would think, but it would do no harm to put forward the suggestion and the school needed an updated uniform anyway.

Beattie knew she would have to prove what she could do to a larger audience, but if viable it could happen. She had a sewing machine already and the finishing touches were personal, no outfit was the same. She wanted to grow her business but doing everything alone would not suffice in the future, should demand increase, but the income and the recognition gained if she was appointed this task would be invaluable. She had a pot containing money she had earned from friends and family and in it were some notes and a few coins, but it wasn't making interest, she needed a savings account.

The headmistress had agreed that the school was due a change and she promised to talk with the powers that be. She also recognised that Beattie being a former student was a definite plus for the school, as this would surely represent the kind of children they had inspired and encouraged. Beattie was effectively still a child herself, but the Head Mistress saw a great future for her and she beamed with her eyes bright as Elodie continued to sit quietly, just listening to them talk until it was time to leave.

Beattie almost skipped home, happily chatting away to her daughter. She knew Elodie couldn't possibly understand but she needed no reply, as her baby just garbled and laughed in an accepted form of approval. Beattie had already contacted a potential factory, and she knew that if she got this order her success could be huge. Later

Beattie and Marguerite discussed at length what shape the project could take; she already had contacts for materials through the haberdashery shop, so they were both optimistic. Maisie was in bed early for once with Colm, both tired out from a day in the garden. It had been a typical Scottish day, always a bit cold and breezy, and the effects of it were like being at the coast all day and returning home exhausted from all the fresh air.

Maisie had been impressed by Beattie's diligence, thought her lucky that Elodie was such an easy child, but Beattie was strict with her even though it wasn't required. Maisie had been content to just wile away the days and hours with her son, her boyfriend Greg doing well at work, no longer a boy but a man with responsibilities. He still continued to try to persuade Maisie that they should strike out alone, but she couldn't find the enthusiasm or the energy. It was easier for her to stay put and she knew without the on hand help she wouldn't have any freedom at all and she just couldn't visualise herself in some little flat, she would hate it. Greg was cross with her, stating that they had to start somewhere and couldn't stay there forever, but Maisie didn't want to try to understand his need to be in charge of his own home and her and Colm. She didn't want to be trapped with him in relative poverty. They had only been brought together by stupidity on both sides, the result of which was their son, and they were both happy with him and being parents, but would they last alone as a couple? Financially, without the house and her family she could not and would not give up her home and Greg could see that he was only wasting his time. The house was amazing so why would he want to leave it? But it wasn't his home, he was just a guest, and he didn't contribute to the upkeep of anything so this couldn't be their permanent home, he needed to strive for something. For now his money was used to buy things, mostly treats and luxuries, though he couldn't even begin to compete with Marguerite who always made sure Maisie didn't go without. Colm was always well dressed too, sporting a Beattie creation or in clothes paid for by her. Beattie had photos of everyone dressed in her creations in her portfolio, the girl was a powerhouse. Maisie was clever academically, she just lacked the desire and confidence needed to achieve, but she was in the perfect place for her for now.

Beattie wasn't particularly interested in the money side of things as it was the status that she craved. If she was really successful she would be rich and that would be a bonus, but having money was not a novelty to her, and she would be too busy to enjoy spending it. Mace, still her boyfriend in the background, continued to visit regularly, but he still lived in England so they weren't together often. There had been a gap in the relationship for a while, but he had decided to accept that Beattie had had a dalliance, the result of which being Elodie, but she wasn't with the father and would never be. He had stayed away, it hadn't been easy, but he could sense that Beattie didn't need or want a permanent man at her side. Their futures were uncertain, though Beattie did not doubt hers and she was taking control, moving forward rapidly, and a kind of relationship had started again between them, but it was really just a matter of convenience and deeper feelings were not involved, at least not on her side.

The girls eventually organised the meeting with their father, insisting that he was to be alone as they didn't want to meet his girlfriend yet, this was just between them. Roly had agreed, not wanting her with him anyway but he was still the same, compartmentalising his life, but it was too soon to be crossing lines that were anything but clear.

Roly was at the coffee shop before the girls and their babies arrived, he had specifically chosen a time which he thought would be quiet and he was one of just a handful of people, that were either sitting and reading a newspaper or chatting quietly. He sat down on a large sofa, a few lounge chairs were opposite and facing a low-level table, and the café door opened, the room immediately filling with the smell of perfume. He was blown away as his daughters entered the café, noticing that they looked so much more grown up now than when he had last seen them. Maisie was a natural mother it seemed, her little boy held close to her but struggling to free himself and get moving, but she held him tight protectively. Beattie was dressed in what could only be one of her own creations, her little girl with bright blonde hair and piercing blue eyes looked up at her grandfather from inside a pushchair and smiled. He was visibly affected, the tears that he hated to allow to appear were teetering, and he quickly found a hanky in his pocket and blew his nose. Colm started to laugh and Maisie put him down on the floor and he toddled over, holding out his chubby little arms to Roly, who crouched and picked him up. Colm hugged him tightly "Granda" he said, and that was his undoing as the tears fell. It was an emotional moment for all of them, why had he wasted all this time? He hadn't been ready for what he now had before him, but he was glad that he had finally taken the step, and he now understood why Marguerite had always tried to tell him that this was all that mattered. After a while, Colm was returned to his mother and Elodie was placed on her grandfather's lap by Beattie where she bounced happily on his knee. The conversation was difficult, but just being together was enough for now.

After the meeting they were all wiped out mentally, absorbed in just staring out of the window and watching the scenery flash by, both babies sleeping as soon as they were on the road, as they returned home by taxi. The taxi man was more of a friend now and he had gotten to know all the family, each of them needing transport at some point for one reason or another. He would always make himself available, made them a priority, like a personal chauffeur almost.

Beattie had booked his taxi tentatively for a meeting with the bank, she didn't know the exact time, but would soon confirm it. Marguerite had said she was too busy at work to take time off to go with her, she knew she could but she let Beattie take control, but she did help with the business plan and Enid had assisted in giving ideas that could help her secure the loan. They had needed the school uniform order, luckily that had been forthcoming, and a substantial deposit had that day been transferred to Marguerites account for now. Beattie needed to open her own bank account as it would be confusing with two businesses, her mother's shop and hers. The cost involved for the materials and the physical work to produce the uniforms would have to be covered initially by Beattie, and it had been quite a substantial task obtaining all the sizes and quantities required. It was an original uniform, specifically for this school alone and not be sold to any other. A prototype of the uniform had been produced for a girl and a boy, and two pupils from the school had been chosen to model the uniform. Photos were taken and printed on to a newsletter that was sent out to all the parents to obtain their views and the feedback had been positive. Beattie was well on her way, all that she needed now was the loan, without which the venture could fail, but failure was not a word that Beattie accepted.

A time now confirmed the taxi was booked to take Beattie to a high-prestige bank meeting in the town. Elodie was with her and they were both dressed in her creations. Maisie had offered to look after Elodie while she went, thinking it was a mistake to take her to the meeting as it was with a business manager, but Beattie had turned down her offer and said that Elodie was to be with her where ever possible. Maisie said she was lucky that Elodie was so easy to manage, but Beattie just said that she wanted Elodie to learn that if she behaved well she would be able to stay with her through everything.

At the bank the manager, whose name was Xavier Moriarty, was a little surprised at his client. Noting that she was very young and had a baby in tow, he immediately expected the meeting to be cut short by something related to the child. But Elodie just sat quietly, playing contentedly with the toys that were strung across her pushchair, whilst Beattie extracted a file full of papers and talked him through her plan, which he couldn't find any fault with. She was a young mother, but very attractive and was clearly going places, he thought would she like to meet him for a drink one evening, but he didn't know if she was single and she had a child.

"Your partner, what does he think?" he asked with a brisk but not unfriendly smile.

"Partner"? Beattie was momentarily flummoxed "Oh no, it's my business, I'm single" she said.

Xavier nodded; this wasn't very professional of him was it? And he continued by confirming that the plan covered all angles and options but would need to put it to his superior first.

"Give me a day or two and I shall call you with the final decision and to discuss facts and figures." He told her as he stood up and shook her hand.

The loan sum was also to include the purchase of the shop, would the bank back a project of this size being put forward by a 17 year old girl? But as she was under 18, the loan had to be guaranteed by her mother.

Beattie was impressed, Xavier was a good-looking man, intelligent, and hadn't said anything to deter her. The meeting had lasted around an hour and in that time Elodie had been given a bottle of milk and some pieces of fruit, followed by a bottle of water, but she had not caused a disturbance. Beattie praised her daughter "good girl, let's go for lunch".

Beattie found herself at her mother's café which amused her, as her father had a café too. For a time Beattie had frequented the all-hours café where she had first got involved with Zachary Elodie's father, but she didn't go there anymore. Her mother had started her liaison with Rodrigo at the cafe where she was now, and she sat outside with Elodie waiting for a waitress to take her order. Café's had featured a lot in their lives for one reason or another.

Later that afternoon Beattie was in the garden with just Elodie, who had recently started to crawl. The garden was a haven and they all enjoyed it, large and rambling with lots of shrubs and abundant with flowers. If they did have to move they would all miss the garden, but her father had not suggested that this was likely to happen. It was a family home, a myriad of bricks in different colours with terracotta the most prominent. From the front it had a large driveway and the fences that had been pure white at one time were now a little grey and flaky. Rodrigo had maintained the shrubs and cut the grass out the back, but the consensus of thought was that less was more and the front garden had been neglected. Beattie watched Elodie, her knees and hands were green now from the damp grass, but she didn't worry about that kind of thing as they could just be washed later. Maisie however always had baby wipes in her pocket to wipe away smudges, but Colm had grown accepting of this and was becoming just as fussy about getting himself dirty as she was. But Elodie was still a picture of good health, soft skin with pink cheeks, her blonde hair had darkened slightly but she was still very fair.

Beattie was anxious in that the loan could still not be approved and she knew it was a large sum for a young girl to ask for, but she was from a wealthy family and her mother was to be the guarantor. Enid had agreed to a lowered price on the shop, said she didn't need the money and would just be happy to leave the shop in the care of Marguerite whom she admired. Enid was a shadowy figure to Beattie as she was rarely seen in the shop, and on occasions where Beattie had taken a taxi to town to meet with her mother for lunch or a coffee, she would have to shut the shop for an hour. Marguerite didn't like to do that, but she justified it with the fact that most days she would stay in the shop and have her lunch there out the back, where she could hear the bell tinkle announcing a customer to attend to.

Marguerite had had to reorganise the shop so the most could be made of the room available. To stock all the uniforms would have been impossible and they didn't need to, but the shop had its own style and it would spoil the ambience to have boxes haphazardly filling every corner. The window had a flat area where not much had been done with it other than placing a few objects related to haberdashery, so Marguerite had suggested that they have two mannequins, a boy and a girl, to advertise the outfits. They were in place now, but for the time being surrounded with artificial flowers and leaves made from felt which attracted a lot of attention. Appointments were to be made to discuss orders and on one day a week Beattie would go with her mother to the shop and stay for a few hours, Elodie could sometimes be left with Maisie but most of the time she would take her. Beattie didn't want to get ahead of herself and take on more than she could handle, but she later learned that people were in no hurry, considering that one of her designs was always worth the wait. To rush the production could destroy the quality of work and her reputation, and they were expensive in a way, which Beattie didn't like as it limited her potential market but this was a fact of life. She couldn't use cheaper materials, though she was clever with cut-offs from the shop which enabled her to reduce the cost slightly. But she designed because she wanted to, new ideas always appearing in her head to put on paper, but real success was always linked to how much money you made.

Beattie hadn't mentioned her plans to her father as she presumed he would think it unrealistic, considering she had barely begun college before she had had to leave. She knew she was hardly equipped to handle a business so he would probably belittle her, though perhaps he would admire her nerve. Maybe she would wait and tell him when she had made her first million she thought as she smiled to herself. Elodie's arrival had unexpectedly pushed her further forward, motivating her to proceed regardless and she wasn't the type of girl to wait, two years at college would have held her back. No doubt she would have learned some things had she have gone, but now she would just have to find out everything she needed to know by herself.

The suggested day or two wait for a decision passed, it had now been a week and Beattie was growing increasingly impatient, wondering if she should just call Xavier herself. She had his business card in her pocket and surely it wouldn't be unprofessional to enquire on how her loan was progressing, if it was not to be then she would need to look elsewhere. She decided to make the call, but a female secretary answered and informed Beattie that he wasn't available at the moment, but she would arrange for him to call her back later on today. Beattie wondered what the secretary might be like, as she found herself feeling a small amount of jealousy, were they close. But why should she care? She had a little time at the moment but once the loan was approved, she would be too busy to even consider a serious boyfriend. Besides, she had Mace, he was her token man and he was more beautiful than ever now. Truthfully she couldn't understand why he hadn't got himself another girlfriend closer to home, he was ambitious and was at college part-time, surely there were lots of nice girls there? And he had a menial job, where he worked every other day and sometimes evenings.

Beattie thought of Maisie, knowing that her sister would not have been able to cope with a long-distance boyfriend and would likely spend all her time torturing herself mercifully, but Beattie didn't think like that. If Mace had wanted to be with someone else he would be already, especially when she had effectively cheated on him and Elodie was a constant reminder of it, but he said it didn't matter now. It had hurt at the time, he had been gutted, devastated even, but he hadn't been accusing. He knew he wasn't able to visit often and it was inevitable that Beattie would go out and possibly meet someone as she was too young to be sat at home all weekend. Mace was great with Elodie, he treated everyone with respect even when it wasn't really deserved, and she couldn't understand why girls were not falling at his feet. He had joked before that it was because he was not a bad boy although he often felt eyes upon him from all directions, but he seemed prepared to wait just for Beattie, maybe for them both to become adults and to see what happened then. At the moment he was only around for a few hours a month, what girl would really be happy with that? But he had said that he forgave her for the past and if he wanted someone else he would tell her, she hadn't given him that courtesy but she left that unsaid. He would always be a part of the Chevelly family because he was Greg's brother and therefore Colm's uncle, and he was loyal, didn't play with people's feelings and he worked hard. It was expensive to travel the distance on the train to Scotland and he would visit more if he could afford it, but he couldn't, he needed to find more work or a job with better pay, but he couldn't let the situation with Beattie just rest. She played on his mind all the time when they were apart and he had been there for her in an abstract way, mainly because he didn't want to frighten her away. But he also didn't want to lay dormant in her mind so a braver competitor could have the chance to take over. He had already almost lost her once before.

CHAPTER 45

Maisie was interested in what looked to be a promising and amazing career for Beattie, she was a bit jealous but she didn't have the single-minded ambition that Beattie had, it was too exhausting for her. Greg was a good father but what they had was not as exciting now as they saw each other every evening and slept in the same bed every night. She found that she was beginning to feel a bit restless now the euphoria of being a mother had eased. She was endlessly fascinated with Colm, but the novelty of spending every day at home was not so luxurious anymore, and she longed for some excitement but where could that lead? She didn't want to be involved in Beattie's business and Beattie would not have wanted her to, but wasn't she to achieve great things too? Where had that girl gone? Maisie considered that she could return to college, but that didn't really appeal to her now as most of the attraction of going there every day had been her Romanian interest. What had happened to Mitac? She wondered, after not having heard anything of him since he had said he was returning to Romania after an episode in England, coincidentally right after her window had been smashed. No blame had been apportioned directly but she knew it had been him. She could have made something out of it, but had decided she understood that he needed to punish her in some way and release his anger towards her for effectively destroying his career. He could have continued but he, like her, had found he was unable to sustain an ongoing interest in the classes after everything that had happened between them. Maisie had kept in contact with the only other boy in the class, who was Spanish, and he had finished college now and had succeeded where Mitac had not. He was working now at a material factory, a Scottish family business, and he had gotten involved with the mill owner's daughter. It looked as though he had possibly landed on his feet, about to become the son-in-law of the owner, and knowing how ambitious these foreign boys could be she wouldn't put it past him to just be with the girl for what he could gain. Mitac had been her boyfriend for a while, but she had not ever thought through being too vain and certain that she was the main attraction, that maybe he also wanted just to marry into money. The idea seemed laughable now, he didn't have the confidence to do that, he didn't fight hard enough for her and he wasn't ruthless enough to continue at college when their relationship faltered. He had returned to his country to deal with supposed family problems on more than one occasion and whatever spare time he had was spent working, as he needed money for his family. This had meant they had little time to spend together and Maisie was the type of person that was not happy unless she was centre stage, and on one occasion when he was away she had met Greg. After that everything had started to deteriorate between them, but that was then and this was now, and she was glad that Mitac hadn't chosen to link up with another Scottish girl. It was easier for her that he had returned to Romania. But now after hearing about Eduardo's current progression, she wondered if Mitac had actually been that interested in her or if he had an ulterior motive for pursuing her. But that aside, she was feeling restless now, and she said as much to her mother whose eyes had opened wide at the mention of it and Maisie noticed a flicker of something that could have been fear. Her mother was too busy for Maisie to want any more from her, it could upset the balance in the household and jeopardise her job, but now Maisie felt something shift in her pink phase that had been almost permanent to the relief of her family, but now she felt purple was threatening. She felt bored, not with Colm she would never be, but irritated with Greg. Perhaps she just needed a night out with Beattie. They only had to ask Marguerite and Rodrigo, they would happily take care of the children, but she knew that Greg would insist he came with her and she would have liked to go alone with her sister. Maisie could see Beattie in the garden now with Elodie, who was so in tune with her mother. Beattie was talented and she was happy for her, which showed that she was less selfish now, but she wasn't sure where she was headed herself and she didn't have the staying power for a business or the inclination. She felt her life had become a bit mundane already and she was a bit concerned about feeling that way, but she didn't want another major change in her life so she hoped that the feeling would only be temporary.

Beattie was now in her room, with Elodie asleep in her cot, when her phone ringing broke the silence. Elodie stirred and opened her eyes briefly but then drifted back to sleep and Beattie left the room quickly. She went into her mother's room and onto the balcony, having said a brief hello in a breathless voice that sounded like the teenager that she was. She kept the caller waiting while she got herself comfortable, having grabbed her papers.

"Sorry, my daughter was asleep so I had to leave the room" she explained, realising it wasn't necessary to remind him again that she was a young mother.

"Miss Chevelly" Xavier said, the conversation taking on a formal note. "Your loan application has been passed on to my manager".

Was the manager not confident in her ability? Perhaps he didn't want to risk the banks money on a child? Beattie worried herself with multiple negative thoughts, even though Xavier had actually said none of this.

He continued advising her. "Your proposal is being brought to the attention of the board" he went on "As this wasn't an everyday enquiry".

Beattie thought her previous perception was close. He then said would she like to meet for a coffee, and she was confused, what was this, a chat up? She felt cross with him.

"For what reason, to discuss the loan"? Her voice was icy. Beattie found that always worked well for her, until she had been swayed by Zachary, and she couldn't afford to be involved or deterred from her path. Xavier must have noticed the change of tone in her voice and he began to speak more seriously.

"Yes, to discuss the loan, a few more details need to be clarified. I thought possibly tomorrow, at a cafe in town"?

Her mother's cafe was suggested.

"Is this usual practice"? She asked him.

"Of course Miss Chevelly, would 10.30am suit?" His tone was more professional now so she accepted.

Should she take Elodie again? This time she felt she needed to project a different image, so she asked Maisie who said that of course she would look after Elodie, and Beattie relayed to her the conversation.

"I think he's looking for a date" Maisie said, confirming Beattie's suspicions. "He could meet with you at the bank and you could just have a coffee in a white plastic cup". They both laughed at that. Maisie also voiced her night out idea and Beattie picked up on her restlessness immediately. Was the pink phase on its way out? Maisie had been so easy to deal with since she had become a mother, the previous abrasive Maisie that caused trouble and upset everyone when things didn't go her way had left. Was she about to return? Beattie was a little pleased as some things about her sister she had missed, but she wondered at the repercussions. They could all only hope it wouldn't lead to a black mood, where everyone treaded carefully around her again until it passed, but that could be a day, a week or even longer.

The next morning Beattie decided that to dress to impress was the way to go. The money was for her designs and to pay for the shop, that was to be an outlet for her work, and this was her chance so she had to wear her best creation. It was daytime so it needed to be appropriate, as she looked through her made outfits that were actually on coat hangers rather than thrown on the floor. She didn't do that so often now, had at least tried to curb the habit, as it only took a minute to return a garment to the wardrobe and now she had Elodie she tried harder. Being a mother had brought out a deeper determination, having someone to think of other than just yourself was a good thing. The dungarees that were Beattie's favourite creation weren't right for this meeting, so a skirt caught her attention. It was a pencil line skirt, but the lines were unequal, and it was black with a stripe across it that joined at the tip of the point at the front of the skirt, the stripe was a mahogany red. She scrambled around in her socks and tights drawer where she thankfully found a suitable pair of sheer black tights with a seam at the back and some boots that were battered leather anklets with a pin thin heel. Could she walk in them? Yes, she would have to, but she put them in a bag for now deciding to wear flats until she got to the Café. Now to find a shirt, no, a plain T shirt, charcoal and a jacket black, that was the best part of the outfit. It fitted tight at the waist and was adorned with large lapels that were in a different colour of leather and the mahogany on the collar picked up the colour of the skirts stripe. Her hair was very long and thick and she left it loose, it was freshly washed and sprayed so a single hair was not out of place. Her make-up had taken ages but it was perfect and she was happy with the overall look, she already looked like a business woman, and she applied her favourite perfume liberally.

Elodie was not too pleased at being left at home and her arms reached out to Beattie as she hugged her and reassured her that she was going to have lots of fun with Maisie and Colm. Elodie was not convinced, she looked as though she might cry, and Beattie felt she would have preferred to just take her but she knew that this time she should go alone. Maisie swiftly took Elodie up in her arms and began bouncing her gently on her knee and, while she was temporarily distracted, Beattie took her chance to slip away.

The taxi was waiting on the driveway and the taxi man told her she looked fantastic as he opened the door for her and the taxi filled with the smell of her perfume. She didn't want to chat today, needed just to think.

"Thanks" she said smiling at him, and he sensed her preoccupation and stayed quiet for the duration of the journey. Before she got out of the taxi she exchanged the sensible shoes for the boots and he waited patiently while she did this.

"I'll call you when I'm ready to return home" she told him as she tottered away feeling unsteady, she was not used to heels these days but it was only a few yards. She had forgotten about the cobbles and she could feel her ankle turning in on her right foot. She was tempted to take them off but was reluctant to spoil the look, immediately regretting it as she was unable to prevent her ankle turning too far and she was sent flying as her papers and her bag flew right into the very person she had intended to impress. She winced in pain and suddenly felt slightly sick as Xavier rushed to her side, having arrived a little early and was already sat outside. She felt a fool as he fussed over her, taking liberties she thought, by brushing imaginary specks off her clothes. She looked down to her tights that were fortunately not snagged.

"Excuse me" she said. "I need to go to the bathroom" And she hobbled away as quickly as she was able. Her boots were in her hands, having removed them outside, and she tried to ignore the amused expression on his face. In the bathroom she put back on her flats, knowing the outfit looked wrong in them so much for showing off, but she had no choice. She checked her make-up in the mirror and straightened her skirt, yes she still looked good, not as good as before but it would have to do. A final spray of perfume and she returned back to the table where Xavier was waiting. He grinned at her, it was infectious, and soon they were both laughing, it couldn't have been less like a business meeting. Once he had composed himself he passed her some forms that had been marked with asterisks and she calmed herself as she read through them meticulously before signing her signature. She had been granted the loan he told her, and she was elated.

"How about a small glass of wine to celebrate"? He suggested.

No, she thought, immediately remembering how relaxed alcohol made you, often finding yourself where you didn't want to be and doing something you shouldn't be doing.

"Just a coffee please" she answered sensibly.

"Yes, I suppose it is a bit early isn't it? And I have a job to go back to" he agreed, ordering himself the same.

They clicked she felt as he was appraising her, genuinely impressed that she had designed the outfit but teasing her about the boots, said they were fabulous, but just for show. She blamed it on the cobbles and he just agreed with her. Beattie had got what she wanted but her ankle was a little swollen, would he pursue her now? He had no reason to contact her now the business had been concluded, but if he was keen he would likely think of something.

As though reading her thoughts Xavier asked bravely "Would you like to meet again Miss Chevelly, for a meal perhaps?"

Beattie thought of her night out with Maisie that had not been arranged yet, should she ask him to that? Beattie considered it but quickly decided against it as Greg would insist on being there and then there would be the issue of Mace.

"Call me" she said, extending a beautifully manicured hand which was swallowed inside his and shaken.

Beattie then left him at the table, having quickly called her taxi man. Keep it brief she thought. She could have stayed longer but she was also keen to relate her news. This was the start of an extensive phase of her life and everything was now settling in to place, would she even have a spare minute?

Beattie waited until Marguerite returned home from work, not wanting to message such momentous news. Her mother and Rodrigo didn't have the afternoons anymore so she had made them both a coffee and taken the mugs out to the garden where they could talk. Marguerite was thrilled for her daughter but a bit concerned it would be hard work, said they must realise the enormity of what they would now be doing. She said she would speak with Enid tomorrow and tell her that they could now buy the shop. Materials for the uniforms would need to be ordered and Beattie would advise the factory, but this was to be done in person and Maisie would look after Elodie. Maisie said she was fine with it all, she would get her chance to do something in the future, and she hugging Beattie while giving her mother a helpless look. Marguerite was already so busy being the owner of the shop and now helping Beattie, she would be pushed but she would do her best not to neglect her other daughter. Beattie had briefly mentioned Xaviar, said how helpful he had been, and Marguerite could tell that she was interested in him but knew this wasn't the time. They had had a coffee together, that was all, it was just business.

CHAPTER 46

Marguerite, later that evening alone with Rodrigo, told him about the intended purchase of the shop and Beattie's designs, of course he knew about them already, everyone did as she spent hours in her room busying away. He was pleased for both her and Beattie, but Marguerite could tell he was concerned that the focus would be taken even further away from him. He already seemed to be fighting for a place but still, hadn't he always known she had a big family? Marguerite reassured him that she was always there with him, no matter where she was or what she was doing, and thank fully he was an ordinary man that required little to be happy. They cuddled close, savouring their quality time together, that they had determined was what it was now.

The next morning, Marguerite called Enid to inform her of the decision to buy the shop and she went there soon after, putting the closed sign on the door while they went through all of the details. Enid was to be paid in full and then Marguerite and Beattie would just be responsible for the repayments to the bank, which would initially be spread over five years. It was a massive commitment but the school uniform order was to be highly profitable. Right now it seemed a certainty that success would be theirs but nothing was ever certain in life, something could always catch you out, so she didn't get ahead of herself.

The next few weeks were extremely busy. Maisie looked after Elodie while Beattie visited the factory, the schools order for fabrics had been completed so the factory could produce the uniforms. Would Maisie like to be her accountant? Beattie had asked, thinking it

211

would be a good idea to get Maisie involved and even though she had no qualifications, she was exceptionally good at maths. Maisie had professed previously that she didn't want to be involved, other than helping by looking after Elodie, but she had studied textiles so in a way their skills were linkable. Maisie decided to accept the offer as she needed to occupy her mind that was currently idle, which could lead anywhere. She would be paid, Beattie had said, but money was not the issue as she didn't really need it, maybe later when the business was secure. And any spare time Maisie had, mostly in the evenings, she now spent working. Greg would take over with Colm and give him his tea, bathe him and get him to bed and he was pleased that Maisie had something positive to do now. He had felt her lack of interest in them recently and the restlessness, but this seemed to have settled her again.

The boys, fortunately, were self-sufficient now and they helped with chores and only had to be asked to look after either of the little ones. They were a busy household but each member was pulling his or her weight, without which the venture could have failed, but all hands had gotten involved in some way.

Beattie made sure Elodie stayed with her when possible, but now she missed the lazy days they were able to share before. She had gone from domesticity, just making her designs as a hobby and selling to friends, to a career with no gentle introduction. But Elodie thrived and she knew, as young as she was that she was to be good otherwise she would have to be left at home. Elodie liked to observe the shop, found it fascinating, and Beattie had given her little pieces of fabric to play with whilst she conducted a meeting with a Lady, no less. Lady Asher, who on a stroll earlier in the week, had noticed the Mannequins in the window of the shop and requested an appointment. She said she had a daughter with a party to go to soon, it was formal, what could Beattie design for her? The price was no object. Beattie sketched as they talked, shortly presenting a flimsy idea of a dress in layers of pale colours. It was slightly over fussy in a way, but she assured Lady Asher that it would be durable and she went on to describe the different fabrics. Her daughter had sensitive skin she told Beattie, showing her a photo of a thin not overly pretty child with large solemn eyes. The dress would make her the Belle of the Ball, and Lady Asher was impressed, so Beattie gave her four business cards not wanting to be too presumptuous but also wanting to seize the opportunity, as her customer would surely know a lot of high end people. Lady Asher put the cards in her bag and invited Beattie to visit her home to take the measurements of her daughter, also insisting she was to bring her daughter as she would be more than welcome, and Elodie smiled at her happily. As soon as she left, Beattie excitedly told Marguerite about her client and her mother could not quite believe how successful Beattie had become in such a short time.

Lady Asher lived in a small Castle, there were quite a few scattered about in the mountains, and the people that lived in them were not necessarily aristocrats. They were not that expensive to buy as most had been neglected, but the owners needed to be wealthy to bring them back to a liveable state and have the money to maintain them.

Maisie felt some envy at the direction Beattie's business was taking her and she said she would have enjoyed dressing up for an occasion such as this. Beattie picked up on it immediately and on impulse suggested that Maisie accompany her, not considering that her client could mind, she could be her assistant. Maisie was almost jumping with joy at the idea of time out from the house, but she wasn't to bring Colm as he wasn't a child to sit quietly. It was a daytime appointment, but Maisie said that Greg had some holiday that he could use so he could take Colm to the park or just walk him in his pushchair so he can view some new scenery. He often insisted that Maisie should get out from the house more, so that's what he thinks

Beattie thought, suddenly sensing that perhaps Greg could leave Maisie but he wouldn't want to leave his son. You should go places with Greg too she said, there's the mountains, picnics. Maisie gave Beattie an odd look, should she be worried?

"He's just being ungrateful, look at how he lives. Colm is happy here, the garden has everything he could need"

Beattie agreed but suggested perhaps she should think a little more of how Greg might feel, as nothing was his.

"You think I should feel sorry for him you mean"? Maisie responded feeling agitated.

Beattie shook her head to say no, and Maisie remembered how he had been so keen to live at the house but he thought it was just temporary and they would get somewhere of their own one day. He could leave but she knew that he wouldn't, he might not be that happy there anymore but he wouldn't leave his son.

"What shall I wear for the appointment?" Maisie asked, changing the subject.

"Just something smart would be fine" Beattie answered and they talked about other things as the question of Greg was put aside. Rash decisions weren't wise, but people often eventually reached a point where what they lost was not as important as what they could gain.

Marguerite was relishing a rare moment alone in the garden with a cigarette lit. This recent good fortune had unnerved her but she reminded herself that this had not come by magic as they had worked for it, though the offer of buying the shop had been unexpected. She had changed all of their lives now, that had previously been on track, she and her husband living out their lives in the traditional way with Maisie at college to eventually work in the textile industry and Beattie following her life in the direction she had expected but soon skipping college altogether. The boys were still at school but with new people, but they easily adapted to enjoy the changes. Roly, had he benefited? He would say no, but Marguerite knew he wasn't suited to the hustle and bustle that she thrived on. This girlfriend Verity was more pliable and from what she had heard they had shared interests, so he could spend his time doing what he wanted now. He saw the children but not often, mainly the boys, and he was in the background which was where he had always been really so that much hadn't changed. The flat had become more of a home now, even though he still lived there alone, in no rush to change the convenient relationship he had with Verity who allowed him to decide on most things. Marguerite thought that Verity was likely the one to make sure Roly did the minimum, remembering birthdays and buying gifts to help keep everything calm on the surface. She did suit him and it seemed she was there in a quiet way, making sure that Roly didn't make any wrong decisions. The house couldn't be sold as to do that would cause him irreparable damage to the work done on restoring the connections to his children and grandchildren.

Beattie hadn't let Zachary see Elodie for a while as she didn't have time to go to parks now and was reluctant for Elodie to be alone with her father, his lifestyle still a concern. The last time they met he had asked if he could take Elodie to show her to some of his family, but this bought a shiver of fear to Beattie. What kind of family did he have? Not wanting to anger him she said that she would have to think about it, but she had not made an arrangement to meet since. She felt unsettled by the idea as she liked everything her way and he knew that, so what could she allow? She was not sure how to handle this delicate situation, to make the wrong decision could be disastrous. Her thoughts on it festered a little at times, on the rare occasion when she had time to think, but she had so much to do that she allowed it not to take on the importance it probably should have. Zachary was not to be put aside.

It was a Sunday and Beattie was out in the garden with her sketchbook in her hand, just doodling away at a few ideas. Maisie had been persuaded out of the house by Greg to go to the park. He had been pleased initially with her involvement in the business, but now found she was always too busy for him. As Beattie's assistant now as well as accountant, Maisie was often called to clients houses in the evenings. Beattie could go alone but Maisie wanted to be involved wherever possible now and they, with Elodie always with them dressed in yet another stunning outfit, were a team she had told him. Greg was possessive about Maisie, afraid that she found him boring now he had quietened, because of responsibilities to his son and to work. He wanted to take her away from what he was starting to feel was an oppressive family. They were all so wrapped in each other's lives and becoming even more so, with Beattie's career and success at the school in procuring the order for the uniforms she had designed. The pupils would be wearing her creations soon and it had brought in a large amount of money that enabled a large portion of the loan to be paid off, and other schools in the area had approached her, liking her style. Maisie was busy working on the accounts and researching different fabrics, even visiting the textile factory where her friend from college the Spanish boy was working, who was engaged to the owner's daughter. He was engaged, but Greg was jealous, did that mean he wouldn't flirt with her? Maisie had laughed when he professed his worries to her. She assured him it was just business, but yes they had lunch together sometimes, they were friends and that's how it worked and she was having fun. That worried him a great deal, but he knew that possessiveness was destructive to a relationship and she had looked at him with her blue-green eyes, daring him to object. He was scared of losing her so had to be careful, remembering how he had lost her before, he knew she could be ruthless if it suited her. She would never stop him seeing Colm, but not to be involved with him daily he couldn't bear, so he let her go her way, what choice did he have?

The boys were with Roly which was unusual for a Sunday, but he apparently had had other plans on Saturday. Marguerite and Rodrigo had gone for a walk in the mountains with a picnic, so Beattie and Elodie were alone in the house for once. Beattie was pleased to have the house to herself and they were in the garden, as usual, and she was engrossed in singing silly songs as Elodie clapped which was a skill she had recently acquired. Disrespectfully, Zachary had gone through the back gate, not bothering to ring the doorbell, but Elodie spotted him first and was now waving her hands frantically. Beattie had her back to the gate so hadn't noticed Zachary enter, and was startled when he suddenly called out to her.

"Beattie, how are ya? I waited for you to call" as he strode over and picked up Elodie, who was visibly thrilled to see him.

"Sorry" Beattie said "I've been so busy".

"Yeah sure, so when can I take Elodie to meet my family"? He asked her again.

And it was said in such a way that Beattie thought he might take Elodie there and then, and she would have no one at hand to assist her to prevent it. She knew she had to compromise and he would never do anything to hurt their daughter, of that she was certain. She didn't have her diary with her and he would probably have laughed if she got that out, so she suggested tomorrow and he looked pleased, having finally got his way. Zachary must have picked up on Beattie's concern, as he then suggested her going with him. She had not expected that, and she considered the way he was looking at her now, did he think he had a chance with her? He had the idea that parents of a child should be together, they were so different.

"We could go like a real family, yeah?" He said, giving her a rare smile, as Beattie noticed the likeness between him and Elodie. Now her life felt further complicated; her work, her relationship with Mace though easily handled and also her interest in Xavier and now Zachary, the father of her child. She decided that she should go as she would be worried sick if he took Elodie alone but she didn't mention that and just said yes. He had waited for her to think it through, so he must understand something of her ways, and he gave

Elodie back to Beattie kissing her briefly on the forehead. He said he would get hold of a car from somewhere and pick them both up at two and Beattie thought about needing a car seat.

"I will get a baby seat too" he said, as though he had read her thoughts again. "Nothing bad is ever going to happen to my girl" and Beattie believed him, but she was a bit concerned for herself. Did he think he could win her over? It seemed he was going to try. Oh how annoying she thought but, like Maisie, she would probably enjoy the effort. After he had gone she picked up Elodie and went with her into the lounge where she put on a children's film to occupy her so she could be left to her thoughts, tortured now at the unexpected turn in attitude from Zachery. She had almost forgotten about Xavier, thinking perhaps she had overestimated his interest in her. She was a single mum with a baby, why would he want the hassle? But it seemed that he did. He had obviously figured out that involving Elodie was the way to win her over, rather than suggesting meeting her alone. She was going with Zachary tomorrow, but Xavier had called and said about arranging a date. As always she had plenty to do but he had suggested a drive to the beach and again she thought about needing a car seat, it would be a long drive. Beattie said she thought that was a bit much for a first date, the coffee date had just been business, and he said he would perhaps save the idea for a future date which suggested he had long term plans for her. Asking her out with Elodie also indicated that he would want something that was more than casual, and so she wracked her brain for ideas what they could do, trying to help him out. After a short pause, both of them thinking, Xavier suggested a barbecue. He lived in a shared house that had an outside area.

"That sounds nice" she said, agreeing to the idea.

"How about today, if you're free?" he asked, putting her on the spot.

Why not, her workload would always be there and it could wait she supposed, so she said yes before she could think of a reason not to. But after the call ended she wished she had thought about it for a bit longer, as she remembered then that Mace would be on his way to her later tonight. She knew he wouldn't think much of her going with Zachary and Elodie tomorrow so she could meet his family, but this was different. She would have to be home before he arrived and now she was disgruntled and feeling guilty. She knew it was only casual towards Mace on her side and he wouldn't restrict or pressure her, but maybe he was playing the long game as they were still very young. Why hadn't she arranged next week with Xavier? But she didn't want to him to lose interest, so she decided she would just go for a few hours and be back in good time. He was someone she knew, he had been a business colleague, she didn't have to justify it really, but did she want more with him? Realistically, she knew she was risking her attention being taken away from her business, but she was good at keeping her cool without being unfriendly and she knew that being over keen rarely worked out. Men liked to be the one to put in all the effort she reminded herself, and she was not even 18 yet but already her own boss and a mother, nobody dictated terms to her. Feeling that she was able to handle the situation now Beattie got to the task she most enjoyed that was what to wear. Deciding on some dungarees, the barbecue was right for them, she then dressed Elodie in a busy t-shirt that was bright yellow with scraps of fabric sewn on to it in clashing colours, with a pink ruffle skirt, white socks and soft pink shoes. Beattie brushed her hair which was just reaching her shoulders now and Elodie was excited, always happy to be out with her mother and enjoying new surroundings. Beattie called the taxi man who was available as always, and she wondered if he cancelled other fares in order to prioritise her family. She would need him to bring her back at five and right now it was 2.30, a couple of hours would be fine.

Xavier was dressed casual, in shorts to the knee and flip flops with a sleeveless white T-shirt, his muscled arms on show, obviously proud of his physique. He welcomed Beattie and Elodie into a small area at the back of a terraced house, it had a hexagonal red bricked patio decorated with a few pots of flowers that looked as though they could do with some water. The barbecue was almost ready to use, and an old wrought iron table with a few chairs was set up with a gaudy parasol, it wasn't smart. Beattie had been excited to meet him but now there she wasn't so sure, it felt shabby and deceitful as she thought of Mace on a train on his way to her now. Zachary also there in her head as tomorrow she and Elodie were to be meeting some of his family members. She felt overwhelmed and far from ready for it all and Xavier sensed her retracting from him. She was a young businesswoman only recently setting out and no doubt her life was further complicated by the absence of a partner to help with the child, but he thought Beattie was acting a little oddly.

Beattie knew it was her fault for being greedy and thinking she could have it all, so she tried her best to engage in the afternoon with some enthusiasm and she thought she had succeeded, but when it was time for her to leave Xavier was visibly upset.

"So soon?" he said, not having done anything but wait on her with food and drink and play with Elodie by rolling a ball to her on a blanket that he had strewn on the lawn. At that moment, not caring that Elodie was watching, he pulled Beattie towards him and into a kiss and her hesitancy faded as she lost herself within it. But the moment was suddenly broken by Elodie, who uncharacteristically started to cry very loudly. Xavier quickly pulled away and the crying stopped immediately as she smiled at them again and they laughed, it was a strange moment.

Xavier reached for Beattie's hands "Can I call you?" he asked, he was asking her permission and she should have said no, didn't she have enough to deal with? But she nodded, deciding to let everything go where ever it was going, she believed fate would decide.

Later that evening it was as if nothing had happened. Mace had arrived at the house and the family had all been looking forward to him being there, and now they were all in their usual places in the lounge with the patio doors open. It was rowdy fun as there really was no room for anyone else and Mace was sitting close to Beattie, with Elodie sat on his lap. He was so friendly to everyone and familiar Beattie thought, as she rested her head against his shoulder. She felt safe with him, knew he wouldn't hurt her, and he should have been enough as right now she didn't need any further complications to take her away from concentrating on her career. She still had tomorrow with Zachary, he couldn't be put off again, but he would likely expect more from her after this and the involvement of his family in Elodie's life. She couldn't have everything her way so she would have to be careful, but perhaps it would all sort itself out. That's what her mother would say, why worry about things that might not happen? And she had a point, she wasn't a worrier, unlike Maisie who got herself into a state about imaginary situations, but she was much calmer again these days, the old Maisie remaining locked within. Beattie's coolness would protect her if she let it, and the next day Mace had a few hours to spare before he had to leave. She had told him that she had to go with Elodie with Zachary, as he had insisted that his daughter should be introduced to her other family. Mace said he understood, what father wouldn't want to show off his daughter, and in different circumstances he could have actually been the father, but he had always been careful and took no chances. Nothing was going to happen to him that he didn't want to, he had plans, and perhaps in time he and she could move forward, but did she even love him? He wasn't usually like this, but he was scared now and he even admitted it to Beattie. She had not realised the true extent of his feelings, his casualness and joviality had just been his way to secure her. It was clever and perhaps he could have succeeded if Xavier hadn't appeared in her life to throw her off. It was early days but feelings were definitely emerging. She had Mace and, yes she loved him, but it didn't feel like the all-consuming love that she thought it should be. Mace didn't think he had to worry about Zachary but they were the parents of Elodie and that made them linked, so anything could happen. Beattie reassured him in that Zachary was difficult, he had to be handled carefully, as there was no limit to what he could do or try to do.

"Let's go for a walk to the local Café, the out of hours?" he suggested. "Or we could go for breakfast in the mountains?"

No, it was too far to go today, another time and we can make a day of it Beattie said and so they went and sat in the garden for a while instead. It was peaceful, just the two of them and Elodie, who was happily crawling amongst the damp grass, her clothes not a concern as she was just in her play clothes for now. They sat quietly with their own thoughts, not needing to talk, it was important to not have to make conversation sometimes and just be.

A little later, Mace reluctantly had to leave, but Beattie knew he would return soon not wanting to wait weeks and he knew that he had to work a bit harder now. He had sensed a slight shift in Beattie, not to mention the fact that she would now be meeting lots of people in connection with her new business. She kissed him goodbye and it was a gentle kiss.

Beattie prepared herself and Elodie, paying attention to every detail, and Zachery arrived in an old car but it was spotless outside and in, he was a fastidious person. A baby seat was already fitted in the back and Elodie was secured safely in it. Beattie got in the front with Zachary and she noticed he smelled nice, dressed casually in some good quality fashionable clothes and she felt aware of him. His blonde hair had been cut very short, but it suited him and his eyes that were so blue pulled her in but she reminded herself of his lifestyle. This put a dampener on any softening in her and he was very perceptive, like he always knew what she was thinking, but he was in a nice mood chatting to her about his family and familiarising her so she wouldn't feel out of place when they arrived. Beattie was able to fit in with all types of people, adjusting her behaviour to suit, but she knew she often gave off an unapproachable vibe and these people were Elodie's family so she would need to make an effort not to be.

It was a long drive, but Beattie had already resolved herself to having to do this, and eventually they parked on a road outside of a small house as Zachary took her hand and held Elodie with his spare. They looked a proper family, neatly turned out for a Sunday afternoon tea. The front door opened and a worn-out-looking woman appeared, Zachary's mother and Elodie's grandmother, and her face broke into a smile on seeing the three of them standing before her. She welcomed them all inside and the house was neat and smelt fresh. A boy and a girl were sat on the sofa beaming at them, but more so at Elodie, professing they thought she looked like a doll. They were all so ordinary, likeable, what had she been so concerned about? It seemed like nothing now and it was a pleasant afternoon. Nobody said anything bad and she was made to feel welcome, Elodie even more so, as she lapped up all the attention, unperturbed by these new people that were her grandmother, uncle and auntie.

On the way back, Zachary was in an excellent mood.

"What do ya think then Beattie? You like em?" he asked.

"Yes" she replied, and she genuinely did.

"Wanna go again sometime?" he said, not mentioning taking Elodie alone.

"Sure" Beattie said, feeling it wasn't really a problem for her now. If Zachary thought he could get her back this way then she would let him try, she didn't have to do anything she didn't want to.

Back home finally, Beattie was tired. She had had a very intense weekend and had a busy week ahead, but as her own boss she knew she could do as much or as little as she wanted. The success with the school uniform had lessened the burden of the loan, so a few days low key would get her head straight. Not to think of the men in any capacity, just to get on with her work, as she had another school showing serious interest in replacing there outdated uniform and an appointment had been arranged for later in the week. Elodie thankfully fell asleep immediately once put in her cot and tucked in. She was growing fast, filling out and starting to make attempts at words. It probably wouldn't be long before she was walking as she had already pulled herself up on the side of the sofa earlier that week, looking proud expecting and getting claps.

Beattie and Maisie wiled away the next few days, with Beattie's designs spread out across the kitchen table and Elodie and Colm watching them. Maisie said she liked the short sleeved pinstripe shirts in the school colour of lilac and white. Beattie had insisted that long sleeves were a hindrance, the cuffs would always get stained and fray, so she had also designed a short sleeve jacket. For the boys, long sleeves had been kept, but the jackets would be lightweight and easy to wear as she remembered how cumbersome her jacket had been and Maisie agreed that comfort was important. Maisie told Beattie that she didn't feel the need for a night out now, she was busy enough dealing with the finances of Beattie's business and that had kept her mind occupied. The school that had made the order this time wasn't a particularly large one, but it would bring in a reasonable profit as there were still 250 pupils needing to be kitted out. They had also wanted overcoats and tracksuits for PE, and the addition of socks, again she had pushed for more colourful socks. They liked the idea of a less severe uniform, so white or grey socks were to be kept, but Beattie could source them and Maisie said she would go alone to the textile factory that her friend worked at this time. She could get him to give them a good deal.

Despite Beattie's previous resolve not to think about them, she discussed all of the men in her life with Maisie. She told her all about Xavier, Mace's increasing attachment which she hadn't been aware of, and also Zachary trying to win her over with happy family scenarios. Maisie laughed, aren't you the popular one now, and Beattie said at least she didn't have that problem anymore now that she was with Greg.

"You are happy with Greg, aren't you Maisie?" Beattie asked her.

"I guess so, but I miss having a few men fighting for me, but it seems that's your turn now!"

And at that they both collapsed into fits of childish laughter, with Elodie and Colm joining in.

The girls had visited the castle a while back now, and it had been an interesting experience. A maid had answered the door, dressed in a black dress with a white apron. A mop cap would have been perfect with the ensemble Beattie found herself thinking, but this was a modern-day Lady and Lord Castle. However they were announced and taken through to a large conservatory where teas and coffees arrived on a tray. The cups and saucers were obviously real bone china, they marvelled, and the tea and coffee pots all solid silver.

The daughter was watching and waiting, sitting nicely on a huge arm chair, ready to be measured for her party dress. Lady Asher decided on a dress that had layers falling neatly onto each other, and Beattie had brought pictures of several different styles, but this one was quite modern and the colours pale hues of pink, purple, orange and yellow. The colours clashed, but the paleness and softness of the material made it less obvious, and Beattie said that with the materials and the time involved in making it, the total cost would be £250. This was accepted by Lady Asher and they went on to chat about her daughter Prunella, who said she was keen on ballet. She was delicate and Beattie, who hadn't thought of dancing clothes before, said that maybe she could design an outfit for it. Prunella's face lit up and Lady Asher, clearly very indulgent of her only child, said for Beattie to work on some designs and she would consider them. She also said that she had passed on the business cards to some friends and they too had shown interest, so would likely be getting in contact with her soon.

Maisie took the measurements of Prunella as her attention to detail was superior to Beattie's, though Beattie missed nothing out when making her creations perfect. Maisie was happy to do this and she liked the feeling of importance it gave her. They had only seen the hall and the conservatory, so couldn't judge how well the Castle had been kept in keeping with the past, but from the outside it looked pristine. A little fewer hard lines within the flower borders would have been nicer, but they were smart with just one colour in each, and the driveway area was filled with chips of pink stones that were fairy tale-like. Perhaps next time they could get the chance to see more of the inside, but it was Lady Asher's home and not a stately house open to the public.

Beattie designed a few ballet outfits, keeping them in pale colours, as bright would be too harsh against the child's pale skin. She needed to keep to pale pinks and purples but there were so many hues of these, perhaps Lady Asher would buy them all. She felt greedy, but her ambition could not be stemmed, and it occurred to her that she needed a seamstress, possibly more than one. It was too much for her to continue making everything alone, but she accepted all enquiries and orders as the rest could be sorted after, there might be times where she had no work at all and there was usually no rush.

The party dress was ready and Lady Asher collected it from the shop, which was presented to her in a haberdashery delights box that had been added to the range of gift wrapping the shop offered. The dress was neatly wrapped in soft tissue and tied with a ribbon, and Beattie had added a card with another ribbon threaded through that read 'Designed by Beattie Chevelly'. It was simple but professional, and the shop itself benefited as clients rarely left without buying something. Marguerite had now got some bone china cups and saucers for client meetings, it was an image that she felt was true to the calibre of her daughter's work, and she had made room for a small white table with two chairs. They tried to keep stock to a minimum, preferring the swatch book as it took up less room, and Enid called in every so often not wanting to impose but naturally curious, and she was always welcomed. She was impressed by the changes in the shop and Beattie's designs. Beattie hadn't ever had her own money as all her needs had been met by her parents, and without her own home she had no outgoings, but Marguerite had said that Beattie was to keep some of the profits for her own personal use. Maybe just a nominal amount, as Beattie wanted to put most of the profits into a savings account that was yet to be organised and she wanted to pay off the loan sooner if possible.

The shop revenue was for food and bills and stock, and Marguerite had been paid a wage before but now she had to pay herself and there was a lot to consider. She kept a close eye on what sold and what didn't and she was aware that new materials should always be available to keep the customers, especially the regulars, coming through the door. It was not easy running a business, attention to detail was so important, and for keeping account of outgoings and sales she had had no training. Marguerite had ideas of how to increase profit, but she had passed this job onto Maisie as doing the finances was very important and she missed nothing.

Marguerite and her daughters were so tightly linked now, and she knew it annoyed Greg, who was always trying to push himself in and he couldn't understand how Rodrigo was not causing a fuss about it. He was leading an easy life he supposed, though missing out on the freedom someone of his age should be enjoying, but he knew he could go out anytime and Marguerite didn't dictate this. That likely removed the desire to want to, and Greg got this with Maisie who enjoyed attention and possessiveness when it suited her, but she would not be told what she could or couldn't do. Greg had started to save his money now as he didn't think it was needed by Maisie or Colm, and he thought that one day he would use it to get the three of them a place of their own. The way everything was now, he couldn't envisage when it might happen, but it satisfied him to watch his savings grow and he didn't smoke cannabis regularly anymore, just the occasional joint. He smoked cigarettes and he knew he drank a little too much as there were always beers in the fridge, so he didn't even have to pay for that. Really he had little cause for complaint, but he felt kept, and in theory he was.

Maisie was alone today, without Colm, as Beattie had said she would look after him this morning and they would have a picnic in the garden. She, like Maisie, thought it unimportant to go to a park when the garden offered all the children needed at this stage of their lives and they were privileged to have that option.

Maisie was dressed stylishly. Her hair, which was very blonde, was a mass of ringlets and today and she wore sparkling clips on either side. She was wearing earrings, small silver hoops, and she had taken care of her make-up. She was meeting with Eduardo, her Spanish friend, at the textile factory. It was only business but she felt freed from her duties as a mother and a girlfriend as she called the taxi man. Every time, she was surprised that he was always free whenever the Chevellys needed a taxi, but it wasn't her problem and it was convenient that he could always be relied upon.

Eduardo had matured and on completing college, been lucky to get taken on as an apprentice at the textile factory that was owned by several generations of Scots. They were usually suspicious of foreigners, but he had got excellent grades and was a flamboyant character, charming, and after a relatively short time he had managed to get the owners daughter to agree to marry him, so now he was almost part of a Scottish family. Maisie hadn't meant to flirt with him, but she couldn't help herself as she was feeling like she had been let off a leash today and he flirted back. It was just fun, Eduardo was never serious, and they were there to discuss business, a lucrative order for the factory. A large amount of fabric was required for Beattie's designs for the Old Lawn School, where the sons and daughters of the Scottish aristocracy were privately educated from age 11 to 16. The order for the uniform was to include coats and these Beattie had designed in several styles to afford individuality to the pupils. It would bring in a considerable profit if Maisie were to get a good deal. Beattie was looking for dark coloured cotton twill with a small check of a lighter colour to be for the skirts, trousers and the short sleeve jacket, which was to become Beattie's trademark and the waistcoats were to be in a lighter colour of the twill for the boys.

Eduardo took Maisie for a tour and she saw that everywhere was a hive of activity with a continual buzz of machines, the air was dusty so many workers wore masks. Lines of machines were electronically operated, but still needed people to put through the material exactly as any snags would mean the material could not be sold. The looms where the fabrics were put together were massive and extremely complicated, and Maisie wished then that she had listened more in her classes, but Eduardo's knowledge was extensive and she admired him for it. It was always hard for a foreigner to get into a decent business, but Eduardo had been right with his attitude of playing the field and not getting seriously involved until his education was complete.

Once Maisie had seen all that she needed, Eduardo said he would take her for lunch, his fiancée wasn't at the factory today and he never said much about her. He now owned a very nice sports car, it wasn't new but it was meticulously maintained and he opened the passenger door graciously for Maisie. It smelt fresh and was pristine, and she got in feeling exhilarated but she checked herself. This was business and he was just an old friend, she knew Greg hated it but tough. This was something she could get used to she thought, business lunches with good looking men.

Soon they were settled in a garden in an out of town pub, with cold drinks and a mixed salad on a sharing platter. They talked of college and of course Mitac was mentioned as Eduardo had kept in contact with him, apparently he had a Romanian girlfriend now and she found herself feeling a little jealous. Of course he would have a girlfriend, they had moved on a long time ago, and now Eduardo flirted continually with her, his expressive eyes teasing. He had always been like this to women, it wasn't just for her, and they were college friends but she pitied his girlfriend. Eduardo really made no pretence of the fact that he liked other women and his girlfriend probably just accepted it, considering that to make an issue would create one. Perhaps she was right, but no doubt he behaved impeccably in his fiancée's company not wanting to risk his future, but gossip could be so damaging. Maisie hadn't had much chance to play the field before motherhood, and she talked a little of Colm, not wanting to sound too 'mumsy'. Obviously she was very proud of her son, she thought maybe he was a little slow in achieving, but Marguerite had said that boys generally were slower to learn than girls. She said he would likely improve gradually, unlike girls whose progress was more rapid, and she should know as she had had two girls and two boys. Colm was a good little boy, he had a temper and still woke at night expecting to be played with, but Greg spent hours trying to settle him letting Maisie sleep even though he was the one who had to get to work early. She knew he was trying to keep her happy but in a way she disliked this attitude, he had been so much more fun before but perhaps she was just being ungrateful. She knew that Greg wanted them to get out of the house, but it wasn't going to happen, and she could see that at some point Greg would find he couldn't bear it any longer so she decided she would have to find a way to make him feel more needed. Maybe he could be involved in the business in some capacity? Maisie would have to discuss it with Beattie, but in time they may not be able to cope without outside help and besides, Greg was family too. He wasn't her husband, but then Rodrigo was not her mother's husband either, but he was definitely part of the family. Mace, where was that going? Maisie wondered. Beattie was clearly interested in Xavier, and Zachary was trying to win her back even though he had dropped her previously. He had said he found a girlfriend a liability and Beattie was never going to hang around like a spare part for his convenience, but they had Elodie now and nobody felt about a child the same way as the biological parents. You could go on about how wonderful your child was to each other, so Zachary had that advantage, and Mace was waiting but Beattie was hard to catch. Maybe Xavier had a chance but Beattie was a girl on a mission, Maisie was now a part of that, and Beattie always acknowledged all of her help but she knew her sister was evolving again, her old self emerging.

CHAPTER 47

Out of the blue, Marguerite found herself thinking of holidays and how she could do with a break. In the past holidays had been always taken place over two weeks of the year, but there had been so much happening recently and so many changes that the idea of a holiday hadn't even crossed her mind but she had been working flat out for months now. The shop sales were increasing with the flow of customers, and she had decided it was too much to cope with alone so she had thought it would be cost-effective to take on an assistant for Saturdays and a local girl had been sourced. Saturdays were the busiest day and sales were potentially lost when Marguerite couldn't get to each customer, even though she acknowledged each one, but they couldn't always wait. So now she was training this girl with a view that, when she left school in July, she could work in the shop in the holidays for a few hours a day and possibly stay on after. If Marguerite were satisfied with her abilities, the idea was that eventually she would be able to take some time off if she wanted or needed to, knowing that the shop would be in good hands. The girl was interested in fabrics, seemed keen to learn and she got on with Beattie being close to her in age. As the owner of the shop now, it was difficult to take time off, she could just close for a few days but was reluctant to resort to that.

Enid still called in regularly and had noticed that Marguerite wasn't looking particularly well and voiced her concerns. Marguerite said that nostalgically she missed her holidays and it would be nice for them all to take a break from their hard work, but didn't want to close the shop even for a week. Enid offered to keep the shop open,

232

it was much busier than it had been previously and she didn't want to be paid as she missed the shop, but was happy in her retirement.

Beattie was at burnout levels, with her daughter to care for and her designs and juggling her various man friends. Zachary was now trailing her with the intent on making them family unit with her and Elodie and had said that maybe they could get a place together. They could afford it, he always had loads of cash and Beattie was making a bundle, but she was horrified at the suggestion. Had she been too accommodating and given him the wrong idea? It was not going to happen, but she felt Zachary's power and it was threatening. She hadn't done anything more with him, Mace was always with her in her head, and he hadn't asked again to have Elodie by himself, he wanted them both. He would hold her hand and try to kiss her and she hadn't stopped him, she would be lying if she didn't admit she wasn't tempted, but she knew it would be a mistake. She had Mace and Xavier hadn't given up on her either, he was messaging her regularly now and suggesting meals or outings but she just fobbed him off with too many commitments which were the truth. She wasn't ready, had too many loose ends to tie, but she felt that she could have something with Xavier but couldn't envisage how. Beattie resorted to her mother's philosophy that situations resolved themselves, and she concentrated on the most important aspects of her life that were her daughter and her work.

Having organised a definite time and checked availability, Marguerite gathered the family together in the lounge and the TV was on in the background for the boys, the little ones asleep in their cots upstairs. She had found a villa, a hotel being too expensive and too complicated as they would all be in different rooms, possibly even on different floors. The villa was in Menorca, close to the beach and it had a small pool. Marguerite recalled all the luxurious holidays they had enjoyed with Roly in the past, now she longed to be somewhere other than there and they deserved it. Maisie and Greg were thrilled at the news, Greg particularly as he and Maisie could have some quality time together. Yes, the family would all still be there, but she wouldn't be flitting off which she was in the habit of doing so more and more now.

Beattie, did she want to invite Mace? Marguerite asked. She said she would prefer it just to be her and Elodie, he likely wouldn't be able to get the time off, but thought she should ask him anyway as he would wonder why he hadn't been invited. He was still her boyfriend and she cared for him, would be lost without him in many ways, so she sent him a message. He replied immediately saying that he had exams the week in question, but he was pleased that she had asked him, that was a relief. So it would be Maisie, Greg and Colm, Beattie and Elodie, the boys and Marguerite and Rodrigo. Rodrigo and Greg would need spending money, but that was all, and it was just a few weeks away, giving Beattie time to complete any outstanding orders. Xavier had asked to meet her before she left and she agreed to a coffee. He said he had missed her and Beattie thought that was funny, they had not met since the Barbecue and she hadn't forgotten the kiss, but they didn't know each other well, what was to miss? She asked him, and he wasn't able to answer but said that he just knew that he really liked her. She liked him too, but in her mind she considered she should be free at her age to kiss someone without having to be concerned with feelings. She had been too busy to think about it but maybe it had played on his mind, everything was always complicated. He didn't know what her situation was other than building her business, which quickly became the topic of conversation along with the holiday. Beattie again wondered what he might be hoping for from her, but she didn't ask then, she wanted a clear head. The holiday would be good, just to enjoy time off with her daughter she told him.

Greg had gone into the loft in search of suitcases that hadn't been used for years and he had found them covered in dust, still with labels from their last destination. He put them in the hall and they had prompted a trip down memory lane that he wasn't part of, so he picked up Colm and left them all to chat amongst themselves. The suitcases were in good condition underneath the dust, as always expensive things endured, and clothes needed to be sourced and washed. They all wanted to go on a shopping spree, something they also hadn't done for a while and had made do with their existing wardrobes as nobody really went anywhere where it mattered. Now swimsuits, bikinis, trunks, T shirts, shorts were needed and Frankie and Maurice had grown so new swimwear was a must.

The flight seats and villa were still available, having checked on Beattie's laptop. Marguerite hadn't known the cost of their previous holidays, which had been increasing with the more exclusive destinations, and this one was only in Europe but was still £4000. She put it on her credit card for now, intending to pay it off at a later date, and they were a large group. Colm would get his own seat but Elodie would be free so would not necessarily be entitled to one. An upgrade was offered to Premier, which meant they would have more room and better meals and this was a treat so she added that too.

A few weeks later their usual taxi, and another belonging to a friend of his as one taxi was not big enough, arrived and they divided themselves between them. Maisie, Greg, Colm and the boys were in one, Marguerite, Rodrigo, Beattie and Elodie in the other. Marguerite had told them all to pack light remembering you hardly needed the amount of clothes and shoes that were usually taken. Passports had had to be acquired for the grandchildren but everyone else had one already. Greg had been on holiday once with friends years back so had obtained his passport then and Rodrigo had previously holidayed with his family and had a year left to run on his. Greg was pleased his savings would be useful now and Rodrigo, who had also lived for free, had more than enough and said he would look forward to treating Marguerite. They were all very excited, the house secured as they watched it retreating behind them, as they journeyed to Inverness airport arriving in good time. It was a tonic for them all to be going somewhere other than Scotland and the Chevelley house.

The flight was smooth and comfortable, having paid extra for premium. The grandchildren were the only first-time fliers and had cried a little on the take-off but they were soon settled with an in-flight movie that was a welcome distraction.

After touchdown, Mahon airport had lots of taxis outside and porters that were keen to make some money. It was fantastic to just feel the sun on their skin, a sense of freedom from their daily lives, and the rise and fall of the babble of Spanish voices and other nationalities blended in. They were all recognisably in the holiday mood, chatting excitedly about the week ahead, as taxis again took them to their villa. It was in the northern part, which was rocky and rugged and less commercialised. The south had more sandy beaches but it would have been more crowded and the little ones were still very young but the villa had a pool. On balance, Marguerite felt the north offered more for the girls and the boys, which included Greg and Rodrigo, and they could go snorkelling and diving. Marguerite was just looking forward to relaxing by the pool as she had travelled extensively before but hadn't been to Minorca. They were all already used to being in the same house, so no rows were likely which could often result when people were forced together in close vicinity. The villa was not as big as the house but it was large enough. The nearby Port Addaia had a few bars and restaurants so they didn't need to go everywhere together, Maisie and Greg had already taken off with Colm as soon as they had placed their cases in the best bedroom. Maisie had looked at Marguerite pleading could she have the room with the extending balcony as didn't she already have that year-round at home? Marguerite had agreed and found a bedroom on the lower floor that lead onto a terrace, she and Rodrigo would have that one. Beattie, accommodating as always, didn't mind as all the rooms were great in their own way, all with en-suite bathrooms, which was special to her as she didn't have one at home. The boys took the last bedroom that was left available, not in the least bit interested as they were just keen to get to the rocky beach and look for shells and crabs. They asked for some money for ice creams and drinks which was a novelty and excited them as it was foreign money they hadn't seen before. They had been too young on previous holidays to be able to go off on their own, but now they ran off dressed in bright summer clothes on an adventure, they were 13 and 11 now.

With some of them gone now, Beattie and Elodie and Marguerite and Rodrigo remained at the villa, happy just to relax by the pool with cold drinks and snacks. The fridge had been stocked up already, so they didn't need to shop for groceries yet. It was so peaceful and they had everything they needed, the time now their own for a short time. Elodie had had sunscreen applied liberally to her fair skin and a bonnet had been put on her head that was neatly tied beneath her chin, so she couldn't pull it off. Beattie popped her in a playpen that she had found in the villa and placed beneath some flowering shrubs in the shade. Elodie was soon asleep, the excitement of the journey had tired her, as the adults laid on sunbeds close by and one by one they too fell asleep. There was a gentle breeze but it was warm, they weren't used to full-on heat but today the temperature was clement, the weather report said tomorrow would be hotter.

Beattie slept on exhausted and Rodrigo, he too had worked hard all year round by cooking and maintaining the garden and Marguerite left him where he was stretched out on a lounger. She went over to Elodie, who was also still sleeping, and picked her up and placed her just inside on some cushions. She had woken momentarily but soon settled, she was a child that seemed to need a lot of sleep, and Marguerite closed the door. Elodie could crawl so you couldn't be too careful as everything was much harder once babies were on the move. Marguerite thought she would prepare lunch for them all, relieve Rodrigo from the cooking today, and Beattie had woken up sensing movement around her and gone into the large airy kitchen to help her. They both looked in the cupboards and the fridge and decided on a salad with cold meat, with cold beers and a coffee for Marguerite. There was a coffee machine and Beattie had fathomed out how to work it.

The large terrace had a huge table with chairs surrounding it and they found plates and cutlery to set it with. Beattie text Maisie to ask her to bring back some fresh bread, there was sliced bread already but she wanted it to be perfect. Rodrigo soon stumbled into the kitchen, expecting to be the chef, but was pleased that he didn't have to be this time. He needed a shower, he was already brown and had said that he tanned easily, he wasn't joking as he appeared after what was probably only 15 minutes looking as though he had been already been there a week. He was wearing thin cotton shorts, flip flops and a white sleeveless top, and Marguerite felt fortunate at her age to have such a young and handsome man and she excused herself to change while Rodrigo quickly showered. Marguerite was still slim, but not painfully so, and she put on a long floaty summer dress while Beattie was busy setting the table and then searching for some salad dressing. Beattie didn't have time to change, but she had no one to impress, she was on holiday and she had none of her men around as they were all back in Scotland or England. She turned her phone off, not wanting to be aware of any problems, and Maisie and Greg appeared hand in hand, Colm holding his father's spare hand. They all sat around the big table chatting and laughing, enjoying the sun, and it was idyllic to all be together, this time on holiday in Minorca.

CHAPTER 48

B ack in Scotland, Roly was thinking of his family on holiday, their first without him. He had been right in thinking that Marguerite would arrange a holiday at some point, it had taken her years but she seemed to be coping financially and now she owned the shop. Beattie too had her own business, Beattie's designs, and the boys had said that she was a hotshot businesswoman now but why hadn't she told him herself? When he asked the boys this, Frankie had just shrugged and said he thought she wouldn't want her father's input, but she had said that when she made her first million she would tell him. That thought didn't excite Frankie, he and all of them always got everything they asked for, it was normal for them to have enough money. He was 13, almost 14 now and growing tall and confident, but Maurice was a lot shorter, still waiting to catch up with his brother. They had told Roly about the holiday as Marguerite hadn't said not to, but she hoped they wouldn't reveal too much. She was still his wife but only by name and they wouldn't be getting back together but there was no rush for him to get a divorce. Roly wasn't planning on marrying again, but Verity had hinted at it and they spent a lot more time together now, out on their bikes or at the club. He didn't really want to remarry, but if he did, did he want to marry her? He was fine with things as they were and he hadn't returned his key to the house and now was his chance to go there while everyone was away, just to poke around. He felt a little guilty for invading their privacy, but it was still his house and he was paying the mortgage and council tax. Really, if Marguerite had the money for holidays, it should be time to make changes on that but truthfully he had had enough drama. His girls, his sons and his grandchildren were still in his life but they didn't meet often as they were always too busy. He was the only one that wasn't so busy now it seemed, just working 9 to 5 on weekdays but no weekends. He did have the occasional meeting after work, but he would send somebody else in his place if he could as he found his ambition had left him now. He had reached a pinnacle and had no desire to rise above it.

In Minorca, the family were relaxing more into their holiday. It was only for a week, but without all the usual chores and work it seemed longer, every day a day just to indulge. They were all getting tanned, Rodrigo now a rich brown in colour, but the boys who were playing in the sun all day were the brownest. Marguerite stayed in the shade mostly but she had still caught it a little. Beattie tanned easily, having olive skin and a naturally dark colouring, but the others were blonde and had to be careful so Maisie wore a sun hat to protect her skin and massive sunglasses. She had found herself thoroughly enjoying her time with Greg, he was more his old self there and he danced attendance on her. Marguerite was pleased about this as she liked him and he was good with Maisie, always taking care not to provoke her. Maisie was a difficult person sometimes, she had mellowed with motherhood but the old Maisie still bubbled beneath the surface. Colm was also made to wear a hat, which he wasn't keen on, but his little chubby arms and legs had turned a light shade of brown. Elodie was kept out of the sun and Beattie was attentive to sunscreen, knowing how the sun could potentially be dangerous and damaging to fair skin, and she was given bottles of water regularly.

It was the fourth day into the holiday when a visitor arrived. Mace had finished his exams and had decided he wanted to surprise Beattie, and he had, but was she pleased? She had been enjoying a break from her life in Scotland, but what could she say? She hugged him, but everyone else was more delighted than she was that he had joined them. Maisie was impressed the most, said that it was a serious effort, so Beattie decided to accept that he was there as he fitted in with them all. She knew the family would be pleased if they made the relationship more permanent but Mace still had college to complete so there was no hurry and he wasn't pushy, knowing Beattie as well as he did. He didn't impose on her and she was able to continue as she had done before his arrival as he sat beside the pool, in white shorts with a cold beer, chatting with everyone and playing with Elodie. They all barely left the Villa and as the days went on it was too hot to go to the town or the beach. In the evenings, when it was cooler, one or more of them would go for a stroll and look around the shops that sold cheap souvenirs and maybe stop for a coffee or a cold drink and the boys found friends on the beach, both old enough now to be out by themselves. Marguerite just gave them a small amount of money each day and they thoroughly enjoyed being able to decide what to spend it on.

When the holiday came to an end they were all very sad to have to leave and return home, but the memories of the holiday would stay with them, to return to and chat about their shared experience time and time again.

Inverness airport had been busy with returning or departing holidaymakers and it was a late evening flight so they were all quiet, alone with their thoughts. Mace travelled back with them, having managed to get a seat on the same plane, and he still had a few more days before he had to get back to England as he had taken a week off work, and Beattie and he had got closer in the few days that he had managed to get to her. Back in Scotland, the same two taxis returned them to their house and back in their own home they found it cold after all the Spanish sun. It was still summer, but the temperature difference was noticeable and they were all exhausted so they left all their cases in the hall for now. The little ones were settled for the night in their cots, and the boys and each couple had gone to their own rooms. Marguerite and Rodrigo were reluctant to return to their everyday lives, having enjoyed being together for a week without interruption, and for Maisie and Greg their relationship had strengthened. Beattie and Mace chatted quietly for a while but they soon slept.

Roly knew that they were all back as Frankie had messaged him to say that they had all had a great time and asked, how was he? And Roly appreciated that he had taken the time out to do that. He had gone to the house when his family were away and it had been an emotional experience, but he felt it had helped him accept that that life had gone now. He hadn't lived there for years but the house looked lived in, a proper family home. It was not pristine as it had once been when he was there, but it seemed a happy home and he was resolved and felt he was ready to move on now. He couldn't sell it, he knew that much, and his flat was alright but he didn't like that it was rented. Perhaps it would be possible to buy it, or maybe something similar, but he didn't feel that he could be bothered to look around. He had lost the feeling of wanting to push himself, just going along with his work now and doing only what he had to do, returning after to the flat and just watching TV. He had worked so hard over the years but now he didn't know who that person was anymore that had once been so hungry for wealth and status, those things had lost their importance now.

CHAPTER 49

At the house, it had taken a day or two to adjust back to reality, but soon the family was operating as before, the holiday now subsided into the background. Marguerite felt much better after the break, with a renewed vigour, and she was keen to find out how the shop had been while she was away. Enid said she had been rushed off her feet and accrued several potential appointments for Beattie's design sales. She said that she thought Marguerite had done so well in the short time she had been the shop owner, and the new range of materials that she had recently sourced had been particularly popular. Lady Astor had ordered some pink and purple plaid as Beattie's designs now included making cushions, as she had been asked and wouldn't turn away the business and she would add her originality to them. They were for Prunella's bedroom as she now liked pink and purple apparently and Lady Astor always indulged her child.

Unbeknownst to Beattie, Mace had been taking photos of her and all of them over a period of time and he had selected the ones that showed off Beattie's designs and forwarded them to a fashion magazine. The magazine was one of those women's magazines for families, and they had said that they liked the photos and would consider a series of features, telling of the young mother who had risen to success. He messaged to tell Beattie, who had been genuinely touched by his gesture, she hadn't thought to do that herself. He really was the best, so thoughtful and so kind, and she hadn't been in contact with Xavier again since her return as she was too consumed with guilt. She truly cared for Mace and she admired his tactics to win her and he was doing well.

Zachary however had managed to get himself arrested, he had been getting too complacent by circulating the same venues for business and the police had been watching him and now he had been called in for questioning. His bedsit had been searched but they had thankfully found nothing that could actually incriminate him, and a few of the local teenagers had been interviewed but denied all knowledge. It was noticeable that the areas frequented by those teenagers had became desolate, so it had helped them as they didn't know of anyone else that they could get drugs from other than him. Zachary's partner in crime, another man who he spent a lot of time with, had also been questioned and it was brought to light that this man was actually someone the police had been looking for some time. Shockingly he had matched the description related to the kidnapping of the boys some years back and Marguerite too had received a visit from the police. She was forced to recall that nasty episode, dragging up again about her car that had been destroyed and the kidnapping. The culprit hadn't been found, but the police had continued to build a case, were all these incidents linked? They asked her. She was reluctant to divulge anything but they had said that the man was a danger to society and capable of anything, was it right to withhold the information? They couldn't make her talk, so they left her to think about it, giving her a number to call should she have anything more to add. Marguerite was horrified as she had not had to think about it for years, she thought it was all over, but the case was still open and wouldn't be closed. She knew it sometimes took years to solve mysteries, and now she recalled the description that she had given when she had been forced to pay the debt that Greg had run up. He had been a full on druggie back then, and it had resulted in threats and her sons den being destroyed, showing them as the target. The boy's didn't play in the den as such anymore, but they sometimes had friends come over and sit in it to chat, play music or video games. Especially in the cold weather when they would just wrap up warm, the Scots were never fazed by cold weather. The boys had been kidnapped from school by an uncle who wasn't, but they never found out who he actually was and thankfully no harm had come to them so she hadn't wanted to do anything more, fearing a reprisal. The police had kept it on file and the town was a sleepy village, but of course there was always a criminal element, and the law wanted the crime solved. Nothing was ever just forgotten.

Marguerite wished it would just go away as who knew what could happen if she agreed to testify against the man. She knew she didn't have to, but at the same time felt that it would be wrong not to protect others from going through the same experience.

Following the visit, Marguerite had gone very quiet for a few days and eventually it became obvious to Beattie, who was busy but still noticed. She had heard about Zachary and that he had gotten away with it for now, assuming he would probably find other ways to sell his products. Beattie remembered the man on her 16th birthday, but she was as reluctant as her mother to dig up the past. If Zachary and this man were connected, had he had something to do with the kidnapping? Marguerite recalled the man in the hall that evening when she had left the £1500 in an envelope, and the door had opened to reveal a shadowy figure that was tall and slim. Beattie voiced her concerns to Marguerite that the man could have been Zachary, as the boys had not met him in the time that she had been seeing him. But Marguerite told Beattie no, the man had been dark-haired and Beattie looked relieved, she had an association with Zachary and he was Elodie's father.

The police had said to Marguerite that they would talk again when she was ready, but emphasised that she had been a victim so wouldn't she want justice? But Marguerite was not a vengeful person, just being happy to get her sons back unscathed, and she would have preferred to forget the whole thing. But did this man use these tactics on others? She didn't know, but perhaps he was an opportunist, noticing one family's wealth and using them to get money. She decided not to act in haste but knew he could possibly hurt other people, but would he know others that could hurt her and her family if she spoke up? It was a truly awful position to be in, the halcyon days were over, no one was allowed to just live happily it seemed.

Beattie was worried about her mother, the glow of their success now tainted, and she thought of Zachary. She knew he would protect Elodie and her with his life and he had said nothing that suggested he could hurt his girl or her. She was the mother of his child, but she knew that he could possibly be in fear of this man himself. She decided to call him and he was sketchy on the phone, but said that it was all crap and made light of it.

"Yeah, he was bad" he said to her. "But if we didn't sell it somebody else would". He said he knew it was a risk and that it was wrong, before she could say it herself if she dared. But he didn't want to say too much on the phone, so he asked, could they meet? Not at the all hours café she said, somewhere else, not his bedsit or her house. Eventually they settled on a little restaurant out of town but he wasn't to pick her up, she would get herself there. She was paranoid as she was connected to him, but not his lifestyle, so she would get a taxi. She told Maisie and asked could she look after Elodie, but she was to say nothing to anyone else and instead just make up a flimsy excuse, something to do with a client meeting to discuss an outfit. Maisie was concerned, they had all been living the high life and feeling ridiculously happy after their holiday, but now it seemed as though that was all going to change.

The taxi man was pleased as always to have the fare and it was to his advantage that, other than Marguerite, none of them had cars or could drive. He had questioned Maisie about it once before but said that it was more cost-effective for them to order a taxi now and then than have the cost of a car. That was probably true but it worked well for him, why did he care? She had asked, and he had laughed, said he was just being curious and Maisie had left it there. They had Marguerite's car and she used it for work, but nobody had asked to learn to drive as they didn't really have the time. They were all flat out already and a taxi was convenient, so why change it?

CHAPTER 50

B eattie dressed with care as she always did, wanting to feel confident. She didn't fear Zachary as such but knew he could turn nasty if he felt threatened. She just wanted his advice and he was flattered, said that of course he wanted to help her, which was another step in the right direction for his happy family plans.

Beattie explained to Zachary what had happened years ago and asked him how well he knew the man.

"He's just a mate, but not really a friend" he answered.

"What does that mean? You don't want to cross him so you pretend he's a mate?" Yes, she got that part. "Is he the same about you do you think?" Beattie continued firing questions.

"Yeah I think so, he wouldn't mess with me, we both deal on the same patch so it's an unspoken agreement I guess" Zachary offered by way of an explanation.

"So, what should we do?" she asked. "If my family crossed him, what could he do?"

"You already know that Beattie" and he looked deep in thought for a few minutes. "Want something to eat and drink?"

Beattie didn't feel hungry but said she would just have a coffee and a salad, and Zachary clicked his fingers. His powers were noticeable as a little waitress scurried over immediately. "A coffee and a salad for my lady please, and a coffee and burger and chips for me" he ordered.

They continued chatting about Elodie while they waited, Beattie giving Zachary an update on her achievements.

"Cheers Beattie" he said suddenly.

"What for?" she raised a quizzical eyebrow, confused at the outburst.

"For letting me have my girl in my life" he answered, and he looked vulnerable for a moment. Under all that bluster there was a softer person that being a father had occasionally brought to the surface. She wanted him to get out of what he did, but she knew he wouldn't, it was his life and he earned a lot in just a few hours. He obviously thought it was worth the risk and she knew he would never intentionally put them at risk, but their association involved them. "You know what Beattie, he is going to disappear soon and find another patch as it's too dodgy for him here now. Nobody makes people take drugs, we kind of encourage it I guess, but ultimately it's their choice".

Beattie could see the truth in that, but it didn't make it right, and she admitted to him that her mother was the type of person that always wanted to do the right thing. She would hate to think that because of her not speaking up, others could be in danger.

"He's not a murderer Beattie, he's clever, he gets money out of people but I don't think he's ever actually hurt anyone" Zachary tried to reassure her.

Beattie wondered if this was true or was he just saying it? Knowing that she would tell her mother and this could put her mind at rest.

"Yeah he's a dealer, not a nice person, but if it wasn't him it would be someone else, the drugs aren't going anywhere".

Beattie said she would tell Marguerite, but she understood what could happen if she spoke out and that they could all be at risk. Zachary's eyes narrowed, they were incredibly blue, and she got the message to leave it as he took one of her hands, admiring her nails which were bright red.

"You're looking good girl" he told her, and she felt the frisson, the danger was potent.

After their meeting, Beattie didn't hear from Zachary again for a while. He seemed to have temporarily disappeared, but she knew he would be back soon enough. Marguerite had been reassured by Beattie and it did seem that doing nothing was the answer, the easier option, but she knew that getting one bad person off the street would only leave a place to be replaced by another, but where did you start? Beattie said it wasn't up to Marguerite to put everything right all the time. Didn't she have enough to do and people to care for? The police had called again, said that they were unable to proceed as the man couldn't be found at this time, but they would contact her again if this changed. The case still wasn't closed and she wished that it was, but it wasn't just about her and Marguerite felt a great sense of relief. The situation wasn't gone, but for now she could get back to her work and re-immerse herself in what was important which was her family and working to look after them all.

The uniforms for the Old Lawn School were ready now, produced by a small retailer's outfitters that had a team of seamstresses. They had had a lull in business recently and Beattie's order had filled the gap. She hadn't got any more enquiries for uniforms but that kind of order involved a lot of work, preparation and sourcing materials. Her line in children's clothes was increasing and these she still made herself, including the dance outfit for Prunella which she had worn at her class immediately and had become the topic of conversation amongst all the girls and their mothers. They all wanted one and Lady Asher had called to tell her, adding that Prunella had got a little cross about it as she didn't want the other girls to have a dress like hers. All Beattie's dresses were different, but she understood, and Lady Asher said that the dress had made a noticeable difference in her daughter. She was a timid child but the dress had given her a confidence boost that had been invaluable. Beattie had also made the cushions, adding an elaborate P for Prunella in a contrasting fabric which glittered with an interwoven silver thread that she had found in her mother's offcuts box in the shop. Marguerite said Beattie could easily sell more cushions, but she could see that they needed to get more organised as they were only just about holding it all together.

Beattie was dealing with each enquiry, taking on all orders without quite knowing how she could follow them through. Neither her nor Marguerite were actually business trained, but they were learning whilst they worked.

Maisie worked on the figures for both the designs and the shop, neat columns showing in going's and out goings. The amount going in was considerably higher than what was going out, but she advised that they needed to specialise in things and not flit, as both her mother and sister had a habit of doing. Were they shop retailers, designers, fashion models or creators of cushions? Maisie had asked and Beattie had laughed, they were all those things, but she agreed that they needed to clarify all the components to be part of the business on a more organised basis and Maisie had that skill. They were paying an outlet to make the uniforms but they should have their own seamstresses now. This had been the original idea should Beattie get another school enquiry and she had, so she would need to look in to it again. It was decided that the link between the shop and the cushions should be a service offered by the shop, so Marguerite would deal with that, and Beattie would continue with her designs for children, changing the mannequins every Saturday but keeping a portfolio of the others and dates of when they had been in the window. That way if someone asked about an outfit that they had seen on a particular week, it could be located easily which was a good idea that was implemented immediately.

The dance outfit Beattie had made for Prunella would feature in the portfolio and any others that sold too. All the outfits were original, but this showed ideas, and the fashion magazine had also shown more interest. Beattie's adult designs had reached a modelling agency, so the branches were spreading out in lots of directions and they couldn't be handled without more structure, but Maisie was keen to keep it within the family. Beattie decided that she would leave Maisie to fathom out how, and told her that she was a very important part of the business as without her dealing with the behind the scenes, the whole thing would have gotten out of control. Maisie was thrilled at this and the result was that in every spare moment she was scribbling facts and figures and ideas. Greg was happy that she had chosen to put her energies into the business, rather than elsewhere, but he knew the chances of them ever getting out of the Chevelly house was as good as non-existent. After the holiday he felt that he and Maisie had strengthened their relationship together, which took effort that was mostly his, but he was satisfied for now.

The shop had an area at the back which wasn't used for anything, it was a paved patio but they didn't have time to sit out there, so they thought this could be converted into a room where the products could be made. Marguerite had surprised Greg, asked could he find a builder and to measure the area behind the shop and research the project, which motivated him to look into what was involved. He didn't have the actual skills for the building, but he could certainly help with the labour and assist by checking out the local builders.

Lady Asher had brought even more work her way and asked Beattie if she would design a gown for herself, which was an honour. She and Maisie had been invited for drinks, and they hadn't yet met Lord Asher but they would that evening. As it was a social and business meeting, Elodie wasn't invited this time so Marguerite and Rodrigo would keep an eye on her. She would just be in her cot and she rarely stirred until morning, continuing to sleep well, and Greg was always on the alert for Colm who chose to play up most nights. Beattie said she thought Greg and Maisie were perhaps too soft with him, but she didn't judge, maybe she was just lucky that Elodie was so pliable and she was smart as she knew that it got her nowhere to make a nuisance of herself. Elodie seemed to be unaware that her mother was out, having fallen asleep earlier than usual after a tiring day toddling around the garden. She had mastered the art of walking, not wanting to sit when she could walk, and she followed Colm around everywhere. He had finally stopped reverting to crawling and was now able to run so Elodie was always way behind, which was comical to watch.

Rodrigo kept the garden under control, the middle was grass and kept short, but the surroundings were wild with lots of hiding places for the children. A swing

hung on the largest tree and they were pushed daily on it, often squabbling to be the first that was usually Colm, and he had to be taken off screaming for Elodie to have her turn. The garden still offered all the entertainment they needed and it was convenient.

Zachary continued to seem out of the race as he had still not contacted Beattie, even to ask about Elodie. He was being watched by the police and they were waiting to catch him. Beattie had no idea where he was but she knew that she could never live with him, he was a villain at heart and she was an inspiring business woman.

Mace also appeared to have decreased his interest, concluding that his college days had lots of exams, and he worked as a barman on some nights and others as a waiter so Beattie assumed he must meet and talk to other girls. He had not returned to the house after the holiday, when he had appeared to want to be with Beattie more to try and make a life with her, but was now distracted, as was she as she barely had a spare second.

Xavier hadn't been in contact for a while but had suddenly started messaging again, just to ask how Beattie was and Elodie. She messaged him back casually, indicating she was busy which she was, and she reminded herself that she didn't really need to be this busy as she was her own boss. They both mentioned that they should meet but neither actually organised anything as truthfully they were both too busy. Xavier had been promoted in his job, and relationships took time as did businesses, but it was about choices left or right, more time for a relationship or more time for a business? Beattie had to strengthen her hold, keep herself out there, but neither of them progressed further and the casual messages continued.

Maisie looked fantastic that evening, wearing a midnight blue dress that was covered in tiny diamond shapes in clusters, another amazing design by Beattie that had taken hours. Beattie was in a rich green dress, slim line that reached mid-calf and her sandals high but the heels solid. Less likely to be a hazard as she recalled the incident with the boots that she had not worn again since. The dress was simple but had been teamed with a belt in a rich yellow silk that was embellished with stones in a myriad of colours. Beattie had decided to push forward with a line of evening wear as Lady Asher had important friends, her children's line now taking second place. Beattie had found a girl in the local vicinity that had proven to be excellent at putting together the basic shape of her designs, leaving Beattie just to add the final touches.

The Castle looked magical at night, surrounded by a glow of hidden lights that also paved the edges of the driveway and the flower borders so that the pink stones glittered. The maid was immaculate in her uniform when she answered the door to Maisie and Beattie and they were shown to a large drawing room. There was a baby grand piano in the corner and shelves of numerous books with an assortment of antique chairs, a low back leather sofa and a long coffee table inlaid with matching leather. The lights were dimmed and piped music played, an old fashioned aura with the benefit of modern technology, and a few other guests had been invited as potential customers, friends of Lady Asher. They were already chatting amongst themselves when they entered, but Maisie and Beattie had no problem fitting in as they had been brought up to fit in to any situation and they enjoyed the evening. The maid brought around flutes of wine and food was served from trays by a male helper, was he the butler? The girl's outfits were admired and Lady Asher was dressed in a plain but expensive dress. She was an intelligent woman, in her 40s with hair a mid-brown with highlights and eyes like her daughter's, large and solemn, a grey blue. Beattie felt her look needed brightening and an idea of the perfect dress for her was visualising in her mind. It would reach to the knee, but flail behind in layers, a waterfall effect falling to the floor to reach a point with simple lines but in a bold colour, rich purple she felt would stand out. She pulled out her pad and began drawing a picture with her descriptions, aware that other women were moving closer to watch her. Lord Asher had disappeared with the other male guests, to smoke possibly and probably bored at all the talk of clothes.

Later on several of the ladies pressed business cards into Beattie and Maisie's hands before they left, as they each went to every guest to say their goodbyes. One of the ladies had a party to attend and another had a conference that had a formal night to follow, where she would need to dress appropriately. Another would like something special to wear whilst on holiday should she go to a club and no limits were suggested regarding budgets. It was a social evening but a lucrative business one and it seemed that the only limit now was how fast Beattie's creations could be turned out but Maisie reminded Beattie that original designs could not be mass produced, the customers would wait. Maisie could source the fabrics whilst Beattie would create the designs, and they were a team with their joint abilities, one being able to do what the other could not.

CHAPTER 51

Eduardo had finished college as the only boy in the class after Mitac had left to return to Romania, and not even Scottish or English but Spanish, he had achieved the highest grades ready to pursue a career. He had already been made aware of the number of textile factories in the vicinity, which employed a large number of the locals, as Scotland was renowned for its quality twills and wools that were one of their major industries. Eduardo had read much about the history of tartans and plaids and how they related to clans. A textile factory had been looking for an apprentice, they hadn't advertised so you just had to be in the know, but when he frequented the local public house he had overheard a conversation between some men about it. He, in his usual friendly way, had casually joined the group and offered to get them all a drink which they had accepted. Eduardo hinted that he was looking for work, subtly dropping in that he had heard that there was a job going at the textile factory.

"The boss, he'd likely not take yah, as you're not a Scot" one told him. But they all admired his confidence so he had been given a name and a contact number.

Eduardo called straight away the next morning, managing to talk the owner into at least meeting with him that day. He dressed in his usual style; a leather jacket with black skinny jeans and boots with a small heel, his shirt silk white with a loose cravat. It was the textile industry and he looked the part, knowing that if he arrived dressed in tartan it would come across as an insult. The Scots considered tartan should only be worn by a Scot, and to wear a kilt would have been even worse as he would not ever have been taken seriously.

The mill owner pulled open a heavy wooden door to let Eduardo into an opulently furnished room. He was a large man, the great-grandson of the founder, and he filled the room with his presence. The mill had been passed down to him through several family generations and Eduardo had cleverly researched about him already. Bhradain McCloud was his name, with wiry red hair and an untamed beard and moustache, his twinkling eyes softening a large red nose. He was a true Scot and they were all whisky drinkers, his accent thick and difficult to understand, but Eduardo had been surrounded by the sound of Scottish voices for two years now, so it wasn't a problem for him to pick up the gist of what was being said. Bhradain observed Eduardo, taking in every detail, but resolved to say that perhaps it was time for some new blood. Eduardo later found out that this was literally the case, as he was the token foreigner, the men at the pub had been right. There was one polish boy but he was just there to sweep up the mess. The mill was a family business steeped in tradition, but the owner had been more than a little impressed by Eduardo and his nerve. He had known a lot about the factory, had read about the family, which worked to his advantage as a Scot wouldn't have done all that. It was just an apprentice position so really Eduardo was overqualified, and he was Spanish but his English was good, so Bhradain decided to give him a chance.

"Why not?" he had said "Let's get you in and started" and he poured two neat Scotches for Eduardo to join him in a toast.

On his way out, Eduardo had bumped into a young woman about his age. She was no more than 5 foot tall, her features elfin with perfectly clear skin, her eyes narrowing, questioning what he was doing there.

"I'll be seeing you soon" he told her. "I'm the new apprentice".

Her face was agog that her father had taken on this boy, not someone he would often choose. This was a first, a non Scot, but this one had obviously charmed her father. He looked interesting and you couldn't pass him in the street and not take a second look as she stared after him, liking what she saw.

Who could he tell? Eduardo wondered. He was so excited, it wasn't much of a job but he had made history. He decided to call Maisie, knowing she would like to hear his news, they were friends at college and since she had left to have her baby they had occasionally met for a coffee, was she free now?

Maisie answered the call immediately. She had Colm of course, but her mother had a rare morning working from home as Beattie was at the shop today and had said to Marguerite to take the day off, so she could stay on with Elodie for a few extra hours and deal with the banking and make sure everything was tidy and the premises securely locked. Maisie asked if she could look after Colm as Eduardo had asked her out for a coffee and Marguerite questioned whether it was wise, but Maisie was barely 20 so she should be entitled to have some time out. She worried that Maisie could go on a flight of fantasy, but she knew that she could do with getting out of the house so she agreed to put aside her work and took Colm into her arms, relaxing into her grandmother role.

Maisie was already dressed nicely as always, just needing to check her make-up and shake her ringlets that couldn't be brushed, and she picked up a bag and slung a jacket over her arm. The taxi man as always was free.

"10 minutes" he told her. Eduardo had suggested a café to meet, she knew the one, and soon she was on her way. Eduardo was already there waiting when she arrived, he had gotten on a bus, and she immediately pulled him into a hug to congratulate him.

"Aren't you the clever one"! She exclaimed as he grinned.

"Not so much, it's a low paid job as an apprentice, but it's a start" he replied.

They both laughed as they sat down together at a table and he described the mill and the owner, the conversation lapsing into college and their shared memories. Eduardo mentioned Mitac as he knew Maisie always liked to know everything, so he told her that he was now doing a very menial job. So much for all those aspirations he had had before Maisie thought, but she didn't feel bad for him, hadn't she too messed it all up? But she no longer cared, times had changed. The meeting was a pleasant break from her routine and she wished Eduardo good luck as it ended, agreeing to catch up again soon.

Maisie wasn't keen to get home, now enjoying being free for a short while, and she decided to have a walk around the town as Greg had only that morning given her a £20 note, just in case she decided to venture out to the park or somewhere with Colm. She was a homebody, he had joked, really needed to get out more, but today she was glad of the cash as she treated herself to a new lipstick and a toy car for Colm to add to his growing collection. She also brought some chocolate for Marguerite, who used to eat it all the time but it was now a treat, and she didn't have to pay for the taxi as her mother had an account set up, which was paid at the end of every month. This had been arranged before, when Marguerite had been paying cash out to him so regularly, and he had suggested it would be easier to budget that way, but Marguerite had had a car for some time now. For a while before she had had to rely on taxis herself, but now the rest of the family called on him, as none of them other than Marguerite could drive and she wasn't always available.

Back at the house, Maisie found her mother in the lounge on the floor entertaining Colm with his cars, and she added the new one. Colm was thrilled and picked it up immediately and she gave Marguerite the chocolate whilst he was distracted for a second. Maisie had been thankful for the break, despairing of the repetitiveness of play with a small child as she got up and sat on the sofa, Colm now engrossed in examining his new car. Maisie said she would make her mother a coffee and it had done her good to go out alone and meet a friend, albeit an attractive one. She told Greg she had gone for a coffee with Eduardo as she didn't like deception. He hadn't looked pleased but he knew not to say too much, he was always on the alert having a jealous nature, though she was virtually always at home so he knew it was irrational. Maisie was not his property, she was his girlfriend she reminded him, but she knew that she wouldn't be pleased herself if Greg met a female friend but she didn't know who he talked to at work, these days she preferred not to torture herself.

Eduardo had arrived in Scotland a few years earlier, leaving behind a small Spanish village that suppressed his potential. With no educational establishments close by, or none that he wouldn't have to pay for, he had decided he must do something with his life other than stagnating. He knew he would miss his family but they unlike him were content to live their days by tradition, earning a small wage, but he wanted and was capable of more. Eduardo was talented and artistic, interested in fabrics and colours, always standing out from the crowd. His family and friends had always been aware that he was meant for better, so they had one day decided to pool all of their limited resources together to get him a plane ticket to Scotland, giving the remainder to him in cash, knowing he would repay them when he was able. He had landed at Inverness airport with little more than his ambition and what had fit in his rucksack. Fortunately the college had been impressed by him, taking one student for each class on a scholarship, and he felt lucky to have been given this opportunity. He knew he would have to pay for his own books, but he found a part-time job which enabled him to do this and also fund a very small bedsit to reside in. Some days he barely had enough money to buy food, but this didn't stand in the way of his ambition. He knew that all the effort he put in now would pay him back 100 times in the future, and whilst he often played with the idea of a girlfriend, he persisted with the chance that he had been given. His family lived off his visual reports of Scotland, which was very different from dusty hot Spain. It was so cold, sometimes even in the summer, as it snowed a lot but the air was fresh and healthy, but he told them that he would return as soon as he had achieved what he had set out to do. Not to stay permanently, but to deliver gifts and to repay all those that had helped him to achieve his dreams.

CHAPTER 52

Frankie had been at senior school for a few years now and Maurice had joined him there, but it was a lot more involved than at the junior's. There were lots of different classes to get to and different teachers, and Maurice found it a bit of a struggle, he preferred the juniors where it was just one teacher to contend with. Frankie had a gang of his own friends now and Maurice had made a few close friends in his tutor group. But Frankie seemed to always be getting into trouble for going against those in authority and was often seen outside the Head Masters office, waiting to be called in for yet another reprimand. Marguerite had recently been called in to discuss a serious incident, involving Frankie punching a boy that was apparently making fun of his younger brother, and she was also informed that Frankie was running wild, always talking in class when he should be paying attention and getting himself into mischief. Without a father around, the headmaster had dared to say he had no role model. Marguerite had replied that of course he still had a father, though admittedly had little to do with him now so she was effectively mother and father, but she was annoyed at his smug suggestion that she might be failing in her role. Maurice however, the headmaster continued, is a very good student that always works to the best of his ability and remains polite to everyone, but he expressed concern in that he could follow in Frankie's footsteps as he was setting a bad example to his younger brother. Marguerite knew that Frankie had taken Maurice with him after school to the park to hang out, kick a ball about and chat, but what else? She wondered. She decided she would have a conversation with her youngest son first. Maurice and Frankie found their own way home on foot, there was a bus but it wasn't far to walk and it was healthy for them to get the exercise.

That evening at bedtime, Marguerite sat on the side of Maurice's bed, continuing the routine that she had started years ago as the boys had previously been talked to together and considered as one, not the two very different boys that they now were. Maurice was reluctant to say anything bad about his brother as he was loyal to a tee, his soft blue eyes looking tearful. Roly had hated this softness in his son, thought he needed to toughen up as he had often said to Marguerite, but this was lost on Maurice, who hadn't known how to reply.

"He gets into fights a lot, maybe he should take up boxing"? He suggested innocently.

Marguerite smiled at the tearstained face that stared up at her, considering his thoughts. "Yes, possibly" she replied. "Did you want to go too"?

She knew he would want to be involved in anything related to his brother and thought it could possibly be a good idea. Maybe he too may one day need to be able to defend himself. Maurice said he did, so Marguerite agreed to look into it and left his bedside to go and chat with Frankie, who didn't like the idea of having to have a serious conversation with his mother as she could always see straight through lies.

"Boxing"? Frankie was surprised at the suggestion.

"Yes, you could use up some of that energy in a positive way and it might be fun, Maurice wants to go with you as well" Marguerite replied.

Frankie laughed "Might toughen him up"!

Did they want to do that? Marguerite considered. He was the one sensitive person in the family. But she decided that it would help Frankie control his anger and could hopefully create some strength in Maurice.

CHAPTER 53

Beattie went to the shop for just two full days a week now, sometimes midweek for a few extra hours or longer if she had an appointment with a customer. She always spent time getting to know her clients and knew well not to hurry as a potential commission could be lost that way. She and Elodie always dressed in one of her own designs, and she had an extensive portfolio now which she had built on over the years that showed off a full range of clothing. Marguerite would sometimes wear something of hers too, but not daily. Beattie had one or two appointments most weeks, but if not she would make calls or work on her laptop. She had created a website where she had posted photos of the uniforms she had designed, others with her clothing line for children or adults, every outfit an original. Marguerite would entertain Elodie if she had no customers herself and it was becoming a successful family business, expanding to cover the costs of all their lives. The large house could have been expensive and difficult to sustain, but with all the residents hands-on, most tasks could be dealt with by one or other of them but the bills and food still had to be paid for.

Beattie was now approaching her 18th birthday in December and she had almost forgotten already what it was like to be young and free. She was enjoying the business and being a mother, but when was the last time she was able to just be a teenager? The last time she had a night out was the cocktail party at the castle, but it was a very grown-up event, business related where she had to be professional.

The assistant Malvina was a small petite girl, as Scottish girls often were, with reddish brown hair tied back in a ponytail and a thin face, her green eyes framed with red eyelashes. She should mascara them Beattie thought, noting that she never seemed to wear any makeup. Malvina worked a few hours a day in the shop now, after being given the job following working through the summer break on a casual basis. This meant Marguerite was now able to leave the shop on errands or just for lunch without having to close. Malvina had said to them that she preferred to be called Mali, and Beattie had said she thought she should use her proper name but knew it wasn't her business. Mali explained it was just what she had got used to being called, and Beattie understood that as she was called Beatrice really but nobody called her that.

Beattie's 18th was decided not to be held in the garden at home, but at Lady Asher's Castle. She had mentioned her upcoming birthday and that she would soon officially be a grown-up, in a conversation when she had been at the Castle delivering the purple dress. The dress had so many more colours, interwoven with silk threads, slithers of silver, ivory pearl, lilac and a dark red. Lady Asher was astounded, claimed it was a masterpiece to have been created by a child. She paid her well and insisted she used her castle as the venue as a thank you for all she had done for Prunella; turning the girl into a small celebrity at her dance classes with the dress she had designed for her. Her daughter had been so quiet before and was barely noticed, but she bubbled now with her hidden personality emerging.

The party would be held in the ballroom, such a grand term, all the rooms in the Castle had names and Lady Asher had said Beattie could invite who ever she wanted. She didn't have a lot of friends really as she was always too busy to find or keep the ones she did have, but she was sure no one would refuse an invitation to the Castle. The ballroom wasn't a big room as the name suggested, but it was just right to accommodate an elite guest list which Beattie preferred anyway as it gave room for dancing. She wanted all those that had been a part of her journey to be there and it wasn't to be formal just fun, with no room for jealousy or worry that certain people would object to others being there. The behaviour would have to be beyond reproach, the party was in a Castle after all, but she felt like she belonged and was answerable to no one so would invite who she chose to.

The business was put on hold now for any new orders to be dealt with in the New Year and Beattie had been very busy making party dresses. She really needed another seamstress to work on the basic shape as she had too many orders for just one, and she would then add the adornments that made it unique using as many different textures colours and decorations as she could, whilst still keeping it classy. Christmas was now approaching fast and the dresses already made were awaiting collection at the shop, but to wait for one of her designs was never an issue as Beattie's creations were worth being patient for.

Maisie observed herself critically in the full-length mirror. Her blonde ringlets falling to her waist, her oval shaped face showing a new maturity now that she was nearly 20, her nose little and neat, a full mouth with large teeth and her smile huge when she revealed it. She had been told before that it had been considered a treat to receive one from her, but of late she was often smiling. She was slim and tall and Greg looked inadequate at her side, being of medium height, so she had to wear flats shoes. He was thin though muscular, but they weren't really a match in appearance. In personality they were both volatile, but Greg had become too quiet recently and Maisie preferred not to be able to get her own way all the time as it just made her walk all over him. Greg was tired but restless. He had been popular before and could have hooked up with a girl that would have allowed him to be a man. He could have supported them in having their own house, rented as he could hardly afford to buy one, and he checked himself now as he thought of all he had given up. Very little really in comparison to what he had gained, he lived well but he didn't feel content despite having caught the girl he had chosen. He was happy with his son but felt continually annoyed that his needs financially were met by his son's grandmother. He could have insisted against it, but somehow you didn't question Marguerite and he was essentially a guest in her house.

Rodrigo was left to himself now mostly, he had his job to continue to cook and work in and around the house. Marguerite tried to involve him in her venture as much she could but he didn't understand business or care about money but he knew she had many people to care for so this was his way of contributing and it was invaluable. Marguerite had no choice, she couldn't let go of the confidence she had now but she was still responsible for all of them. They depended on her and she had done her best to keep up with them all by being attentive to changes in the moods, but not to the extent she had done before.

When discussing the party, Rodrigo said he felt he wouldn't fit in and would feel out of place at the Castle but Frankie and Maurice wanted to go, so it was decided that Marguerite and Maisie would arrive un-partnered and the men would stay at home with the children. Beattie had invitations made that had been designed by Maisie, another possible business idea that could be Maisie's alone. She matched Beattie with her skills, different but equally necessary in their own way. Maisie felt she was growing away from Greg, and in truth he was no match for her. He had tried to aspire to greater things and had had some success with the building project, but basically he was an ordinary person wanting a normal life and he was out of her league. Maisie had mentioned that she wanted to invite Eduardo to the party. He had been a great support to their business but Beattie didn't know him well but knew he had caused a fight when they had their night out. Maisie assured her that there was nothing between them and he would behave, he was a player,

SHE CAN, CAN'T SHE?

just having a bit of fun and not anticipating the results of his actions. Neither of them knew his fiancée, but he had given cost-effective deals on fabrics so there was to be an invitation just for him.

Xavier was also invited as he was the man who gave the loan and Enid was delighted to be involved. Then there was Malvina, recently on board but still a part of the continuing success story. Mace had been distant of late, but whatever they were now he was still a part of Beattie's life and she wanted him there. Greg was again annoyed, his brother was always accepted in any circle and sometimes he hated how nice and good looking he was, always saying and doing the right thing, whereas it seemed he could not. He didn't know who else was on the guest list, he knew Eduardo was a business associate but he preferred to spare himself by not asking if he had received an invite. Mace had talked to Greg about Maisie, she was going to attract attention as would Beattie, but that was the penalty of being lucky enough to be her boyfriend, and hadn't he been the one to win her over Mitac?

Zachary was again absent, since being seen on the night out that none of them liked to refer to and Maisie had forgiven Greg for his show of jealousy, which had been unintentional on her part. Zachery offered no indication as to where he had gone, likely on purpose, as no one could tell what they didn't know. He had managed a few messages asking about Elodie, but he would hardly be a suitable guest to be invited to a Castle but Beattie knew he would have pulled it off, adapting his behaviour to suit situations. He was a presence that couldn't be ignored, but she didn't have to consider him now as he was not around. Beattie wanted her father there which was a bold move, but not Verity, for no more than one simple reason in that it would make it more awkward. Beattie didn't know her and she knew her mother would have felt uncomfortable as she would be at the party without Rodrigo. Roly didn't object, he preferred not to involve Verity, and he was impressed that the party was to be held at the Castle of Lady Asher. Even he had to admit that his daughters and no less his wife were a success. It was a carefully selected guest list, very different from Beattie's 16th, which had included uninvited attendants, drug addicts and suppliers. They had all learnt from their mistakes and their experiences and now moved in higher circles. The party was Beattie's birthday, but ultimately it was to show how far they had come and all the support they had in getting there. Roly had not struck the blow that would have changed the course of their lives by selling the house, and they knew that without that it would have been a bigger struggle. He had stepped aside, giving them all that they had needed at the time by making himself absent. Leaving each of them to make their own mistakes and learn and grow and reach the destinations which they were destined for, now they were grateful for that as any bitterness resided.

CHAPTER 54

On the night of the party, it was snowing. The garden had become a brilliant white wonderland, the trees and shrubs glistening from being heavily weighted down with snow. Rodrigo was now feeling a bit sad that he wasn't going to the party as he watched Marguerite carefully getting ready and he thought she looked fantastic of course. She was modelling one of Beattie's latest designs and her long dark hair was freshly washed, hanging loose but still a little damp. She had gotten very thin again, returning to her former slim shape and she looked healthy if a little tired, but content. Rodrigo knew that Roly was to be at the party tonight but Marguerite assured him that he was in no way a threat to him. She would have preferred Beattie not to have invited Roly really, but Beattie wanted him there. Now it felt wrong that Rodrigo was not going to be with her but Verity was not going to be there either, so they were there just as parents to Beattie. Rodrigo assured her that he understood and he genuinely did as he was the one living with her now. He considered himself fortunate to be in the house with this wonderful family and he was scared it could get snatched away, but this he left unsaid. It was Beattie's day and he knew Marguerite would not want to arrive feeling that she had let him down in some way so he had just said that she was to enjoy the evening, and hadn't they defied tradition anyway? Proving themselves to all those that had shown negativity towards their relationship, but who really cared what people thought? Though neither he, nor she, had yet introduced the other to their extended family that was his mother and her parents. But Marguerite suddenly felt closer to him now, emotional in the fact that her daughter had become so successful and was only still a teenager. Maisie too was becoming more mature, with less focus on herself, though Marguerite was a little concerned that she had outgrown Greg but the relationship continued for now. Greg wasn't going to be at the party either, instead staying with the children and Rodrigo, for a few beers and a joint no doubt.

Maisie said they should have arranged a carriage rather than a taxi as it was a much more appropriate form of transportation to a Castle, and it was snowing relentlessly now but nothing would stop them from getting to the party. Beattie was in a silver dress with sheer stockings and high-heeled anklets that were carried with her in a silver bag that had a fine heel, but for now she was wearing her Ugg boots. Maisie was in a gold dress that was pinched in at the waist with a black leather belt that was studded with gold and silver stones, sheer tights and some very high heeled shoes which she seemed to have no trouble walking in. Greg watched her as though she was a goddess as she walked slowly to the taxi. The taxi man was also dressed for the occasion, having been a big part of Beattie's success by always being available to her and to the family. He opened the car door for Maisie and she carefully stepped in, pulling her long legs with the party shoes inside. They had insisted that he should stay at the party and be there to take them all home, it was a precarious night, but this at least assured that they would be back home tonight.

Greg felt furious, he knew it was wrong and that he should be there too but he had had to stay at home. He knew there were many reasons why he wasn't welcome, Maisie's father for one, who had still not even met the boy that had got his eldest daughter pregnant. Roly had still not realised that they had actually met briefly a while back, when Roly had appeared unexpectedly and a fight between him and Rodrigo had resulted in Marguerite getting hurt. But Rodrigo was staying at home too, and he could see that he and Rodrigo would have caused them all to look back and that was history now. This is Beattie's night, Rodrigo reassured him with a grin, we would just be like a pair of spare parts, and Greg accepted that this was probably true. It was just a party with close friends and acquaintances and it wasn't a threat to them.

The little ones were now tucked away in their cots, Greg and Rodrigo outside with a joint. It had stopped snowing but they had their coats and boots on and it wasn't that cold. They didn't get much chance to talk alone but they were both in a fortunate situation and they knew it, so Rodrigo pushed away Greg's moaning by saying that it was up to him to make the effort to keep Maisie and not to just back off. Rodrigo was happy to be a kept man, he knew he did a lot for Marguerite and she wouldn't have been able to handle everything without him. Suddenly he felt more secure, he knew he didn't have money and he didn't have class, but he had many other more important values to offer. He was an excellent cook and he was also a gardener, a painter, a babysitter and he was invaluable to them all, Marguerite needed him as much as he needed her so he did not need to worry.

"But does Maisie need me"? Greg asked, even though he knew that she did. He filled the gaps with Colm at night, he was the one sitting by his cot; talking, soothing. Maisie was a good mother but she didn't have the patience with Colm that he did. Maybe she did need him, he reassured himself, as the boys decided to enjoy their night at the Chevelly house without the family for once, other than the children who were fast asleep. An air of joviality prevailed as they declared 'Happy 18th Birthday' to Beattie, by raising their glasses and taking puffs on a joint in a form of celebration between themselves.

Beattie put on her shoes as she entered the Castle and the maid, dressed in uniform, bobbed a curtsy which was almost comical. She took Beattie's shawl and Maisie's too, Marguerite was wearing a long line jacket but she opted to keep it on and the boys were both in black suits with bow ties that were Beattie's creations. Black with blue swirls for Frankie, his hair was gelled and he had good even features that promised he was to become a very good looking man. Maurice, his bow tie with purple swirls, was still very young looking and his features soft. His hair was gelled too and he had a round face that was engaging and friendly as he grinned at everyone. They both so liked to be out at new places but a Castle was a first.

The ballroom was decorated for Christmas, balloons red and green but saying 18 in keeping with the birthday theme and a huge banner read 'Congratulations! 18 today Beattie'. Maisie took photos and sent some to Greg so he could somewhat be a part of the party, thinking briefly of him and wishing him to have a fun night with Rodrigo. He replied after a few minutes saying only "yeah", but a few minutes later added "Have a good night my Princess". Maisie thought perhaps he had gotten a tip off from Rodrigo as he always knew what to say and managed to keep jealousy out of his relationship with Marguerite. She pondered that two powerful people in a relationship was not usually a good thing, so maybe her relationship with Greg was balanced and that was probably the same with Marguerite and Rodrigo.

The ballroom filled with people and Beattie was happy to welcome them all as she was given gifts that she put in a box provided by Lady Asher to be opened later tonight or most likely tomorrow. Mace had managed to get himself there, which had been no mean feat with train delays, and he looked so incredibly handsome that he took your breath away. Maisie whispered to Beattie, how could you not want him? And Beattie looked at Mace, who was smiling with his perfect white teeth on show. She knew that the chemistry should be there in spades, but that was just not how their relationship was and she couldn't explain it, he was the perfect gentleman fitting with the surroundings effortlessly charming everyone.

Enid, dressed in a black party dress with red spots and flat court style shoes looked stylish as she sat down in one of the upright chairs, enjoying the party unfolding by watching and admiring the beautiful guests, just glad to be a part of it. Old friends, new business associates and the family and the taxi man who stopped for a while to chat to Enid. Lady Asher and her husband were the perfect hosts and Beattie was free to mingle as the maid hovered, refilling glasses the moment they were empty and food was handed around as extra staff had been employed for the evening. There was no sign of Xavier, Beattie thought maybe he had decided not to attend but it was unlikely as he would have at least let her know.

Roly was dressed smartly, in a tailored charcoal grey suit with a white shirt and also a bow tie. He observed his family, proud of them now, each one knowing how to behave in any company as they always had. Marguerite went to speak with him after Beattie had chatted with her father and accepted a gift from him, but she hadn't heard the conversation between them.

"Well" he said "A fine display tonight and you look well Marguerite".

She returned the compliment and the conversation was stilted, but it was Beattie's night and she knew it would make her happy to see her parents acting civilised and neither of them wanted anything to ruin her party so they kept it brief.

Suddenly Xavier appeared, breathless and apologising to Beattie by explaining that his car had decided not to start so he had ordered a taxi, which he should have done anyway, but had had to wait. They had kept in contact and were at the getting-to-know-each-other stage. It was a slight risk to have him at the party with Mace, but Mace would not question her as the man was just a business associate and Beattie left him talking with Eduardo, who was dressed particularly outrageously tonight. Xavier's outfit, though very trendy, looked safe in comparison.

Music was playing, it was modern, and everyone was dancing. The atmosphere was good and an area just behind the ballroom had been designated for smokers. Maisie had gone there with her mother so she could have a cigarette, and it still seemed odd that her mother was smoking now. What do you think, Xavier or Mace for Beattie? She asked her and Marguerite laughed. "I couldn't say" she said. Xavier was tall, well-dressed and had a good job, Mace needed no explanation as he was too easy on the eye, but she suddenly held her hands up in admission as she knew what they were both thinking. Looks were important, but without that extra undefinable ingredient, it didn't matter. They knew Mace would not do anything to spoil Beattie's evening, but did he know about Xavier? And what did he get up to when he was back in England? It was hard to believe he wouldn't have a string of admirers. Beattie was glamorous and could get any man she wanted Maisie thought, but it wasn't true that looks alone would ever be enough.

Xavier was dancing with Beattie now, Eduardo with Maisie, clearly no thought for his fiancée tonight as he was doing some kind of flamenco dance that Maisie was easily picking up the steps of, they looked impressive together. Eduardo was tall, but Maisie was taller with her high heels on and realising that she had taken them off, which the maid noticed and quickly put somewhere safe on her behalf. They put on quite a show, Maisie's blonde hair flying freely and Eduardo's feet tapping impressively on the woodblock floor. Marguerite could for see the potential trouble, factory owner's daughter in the picture or not. Greg couldn't possibly match up to this Spanish exotic boy that was more Maisie's type, but then on the other hand Greg was the father of her son. Roly was just watching from the side lines, taking it all in, and also watching Beattie with the blonde man. He looked decent enough he thought, but Maisie was dancing with a foreigner and he didn't quite know what to think about that, didn't she have a boyfriend already? And he was sure that this man was not him. He scanned the rest of the room and noted that his sons were nowhere to be seen, they had been shown to the games room and were there now with Prunella and one of her friends.

CHAPTER 55

Later on in the evening, Lady Asher had a cake brought into the ballroom by the maid. It was a large birthday cake on a silver plate and 18 huge candles were lit on it.

"Make a wish Beattie"! She exclaimed.

What could she wish for? In her head she thought of a secret wish, nobody needed to know what it was and besides, hadn't she got her wish already? She blew out all the candles in one go and everyone cheered.

"Speech"! Someone shouted. Beattie hadn't prepared one but she was standing on a raised area like a stage and all eyes were upon her now, so she took a deep breath and spoke out ad hoc to her guests.

"Thank you so much to each and every one of you, you have all played an important part in helping me to fulfil my Fashion Designer dream, which started when I was about 2 years old so my mother tells me. I know I am a very fortunate girl that has so many things to be grateful for, including all of you being here today to help me celebrate both my birthday, and I hope you all have a great night"!

Beattie then got down quickly before she became emotional, always wanting to appear in control, as thunderous clapping and cheering followed. The music continued quietly and gradually guests began to disperse. The snow outside had settled but a line of taxi's waited outside undeterred, snow was a normal thing in Scotland so the taxi's all had snow chains. Beattie's gifts and cake box was arranged carefully in the boot of the taxi, slices of cake beautifully wrapped inside individual boxes for Rodrigo, Greg and the children also placed inside. Mace was returning with them as he would stay for a few days, possibly even until Christmas if the snow continued as it was difficult for the trains to operate.

Back at the house they found Rodrigo and Greg, one sprawled out on the sofa and the other in an armchair, beer cans littered around them on the carpet. They had had a good night it seemed, and Maisie decided to leave Greg where he was. She had had such a wonderful evening but didn't want to talk to him about it now so she went straight upstairs, stopping to check in on Colm who was cosily wrapped in a soft blue blanket with a bare foot sticking out. She didn't dare touch him as she knew he could easily wake up, so she tiptoed back out.

Marguerite also went alone to her room, it had been a perfect evening, and she slipped out of her dress and laid it neatly on a chair. Beattie's creation was to be treated with care, her shoes under the seat, and feeling tired she sunk gratefully into her bed.

Both the boys had fallen asleep in the taxi so they were groggy and barely aware of getting to their rooms, but they too had had a fun night.

Mace was with Beattie, snuggled close to each other but still in their clothes, intending to chat a while and then sleep. Elodie was sleeping, undisturbed by Beattie and Mace, who fell asleep instantly, which left Beattie alone to consider her birthday night. She was 18, an adult now, and she looked at Mace's beautiful face and wondered why she was still not sure of him. They had stuck with each other through out, him returning for all important occasions, and he cared deeply for her and she knew that she did for him, but what was it that was missing between them? Maybe they were just still too young she thought, as she too slipped in to a deep sleep.

CHAPTER 56

The next morning, Marguerite decided that work could wait. It was her shop after all, so she quickly put a message on the shop answer phone to inform anyone that called that the shop would be open for business tomorrow. It was a productive time of year with Christmas such a short time away now and the snow had gotten heavy. A few customers could still have ventured out, but they would understand the shop being closed and likely return tomorrow regardless. Marguerite always managed to drive in the snow without too much trouble.

Rodrigo must have stayed downstairs all night and now she could smell food cooking. Perhaps the alcohol last night had made him hungry, she knew the weed made him eat sweets. Marguerite found her dressing gown on the side of the bathtub, the smell of coffee was strong and inviting, and she went downstairs to find Rodrigo still dressed in last night's clothes and looking bleary-eyed.

"Did you enjoy your evening last night"? She asked him as she smiled "Looks like you did"!

"Yeah, it got a bit heavy" he answered, looking a bit shame faced. "Still checked on the baby though" he added, just so Marguerite would know that he had not gotten too drunk or too stoned to forget about Elodie.

Besides, Greg was there too and Colm was his responsibility. Elodie usually slept well but you never knew.

"How about the party"? He asked Marguerite.

"Very grand" she said.

Rodrigo laughed as he imagined the Castle. The girls moved amongst the aristocracy now. Rodrigo put a pile of toast on a plate next to some butter and jam and telling Marguerite to help herself, he placed a strong coffee in front of her. It was so cosy just the two of them.

"No work"? He asked, noting her attire.

"No, not today, I needed a day off" she replied.

Rodrigo smiled, revealing his gappy teeth. He missed their lazy afternoons and the lazy mornings were rare too nowadays. Marguerite lit a cigarette inside, she knew she shouldn't but she couldn't go outside to smoke today, so she shut the door and opened the kitchen window. It was foggy out and the sky was grey, more snow was on its way, definitely a day to stay at home.

Greg had returned to the bedroom in the early hours and was a bit worse for wear, like Rodrigo. Maisie on the other hand was in an indulgent mood after enjoying her night of freedom. Eduardo was hot, and she had thoroughly enjoyed dancing with him. She knew he was trouble and probably wouldn't think twice about cheating on his girlfriend, but it would just be a fling for him and Maisie didn't want that. Why would she want to upset the status quo? It wasn't ideal for Greg, she knew that, but she was happy with the way her life was going and she had so many options now and she decided to give Greg a good morning treat. He looked like he had lots of questions that he was going to ask about the night but she skilfully lead him off the subject and he decided he didn't need to know anyway. Oddly he seemed to actually trust Maisie, accepting she might flirt but that was all, and she was a mother now. That morning even Colm had indulged them by sleeping on as they enjoyed each other.

The boys didn't appear downstairs until midday. No school for them today Marguerite decided and it would probably be shut anyway, but even if it wasn't they wouldn't question why some pupils hadn't turned up. Several lived a little way out so it was ultimately the parents' decision. On being told they could stay home today, the boys disappeared straight into the garden to build a snowman with Colm who had been dressed in warm clothes, a bobble hat, gloves and bright blue boots. When they had finished the snowman they began to have a snowball fight, still kids for a while longer, and even Greg had appeared looking chirpy and joined in.

Beattie was in the lounge with Mace, opening her gifts that were all so beautifully wrapped with little cards attached to them saying who had given each one. She received her favourite perfume from Mace who had also given her a small box, which when he had taken it out of his pocket she had panicked. It couldn't be, he was still sat on the sofa he wouldn't be this casual about something like that he would perform. Mace watched her, picking up on her line of thinking, but the box revealed two tiny diamond stud earrings and Beattie hoped the relief she felt wasn't too noticeable. She put her arms around his neck, taking in his fresh smell, she did love him and the words were just resting on her lips as he whispered into her ear that one day it would be what she had thought it was. He went quiet for a moment then hugged her quickly and pulled away.

"Come on then Beattie, what else is in these boxes"? He said, changing the subject.

Beattie returned to the unopened gifts and slowly began opening another, not wanting to rush. It was thoughtfully chosen with her taste in mind, she knew she wasn't easy to buy for, but it was a gorgeous fluffy dressing gown. Her old one was a little tatty now so a replacement was due. Next was another gift from Marguerite, a silver watch. The card attached read 'time is valuable' and also said that it was from Rodrigo as well as her. The watch had a large face with hundreds of tiny diamonds lining the edges and it had been engraved on the reverse with the date and Happy 18th Birthday Beattie. She had also received lots of other things, including a leather-bound appointment book from Enid. Everything was on phones now, but she thought it would look impressive on her desk at work. Roly too had pushed the boat out and surprised Beattie with a course of driving lessons. He wrote on the card that he had done the same for Maisie, as he hadn't acknowledged her 18th birthday with a significant gift, but as it was her birthday and not Maisie's he had also written her a cheque. £500 to spend as she wished, Beattie was thrown. She had her own money now but still, she could save it, and who knew when she might find some extra money useful, fortunes could always change overnight. Beattie decided she would leave the last few gifts to open later so she and Mace got Elodie dressed in to a snowsuit and went out into the garden to play in the snow with the others.

Whilst everyone was playing outside, Maisie had been alarmed by a visitor at the door for her. It was a tiny woman, about her age, which turned out to be Eduardo's fiancée. She was feisty in the way that Scottish girls were with her hair a bright shade of auburn. She looked delicate, but Maisie could tell she was anything but, as she nervously went out to the front garden with her. It was chilly outside, but they could talk privately there and anyway the Scots didn't concern themselves with the cold, they were a tough breed. Maisie wondered why the woman was there, apparently a date for the wedding had been set for her and Eduardo, but how did this involve Maisie? Was it about her dancing with her fiancée? Surely she wouldn't be here about that, it was a business event and nothing more had happened. Growing more confused, Maisie waited for an explanation.

"I hear you print invitations? I read it on a website and thought it would be nice to keep it local" the woman finally told her.

Maisie gave her a spectacular grin and the woman looked confused for a moment before saying "You thought it was about Eduardo didn't you. He's the biggest flirt, I know, but hey he is what he is"!

Maisie smiled again at this. She was right, maybe it was the sneaky ones you had to worry about, and Greg was acting a bit like that lately she thought.

The wedding was to be held in a Castle and they would of course need bridesmaid dresses and a wedding gown.

"Your sister I know is very clever, but I thought I would start with you as it's not for a while yet" she told Maisie.

Athdara was her name and Maisie sort of admired her. Making a friend of her was perhaps her way of making sure that Maisie didn't get any ideas about her man, even though she claimed her reason for coming was about the invitations. She and Athdara chatted for a bit about foreign men and Maisie told her she had had a Romanian boyfriend once.

"They are a caution aren't they" Athdara said.

Maisie agreed, but sometimes different was good and exciting, and she touched on a few issues she had had with Mitac, like his family. Athdara said Eduardo hadn't visited him since he returned home. They would still invite him to the wedding, but doubted he would be able to come as it would be too expensive for him, and even though Eduardo was now working his way up in the factory, he was still not that well paid. Athdara was a good match for Eduardo it seemed, as Maisie went through some options of invitation styles. Athdara said she would decide herself as she knew Eduardo wouldn't be that interested, though he would probably want to choose his own shirt or something for the wedding.

Keep your friends close and your enemies closer so the saying goes, but they seemed to actually get on quite well and Maisie's only interest in Eduardo really was as a friend and a business contact. Never cross one with the other was the golden rule.

Back inside, Marguerite and Rodrigo had returned to their room to enjoy a few more hours alone together. Everyone else seemed happy too and it felt good. Christmas was approaching again and there was always a lot to do in preparation for it. Big families, big houses and big businesses meant they could never say they had nothing to do.

CHAPTER 57

The next day the shop wasn't busy with customers, so Beattie was working on an order for hats. This was not an area that she was much interested in, but it brought in extra business and money. The shop was a mess and Elodie was now sitting amongst the scraps of material playing, occupied so that her mother could work.

Beattie had been asked to design a dress for a child for a themed wedding. The girl's Aunt was getting married and the Mother wanted something a bit different and unique. She had told Beattie it was was to be colour coded in black and white and a Hollywood theme and this was the only given specifications, but Beattie was used to letting her imagination take hold with different fabrics and decorations. Again, there appeared to be no limit on the price as the customer hadn't given a budget, but she didn't like to exclude people on that basis. Beattie had suggested adding jewels, to which the woman's expression had changed to uncertainty. Or sequins perhaps? Not too many, but just enough to add an element of colour. She then pushed her luck by asking what the mother would be wearing herself, but she had said that she already had a suitable dress in mind and couldn't afford to have another one made. She also told her that the flowers in the church, the bride's bouquet and the bridesmaid's posies, were to add colour so it would not be all black and white. Beattie then asked if she might like a jacket made instead, or a hat, as she had made a few already as experiments. One was black and already adorned coincidentally with white stones, so she quickly showed this to her customer.

"Oh yes, that looks fabulous, how much is it please"? She asked with her eyes huge in anticipation and was clearly delighted when

Beattie said it would be just £25 for her. She would usually charge double that, but it was good for business and it had proved to be a good move as the next day she had called in to the shop again.

Marguerite had taken the order this time, but apparently her husband, Mother and Aunt would now all like a hat made but Beattie knew she was honour bound to match the price of the first hat. She couldn't charge £50 each now but still, who knew where it could lead and she would make a profit in the long run. Beattie had another base hat already made, so it was kind of a cheat, but with scarves and stones added to it the effect was clever and she was careful to make use of the materials left over from other projects. Beattie had continued to take on every order requested without considering if she would have the time. You never knew when things might change or when there could be a stint of no orders at all and designing her dresses was never easy and had always involved pushing them to sell. No designer was guaranteed a place in any show, the quality and originality had to be improved every time.

Mace was due to visit again at the weekend and the two of them were going for a rare evening out, with Maisie and Greg. Marguerite and Rodrigo were always at home in the evening and the children, Elodie at least, would be in bed early. Colm was still more of a problem with sleeping, but he chose to be difficult with Greg mostly. The venue was a bar and strictly speaking, Beattie was too young to drink, but the owner didn't ask for identification and she wasn't a big drinker anyway as she had pretty much stopped after Elodie was born. Also to have a hangover or bleary eyes was not how she wanted to be seen as her work was detailed, she had a lot of orders to complete and so she preferred not to have to take time off.

As they all alighted from the taxi, to Beattie's horror, who should be outside it but Zachary? He was obviously back in the area, but with a new partner in crime now. They were being very discreet and, if you didn't know about him already, you wouldn't suspect a thing as they just mingled naturally with people in a friendly manner. Beattie could see that if you looked closely enough, a quick exchange of money and packages could be noticed, but that was probably just because she knew about it.

Zachary looked different, his hair was much longer now and he was wearing a stylish hat with smart chequered tailored trousers, a casual jacket and loafers. He was not so easy to recognise, but why had he returned? Beattie thought perhaps because of her, but more likely Elodie, would be the main reason. Beattie suddenly felt wrong-footed and awkward as she was with Mace and unsure of what his or Zachary's reaction would be at meeting the other in person. If she had been alone it wouldn't have mattered so much. Mace smoked weed sometimes and Beattie reassured herself that he probably wouldn't care what Zachery did, but suddenly his fingers began pressing hard into Beattie's shoulder as he pulled her close to him but still managed to portray himself, as always, as the perfect gentlemen.

Mace just smiled casually at Zachery, who was giving him the once over now, probably considering him a weak character but Mace was physically fit and able to defend himself if pushed but he preferred not to make a show in public. In his opinion, Zachary wasn't good enough to even talk to Beattie, let alone have a child with her and she too gave Zachary a cool look. Ultimately, Beattie held all the cards as she could withhold Elodie from him anytime she wanted to but she wouldn't as she wasn't cruel enough, but he seemed to sense the warning. His blue eyes were steely cold as always and Beattie felt a sudden chill down her spine, she knew he was not to be crossed and even though she was effectively in a position of power, she knew he would hate that she was with Mace now, a man that nobody could fault.

Zachary took in Beattie's appearance. She was dressed in casual jeans, boots to the knee and a tight white jumper. The boy next to her looked like a model he thought and together they looked a striking match, both dark-haired and well dressed and he could see that she could really go places with him. He suddenly felt sick with jealousy but kept his stance, nodding in acknowledgement as he walked away to continue going about his business. He knew he was not in a position to attract attention, but he still couldn't resist sending a text message to Beattie asking who she was with, to which she had replied that it was none of his business, but then softened the blow by adding that she would arrange to talk to him soon. He would have to be satisfied with that, as she turned her phone off for the rest of the evening just in case.

Mace didn't mention anything about Zachary, but he could tell he was a real bad boy and thought that Elodie was very like him in appearance, there was no mistaking that she was his daughter. He was surprised that Beattie had been taken in by him but also understood that she had been very young and naive. She was still young now but had taken on a new maturity, excelling with her designs so she could go far in life, far away from him too he hoped. Zachary was the polar opposite to Mace. Blonde and blue eyed with a different disposition and different aspirations for life, making easy money which would result in heavy punishment if he got caught. But did Mace envy his bravado a little? He liked to play it safe, but did that get you where you wanted to be in life? He preferred to keep within the law and besides, he was the one with Beattie on his arm tonight.

Greg wasn't getting off lightly that evening either it seemed as Eduardo suddenly appeared and rushed over to greet Maisie to ask if she would dance with him again tonight. He nodded at Greg in acknowledgement and received a glare back which only fuelled his sense of fun, but he wasn't intending to cause a problem for Maisie. She said she would later, but as they had just arrived she should have a dance with Greg first. Eduardo wasn't offended, he seemed to be out alone, but didn't he have a girlfriend? Maisie knew that wouldn't stop him as he would always do what suited him, though to upset the bosses daughter would not be in his interest. He should probably have kept the two areas of his life separate, and his fiancée wasn't really his type in truth. He cared for her, but he cared more for his career and he only hadn't pursued an interest in Maisie at college as she was taken and he knew she was a girl that didn't play.

Maisie, acutely aware of Eduardo's eyes on her now, was unable to relax as Greg danced with her. Greg had his own style and she herself was barefoot. She liked heels and she could walk like a pro in them, but dancing in them made her feet sore. The floor felt cool and the music was lively as she tried to forget Eduardo was there. It would have been a great night, but Greg not saying hello like a normal person had clearly caused friction. Did Maisie even feel attracted to Eduardo? He was a colourful character and she knew he was only playing, but he was clearly enjoying Greg's obvious discomfort. Maisie felt the tension rising and she couldn't lie that it surfaced hidden feelings of power that she liked to think she had. She was not like Beattie, who wouldn't have let this situation happen at all and Eduardo wouldn't have dared to ask Beattie for a dance as he would likely feel outclassed by her. Maisie was the entertainment value for him tonight, but more so Greg, who Eduardo didn't particularly like. He wasn't impressed by Greg, he was too skinny and he looked common, probably a fighter and hardly a match for Maisie, who had towered over him in her high heels and even without heels was still taller.

Eduardo eventually approached them and tapped Greg on the shoulder, deciding he had waited long enough.

"So come on, let me have a dance with your girl now"

He had acknowledged that at least, but before getting a reply he whisked Maisie away in to his arms to dance.

Maisie was a little drunk so she quickly got lost in the music and the atmosphere; Eduardo really was an excellent dancer and they were great at dancing together. But a few minutes later she caught a glimpse of Greg's tortured face, realising he was about to lose control but it was too late as Eduardo was suddenly grabbed and pulled from the tight hold he had had on Maisie. Greg pushed Eduardo and got close to his face, he was drunk but Eduardo hadn't expected this. Should Maisie feel guilty? She had had a choice she supposed, she could have said no to him, but it was only dancing. In that moment Greg landed a punch and the other dancers surrounded them, circling the two men and anticipating a real good fist fight, but Eduardo had been so taken aback that he didn't have the chance to retaliate. It could get back to his employer he panicked now, arriving at work with a black eye or worse he knew he would be asked too many questions. Who was in here tonight that could report back? He thought as he looked around. There were a lot of workers at the factory and he didn't know them all yet, one of them could easily be there.

Greg was furious, all his pent-up emotion surfacing and his feelings of inadequacy. He felt he couldn't compete and he knew Maisie would prefer this boy to him given the chance, hadn't she already shown a liking for foreign men before? He thought then of the boy from college, yet he had won her from him. He knew Maisie would be angry at him now for this, maybe even tell him to go, Father of her son or not, but Mace saved the day as always by quickly ordering Eduardo away.

"Fun's over" he said, giving him a 'leave while you can look'. He thought it was all ridiculous, Greg knew Maisie had been in Eduardo's class for almost two years and he hardly had a chance on a night out with Greg there. Mace took Greg to one side, talking to him quietly and calming him down, but the evening was over now and it didn't help that Zachary was still skulking outside when they left the bar. Beattie had already called for their taxi but they had to wait, he was busier this time of year, so they all stood with Maisie crying and Greg looking sheepish. Beattie felt Zachery's eyes observing them all, probably misjudging the situation but sensing

288

disharmony as that much was clear, and he gave Beattie a sceptical look but she didn't choose to enlighten him. Mace had his arm around her shoulders possessively, tensions were still high, and they all breathed a sigh of relief when the taxi arrived. It was safer just to stay at home, their rare night out tarnished.

Back at the house, Maisie ignored Greg's pleas with her that he was sorry he had ruined the evening. He was such a baby she said, going on to tell him that his behaviour had been beyond immature, even though she knew full well that she would have found it difficult if Greg had danced with another girl in front of her. But Maisie still defended herself in that she hadn't encouraged Eduardo, she just didn't refuse him, but she didn't fancy him, he was just an excellent dancer. He was a player, a troublemaker, only out for a bit of mischief and fun and he just wanted a decent dance partner. He had a girlfriend already, a fiancée in fact, who was the very wealthy Mill owner's daughter no less, but it seemed unreasonable for her not to be able to speak with other boys, and him other girls. Didn't he speak to other girls at work? She reasoned, and in that moment Greg looked pitiful. Ultimately people stay together because they want to and they had chosen each other, but being everything to one person was a difficult task and the foreign boys appeared to see things differently. Loyalty to one woman was not perceived in the same way, but for the Scots and the English it was all or nothing, so Eduardo best lookout Greg thought.

The next day, unexpectedly and certainly not welcome, Marguerite received a visit from Roly at the shop. She was alone, not busy but it was still early, and he was casually dressed which was not like him on a weekday. No work? She asked him. His demeanour was less rigid, perhaps it had been better for him to be away from her and them, but what did he want? She asked. Thinking Christmas was a few days away and he had already made arrangements directly with the girls, but with the boys it was pretty much a standard arrangement. Marguerite hadn't seen Roly in close proximity for a very long time and she felt it was wrong of him to have stepped into her new life now by just turning up at the shop unannounced, but she question herself now as to why she was feeling nervous.

"Time for a coffee?" he asked her, his smile giving a hint of friendliness. He clearly wanted something she probably wouldn't want to give, but what could she say as he still paid the mortgage and council tax for the house. She found a card saying the shop would be open again in an hour, that covered lunch even though it was a bit early for that but she put it on the door anyway and got her coat, changed her shoes to boots and picked up her bag and locked the shop. She felt proud of herself, her very own shop, and she thought about how she had exceeded his expectations as they walked together to find a place for coffee. It felt odd to be at his side, so strange that you can spend a large part of your life with someone to find you have nothing to say to each other. Roly seemed similarly affected. It was too cold to sit outside and Marguerite didn't want to go to her café so when she noticed he was walking that way she finally spoke.

"There's a small coffee shop around the corner, we can go there".

It was one that she rarely frequented but Roly had shrugged in acceptance, following her change in direction. The bell tinkled as the door opened. It was homely, old fashioned and warm and they were immediately greeted with a 'Happy Christmas' as it was almost, and the shop was heavily decorated with Christmas cheer. The tables were a plain dark wood with a red candle placed centrally on each one and the chairs were high backed but cosy, with checked cushions that took away the hardness of the seats. Roly ordered Marguerite a coffee without asking, what if she had changed her preference? She hadn't, but she would have liked to have been asked. Once he had sat back down Roly got straight to the point, saving her any more unwanted anticipation. He said that he thought it was about time he was able to have all his family, HER family she thought in her head, but yes they were his children too, for Christmas Day this year. She could hardly bare to think how the house would feel without them all. She knew he could insist, but really he had no right, and he was actually asking her if she could ask them for him, knowing they would refuse if he asked them himself. Verity doesn't know the children at all he explained. Does she need to? Marguerite thought. But she understood that Roly would want her to know them as after all, didn't Rodrigo know all her children and even her grandchildren? She wanted to be selfish and refuse, she knew the children would realise what a big thing this would be for her to allow this to happen, but he continued. He said his flat was small, too small to accommodate them all, so Verity had suggested a cottage rental over the Christmas period and he didn't want to refuse her as she had gotten so little from him up until now. No surprise there Marguerite thought nastily but kept her mouth shut. It's in Scotland he went on. Yes, there were lots of cottages dotted here and there that she knew of, but picturing her children and grandchildren in one of them with Roly and this woman made her feel sick. Christmas was just days away, and she had planned the day already. What would the girls think, and the boys too? Christmas with a stranger, as that was how they thought of Verity at the moment. Marguerite chose not to reply straight away as she sipped her coffee. Rodrigo was going to his family for Christmas this year too as he hadn't been for years. Was Greg to be invited too? She asked Roly, who still hadn't even met the father of his grandson, but he looked at her strangely.

"No, I don't want him there" he answered her, his expression closed. So he was still the same Roly after all. Marguerite didn't want to appear upset as she knew Maisie would be, and what about Colm? She considered suggesting Boxing Day instead, but that would make her look vulnerable and as though she couldn't spend one Christmas day away from her children. But she would be alone as Greg would probably go to England for a rare visit to his own family, who was nothing to the rest of them as it was too far away to build a rapport. Christmas alone, well Roly would say he had had one, but did he even care if Marguerite would be upset about it? She had the children all the time, not that he would want that, but she knew she couldn't really refuse him when he had, as good as, let her have the house even though she lived there with her younger partner now. He deserved to have this and she knew it, she would be fine, it was just one day and there was still Boxing Day, they would have their Christmas then. Roly was waiting and watching, likely already knowing her thoughts.

"Ok. But only if the children agree" she said.

His face lit up "Thank you!" as he gave her a genuine smile.

That evening was like a conference, the kitchen table was to be the place to have the conversation. Beattie was the first to respond to her Mother, who had relayed to them their Father's proposition. She knew more than any of them how hard this would be for her Mother, but hadn't she had it all her way so far? She pointed this out to them, sensibly but not unkindly, and anything the others might have added was left unsaid. Beattie had decided for them of course. They would be there in the morning, have a good breakfast together, but keep the exchange of gifts until Boxing Day. It would be different, but that was good wasn't it? They would have two Christmases now. She knew that Rodrigo was going to his family, who had since been neglected in favour of Marguerite on so many occasions, and Greg's too. Shouldn't he go to England to his family? Didn't they deserve to have their son there? They didn't know their grandson, other than photos and video calls, but Maisie was not about to let him take Colm without her. Maybe in the future they would all go? It was ridiculous really, how involved they all were with only each other yet selfish to their partners' families. Surely Zachary would want to have Elodie for a Christmas day too? He would insist that Beattie goes with him. But again, this was in the future.

"Just think how busy you always are Mum, it would be a day to yourself" She knew Marguerite would not relish that, but it was just a day, just a few hours even if they came back possibly in the evening.

It was confirmed with Roly, he said that he and Verity would go to the cottage on Christmas Eve and he would pay for their taxi to the cottage and back. The children were a little excited at the idea of the cottage, despite being a different Christmas to ones they had been used to, but change didn't seem to bother them. The boys in particular always enjoyed a new experience, but even they were a bit fazed that Verity was going to be there as they didn't know her yet, but still, they had accepted Rodrigo so they should all at least try to do the same for Verity. It was just that perhaps Christmas Day was not the best day for it.

On Christmas Eve they had all been invited to the Castle for drinks, it was a lunch time venue. This time Maisie, not spending Christmas Day with Greg, decided that she would take him but Beattie said she would go alone, not wanting to cause friction by suggesting maybe Xavier came instead as her plus one. Rodrigo had said no when asked if he would he like to go and Marguerite had said that she wouldn't go either, but he insisted that she wasn't to miss it. He still had his own gifts to wrap so he would be fine, plus someone had to babysit he pointed out. They could have taken the children or even asked Enid to help, but it was Christmas Eve so she would likely be busy and it was easier just to keep the children at home and Greg would then be free to catch his train later that evening. Mace had already left a few days after Beattie's birthday as the snow had cleared. He had expected to return for Christmas, but that had changed now with Greg going back home to England, so he would spend a few days there now and return before the New Year with him.

Greg was pleased to be invited to the Castle, not having been before, and after his show the other night he had vowed to do Maisie proud. He dressed with care and Maisie was suitably impressed at his tailored suit, his blonde hair gelled. The boys had insisted they wanted to go too as they had enjoyed being there before and really liked the games room and wanted to be reacquainted with Prunella, who they had now struck a friendship with. Greg would no doubt be feeling a bit worse for wear after a few drinks but he could sleep the whole way back to England, it was a long journey.

Christmas morning was hectic. Rodrigo had left the night before to go to his mothers, who had been delighted to have him there alone. Greg's parents were also amazed that Greg had decided to be unselfish for once and spend it with them, though he wouldn't have gone if Maisie wasn't going to her father's Christmas cottage. This meant it was just Marguerite, the girls, the boys and the grandchildren at breakfast and it was nice to be just them. When the taxi arrived she suddenly felt extraordinarily tired and not sorry that she wasn't to spend the day helping with the Christmas dinner that Rodrigo would mostly have cooked. He too was probably glad not to have that task that had become a daily chore and, as much as he liked to cook, a break must have been welcome.

Once they had all left it was very quiet. Marguerite felt nostalgic for Christmases past, thinking back on when the children were small and how excited they had been. She went into the lounge then and opened the patio doors. It wasn't that cold, but she wrapped herself in a huge cardigan and just for today she smoked in the lounge. She sat in a chair close to the doors and put some music on to break the stillness. She was a little sleepy now as she had had a big breakfast, which she had surprisingly enjoyed. Shouldn't everyone spend Christmas Day alone at least once? She had given a gift to her family already, the gift of freedom, and she had wished each of them a wonderful day. The actual gift giving to each other would be tomorrow. Marguerite put out her cigarette and, with the music playing in the background, looked out to the garden. It was covered with a blanket of snow, a perfect Christmas picture, as she found herself dozing off, the nectar air filling the room.

The boys and the overexcited toddlers had no real perception of Christmas, but Maisie and Beattie felt upset leaving their mother alone. She had seemed fine so perhaps a break from them, and they from her, was a good thing. Greg had often asked if they could even function without each other, he always felt like a spare part and not a useful one at that. They were all connected by more than just being family, they all worked together, but did they have to live together too? He had often asked this question, but what about him, where did he fit in? He felt he was just there, looking after Colm when it suited as Maisie never really considered what he might want. But he had known how she was and still chose her, but what now? He wanted her to be different but he knew she could easily manage without him. She had once cruelly said that he could leave if he wanted. She wasn't responsible for his life or his happiness as that was for him to work out. He was exasperated that she didn't even want to think about how they might change or improve anything, but he knew he couldn't compete with her family.

Beattie knew her mother would be fine for the day. Honestly, how she had tolerated all that pressure she sometimes didn't know, but she probably needed the space to think. Were they all going to be there all their lives? Her business was linked to the shop and it was expanding, but it was unrealistic to think it could be contained by just the two of them and Maisie. The individual designs could be made by a team of seamstresses, but she needed to find them, and they must be highly skilled as the designs were often complicated. She had been asked if she could do fashion shows now too, but it all gave her a headache. She was only 18 yet not able to do anything other than work but she started this, not expecting truthfully for it to diversify into as many areas as it had. Now it was Christmas and there she was without a partner, her sister not able to bring hers due to their narrow-minded father, and so they were spending one of the most important days of the year with her father and his girlfriend. His actions had been forgiven in so much as they still included him in their lives, but they had not forgotten and he was partially the reason they all strived to be better, just to prove him wrong.

Frankie didn't care that he wasn't at home for Christmas, but he was not interested in pretending to someone he didn't know that he was having a good time. His father's girlfriend, he didn't like to think too much of her in that way, his mother with a younger man when all of his friends' mothers had husbands of a similar age to them. It seemed his family had to be different. Maurice however was upset, he wanted to go home, but their father was pleased they were there even though he looked nervous and didn't know what to do with them all. Maurice had been young, but he remembered how his dad had always been working and had rarely spent time with any of them. Verity was standing next to him now looking equally unnerved, observing the reluctance of his children and two grandchildren to be here today. They were Marguerite's family and she was alone today whilst her children gave their father the chance to play happy families. She was a generous person, Verity decided, and she was brave in that she had dared to change her life and pulled herself forward and now she had her shop, how could she compete?

The children, bearing gifts in Christmas-themed bags, had stepped into the cottage. Christmas day had begun, but they looked as though they would all prefer to get back in a taxi and go home. The cottage was very Christmassy, it was warm and beautifully decorated with piles of presents beneath the tree, a perfect setting for a traditional family Christmas, but they weren't that. Beattie, as always the one to take control, chivvied everyone in to find somewhere to sit. They all opted to sit in a line on the sofa, with Colm on the floor next to his mother and Elodie by Beattie who was now getting out all the gifts and putting them at the sides of the others.

Beattie chatted about inconsequential things, trying to bring each person into the conversation, whilst Verity served drinks. Alcohol for the adults, which immediately calmed Maisie and made Beattie even more talkative, but it was infectious and the atmosphere soon became jollier. Roly had a few drinks and even Verity had hurriedly consumed a glass of wine and was now looking a bit pink.

Colm and Elodie loved having so much to explore and the Christmas tree was looking to be the next likely prospect. Colm had to be restrained from it, but Elodie picked up on her mother's expression and immediately moved her hand away as a bottle of juice was given to her and a bar of chocolate to Colm. Maisie quickly pulled some wipes out of her bag ready to contain any mess. How were they going to get through this? It felt like a mistake but they were there now. Roly didn't have a clue and was probably thinking how he and Verity could have sat in front of the TV in relative peace, instead it was chaotic, but it was Christmas.

Greg had arrived in England at his old home. It was a suburban semi-detached house where his father lived with his girlfriend, but she had gone to visit her own relatives today. Greg's mother did not want to miss out on seeing her son so she was spending Christmas day with her ex-husband, which was an odd arrangement. Mace looked out of place there he suited the Chevelly household more. He looked like he belonged there, unlike Greg who appeared to have been whisked into some kind of surreal environment. He thought of Maisie. He knew he had won her, but had she really wanted him?

Later in the day some old friends, probably weary of just their own families company, had called round and they had all gotten pretty drunk. Greg's mother was a drinker, unlike Marguerite who had never experienced an interest. An old girlfriend of Greg's that was single again was sat next to him now on the sofa. She was blonde, skinny and over made up and more his type in truth Mace thought, suddenly concerned about his brother. Was he about to mess up what was probably the best thing that had ever happened to him, for some old girlfriend he had abandoned years ago? Returning to the past didn't usually turn out well and the relationship had already run its course before. If Maisie suspected anything, and she was very perceptive, Mace would have to cover for his brother. As far as he knew he hadn't actually moved in on her, but Greg was apparently still in contact with this girl as she had told him herself with a superior attitude, despite already knowing what a good life Greg had back in Scotland. It was just jealousy wasn't it between girls, and spite, wanting to show a man that that they were more fun despite him already being taken by another. Why be with her when he could be with me? But she was nothing compared to the statuesque Maisie and Mace hoped Greg wouldn't risk it. Maisie had already let him back once, she wouldn't do it again, and she definitely would not take kindly to being replaced by this girl that she would likely consider inferior. Besides, the ex-girlfriend was probably just playing with Greg, but he was clearly flattered by the attention and responding to it, instead of building on what he already had. The girl likely just had no other man available, but that would soon change and then she would just push Greg aside. Mace knew her type and Greg was an idiot, but he was still his brother.

Beattie too was not far from his thoughts, always there even though he was too far away. Mace knew she cared for him but how much? She was sceptical about the endurance of love and believed that fate would decide. They were still young, she had too much to do first, and she was always thinking about her next move as she wanted to be widely recognised in her field and that took continual pushing and hard work. He had helped her with the Fashion magazine, a gesture that would put him ahead of some other potential man, and he was always on the alert, surprising her with random messages and arriving at the house at short notice. The family thought he was good for Beattie and Greg had nastily said that he fitted in better, unlike him who was the poor relation. Mace had just said it was up to him to prove himself, to which he said he had tried. He had got promoted at work, helped with the building project and he was a good father, all of which was admirable but clearly still not enough. Greg had said it was alright for Mace, but he too had had to work continuously to keep Beattie's interest, not giving her a chance to replace him and pulling her back before another man had a chance to catch her. But ultimately he knew that wouldn't happen unless she wanted to be caught. He knew how she thought of him, too nice and not a threat to her life or her career, but she was wrong in some ways as he was a serious person really with aspirations of his own. He drove himself and, much like Beattie, he was the person in the family to advise and make the decisions that no one else wanted to make. She would want to be with a successful man and Mace intended to be just that. He knew to keep the contact going, catch her by surprise and bring her back to him before another man could capture her.

Today his role was a bit like Beattie's as they were the ones to hold the day together. She at her father's trying to make the day successful against the odds, and he making sure that Greg didn't do anything stupid under the influence. He despaired of his brother, living a life he didn't appreciate and probably didn't want as he would probably prefer an easier option. Maisie would never be that, she would always press the wrong buttons and expect more from him than he was able to give. Colm was their only reason to be together really, did they even love each other? Not in that all-consuming way, that was clear, but did Mace love Beattie like that? They could be a good couple he thought, but Beattie would never make a man her priority.

Rodrigo was tired, like Marguerite. The house was greedy and he was always kept busy with something. He was a laid-back person who preferred simple things. He liked his weed but he didn't much care for his job. What was he doing really? But he was grateful for the break. Marguerite was a businesswoman now and she was getting wealthier, where did he fit in in that? She had tried to get him involved, but it had been half-hearted on his part as the project was incomplete. He had made some wrong choices and he should get back to it really, finish what he had started.

Marguerite awoke late. The day was almost over, what a farce really. She thought of each of her children and the grandchildren with Roly and his new partner, Rodrigo with his family and, at last, Greg too in England with his family and Mace. She lit a cigarette, still sitting by the door, but it was dark now as she wondered when the last time was that she had had time like this to herself. All that had happened had been exciting, but she felt grateful for now just to be alone with her thoughts.

Suddenly her phone beeped, she had received a message from Beattie to say that Colm and Elodie were now upstairs, asleep in cots that Roly had actually thought to hire, both exhausted from the day. They all were. Beattie said it had been full on trying to protect the cottage from the hands of Colm and Elodie, who had both ended up being sick after dinner which hadn't gone down well, as Verity was anxious not to leave a mark on the cottage. They were all too tired to come back that evening but they had wanted to make sure Marguerite was alright and let her know they were all looking forward to their Christmas Day tomorrow. Marguerite replied saying that she was fine and would be ready for them all and Beattie asked her what she had done with her day and said she was sorry that they had left her alone. Marguerite reassured her that she had in fact benefitted from the day to herself but hoped they had all had a good day. Beattie said she thought she had given the performance of her life and Verity had tried her best to accommodate them, but she was unused to so many people and had seemed visibly relieved when the little ones had gone to bed. The boys were still up watching TV and Maisie was annoyed as Greg had been incognito all day. Mace had called Beattie, said that Greg was very drunk, as well as everyone else. He had had a few too, but he had to be on the alert he had told Beattie, and she had to laugh at that as she was usually the person to do that in her family, when Marguerite wasn't around. They needed to keep everything and everyone from messing up, not that they had not lost control themselves before.

Marguerite had also heard from Rodrigo, he was having a good time and was going to stay on a few days with his family to visit a few people he hadn't seen for a while, but he would be back when he was ready. This was a new situation for the two of them. Marguerite had always been flexible, expecting him to spend time with his family or go out with friends, but until now he hadn't been interested. Would his family try turning him against her? Was he tiring of her and his situation? As like Greg, she considered, Rodrigo was in a life that wasn't really a natural fit for him either.

Lady Asher was having a party at New Year's. Marguerite and Beattie and her family were always on the guest list, but New Year's Day they could spend together and of course there was still Boxing Day tomorrow first. Marguerite put her phone aside and went into the kitchen to make a meal for one which she hurriedly put together, and a coffee. Tomorrow she would be faced with having to cook a meal for everyone herself without Rodrigo, but it didn't have to be anything too complicated. The house was already tidy having got it that way for Christmas and of course it had remained so, with just her in it.

CHAPTER 58

Maisie had received a course of driving lessons as a gift from Roly. It was a skill she did not really need as there was already a car at the house, but only her mother drove and she used it for work. Maisie didn't go out much and when she did, the taxi man was always available, but she was always busy with Colm and the work she did on her laptop at home. She would ask Greg to look after Colm so she could go out to business meetings occasionally but he worked too and had tried in the beginning to give money to the household income, but it had been refused, and he hadn't pushed it. Now he was saving for when they might leave, but he knew that was unlikely to happen. Maisie went out if she chose to, but he didn't socialise much and his life outside of work was at the house. The two of them shared a bedroom with an en suite and a television, and they were able to play music, but Maisie was always with her sister discussing business or just talking, or sometimes out with her when she felt she could stand no more of the same four walls. Colm had his own room too but they could still all use the rest of the house. Meals were sometimes difficult but they managed, and of course barbecues were frequent as it was easier. Greg hadn't minded at first, it had been what he wanted, living in a house where they had their own room and it had been his decision.

Maisie spent more and more time working on the accounts, which was her contribution to the expense of the house, and this she did in the garden when possible. The garden was fantastic, Colm and Elodie loved to play there, it was all so perfect and Greg hated it for that very reason. He thought Maisie should be saving with him to move somewhere as a family, but she still claimed they were too young, and why would they want to? Not for a few more years at least she had reasoned, and only then would it have to be to somewhere that was up to the standards she was used to.

Greg was just an average boy, from an ordinary background, but he had chosen to pursue Maisie and now they had a son, but would he have stayed with her otherwise? Those factors didn't matter now and, other than for his son, he felt no reason to stay but that was a big decision he was not yet ready to make. From an outsiders point of view he had an easy life, but truthfully it just wasn't what he wanted anymore. He wouldn't be pleased about Maisie being given driving lessons and would probably be sarcastic and say she had no need for them. But really he would be jealous of her, and that in itself wasn't right, weren't you were supposed to want your partner to be happy? Just not at the expense of your own happiness. He had a bicycle, which he used for work that he had brought when Colm was born. They had been so happy back then but now, despite living in the same house, they were rarely together. Greg would say that she, along with her other siblings, just got everything handed to them on a plate. She had everything her way but he was still just an outsider that had only been accepted because he was Colm's father and her boyfriend, not for himself. He played no productive role in the house, even though Maisie had said many times that there was always work to be done around the house. He wouldn't go out of his way to look for chores, but also wouldn't refuse if he was asked to do something specific. He just wanted his own place, but Maisie was taking more than she was giving where Greg was concerned but Colm didn't seem to be effected, he was happy spending his time in the garden or the house, and their taxi friend was always available if they needed to go anywhere.

Maisie pulled on her coat and went into the garden where everyone, except Marguerite and Rodrigo, were playing in the snow. She watched Beattie with Mace, their dark heads close with Elodie's blonde head a stark contrast between them, as they crouched in the garden to pick up handfuls of snow to make snowballs. She thought Beattie should take care not to lose Mace, he wasn't just good looking, he was kind and he understood Beattie and he was so good with Elodie, despite not being his own, but Beattie said the spark was missing. There was always something missing wasn't there? Did you ever get everything all in one man and did they ever find it all in one woman? Beattie said she was just starting out really. Look at their mother, who had broken away from her marriage after many years. But it hadn't been a mistake Maisie pointed out, with a newfound wisdom she appeared to have acquired of late, a new perception of how other people might be feeling. Their parents had simply just grown apart and Marguerite was with Rodrigo now, but really how could they last? Surely he would, in time perhaps, want something different?

Rodrigo was at the moment steeped in domesticity, but he felt comfortable and was grateful for the snatches of company he got from Marguerite in between it all. The financial burden was lessoning, but the work involved in keeping it under control increased with the business expanding. They had a bit of a break now, but in the New Year they would be back pushing the boundaries once again. It wasn't just about the money though it was about the potential, after Marguerites stifling it for years and Maisie's hidden by being obsessed with boys. Now she had a man that cared for her and understood her reasons for not wanting to move out, even though he didn't share the same view. He took it as he was just not that important to her, but he remained hands on with Colm and worked hard. Really he deserved more from her, Maisie had thought in the time they had spent apart over Christmas, and she resolved to treat him better. But was it too late? He seemed different after going back home to his parents and she noticed he was on his phone a lot more, but when she had commented on it he just said he was messaging some old friends that he had been reacquainted with. It seemed a reasonable explanation, but he didn't seem to care that she was busy anymore and alarm bells sounded. He knew how it was, if Maisie felt neglected she would have looked elsewhere, but now she thought different, it was too easy to just give up and let someone get away. She knew he felt stuck, outclassed, but did that kind of thing really matter? Maybe not in the beginning, but eventually it did, when a similar class, level of intelligence and matching life aspirations did more to keep a couple together.

Beattie was always ambitious and knew what she wanted and where she was going, and because of Elodie she had started her career officially, but she had always been designing and sometimes sold her work. Two years earlier, without college, she was single minded but now she had control and could keep herself motivated. Mace was good for her as a boyfriend, but she didn't spend much time with him and he too was ambitious. Who knew, maybe Xavier was interested in Beattie, but he had to wait it out. Zachary too would have wanted Beattie and Elodie to make a life with him, but Beattie would never put herself and Elodie in danger. She knew he would protect them, but they could never feel secure in that lifestyle so he would have had to change drastically and he wouldn't of course. People can adapt, but ultimately they always return to themselves and Zachary liked to live life on the edge, he would be bored with traditional Beattie too was not going to have an ordinary or traditional life, but she didn't want a dangerous one. Her success had started, but it had not yet reached the level at where it could eventually go so she wasn't ready for domesticity and she had a child already, but didn't think she would ever want another.

Just a few days into the New Year, Beattie had unexpectedly heard from Xavier. Apart from the barbecue and a coffee in town before she went on holiday last year, they only exchanged a message here and there, saying nothing significant, only once suggesting they should meet but that came to nothing. He had been quiet, probably trying to fathom a way into her life but didn't know how. She hadn't given much away about any man, but did he think that the father of her child was a possible long term relationship? She was on the fence herself and had said as much when they last met, said she was too young for serious, serious was business. They both laughed at that. He hadn't sent flowers, was she even a girl that liked that? He didn't think so, it was too predictable and any man could do that, just pick up the phone to order whilst somebody else delivered them. He knew she wouldn't be impressed, but he knew she had contacts that could pop up in her life at any time. He knew about her various side lines and aspirations, businesses and even the magazine and she had her aristocratic connections as she was a girl on the move, if he wasn't careful she would likely soon be off his horizon altogether. But they had barely got off the starting block. He messaged her now and said he had another week before the bank opened, an extended new year, so would she like to spend a day with him getting to know each other better? Just a coffee next week and if she accepted she was to name the day. Beattie hadn't replied immediately as she felt unsure, reluctant to start something that she really hadn't the time for and wasn't free to pursue. It was a slow game with Xavier and her conscience and loyalty to Mace hindered her, but she reminded herself that she was only 18 and surely too young to be turning down possibilities so she replied then before she could think any further on it. Wednesday she said in acceptance, and waited an hour for his response, they were both playing the same game. He said yes, Wednesday is good, bring your passport and meet me at the airport. Forgetting the game she immediately replied, meet you where?! He called her then and she answered, what is this meet at the airport for a coffee? She demanded to know but he claimed it was a surprise, just a day out, but he didn't want to say any more and give it away so she was just to be at the airport by six that morning and she agreed hesitantly before putting the phone down.

Beattie hadn't seen Mace for a while, or even received a message from him. Greg was behaving oddly too and likely wouldn't want to answer any awkward questions that she might want to ask him on Maisie's behalf. No doubt Mace knew what was behind it and that was why he was avoiding her, so she couldn't resist meeting with Xavier to maybe check him off the list. It was never going to be easy, and she sometimes thought Mace should date other girls and her other boys and now she was going to, but what did he get up to when they weren't together? The distance meant they couldn't see each other that often, and she was always pleased to be with him when she was, but she wasn't accountable to him or him to her. Just at that moment a message arrived from Mace, the sixth sense, "I miss you, Beattie". She couldn't reply, suddenly feeling guilty.

That was how she reacted when she met with Xavier. She was thinking she shouldn't, but not being able to resist and to lose him could be a mistake. She didn't know him well enough, but she knew what she had with Mace, who had forgiven her for the night Elodie had been conceived and that was huge, but if she messed up again he likely wouldn't. Beattie reminded herself then that this was nothing, at least not yet, so she felt bound to follow it through and reasoned that by doing so, she would know if Mace was to be her ever after or if Xavier could be. Really, she was free to meet anyone and so was he, the only restrictions were the ones that they gave themselves. She messaged Mace back, you to, yes of course she did miss him, and he returned her text with how much. Why was he doing this now? Lots she said bluntly, and that was the extent of their conversation, but there had been a bit of reassurance on both sides she supposed.

Beattie had asked Maisie to look after Elodie and not to say anything to Greg. Maisie had said that Greg probably wouldn't be interested anyway, he was too self-occupied. He was envious of his brother, but he probably wouldn't think much of Beattie being out and Maisie looking after Elodie. It wasn't that unusual. Mace would have looked out for his brother and defend him, but would that be reciprocated by Greg? What did Maisie think about a coffee with Xavier? Somewhere out of Scotland sounded too intriguing to miss, but she wasn't sure that Beattie should be overcomplicating her life even though she could understand the attraction. She had met recently with another man, Eduardo, she still didn't fancy him, but who knew what could change under certain circumstances. Maisie should be learning to drive, the costs of taxis was mounting up now they had begun going out more, and now another taxi was needed to take Beattie to the airport. Maisie promised to look into it, perhaps they could share a car and both learn. It was an option. So, the coffee meeting involved her passport, Maisie had reassured Beattie by saying she should think herself lucky and of course she should go, why deny yourself of some fun? And that made Beattie relax enough to order the taxi. The taxi man was available at 4am, why wouldn't he be at that time? He did sometimes have airport drop offs early or very late, but it was not a problem. It's a traffic free drive he joked, and asked would she need a return taxi home? But she didn't know yet and had no idea of the timings.

Marguerite was sceptical when informed about Beattie's coffee day but didn't show it, it sounded exciting and her daughter worked most of the time so it would give her a much needed and well deserved break. But Beattie said what she did for work was fun, and what else would she do? She had effectively been working since she was about five years old, always with a pencil in her hand, sketching out what she wanted to do for a living.

Beattie was wide awake at 2am, she had hardly slept, and she didn't turn on the lights as she grabbed what she thought would be suitable and comfortable, only to find once in the light, that she had pulled out an ugly tweed jacket. She didn't want to risk returning to the room in case she woke Elodie, she would then know her mother was going out without her and likely wake the whole household.

Then everyone would want to know why she was sneaking out of the house at this time. She suddenly felt guilty, wondering at her foolishness as she went into the bathroom and put on an old pair of jeans with a strange orange jumper, which she had thought was red in the dark. But somehow the ensemble worked and she didn't really care. She didn't want to look like she had gone to a lot of trouble for him anyway and the tweed jacket effectively completed the look. Her boots were old, but they had been expensive and were comfortable. Elodie shouldn't wake until about seven, but it felt wrong leaving her alone in the room. Her blonde hair was spread out messily, her chubby little hands gripping her blanket. Beattie was leaving the country and she suddenly panicked at the thought of it, but it was only for a day and who knew, in the future she may have to make business trips out of the country.

Beattie tiptoed downstairs to the kitchen, where the lights beneath the cupboards gave off a warm glow, she sipped on some fruit juice and at four she left the sleeping household. Walking out into the darkness, the taxi was just a black shadowy outline, and again she pondered why she was doing this but still got in. The taxi man was right about no traffic, they were a lone car on the roads, but when they got closer to the airport a few had joined them. Her passport was in her bag along with some cash, Scottish pounds but the country they were going to would most likely need euros. How far could they get in a day? Most of Europe used euros now. She doubted she would really need money, maybe she would want to buy souvenirs wherever they were going but they were too big of a household for more gifts and there likely wouldn't be enough time for shopping. Besides, then they would all want to know too much and honestly, she was supposed to be enjoying this not worrying about everyone else.

The sliding doors in to the airport opened automatically, and Beattie spotted Xavier straight away. He was tall and fair, dressed in jeans with a casual leather jacket and brogues. He appraised her outfit as he approached, noticing she always dressed with such originality, and he didn't hug or kiss Beattie to greet her, just respectfully guided her by lightly holding her arm. Taking her through to the lounge, which was already open, the smell of coffee was heady. Do you need a caffeine fix too? He asked her, still giving nothing away, but when they checked in it finally became clear of the destination. They were going to Paris. She allowed herself then to feel some excitement, she knew she wouldn't be here if she didn't want to be. It had taken some considerable effort initially, to let go of any concerns about why she shouldn't go and change those thoughts to reasons why she should.

It was only a short flight, and they touched down at Charles de Gaulle airport at 9:30am with a whole day ahead to explore. Right outside the terminal, they got into a taxi, yet again she was in one she noted, but they could view the sights through the window. Just a taster Xavier said and then they would stop at a venue of her choice for breakfast. She was a bit sleepy now, as was he, and they sat close to each other in silence. It wasn't until he shook her gently that she realised she had fallen asleep on his shoulder, he too had fallen asleep. Both annoyed they had already lost some precious time they stopped outside a café with tables and parasols, both agreeing it looked appealing. It was a pleasant though chilly day, but compared to Scotland it felt warm. The city of Paris was alive with people going about their day, lots of cyclists and cars, and the air offered an overwhelming enticement of food and lots of babbling voices. The city was always busy, regardless of time.

What would she like to eat? He asked, both of them even hungrier after their nap. Beattie checked the menu and opted for croissants and macaroons to start with an omelette to follow, some fruit juice and a coffee. A petite little waitress rushed over, the French like the Scots were slightly built but this didn't hold out for her family. She had black hair tied up neatly away from her face, her make up perfect with her lips coated neatly in bright red lipstick and she was dressed smartly, a pencil black skirt with a patterned apron and a crisp white shirt.

"Bonjour"! She exclaimed smiling briefly, and then professionally took their order.

Beattie couldn't quite believe she was there, in another country so unexpectedly, but she was flattered by Xavier's lavish attempt at winning her over. This gesture would have been expensive and he was beaming at her now, he could clearly tell that she was more than pleased. What girl wouldn't be?

After breakfast they got back in to yet another taxi to view some of the sites they had missed earlier; The Eiffel Tower and The Louvre, then through the Champs-Élysées to the fashion houses. One day her designs could even be for sale there Beattie thought, it was a pleasant daydream and the perfect end to a wonderful day and shortly after, they headed back to the airport. She had had a truly memorable day and Xavier had been the perfect host, only holding her hand briefly to assist her on some steps but otherwise leaving her free to browse. At times when they walked, his arm would hang casually around her shoulders, but on their return to the airport he decided to take her fully into his arms. She was intoxicated by the day and fell easily into his kiss, their second kiss. It was a slow game but it heightened the stakes and before she knew it they were on the plane back to Scotland, just casually drinking champagne and chatting nonchalantly about the day. They alighted quickly, having no baggage other than a few bags full of token chocolates and sweets for her family. They walked straight out into the cold air, where Beattie found Xavier had his car parked in the car park. Could he not have offered to collect her that morning? She asked him. But he said no as that would have obligated her to go should she have changed her mind, that way she was free to make her own decision if to turn up or not. Now, Xavier returned her home. Elodie would be asleep as it was late, about 10pm, and she hoped she had been alright waking up without her mother that morning.

Xavier didn't try to kiss Beattie again, he respected that they were right outside her house and that she might not want him to and instead intended to leave her, with thoughts of him and the day lingering. Thank you so much she said and to his surprise she leaned over to kiss him, just a whisper of a touch on the lips, before she got out and walked towards the house. As he was driving out of the driveway he turned back to look at her and she could vaguely see his face, but not his expression. How did she feel? She wasn't quite sure. Happy, yes, happy was how she felt.

As the days went by, Xavier became increasingly interested in meeting her again, but he didn't know quite how to get her. He knew that one wrong move and he could be out of the race, but he too was a Scot so that was already a plus for him and he was respectable too, but was that enough? He knew Beattie had fallen before for a bad boy, didn't all the girls when they were young, but they didn't usually decide on a life with them if they could help it. But she was unfortunately linked to that bad boy now as he was the father of her child and that was a strong tie. Beattie didn't like interrogation, and he knew that she wanted to be admired for her success. It wasn't about looking better or being the most successful, just wanting to achieve her potential, but he was sure she had a boyfriend already that must not be around that much. He hadn't been mentioned and that probably suited her, this way she had control over herself and that was her power.

The coffee in Paris had wowed her, Xavier had a good job with exciting prospects and he could afford to do more of the same, but that was done now, he needed to think again. She was young, too young really and yet she was already a mother and a businesswoman. She was a grown up in so many ways and it was likely to be a soft approach that would be needed with her, yet he had thought she wanted to be blown away. Beattie had touched on the subject of her mother who had a young partner, but he suited her by allowing her to retain her individuality. He understood then that that was a trait that must also be important to her. She had also said that her sister

Maisie was a loose cannon, just happy for now with motherhood which tamed her wild side, along with helping Beattie with the business. She was also now side-lining everything with producing invitation cards. Beattie liked to talk about her family, he noticed, when she was telling him that she also had two younger brothers, but giving little away about them. How could he top his day out in Paris? He would have to think on it and he was determined, but sometimes overthinking things took away the spontaneity, and he was sure that Beattie had liked that.

Over Christmas, Zachary was unable to meet with Beattie and Elodie. Because of his way of life, he was hiding, being extra careful not to bring attention in from unwanted areas. It wasn't a career, but it was his way of life and it excited him. You worked your way up in a different way, but he had to be the most feared to make sure he got paid and make sure that everybody knew who they were dealing with. He knew what he did was wrong, and someone else could easily replace him if he were to find a regular way of making a living. Sometimes he did do normal work, mostly labouring, but it was just a smokescreen. He would, and had, resorted to nasty methods to get debts paid and if it all failed he could get his liberty taken from him. He liked living on the edge, but now it mattered he had other considerations. He had a daughter now and he was always very careful to keep her and Beattie out of that side of his life. He recently had a narrow escape himself and he knew Beattie would not want to put herself or her child, their child, at risk. She was building a respectable career now as a fashion designer, and Zachary often pondered over the idea of her name being linked to a bad boy in the fashion magazines. Perhaps it would help with publicity? People liked drama he thought as he smiled to himself, he knew he could be anything he wanted, he fooled people all the time.

Beattie occasionally allowed Zachary some time with Elodie and her, but she was always extra careful as she knew he could be unpredictable. That boy at the club Zachary had seen her with that evening, how could he compete? Boys like that stood out, confident and exceptionally good looking, but really what else did he have going for him? He probably had no sense of adventure, wanting to play it safe by being good. He thought that perhaps Beattie could still be tempted by him, but her better judgement held out. He noticed her looking at him sometimes, but what could he do to put himself ahead of any other potential man? He would have to think of something, a kind of cover, but she was smart and would likely see right through it. Beattie was quite a girl, a woman now in fact, but was he prepared to make the necessary changes, or at least pull off appearing to have made them? He knew that they would have to be visible, but he felt that he could potentially be an asset to her, but in ways that she didn't yet realise. He could put himself in any situation and adapt, which he was sure was something that she liked in him, and he was impressive and had a strong presence, as did she. They could be a match and they looked good together, her dark and him blonde, unlike the other guy who was as dark as her. They too had looked an outstanding couple, catching attention, but her and Zachary would and could be that too. It wouldn't take much, he thought, perhaps the race wasn't over yet and he could still be in with a chance.

In Romania, Christmas had finished for Mitac, but it had been fun. Dinner was outside for special occasions and most other times, any excuse, but everyone dressed warmly as it was very cold. It was equally so in Scotland, Mitac liked that and it was one of the reasons why he had chosen it. In Romania the meals were cooked barbecue style and extensive. The women would prepare the potatoes, salads and desserts whilst the men would cook the heavily seasoned meat and they would all gather together, extended families and neighbours, to play traditional music and drink, dance and eat. He liked a lot of the Romanian life, but he didn't like his menial job. He had planned to be educated and a success, but now he had a limpet girlfriend who would dance attendance on him and his family too always wanted something from him and he felt he had failed in his mission. What was Maisie doing now? He wondered. She was a mother now. But more importantly, what was she feeling? He knew her life was with that boy Greg, the father of her child, but Eduardo had mentioned that he had met with Maisie sometimes. He had even been to a party at a Castle, Mitac was impressed by this. Apparently it was her sister Beattie's birthday party and Eduardo told Mitac that he had danced with Maisie. Eduardo wasn't one to hold back on details, and he was gloating a bit, but kindly. He had also said he had gotten engaged to a Scottish girl and, broken with tradition, was now working in a textile factory that had previously only accepted Scots. His mentioning of all of this had fuelled Mitac to want to return. There were other possibilities, but didn't he have a girlfriend now? Eduardo said, and he said yes, but she wasn't Maisie and he got that.

Eduardo always preferred not to allow himself to get attached emotionally, it was too restricting and he didn't want to get hurt. He had already been hurt once in the past, he never told Mitac exactly what had happened, only that it was just easier not to care. Mitac understood, but he also believed that to not truly love the person you spend your life with, was to deny yourself the most important part of life. He was a stupid hopeless romantic but it destroyed everything that was good. He did have a girlfriend and she was a good girl, good enough, and Eduardo could have said something similar about his fiancée but the difference was that his girl was more of just a way in, to get him where he wanted, but he liked her well enough. He told Mitac this, who responded by saying that his girlfriend would probably want to give him children soon, and then he would be caught up with needing to provide even more support. She wasn't what he had planned, or who he would want to spend his whole life with really. He was young, surely this couldn't be it? He could go to Scotland to visit, he suggested to Eduardo, but he would have to get some money together first. He knew he would probably be a fool to return, it wasn't usually a good idea to go back, and for what? But he had to get away, it was suffocating him there and Eduardo understood. He too could never return to his Spanish village to stay permanently again. Furthermore, Eduardo had said that the father of Maisie's child hadn't even been at the party, apparently he wasn't allowed as her father was there. So this boy was English, but he clearly had still not been accepted, so what chance did he have in becoming a part of her family? Perhaps if he had something more to offer, and the father was gone from the house now anyway. He remembered then that evening when Maisie had got upset, when her father had gone to the house unannounced and spoken with her mother. He could see that Marguerite would be more accepting of him. She saw qualities in Mitac that Maisie had not seen, and anyway, he had to get away from the girl he was with before a child arrived. Whether it was right or not, he had to go before he was trapped without a choice, and he decided that as soon as he could he would be on a plane returning to Scotland. He would have to end his relationship with the girl, take no chances, and she would likely be upset but he couldn't help that. She deserved a better partner anyway he reasoned, someone that didn't resent or reject her.

When the time came for him to leave, the girl asked Mitac if he would ever be back and he felt cruel saying it, but he said not for her. She was angry with him, said she would not wait in case he changed his mind, she wanted to punish him. He understood and said he was sorry, to which she responded by shouting at him that he was an idiot as she walked away without looking back. He had no real feelings for her and she always knew that, but she was still prepared to accept it as long as she was provided for. Mitac thought then of the Scottish girls, they expected so much more, they had more respect for themselves.

Maisie had at times thought she would like another child, but at the moment she was using her skills to have the finances of the business under her control. She did most of the ordering of the fabrics and was currently designing a bespoke invitation cards line alongside. Lady Asher knew a lot of wealthy people that still used this method, plus there was always a market for wedding invitations. It was just a side line but right now she felt she had everything she needed, but she was aware that Greg was likely to leave at some point in the near future and she wasn't really sure how she felt about it.

Frankie, now 14, was being difficult. The boxing had been an idea that was meant to help him, when he had started to become a child they didn't recognise, but now he claimed that boxing no longer controlled his anger but instead fuelled it and he was getting angrier every time he went. He couldn't exactly pinpoint what the problem was but he thought it was his father mostly and he wanted to take revenge. He knew he was of no use to him, or any of them for that matter, and Roly only seemed to be interested in his girlfriend now anyway. He did take him and his brother out sometimes, but he was bored of all that now, he wanted a real father. He wanted to voice his feelings but he knew this would likely upset him, or he might just smirk as he recalled his mum saying once, now he too had noticed it. He longed for a father he could actually talk to, and Marguerite had tried to make Roly aware of that but he never wanted to listen. He hadn't changed, he had just removed himself from a difficult situation, and quite honestly if he could have had his way or changed things, he probably wouldn't now.

Frankie just wanted to be treated like an individual, not part of the duo that was Frankie and Maurice, just as Frankie. Was he not a person in his own right? He wanted to visit his father alone sometimes, maybe even his grand-parents, and he was sure that even Maurice would like some one on one time just for him too. Marguerite would always talk with him every evening but Frankie thought it childish now and just said that he was fine whenever she asked. He knew he could tell her anything but sometimes he just wanted a male point of view, and Rodrigo was a laugh but he wasn't one for serious talks. Let's have a kick about he would say, and of course he would get Maurice involved too as nobody liked to upset him, but he was tougher than people gave him credit for. He was annoyingly good at boxing too, it had been a surprise that he was so skilled in it and perhaps he would even become a professional one day. Frankie however, he just got carried away and needed more control over his punches. Maybe boxing wasn't for him. But what was he good at? The rest of his family were all so clever that sometimes he felt like he must be the only one that was stupid. He could relate to Greg more, but he was acting weird at the moment, and he too couldn't compete with the others either. But Frankie didn't tell Greg this as he was too wrapped up in his own worries. What did he have to worry about? But Frankie knew that people weren't always what they appeared to be on the surface. His father had always expected them to behave well and, because of the success of the business, Maisie and Beattie had gone up in his estimations. He wasn't a father that coped well with underachieving children, but Frankie still had his mother. She must be so relieved not to have to live up to his high standards anymore, he thought. She had her own standards, but for important things, and she would never judge someone for not being brainy or talented. He was just an ordinary person, what was wrong with that? A lot it seemed, as far as Roly was concerned. Frankie would have liked to go out with him, be a pillion rider on his bike, or a passenger in his car. He really liked cars, but Roly was so fussy. He wouldn't throw litter in the car if that was his concern, he just wanted to hear the roar of the engine and feel the wind in his hair when the roof was down. If he wasn't allowed to eat in the car, that didn't matter, but everything about his father was always so straight, uncompromising and cold. Sometimes he just wanted to shout at him, and he knew one day soon he was going to have to vent it out.

Marguerite on the other hand couldn't care less about the odd stray crisp packet. She said a car was just a tool that got them where they needed to go, but Roly had recently upgraded his sports car to a newer model. It was the same Cobalt blue, but inside it smelt fantastic, of brand new leather, and it was much faster and flashier than the last one. Style, yes, Roly had that, but Frankie and Maurice were full on teenagers now. They were no longer good for providing insider information that was so innocently given before. But what did that matter now anyway?

Frankie was starting to notice girls and he was keen to show off his fighting skills but not with his fists, more often it was a kick in the shins or to the knee as that got them to the floor every time. Maurice was happy, he liked boxing and knew he was good at it, it didn't make him angry. Unlike Frankie who seemed to uncontrollably beat his unfortunate partner without mercy and he had repeatedly been called up on it by the trainer. Maurice was getting muscly and he looked more like a boxer physically, being shorter and stockier despite having a soft nose. Frankie's was long and thin and his eyes dark. He had a character face his mother had said, and the girls at school seemed to like it, thinking of him as the bad boy in his family. Both he and Maisie were the volatile ones, but Beattie and Maurice were more interested in keeping other people happy, like their mother. Their father, he was nasty if truth be told under the fake ness, but Maurice was growing in confidence and had the skills. He was being suggested for the junior league, and Frankie was chuffed for him, but wasn't he supposed to be the boxer? Now his dream had been taken over by his younger brother, like Maisie who had been involved in the rise to fame but ultimately it was Beattie, the younger sister that was the leader.

Frankie didn't have the boxer physique. He was thin and tall and he also lacked the patience to land punches in the right places, but he had enthusiasm and that went a long way under the right circumstances. Maurice felt good and calm, but Frankie was always complaining. Marguerite had said it was just his age, but he didn't feel like that was it, he might do in a year or two she had said. But no, he didn't think like that, or like that kind of feeling and he wasn't soft enough, even though he had been a sensitive child. Hopefully he wouldn't get Maurice into trouble, but until now a lot of the fights had only been because he was protecting his brother. Maurice was able to do this himself, but he wouldn't want to street fight, that was more Frankie's scene.

Roly had another life now, apart from the family he had, but he realised a long time ago that there was no way back. But, what a clever family his family were and had now proved themselves to be. Roly was still seeing Verity, but she didn't yet live with him and he was in no rush. Hadn't he been tied to a woman for years and years already? He didn't want that yet, so Verity and he just holidayed together and enjoyed their motorbikes. She hadn't been given the chance to know his children before they had spent Christmas Day with them, which had then extended to an overnight stay, as they had gone back Boxing Day to spend the day with their mother. Verity had been nice enough, but she knew she would be reluctant to have the family all together again. They didn't have room in the flat, and the children were too wrapped up in their own lives to give her any serious consideration. She was their father's girlfriend and that was all, it didn't really concern them.

Marguerite was happy with how things were progressing. Her sons were diversifying into two very different individuals that no longer wanted to be just 'the boys' and were no longer just playing outside, but actually having quite an impact on the house. They were not so compliant anymore, especially Frankie, but that was normal for him. The grandchildren were developing new skills every day and they added so much fun and laughter to the house, still enjoying much of their time in the garden which was wild and colourful with flowers. Marguerite had no cause for complaint, but she felt like things were shifting between her and Rodrigo. He was visiting his family and friends more regularly now and he seemed less keen to help around the house. The intensity at the beginning of the relationship had lessened, but she knew that that was going to happen eventually, it couldn't be like that forever. Still, she had the shop and with that it seemed like there was no room for anything more than her work and her family. Time for Rodrigo was becoming increasingly hard to find. When she was just a part time employee and not the owner it was manageable but now their quality time was limited. She felt confused as she had allowed a man to control her before, but Rodrigo had consumed her and she felt a little sad that that excitement had worn off. Where would it go now? She would have to make more time for him, there were ways, but she enjoyed her work and it was vital to her.

Maisie and Greg were drifting apart too. He was going to visit his family again, but he hadn't suggested that Maisie and Colm went with him which suggested something was amiss. But little did she know, that Mitac was now on a plane back to Scotland.

Beattie's designs were so successful now that they had had to find more premises for their production and she had a photoshoot in London with a high end magazine. Still single for now, but whom could be her chosen partner in the future? Unlikely to be Zachery, but possibly Mace or maybe even Xavier, who was still lurking in the background, or perhaps someone completely different altogether. Either way, with or without a man, Beattie was on the road to riches and Maisie was following on her coat tails.